FIRE FALLING

FIRE FALLING

BOOK TWO OF AIR AWAKENS

ELISE KOVA

Silver Wing Press

Published by Silver Wing Press

Cover Artwork by Merilliza Chan
Editing by Monica Wanat

ISBN (paperback): 9781619849525
ISBN (hardcover): 9781619849532
eISBN: 9781619849518

Library of Congress Control Number:

Printed in the U.S.A

For my biggest fans:
Mom, Dad, and Mer.
The people who I owe everything to—literally.

TABLE OF CONTENTS

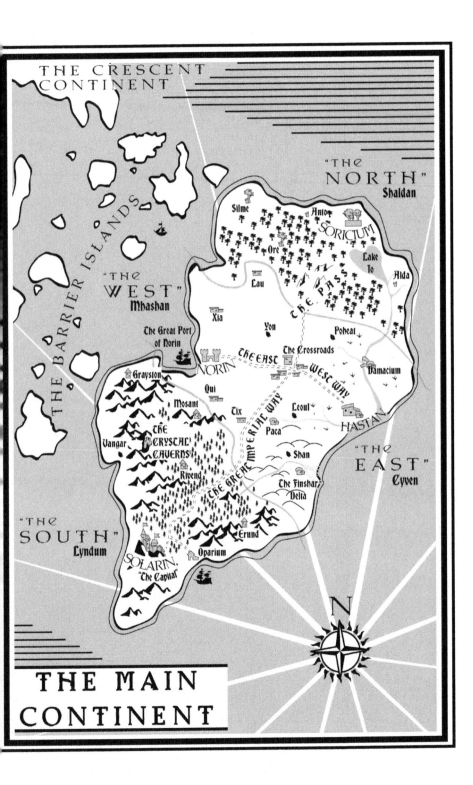

THE CRESCENT
CONTINENT

"THE
NORTH"
Shaldan

THE BARRIER ISLANDS

Silme

Anto
GORICIUM

Ore

Lake
Io
Alda

"THE
WEST"
Mhashan

Lau

THE PASS

Xia

Yon

Poheat

The Great Port
of Norin

The Crossroads

THE EAST

NORIN

WEST WAY

Damacium

Qui

Grayston

Mosant

Tix

Leoul

HASTAN

Vangar

THE
CRYSTAL
CAVERNS

Paca

THE GREAT IMPERIAL WAY

Shan

"THE
EAST"
Cyven

Riveng

The Finshar
Delta

"THE
SOUTH"
Lyndum

Erund

SOLARIN,
"The Capital"

Oparium

N

THE MAIN
CONTINENT

CHAPTER 1

*T*HE WORLD WAS *an inferno.*
Thick smoke. Ash. Blistering heat.
Vhalla dashed between shadowed figures. Faster and faster, she ran through the night, from one horrific scene to the next, as though she was running toward the end of the world itself. The dark, faceless people began to close in around her, hindering her, smothering her.

Tears already stained her cheeks when she reached out a hand to push away the first. The apparition gave a blood-curdling scream before being ripped apart, dissolving into wind-like smoke. Her fingertips rested upon the next—another scream. She didn't want to go farther, but her heart drummed out a single word—faster, faster, faster.

So Vhalla ran. She ran, and each shadowed apparition she came into contact with dissolved into the darkness that slowly encroached upon her. Nothing could hinder the dying cries of the shadow people, cries echoing to her very soul—not the palms pressed over her ears, not even her own screams.

And suddenly, silence.

Vhalla lowered her hands slowly, peeling one eye open, and then the next. There was nothing behind her, nothing beside her; the path before her was illuminated by one last glittering flame, consuming a building that had collapsed in on itself. Pulled by an invisible force, her feet dragged one inch, then the next, toward the rubble. She was already too late. She was too late every time, every night.

Vhalla began pulling the rubble aside, one large block at a time. The flames licked around her hands, but they didn't burn her. They didn't even feel hot. He was at the bottom, waiting for her, and Vhalla took the battered and bloody body of her dead friend into her arms, weeping until her throat was raw.

"Sareem," she sobbed into his gory shoulder. "I promise, next time, I'll be faster. Please, don't wait for me."

His hands sprung to life, gripping her arms. With sudden force the man reversed their positions, slamming her down against the ground, his carcass pressing her to the cobblestone street. Half of his face was nothing more than a gory pulp that dripped blood onto her shoulder.

"Vhalla," he hissed. Part of his jaw was gone and the remaining bone moved at an awkward slant. "Why didn't you come?"

"I tried!" she cried, begging. "I'm sorry, Sareem, I'm sorry!"

"You weren't there." The corpse of her friend leaned forward, nearly touching her face. "You weren't there, and I died because of you."

"I'm sorry!" Vhalla screamed.

"You were with him.*" His grip cut off the blood to her arms, and Vhalla's fingers went numb. "You were with him!" He shook her. "Where is he now? Where is he now?" her childhood friend demanded, shaking her body like a ragdoll, her head slamming on the ground.*

Vhalla struggled against the arms holding her as they shook her again.

"No, no! I tried to save you!" she sobbed.

"Vhalla, wake up!" A different voice commanded, and Vhalla's eyes shot open.

Larel's palms ran up and down Vhalla's arms. Her dark Western eyes were rife with concern. Vhalla blinked up at her, removing the image of her dead friend. The memory of Sareem sent her stomach heaving, and Vhalla rolled to the side of the bed, vomiting into a carefully placed bedpan.

"This is the third night in a row," said a voice from the door. The same voice she'd heard the past two nights.

Vhalla looked up, wiping spittle from her chin. A sorcerer stood there, and he didn't exactly look pleased.

"Cut her some slack." Larel was not amused.

"Cut me some slack." The person yawned, but heeded the warning tones in Larel's voice with one pointed glare back in Vhalla's direction. A slamming of the door punctuated his departure.

Vhalla coughed a final time, her mental and physical stability returning the longer she was out of the dream. Pulling herself into a seated position, Vhalla rubbed her palms against her eyes and blinked away the last remnants of the vision.

"Vhalla," Larel whispered softly, placing her palm on the crown of Vhalla's head. The other woman sat on the bed and pulled Vhalla into her arms.

"I'm okay. I'm fine, I'm fine," Vhalla murmured into the soft comfort of her friend.

"I'll stay."

"No, you can't stay every night." Vhalla shook her head, but didn't shrug off the soothing palm stroking her tangled mess of brown hair.

"Who says?" The woman assumed her position between Vhalla and the wall. It was cramped with the two of them, but Vhalla was too exhausted to object.

They lay facing each other, hands held tightly. Vhalla squinted in the darkness, using the faint light of the moon to make out Larel's face. The other woman stared back. As a Firebearer, Larel could summon a flame with a thought and give them light, but she didn't.

"Larel," Vhalla whimpered softly.

"You should get some sleep." Larel knew of Vhalla's imminent collapse just by the tone of her voice.

"Tomorrow's the last day." After the dream, her emotions were like an avalanche rushing toward the edge of a cliff. Vhalla was hopeless to do anything other than ride it out. She'd been hopeless at everything since her trial five days ago.

"It is, and Major Reale will only work you harder." Larel's voice was an extension of her resolve, as immovable as a mountain. She was the only grounding rock Vhalla had left.

"What's the point?" Vhalla whispered through quivering lips. "I'm dead the moment we see real combat." Originally, Vhalla had fantasized about what she would meet in the North— the war-torn land where she was commanded to march as a conscripted soldier of the Empire. But dreams and guilt had worn at her resolve until only a husk remained.

"You are not," Larel insisted.

"I can barely do anything!" Her voice was pathetic, even to her own ears. But Vhalla was beyond caring. She'd summoned a false strength to make it through her trial, but it was gone now.

"Hush," Larel ordered. The matter was no longer up for discussion. "You *must* sleep."

Vhalla pressed her lips together. "Will you wake me?" she asked finally.

"I will," Larel responded, as she did every night.

"I don't know how I'll sleep without you on the march," Vhalla murmured softly.

"Don't worry about that now, just rest."

Larel kissed Vhalla's knuckles softly, and Vhalla finally relented, closing her eyes.

Sleep was short, but it happened. Larel only woke Vhalla

once more. It was an improvement from the previous four nights.

In the daylight Larel had the courtesy not to say anything about Vhalla's night terrors. With the arrival of dawn, she departed Vhalla's room quietly, leaving the Eastern woman to dress and prepare for the day.

Vhalla's whole body felt stiff and sore, which made dressing take twice as long as normal. She rolled her shoulders and tilted her head from side to side as she shrugged on her black robe. Her reflection caught her attention: dark brown eyes flecked with gold were set upon a gaunt face and accentuated by dark circles. Even the usual Eastern tan of her skin had turned ashen. Vhalla raised a hand to her short hair, remembering the afternoon following her verdict when she'd cut it all off.

"I hate it," Vhalla declared, not sure if she was speaking to her hair or her reflection as a whole.

Her feet carried her against the stream of people heading toward the kitchens. She wasn't hungry. Vhalla didn't think she'd manage a bite today. She had one day left before she'd march away from everything she had ever known. Her normally small appetite had shriveled to a rock hard pit.

She entered the training rooms of the Tower, which encompassed the center of an entire level. The circular room was lined with a low outer wall that acted as a barrier for spectators and waiting trainees.

A woman already stood in the room behind a high desk.

"Major," Vhalla called as she entered.

"Yarl." Major Reale was a Southern woman who was built out of steel and was just as warm. A metal eyepatch had been melted directly onto her bone, covering her left eye. "You're early."

"I can't stay away," Vhalla retorted with a sarcastic tone, a tone that was beginning to permanently slip between her words.

Vhalla didn't know where it came from, and she was too tired to care.

"Well, you're not working with me today." The major glanced up only briefly before returning to marking up the papers on the desk.

"I'm not?" Vhalla didn't know where else she'd go. She couldn't leave the Tower per the Senate's orders. She was still property of the crown until she saw the war in the North to its conclusion—or she died.

"The minister wants to see you."

Vhalla knew a dismissal when she heard it, and Major Reale wasn't exactly the friendliest of women to be around.

With breakfast underway, the Tower hallway was empty. Most of the residents packed into the kitchens a few levels up. As she passed the mess hall, the noise washed over her, but Vhalla was too numb to hear it.

Past her room and almost at the top of the Tower was the Minister of Sorcery's office and quarters. All other doors held a name plaque on their fronts bearing the resident's name. But the one before her had the symbol of the Tower of Sorcerers cast in silver, a dragon curling in on itself split in two: the Broken Moon.

Her eyes drifted upward.

There was one more door, just visible on the curve of the sloping hallway. It was completely unmarked. And, while no one could confirm with any certainty, Vhalla could only suspect who it belonged to. She hadn't seen or heard from her phantom in days and had no way of reaching out to him, no matter how badly her poorer judgment begged her to. Vhalla swallowed and knocked on the door in front of her before the bad idea to proceed to the next door could overcome her.

"Just a moment," a voice called from within. The door swung open and a Southern man with short-cut blonde hair and icy blue eyes greeted her, the goatee around his mouth curling into a smile. "Vhalla, come in, come in," Minister Victor ushered.

She was welcomed into the lavish office; it was a level of wealth that she was still unaccustomed to. Plush cerulean carpet beneath her booted feet reminded her of the Imperial Library in a physically painful way. Vhalla quickly sat at one of the three chairs situated before the desk.

"I was just finishing my breakfast. Are you hungry?" He motioned to a plate filled with an assortment of pastries.

"No." Vhalla shook her head, bringing her hands together and wringing her fingers.

"No?" The minister cocked his head. "You couldn't have eaten."

"I'm not hungry."

"Now, Vhalla," he scolded in a familial tone. "You need to keep up your strength."

She stared at the muffin in his extended hand. Her training won out, and Vhalla listened to the man above her station. She picked at it listlessly, but that seemed to be enough for the minister.

"So tomorrow is the day," he stated obviously.

"It is." Vhalla nodded.

"I'd like to go over one or two things with you, before you march." Vhalla continued to pick at her food as he spoke. "Foremost, I want you to know that no one in the Tower harbors any ill will toward you."

Vhalla had a few bruises from Major Reale's training that could beg to differ, but she busied her mouth with the muffin.

"I have informed all of the Black Legion that you are to be kept under close watch and be defended at all times," Victor continued. "As the first Windwalker in nearly a hundred and fifty years I'd like to see you live long enough to study in the Tower."

"Have you informed the Senate of this decision? I'm fairly certain they want me dead," Vhalla replied numbly.

"Resentment doesn't suit you." The minister leaned back in his chair, pressing his fingers together.

"Excuse me," Vhalla mumbled a half-hearted apology and snuck the partly eaten muffin back onto the minister's plate.

"You need to return alive, Vhalla." Minister Victor regarded her thoughtfully. "I need you to believe that you will be able to do this."

Vhalla didn't know how she could be expected to keep herself alive when she could barely manage magic. *Mother*, she could barely manage to close her eyes for more than a few minutes without horrors haunting her. "Very well," Vhalla feigned agreement.

The minister only sighed at her response. "Will it help you if I give purpose to your days?" Minister Victor leaned forward, his elbows on his desk as though he was to impart a great secret upon her. "There is something I need . . . and only you, as a Windwalker, can retrieve it."

Vhalla instinctually sat straighter. "What?" She finally asked as the words were left hovering in the air.

"There is something very powerful hidden in the North. The longer it sits unattended, the greater the likelihood of it falling into the wrong hands or being used against our forces, should the Northern clans understand what they possess."

Vhalla wondered how this was supposed to help her. "What is it?" Curiosity won the war of her emotions.

"It's an ancient weapon from a different time, a time when magic was wilder and more divine." He paused, mulling over his next words. "It is an axe that is said to be able to sever anything, even a soul."

"Why would such a thing exist?" Vhalla struggled to think of a reason.

"Well, the latest records of it read as much fact as fiction." The minister rubbed his goatee in thought.

"How are you sure it's real?"

"I have it on very good faith it is." The minister returned to the point, "I need you to retrieve it and bring it back here." He tapped his desk.

"But if it's so dangerous . . ." Vhalla mused aloud. She felt like she was missing an important piece of information, but the minister was uninterested in imparting it to her.

"As I said, we want to keep it from the wrong hands. Beyond that, it would make the wielder *nearly invincible*." Minister Victor let that hang and Vhalla was smart enough to piece together what he was trying to tell her. If the wielder was nearly invincible, and she managed to find it, then perhaps she could make it out of the North alive. "Will you help me with this, Vhalla?"

She hesitated for one last, long moment. Vhalla stared into the minister's icy blue eyes, the eyes of the man who had kidnapped her when they had first met. But they were also the eyes of a man who had harbored her, healed her, and protected her when the world was ready to tear her limb from limb. The Tower was a mysterious place, but she knew sincerity when she saw it.

"Of course, minister," Vhalla said obediently.

The Tower took care of its own.

CHAPTER 2

VHALLA DID NOT sleep that night. She stayed awake, fighting through the uneasy hours with a book that she quickly realized she'd never finish. Closing it with a soft sigh, Vhalla tucked it away in her wardrobe as the sky began to lighten.

Two large panes of glass acted as both windows and doors, opening to the railed strip of stone that served as her secondary gateway to the world—what would generously be called a balcony. The beginnings of a bad winter flowed into the city at the end of each breeze. Vhalla let the chill numb her cheeks as she watched the edge of the horizon slowly turn crimson with the Mother Sun's waking.

A knock on her door pulled Vhalla's attentions inside. Larel had told her that she'd be bringing Vhalla's armor and helping her clip it on for the first time. Vhalla took a deep breath, trying to muster up the scraps of courage she had scavenged the night before.

The air vanished from her lungs with a soft choking noise at the person who awaited her.

His hair was as black as midnight. His eyes were crafted from piercing darkness and were perched upon high cheekbones carved from flawless alabaster skin. He wore meticulously crafted and finely pressed clothes—not a single stitch out of place. He was the opposite of the haggard woman whose clothes hung more limply with each day. But it was only expected as he was the crown prince.

Vhalla stood helplessly before him, and he seemed just as lost at the sight of her. Neither spoke.

Vhalla realized, very self-consciously, that this was the first time he'd seen her since she cut her hair. Short hair or no, could he even bear the sight of her any longer?

"I have your armor." His low voice resonated smoothly across her restless mind.

Vhalla heard the demand in the statement, moving aside so he could maneuver a small wooden armor stand into her room.

The sound of the door shutting behind him sent a nervous shiver up her spine. The last time Vhalla had been alone with the prince was the day of her verdict. The last time she'd seen him she was being escorted out of a courtroom by two armed guards, her sentence having been read—a sentence that gave the prince the ability to kill her should she disobey.

But Aldrik wouldn't kill her. The way he looked at her revealed that certainty. He couldn't kill her, if the magical force—the Bond—between them was real.

"Where's Larel?" Vhalla wanted to smash her face against the wall. *That was what she decided to say?*

"I thought I might help you." It was awkward, everything between them felt awkward. It was as though five years, not five days, had passed.

Everything had changed.

"I can't deny you, my prince." Vhalla brought her hands together, fidgeting.

Instead of his usual scolding of her restless tic, the prince took her fingers in his.

"Why the formality?" he asked softly, slipping the gloves onto her hands.

"Because . . ." The words stuck in her throat.

"Just Aldrik is fine," the prince reminded her.

She nodded mutely, still working through the knot of syllables behind her lips. With both gloves on, Aldrik passed her a chainmail tunic. Its sleeves were full, extending to the top of her gloves. Vhalla was surprised to find it had a hood fashioned of tiny links. Her hair fell just above where it pooled at the back of her neck. The weight of his stare brought her eyes to his, and Vhalla's hand fell from where it played with the ends of her hair.

"You had it cut." His hands paused on the armor.

"I cut it," she corrected, staring at a corner of the room. It felt as though she was on trial all over again.

"I like it," Aldrik said after what seemed like an eternity.

"You do?" Her mouth fell open in dumb shock.

"Long or short . . . suits you." The prince gave a small shrug.

Vhalla didn't point out the fact that he had just contradicted himself. Her insides were in turmoil, and she suddenly felt like crying. *He liked it?* What about her was left to like?

The armor she slipped into was crafted out of small scales of black steel. It hung to mid-thigh and had shoulder coverings that only minimally hindered her movement. Her heart raced with conflicted emotion as she watched the prince's long fingers demonstrate the locations of latches up the front of the armor.

"It is just the greaves and gauntlets then." Aldrik motioned to the remaining pieces on the stand. She nodded silently. The prince hovered for a long moment before making for the door. "I need to prepare myself."

"Aldrik." Vhalla's barely trembling hand clasped his coat sleeve before she even realized it had moved.

"Vhalla?" He stopped all movement in an instant, and his eyes searched hers.

"I can't," she whispered.

Pain flashed across the prince's face, riding on the wave of realization of what her words meant. "You can." Aldrik turned slowly, as though she was a wild animal, easily spooked. One warm hand encompassed hers; it was a delicate touch that seemed to carry the weight of the world in it.

"I-I'm awful at everything, and I—"

"Do you remember what I told you?" he asked as though he could sense her emotions were about to overrun her. "On the last day of your trial?"

"I do." She remembered her palm pressed firmly against his side, on a spot that had been a lethal wound not more than a year before when he'd come riding into her life during a summer's thunderstorm. He would have died from that wound if she had not saved him with her sorcery, inadvertently forming the magical Bond that now lived between them.

"Vhalla, I—" A door slammed in the hallway and the sound of footsteps heavy with armor faded down the hall. Aldrik engaged in a staring contest with the door. "I must go."

She nodded.

"I will see you soon, for the march."

Which of them was he reassuring?

Vhalla nodded again.

"We have a long time before reaching the North. I will personally make sure you are ready," the prince swore, accepting responsibility for her.

"Thank you." The words didn't seem enough, but they were all she had to give and Aldrik accepted them before silently escaping.

She stood for several long breaths, trying to calm the tempest that blew within her chest. As close to ready as she'd ever be, Vhalla grabbed the small bag she'd been told to pack her personal effects in. Tucked away in her wardrobe were Aldrik's notes, Larel's bracelet, and three letters addressed to her old master in the library, her friend Roan, and her father. She'd told Fritz, the Tower's de facto librarian, and his friend Grahm about their existence. If the worst befell her, those letters would be sent.

Her eyes caught the mirror once more, and Vhalla spared another minute. She didn't recognize the woman who stared back at her. Hollow eyes and wild hair were framed by black armor. It was the visage of a warrior and a sorcerer.

Taking a deep breath, Vhalla plunged into the hall and didn't look back. She didn't even bother to lock her door. The sloping spiral was full of people, but none seemed interested in speaking and only the chorus of armor filled the air. Their plate was of a similar make to hers, but it didn't look half as fine. Vhalla made note of the small gold embellishment along the front of her steel. One or two other people seemed to notice the same, but said nothing.

The hall ended in a large foyer at the base of the Tower, the only public entrance. Vhalla leaned against the outer wall, speaking to no one. The Tower had been kind to her, overall. But she only had two true friends among them, and they were still asleep in their beds.

Vhalla felt a pang of loneliness. The room was full of the stereotypical black hair and olive skin of the West, the yellow tan and plain brown features of the East, and the pale skin and golden haired people of the South. They were all mixes of eyes and hair she knew, and yet none of them were familiar.

Some of the other soldiers chatted away nervously. Others were too calm for this to be their first tour. Even though Aldrik had said otherwise, she was alone. Vhalla stared at her toes— she brought death and destruction; *it was better this way.*

Over her self-pity Vhalla heard the makings of a familiar voice.

"See, I told you we wouldn't be late," a man was saying.

"We would have been if I hadn't dragged you from bed," a woman responded.

"You can stop with the dragging now."

Vhalla's head snapped up to see Larel leading Fritz into the room, a firm grip on his arm. Vhalla's eyes widened. They were dressed much the same as everyone else, completely done up in armor.

"Fritz, Larel?" she called out to them timidly.

"Vhal!" The Southern man with the wild blonde hair waved in excitement as he passed Larel in a rush, leaving the other woman to leisurely follow behind.

"What are you doing here?" Vhalla asked, dumbfounded as they put their own packs on the floor.

"Isn't it obvious?" he responded, smoothing down his unruly curls. "We're coming with you."

"But neither of you are in the military," she objected.

"We're brand new recruits." He grinned.

Vhalla turned to Larel for some sense.

"You didn't think I'd let my first apprentice run off to war without me, did you?" Larel scolded gently without any mention of the prince showing up in her stead earlier. "What kind of mentor do you think I am?" She crossed her arms on her chest.

"You-you can't." Vhalla's heart began to race. She put her hands on Fritz's shoulders and saw a different set of Southern blue eyes staring back at her. The eyes of a man whom she'd grown up with, who had been a dear friend; they were eyes that now belonged to a dead man. "I can't have any more people die on my account." Vhalla focused all her effort on keeping her voice from breaking.

"Don't treat us like we're children." Larel rolled her eyes.

Fritz grabbed Vhalla's hands. "It's not your job to protect us. We know what we're doing." He squeezed her fingers gently. Vhalla felt a hopelessness rising in her. "You're idiots," Vhalla breathed.

Fritz laughed. "I've been called worse." He grinned, "Larel?"

"Much worse," the Westerner replied with a smirk.

"You look fantastic, by the way, Vhal!" Fritz held out her arms between them to inspect Vhalla's armor. "It's no wonder; you are our Windwalker."

Vhalla allowed Fritz to fuss and Larel to hum and smile. These had been the only people over the past few days who had made her feel close to human, and while she was in numb shock at the sight of them wearing armor, there was a little selfish streak that secretly rejoiced. Vhalla looked at Larel from the corners of her eyes, halfheartedly responding to Fritz.

The overexcited Southerner was silenced as a hush fell over the room. Major Reale strode in, also clad in black with an obsidian cape streaming down her back. A silver Broken Moon was emblazoned upon it. Vhalla saluted with the rest of the room, bringing her fists to her chest, knuckles together. She turned one hand down, the other pointing up, still connected at the wrist to mimic the imagery.

The moon was the point in which the day and night met, light in the darkness where it did not belong. Within it, the Father was said to have entrapped a creature of pure chaos. The Broken Moon of the Tower represented strength, that those who bore the mark would possess magic strong enough to pierce the heavens and put an end to what the Gods had started eons ago.

Vhalla had been too tired since joining the Tower to give the imagery much thought beyond learning its meaning. But the longer she'd considered the symbol, the more it seemed to fit her. There was something severed and rough about her, something tainted and, yet, at the same time those jagged pieces were the makings of something fearsome. She'd wanted to become someone the Senate would fear. *Why not shatter the sky?*

"Well, isn't this a sorry lot I have the esteemed honor of leading to war?" The major took in the room. "Who here marches for glory?"

The room rose in an instant cry of affirmation.

"Get out of my sight," the woman growled, instantly silencing the previously joyous soldiers. She cut down their resolve with a scan of her good eye. "I have no room for heroes under my command. Most of you will march to a thankless death. Your comrades in silver will fear you, they'll hate you, and they'll ignore your accomplishments and claim your victories."

Vhalla's mind drifted to the Senate, hearing a very different "they" in the woman's words.

"But, for those of you who aren't completely daft," Major Reale taunted with a wild grin crossing her lips. "For those of you who can meet our enemy with as much cruelty, as much cunning, and as much skill, maybe you'll see the end of this war. So stand with me, stand with your brothers and sisters in black. We ride toward the horizon of victory, and whoever cannot see the path there should leave now."

The major strode out of the Tower and didn't look back to see if anyone was following her.

Everyone was.

As the sunlight hit Vhalla's face, she looked behind her and up at the Tower, which cast a dark shadow until it became one with the mountainside castle.

Home. This magnificent palace had been her home since she was eleven. She'd came to it as a farmer's daughter, and now she'd leave it as a soldier. Vhalla shrugged the pack on her shoulder, gripping the leather straps tightly. She tried to ball up the nerves, fears, and insecurity and suppress it into some dark hole deep within her.

They walked through an inner path down to the stables. No one said a word. The sounds of the palace waking, and the Black Legion's armor clanking, soon joined the symphony of horses and men below.

The stables surpassed her wildest imagination. Hundreds of people filled every possible space. Each was plated in silver armor. Some were readying steeds, others were preparing carts.

Her awe was broken when the major barked a sharp order, sending Vhalla toward a side stall. She hadn't expected to have her own mount. Vhalla's steed was a mostly-black stallion with a white patch on its forehead. She patted its neck, and it shook a dark mane in dramatic protest. A bit of fire in the beast would suit her well, she decided. A young stable boy who gave her a wide berth worked quickly to saddle and bridle the mount. There was the echo of a voice in her that wanted to reassure the clearly fearful child, but Vhalla couldn't find the strength to comfort anyone else. She was too dark inside to even smile, so it was no surprise that she nearly startled the boy to death when she spoke.

"What's his name?"

"It-it's a new one. I saw 'im just this week. Don't think he 'as a name." The boy finished tacking the horse and attaching one small saddlebag on either side. One was stocked with rations, and Vhalla's meager possessions fit into the other—with some space left over.

She walked to the front of the horse and considered the beast. "Lightning," she decided. It wasn't very original, but it needed a name, and Lightning was as good as any. Lightning was fire in the sky, lightning was brilliant, lightning was fast, and lightning cut the heavens.

Putting her left foot in the stirrup, she swung her right over easily, taking the reins. Vhalla had never been taught how to properly ride, but a horse or two was something her family always kept for the farm. From a young age she'd rode astride, so sitting in a saddle seemed a natural stance. Vhalla glanced around at the other recruits; it wasn't so natural for many.

Taking the reins in one hand, she put her heels to the beast's sides and steered him out of the stable stall. Her armor clanked as she found the rhythm of the horse. Vhalla rode over to where the major was beginning to form the line.

"Major," she said.

"Good to see you know your way around a horse." The major assessed Vhalla from her feet in the stirrups to her grip on the reins. "You'll be close to center, Yarl, at my right." Referring to Fritz and Larel by their last names, she added, "Charem next to you, then Neiress. Then everyone else whom I can trust to not die promptly in a scuffle will be on the outside and rear."

Vhalla placed her horse in line with enough space on both sides. There was a small commotion behind her, and Vhalla turned in her saddle. The palace's giant ceremonial doors opened with the clanking and grinding of a large chain, and the Imperial family marched into the sun.

Prince Baldair wore his golden armor, and it shone brilliantly against the light. The Emperor wore a similar suit with large plate but all in white. Aldrik stood in stark contrast. He wore black scale that covered his entire body, similar to what Vhalla wore. Strapped atop the scale mail were large black plates rimmed in gold, which went from his hands to his elbows, his feet to his knees, on his shoulders, and upper chest. All three held helmets tucked under their arms and wore long white cloaks that flapped around their upper calves.

He looked nothing like the prince she'd seen barely hours before. But he was still utterly familiar to her.

The other members of the Imperial family had their horses brought out to them, but no one seemed interested in bringing

Aldrik his. He approached the stomping beast and calmed it with a hand, leading it from its stall.

Vhalla's stare was broken as Larel and Fritz rode over.

"Charem, Yarl's right. Neiress, after," the major barked, and Fritz and Larel fell in line around Vhalla.

"You're holding the reins too tightly," Vhalla advised quietly over Fritz to Larel, who seemed to be having trouble controlling her horse. Larel gave her an appreciative glance. Even though Vhalla would have rather them be safe in the Tower, she was glad to have her friends near her.

She began to notice strange glances from the other soldiers as more fell into line. There was a definite break between those dressed in silver and white and those dressed in silver and black. Friends were going to be in short supply on the march.

A quiet swept up from behind her, and the major turned. Aldrik sat atop his large War-strider, riding through the gap to Major Reale.

"My prince." The major bowed her head.

"Major Reale." Aldrik's voice was sharp. "How many do we have?" His eyes scanned through the recruits.

"Just shy of fifty," the major reported, confirming Vhalla's suspicions that they were the smallest group.

"Then I want just shy of fifty coming home." The prince took the reins in his hands as the major nodded. He directed his horse through the ranks, heading toward the front, but spared the second for a glance at Vhalla. Their eyes met, and his face relaxed a fraction, a conflicting mess of emotions building behind his stare.

Vhalla hardened her gaze as much as she could and gave him a small nod. He put his heels to his horse and posted a trot to the front of the line.

The time for sadness and pity was over. The girl who had come to the palace at eleven and lived her life in the library was dead; she'd been killed by the Senators whom she'd always been taught were sworn to protect her. The woman sitting in the saddle now had to find a heart crafted of black steel. She had to survive if for no other reason than to spite the world.

The host was in place, and the men and women shifted in their saddles. Vhalla clutched her reins tightly. *She could do this*, she told herself over the mental lies that her knees weren't shaking in the stirrups.

"Open the gates!" the Emperor boomed.

The lower gates groaned to life, opening for the hoard of warriors behind them. The Emperor led the march as the host spilled out into the mountaintop city with a thunderous rumble. Somewhere at the front soldiers began to cry, a wordless shout of bloodlust, fear, victory, and hope.

Vhalla did not make a sound.

Chapter 3

T HE DIN OF the horses' hooves on the cobblestone streets filled her ears. They set a brisk pace down the city and through the assembled crowds. More than one person stared with morbid curiosity or fear as the Black Legion passed, and Vhalla struggled not to give the masses any heed.

But, despite her best efforts, her eyes wandered; Vhalla was faced with a mix of horror, fear, and anger. Sorcerers, they were outcasts and unwanted creatures and—as far as many of the crowd were concerned—they had overstepped their boundaries the moment they left the Tower. More than once, someone was bold enough to throw something at them, though it normally missed and hit a pole-armed soldier at their front or an archer at their backs. The Black Legion was much smaller than the other groups.

By the increasing damage to the city, Vhalla realized they were close to the square of Sun and Moon. It had only been a few days since the already infamous Night of Fire and Wind, and most things were still in disrepair. Guilt swelled within her to near dizzying levels.

As they reached the lower wall of the city the houses became shorter, less opulent. It made the wall all the more impressive. The capital's first line of defense was a massive structure that utilized natural features and stone of the mountain. The drawbridge of the main gate was already being lowered for the host to march through.

"Ride close!" Major Reale called from her left.

Vhalla steered her horse close to the center of the column, and they passed through the gate. The city continued to stretch on beyond the wall on the other side of the moat, a moat that would remain dry throughout the winter months. Even poorer homes lined the mountainside to the valley below.

The road they marched upon eventually came to a T against the Great Imperial Way, a road that ran from the border of the Empire in the North to the sea in the South. The host turned left and began to head in a northwestern direction. Laid stones made their path wide enough that the entire host could ride and march abreast, eleven to fifteen men side-by-side.

It wasn't until they hit the forest that a horn blew long and low. The whole of the host slowed their pace, and the leaders called for a change in formation.

Major Reale waved out her arm to the right. "Make a space," she called, and they obliged.

Vhalla focused ahead; the whole army kept on while cleaving a hole down the middle. Aldrik, to his father's left, slowed his horse and the soldiers marched forward around him. Then the Emperor stopped his mount, and finally the golden prince. The Imperial family fell into place among the ranks.

Prince Baldair stayed in the middle front with all the sword-bearing soldiers. The Emperor rode behind him among the pole-arms. A few rows after was Vhalla and the crown prince, who now occupied the space between her and the major. His War-strider was a large creature, and her waist was on the same level as Aldrik's knee.

She glanced up at him, and caught his eyes on her at the same time. Vhalla gave a small bow of her head.

"My prince," she said respectfully. He barely nodded and turned back to the major. Vhalla looked forward. She wanted to believe that it was simply chance how the formation had lined up, but she was too smart for that. The man to her left gave nothing to chance.

In truth, she was fairly certain it was the safest place to be in the host—near the center, next to one of the most powerful sorcerers alive. Vhalla told herself that relief was the reason for the warmth that relaxed her shoulders at the thought that he'd be near her.

The legions had slowed to little more than a walk and the banners were struck. The time for pomp had ended, and everyone seemed to settle in for the long trip north. The war had been raging for four long years, and victory was one winter away. At least, the Emperor had said such.

Vhalla glanced behind her; in between the two back legions moved supply carts. It seemed a large amount of supplies for a victory that was only supposed to take a few months. She mused if the Emperor hadn't been entirely true in his time estimates.

The forest became denser, and soon they rarely passed any houses. Occasionally game and hunting trails stretched out from the road, but there was little else. The trees fractured the light from the Mother Sun, splotching the road ahead. Chatter began to fill the air, and it was a fairly peaceful ride.

But Vhalla didn't know if she could feel peaceful, she didn't know if she could sit easily in her saddle and prattle on about this or that. Every shift in her armor reminded her why she was there. She was a soldier now, *property of the crown*.

"How long has it been since you've been out of the city?" Fritz asked. The Southerner had other plans than to let her sit silently and wallow in her misfortune.

"It's been a while," Vhalla finally replied.

"Really?" he seemed genuinely surprised. "How often do you go home?"

"The last time I went home . . ." Vhalla's words trailed off, thinking of a farmhouse amid a field of golden wheat. She'd sent a letter to her father just a few days ago, trying to get word to him faster than rumors could fly. The thought put a lump in her throat, as though she'd somehow tarnished the happy memories her family had made in their home with her sorcery and crimes. "For my coming of age, I think?"

"What?" Fritz was aghast. "Fifteen? It's been three years since you went home? My mother and sisters would have my skin if I didn't come home for three years." Fritz laughed his infectious laugh.

Vhalla cracked a smile. "You have sisters?" As an only child she sometimes wondered what it'd be like to have a sibling.

"Four of them," Larel chimed in from Fritz's right. She seemed to be much more comfortable on the horse now that it was barely moving. "And you should see them all together. Thank the Mother they're not all sorcerers or it would be the Charem family against the world."

"You've met them?" Vhalla's curiosity compelled her to ask.

"Once." Larel nodded.

"How long have you known each other?"

The two exchanged a look before turning back to Vhalla.

"Seven years," Larel said.

"Eight years," Fritz proclaimed.

They both glared at each other.

"No, it's seven. You came the year after my coming of age." Larel counted on her fingers.

"No, eight, I just turned thirteen," Fritz argued.

"Yes, you turned thirteen, but after we met."

"You two remind me of an old friend and me," Vhalla mused softly.

"Who?" Fritz asked, oblivious to the sorrow that laced her words.

"His name was Sareem." She fussed with Lightning's mane.

"Is he at the palace?" Fritz tilted his head.

"He died on the Night of Fire and Wind." Vhalla was momentarily assaulted by her nightly visions of her friend's battered and broken body. *It was her fault.* She'd been too slow and he'd been waiting for her.

"I'm sorry, Vhal. Was he someone special?" Fritz asked, pulling Vhalla from her self-inflicted mental abuse.

"He was a good friend—special, like a brother." Vhalla physically shook the images from her head, feeling another set of eyes fall on her from her left. Her sanity couldn't handle another question on Sareem so she decided to take control of the conversation. "How long will we ride today?"

"Another two or three hours," said a voice, dark as midnight.

Vhalla turned and looked up at the crown prince. "That's all?"

Aldrik nodded. "It will take some time for a host this size to stop and set up camp. We don't want to do it in the dark."

Vhalla nodded and turned away before she became too entranced by him. Fritz and Larel began to talk between them, but Vhalla excluded herself from the conversation. She felt exhausted and passed the rest of the day in a daze.

When the sun was two-thirds of the way through the sky, the trumpet bellowed twice, calling for an all-stop.

"Make camp on the left side," Major Reale barked, and the Black Legion followed her order.

Aldrik split off and dismounted between the Black Legion and the pole-arms. His father's tent was erected in the center of the forward legion, and Aldrik's went up at the edge.

The more experienced soldiers who knew what to do began to set up tents. The Imperial family members' tents were significantly larger and rose up in a square with a pyramid roof. Groups of people ran over to assist each royal in setting up their temporary home.

It was a nice feeling to be out of the saddle. Vhalla stretched out her legs, ignoring the stiff ache, as she tied Lightning to a low-hanging tree branch. But she suspected the horse was smart enough not to run.

"Vhalla, we're sharing," Larel called, walking over to her with a bundle of canvas in her hands.

Relief settled over her as Vhalla pulled her bedroll off Lightning's saddle. *Larel was with her.* She felt guilty that the woman had become her keeper, but Vhalla was too mentally and physically exhausted to waste much energy on such a small guilt.

Seasoned soldiers took personal effects from their saddlebags, like blankets or small pillows, and made themselves comfortable in their cramped spaces. Some regarded her with curiosity, some ambivalence, which was better than the one or two dirty glances she received even within the Black Legion.

Larel drove two posts, which suspended a length of canvas, into the ground. The product was a simple triangular tent. Privacy came in the form of two flaps in the front and back that could be tied closed. It was barely big enough for their two bedrolls.

"Dinner will be ready soon," Larel announced after they'd finished settling.

"What's for dinner?" Vhalla followed the Western woman as she walked toward one of the fire pits.

"Whatever the hunters can find with speed," Larel answered.

Tonight that appeared to be a few deer, hare, and pheasant that already dripped fat into the fires from the turning spits. Vhalla received a shred of meat directly into her palm. She thought back to the lunch she'd shared with Prince Baldair at his formal table. Was he eating with his fingers now also?

"It's not half bad," Vhalla mused as she gnawed half-heartedly on a corner of the meat.

"I've always heard the Southern Forest was the easiest stretch of the march." Larel tore off a strip with her teeth, eating ravenously. "The soldiers say that the Western Waste makes up for it in difficulty, and if we dip into our rations now we'll never make it through the desert."

Suddenly everyone was on their feet, giving the salute of the Black Legion. Vhalla was slower in bringing her fists to her chest. The crown prince walked up to the circle, his hands folded behind his back in a commanding stance. After a long moment of assessment, he gave a nod and the company relaxed. Aldrik walked over to the far corner and sat down next to a woman whom Vhalla had never seen.

Her skin was a deep tan color, not quite chocolatey, more like the color of a black tea that had been steeped for too long. Her hair was the same texture as the Northerners, and Vhalla instantly felt uncomfortable. Vhalla put her fingertips to her cheek, touching the faint red line of recently healed skin, remembering the Night of Fire and Wind. The woman's hair curled like corkscrews in every direction, and she wore a red bandana around her forehead that pushed it back. She had angular features and striking green eyes. Vhalla's uneasiness aside, the woman was rather beautiful.

She watched the odd exchange as the watercolor sky grew inky black. Aldrik sat with one knee up, an arm propped on it. He had removed his cape and sat leisurely in his armor. The woman was laughing, and Vhalla even saw a smile sneak across Aldrik's cheeks from time to time. It was a smile that Vhalla had only ever seen given to her.

"Who is that?" Vhalla spoke so she couldn't hear the whisper of his throaty laughter with the other woman on the wind.

"Who?" Larel tried to squint across the fire pit.

"The woman the prince is talking to. I've never seen her before." If the woman had been in the Tower, it was amazing that Vhalla had missed it. The woman's appearance alone made her uneasy.

"Ah, her." Larel seemed to get a good look. "Fritz, you know her?"

"Her?" Fritz glanced now too and shook his head. "I'm not sure. I think I heard they were bringing people who knew about the North."

"Do you think we can trust her?" Vhalla asked, unable to shake the unsettling feeling.

"The prince apparently does," Larel replied with a shrug.

Vhalla returned her focus to the two in question. Their discussion seemed to have changed to something more heated, and they were arguing back and forth. Aldrik shifted and, as though he sensed her stare, two dark eyes caught her. Vhalla quickly averted her gaze.

For the remainder of the meal, she made it a point to avoid looking at him. Vhalla picked at her meat. Surely it was a discussion about the North, if that was why this woman travelled with them. Though the casual smiles and relaxed stances made it seem like war wasn't the subject of conversation.

"Eat, Vhalla," Larel instructed. "You'll need your energy."

Vhalla forced half of the meal down like it was medicine. Her desire for social interaction vanished, and she stood.

"I'm going to tuck in," she announced to her friends.

"We have a long ride tomorrow," Larel agreed.

"See you in the morning," Fritz said with a smile.

Vhalla turned and walked away, not tired in the slightest.

Chapter 4

S HE WAS TRAPPED in the labyrinth of her nightmares. Every shadowed figure cracked and turned into fog, dissipating at her touch. She ran past them all, feeling the wind roar on the edge of her consciousness. Vhalla ran screaming through the darkness and fire.

Two arms heaved her upright, shaking her awake.

Vhalla immediately wrestled with the other body, trying to tear herself away from the person's grip. Her forehead was slick with sweat, and her clothes were nearly soaked. Wind howled through the mountains, heralding one of the last storms of summer.

"Vhalla, *stop.*" Larel pulled Vhalla into her arms, pressing Vhalla's face into her chest and shielding her from the world. "You're okay, you're all right. I'm here."

Vhalla shivered, clinging to Larel as she had every other night she'd woken like this. Her blanket seemed less tangled around her legs; the other woman could wake her from her night terrors faster when she was only an arm's length away. Vhalla pressed her face into the Westerner, reminding herself that the person she was holding was not the mangled body of her lost friend.

"Sorry," Vhalla muttered when she was finally ready to face the world again.

"You've nothing to apologize for." Larel said it in such a way that Vhalla believed it.

As it was near dawn, they decided not to go back to sleep. They assisted each other in clipping on their armor before breaking down the tent. Vhalla's skin felt hot and cold all over. It was as though she could still feel the heat of the fire from the nightmare, the chill of the screams in the darkness. If she couldn't make it through one night, how could she make it through war?

"Do you want to talk about it?" Larel asked. It wasn't the first time the woman had posed the question.

"No," Vhalla replied, having no interest in sharing the darkness that brewed in her as ominously as the storm clouds on the dawn's horizon.

"Good morning," an unfamiliar voice chimed, halting any further inquiry from Larel.

Vhalla could've thanked the person were it not for the face that belonged to the voice. She paused, mid-fold on the tent canvas, staring at the emerald eyes that shone brightly in the early morning light.

"Good morning," Vhalla greeted quietly. Seeing this woman and her Northern features so close after her nightmares instantly unsettled Vhalla.

"Good morning," Larel responded politely. "Can we help you?"

"Vhalla Yarl, the Windwalker." It wasn't a question, and it made Vhalla feel anxious. "I don't know what I expected from the stories, but it was not you," she said with a laugh.

Vhalla stood slowly.

"And you are?" Larel asked.

"Oh, where are my manners? Elecia." She stuck out her hand for Larel, then Vhalla. Vhalla took it after only a brief moment's hesitation. "Say, you sure you really made that windstorm everyone tells me about? You look like you'd be blown over by a good breeze." Elecia laughed and, despite being a sweet sound, it made Vhalla's teeth grind together.

"I did; just ask any of the Senators. I know one or two who would be happy to give you a colorful account of the night." Vhalla turned her back on the woman, strapping her bedroll to Lightning's saddle. She didn't care if she was being rude. This woman was the last person with whom she'd discuss the Night of Fire and Wind.

"Well, I guess we will see," she said cheerfully. "The crown prince asked me to deliver a message."

Vhalla paused. Aldrik was sending messages through this woman? She barely looked any older than Vhalla.

"He is going to assist you with your training starting this evening."

Vhalla managed to hold her tongue and give the woman a nod.

"Excellent." The woman clapped her hands together. "Right then, see you ladies later." She was gone before either had an opportunity to respond.

Vhalla pressed her eyes closed and swallowed down the nausea the sight the woman evoked. She was disgusted with herself. "I'm going to take these to the cart," Vhalla announced, grabbing up the tent poles. "I could use a walk."

Larel nodded mutely and picked up the canvas, taking it to her saddlebag before repeating the process with her bedroll.

Vhalla took a few deep breaths, reminding herself she had no reason to be angry. Aldrik was likely busy, and he was talking to Elecia last night. He mentioned it and asked her for a favor, Vhalla explained away in her head. She should be happy, excited even, to train with Aldrik. But the woman's words echoed in her mind: *See you later.* Did that mean Elecia was going to be there, too? Or was it just a colloquial saying? Why was she even talking so casually to Aldrik in the first place?

Vhalla waited in line at the cart to return the tent poles. The sun had almost come up—scaring away the storm clouds in the process—and the host was likely to begin their march soon.

"Thanks," she mumbled to the man loading the cart. Vhalla turned and bumped into a large man with light brown hair. "Sorry," she muttered, keeping her face down. Vhalla stepped around him to head back to her section of camp when a large hand clasped down on her shoulder.

"Well, don't you think you're special, *black armor*?" he sneered, yanking her back.

Vhalla stumbled. "I said I was sorry." She looked up at the man in annoyance; this was not the morning to test her patience.

"Really? I didn't hear you." He leaned down.

"I'm sorry," she forced through grit teeth, not wanting to make a scene before the small crowd gathering.

"It's bad enough we have to deal with the Black Legion at all," the man grumbled. "Now I've to take sass from little girls?"

Vhalla frowned.

An armored arm slung itself around her shoulder, and Vhalla blinked in surprise. "Now, now, don't take it personally, Vhalla. Grun here hasn't eaten yet, and he's really grumpy in the morning," Daniel said with a grin.

"Come on, Grun," Craig came up on the other side of the man. "Let's get some food in that giant gut of yours."

She hadn't seen the two soldiers since her trial. They'd been her guards when she was in holding, *the good ones*. Daniel was an Easterner like her, amber-tinted tan skin and full-bodied dark brown hair. Craig's wavy blonde hair and paler complexion marked him as a Southerner. She'd immediately liked both of them, and this morning was one more reason to add to that growing list.

"Eat with us, Vhalla?" Daniel asked.

"I'm not sure if that's such a good idea." She glanced over at the large man Craig was escorting away.

"Nonsense!" Craig called, and soon she was being led toward the front of the host.

"What are you two doing here?" she asked Daniel as he removed his arm from her shoulders. Craig took the behemoth a far distance ahead before rejoining them.

"We're soldiers." Daniel chuckled, the movement tossing his nearly shoulder-length hair. "I'd say we belong here more than you, Miss Windwalker."

"You're not palace guards?" she asked with genuine surprise. He shook his head and raised up his arm. One of his gauntlets was plated in gold, the metal on his forearm catching the glint of the morning's light. "We're Golden Guard," he explained.

Vhalla had heard of Prince Baldair's personal squadron before; they were rumored to be the best of the best with only the finest lords and ladies serving among them.

As she focused on his arm he focused on her. "I like your hair; you clean up rather nice."

She raised a hand to the frayed ends of her hair that barely touched the chainmail hood of her armor. Her hair was awful. Vhalla scowled as a hunk of cold meat was shoved into her palm. It was a little charred on one side and the natural fats had coagulated into a jelly-like film that she scraped off onto the ground as they sat around the still-smoldering remains of a fire.

"I don't think people like that I'm here." Other soldiers gave her looks, but none were brave enough to approach with two members of Prince Baldair's highest order at her sides.

"Don't you think that's half the fun?" Craig asked with a small grin.

She shook her head.

"Plus, we look *so exotic* with our Black Legion friend." Daniel took a large bite of his meat.

"Where are you both from?" Vhalla asked, picking at her own food.

"The capital," Craig said, unsurprisingly.

"Cyven," Daniel announced.

"Where in Cyven?" She was sincerely interested in anyone from the East.

"Most people don't know it. It's a small town." Daniel laughed when he saw the squint she was giving him and proceeded, "It's called Paca."

"Paca!" she gasped.

"You know it?" He raised his eyebrows.

"I'm from Leoul."

"*No.*" He seemed as excited as she felt.

"Yes! Yes! I went to the Festival of the Sun in Paca every year with my mum and papa." Vhalla felt the sweet pang of nostalgia.

"With the old lady who sells the candied nuts?" he asked in disbelief.

"And the man who never stopped singing?" Vhalla affirmed.

"*Oh Paaaaaaaca, don't you go astray!*" Daniel put his hand to his chest and belted before they both collapsed into a fit of laughter. "You really do know!" He flashed her a dazzling smile that was too infectious not to return.

"Oh, how adorable. You finally have someone who understands your love of farm animals." Craig's tease was ignored.

Daniel's focus was only on Vhalla.

"My family's farm is about a half day's ride to the Hot Pot Inn. We'd stay there for the festival," she explained.

"I knew the family who owned the inn. I'd work there sometimes when Dad didn't need a hand in the fields. I wonder if we ever met." Daniel gave the matter serious thought.

"Who knows?" Vhalla shrugged and occupied her mouth with a strip of meat. She didn't remember any young boys in particular, but she didn't want to discourage Daniel. It was nice to have a connection to home.

"Get ready to move out," Prince Baldair boomed as he strolled through the ranks.

"I should go." She stood, passing her mostly untouched breakfast to an eager Craig.

"Ride with us today?" Daniel invited.

"I don't think I can," Vhalla said uncertainly.

"They're only strict about the formation for show. They won't care now." Craig was already halfway through her portion.

Vhalla opened her mouth to answer as she felt footsteps thunder over the ground behind her.

"You're far from home."

"My prince." Vhalla turned, giving Prince Baldair a bow. She found his presence uncomfortable. First he'd been nothing more to her than the Heartbreaker Prince, a man straight from the lore of servants. A man she'd only briefly met in the library by chance. Then, he'd been Aldrik's brother, and her conspirator in sneaking her into the gala at the end of the last Festival of the Sun. That had also been the Night of Fire and Wind. The last time she'd seen Prince Baldair he'd been tending to her wounds at Aldrik's command. *What did he think of her now?* "I was just about to return."

"Baldair." Daniel stood, wiping his palms on his pants, surprisingly relaxed in the presence of his prince and commander. "Would it be trouble if Vhalla rode with us today?"

"You well know it'll be trouble from the other soldiers if she is around." Baldair laughed as if the idea was more amusing than off-putting. "But I don't mind, if her superiors don't take issue." The prince gave Vhalla a grin as he paused over the word *superiors*.

"We'll see . . ." Vhalla avoided his presumptuous gaze.

"One of you two walk her back? I don't want trouble one day out," the prince demanded, smartly aware of the tensions surrounding her presence.

"I will," Daniel volunteered first.

"Excellent." Prince Baldair gave a nod and left.

"Shall we?" Daniel took a step toward the Black Legion.

"See you later, Miss Windwalker," Craig bid her farewell with a smile.

"Take care, Craig." Vhalla waved and fell in step with Daniel. The camp was almost completely broken down as they walked back. Remnants of fires were doused, and people were beginning to mount their horses. The short walk was filled with talk of how his family grew potatoes and hers wheat, and the processes for each. Despite the circumstances under which they met, Vhalla felt an instant connection with her fellow Easterner.

When they came upon the Black Legion she noticed Aldrik's tent had almost been completely loaded up into the cart with the rest of the Imperial items, but she didn't see the man anywhere.

"Don't let the other soldiers bother you," Daniel said, coming to a stop. "They're not bad people, they're just—" he paused, looking to the heavens for inspiration, "—a little stupid."

Vhalla grinned.

"Vhal!" Fritz ran over. "We were looking for you." He practically skidded to a halt to give her escort a full assessment.

"Fritz, this is Daniel. Daniel, Fritz," she introduced.

Daniel extended his palm in greeting.

"You best be nice to our Vhal!" Fritz said, ignoring Daniel's hand and pointing in his face.

"My, you didn't warn me you had bodyguards," Daniel chuckled, taking Fritz's hand from his face and shaking it. "You have my word, only kindness and care from me." The low draw of a horn echoed through the forest and the last soldiers fell into place like a great migration. "Oops, must get back. Come up and ride with us if you can!" Daniel called, already hurrying to the front.

"He's *cute*," Fritz swooned.

"Fritz!" Vhalla scolded.

"What? Don't tell me you didn't notice." Fritz rolled his eyes. In truth, Vhalla hadn't. She ran back over to Lightning to find Larel already on horseback, waiting along with Fritz's mount. "Sorry," she apologized.

"Yet again, Vhalla, you have nothing to be sorry for." Larel's smiled brightly. "You seem to be in better spirits."

Vhalla mounted Lightning with a nod, concealing a guilty smile. She *had* enjoyed herself.

It turned out to be just as Craig and Daniel had said. The host was a slightly structured mass today compared to the neat rows and careful placement of the day before. But she, Fritz, and Larel gravitated to the same place in line. The two were instantly involved in some heated debate that carried over from breakfast and Vhalla drifted in and out of the conversation, thinking about Daniel's and Craig's offer.

It wasn't until Aldrik shifted in his saddle that she even realized he was there.

Vhalla turned and her mouth dropped agape. "Your . . . *hair*." It was a thought that escaped as sound. His raven hair was limp, falling perfectly straight around his face. The prince had long bangs that tapered in front, falling below his eyebrows, and messy cut layers throughout. They were elements of an Aldrik that Vhalla had no idea even existed, so different from how he usually wore his hair in the palace.

He glanced at her, momentary annoyance furrowing his brow. "You did not really think I would take time to fix my hair while at war, did you?" Aldrik's low tones betrayed his amusement, and it instantly placed her under a spell.

"Well, I may like it," Vhalla mused. His coy smirk encouraged boldness.

Aldrik paused briefly, his lips parted. She caught his ebony eyes and Aldrik looked forward quickly, as if unable to handle being the sole recipient of her consideration. "I trust Elecia got my message to you?"

Vhalla sobered quickly at the other woman's name. "She did. Training?"

"Major Reale said she had begun to work with you, but you still have a ways to go. I would rather oversee your progress personally."

Had he said those words to anyone else they likely would have inspired dread. But for Vhalla, they had an odd comfort.

"Of course, my puppet master." She had meant to reference her old fears lightly, so it surprised Vhalla to see Aldrik staring at her with a deep intensity.

"If you want me to remove myself from your life, all you have to do is say the word." There was no levity to his declaration.

Vhalla quickly looked askance, saving them from impropriety and hiding the blush that had found its way to her cheeks at his apparent attentions.

"I think," she started softly, "that I like playing with fire."

He gave her a long stare from the corner of his eyes. She couldn't make out his expression without turning her head, but what she could see was confusing and made her stomach bubble.

Chapter 5

NOT LONG AFTER the host stopped that afternoon, Elecia made her way to Vhalla and Larel's mostly-finished tent. Fritz stood from where he had just finished unfurling his bedroll.

The sight of the woman still sent prickles up Vhalla's neck—a phantom warning.

"Vhalla, Larel, Fritz," she said with a smile, oblivious to Vhalla's unease. "The prince is waiting, and I would rather not lose first pick for dinner."

"Where are we going?" Vhalla asked, the last to fall into step behind Elecia.

"Out far enough away that we won't be disturbed." They were already halfway to the edge of camp.

"So, where are you from?" Larel struck up conversation.

"Norin." Elecia didn't even look back to give her response.

"*Fiarum Evantes*," Larel said, reverently.

Vhalla looked over at her friend in surprise. She had never heard anyone speak anything other than Southern Common. The old tongues were a fading memory across the land, cemented by the advancement of the Solaris Empire. She could only assume Larel's words to be the language of Mhashan, the old Kingdom of the West.

"*Kotun un Nox*," Elecia responded, her tone shifting to a deeper register, less haughty than the lofty accent she'd used before.

"Norin is a beautiful city," Larel mused politely, referring to the Western capital.

"It is." Elecia nodded.

Vhalla began to feel her unease thaw. She had no reason to distrust Elecia. In fact, she had every reason to trust her. Clearly Aldrik did, and that should be more than enough reason for Vhalla. Furthermore, if she was from Norin, that made her Western and not Northern as Vhalla had first suspected. She took a deep breath. "I'm from—"

"Cyven, Leoul," the curly-haired woman cut off Vhalla with a glance.

"Yes." Vhalla frowned slightly, her fluster returning. "How did you know?"

"It's my business to know, Vhalla Yarl," Elecia replied smugly.

Fritz linked his arm protectively with Vhalla's, as if sensing the dread that overtook her. She realized that they were very alone with Elecia. And, even if the other woman said she was from the West and spoke with the old tongue, she was so Northern-looking that it made Vhalla more uncomfortable than she wanted to admit.

Were it not for Fritz and Larel being with her, she may have snapped.

"About time," Aldrik's voice echoed from across a small clearing. He leaned against a tree, his arms crossed over his chest. "Thank you for fetching them, Elecia. You can go now."

Vhalla wondered briefly why Aldrik was not escorting them himself. Were their meetings secret?

"Nope," Elecia practically sung. "I am not your errand girl. I want to stay."

"Fine." Aldrik rolled his eyes, resigned.

Vhalla brought her hands together, lacing and unlacing her fingers. Elecia had refused him openly, publicly, coyly—and he had let her. As Elecia stepped to Aldrik's left, it dawned on Vhalla that the woman acted as the same way Vhalla did around the prince. Vhalla bit her lip; perhaps Aldrik was more familiar with Elecia than he was with her.

"Vhalla," Aldrik's voice summoned her attention. "I want you to see what you are working toward. Reale has informed me that you have yet to master the basics."

Vhalla nodded and ignored Elecia's smug snort.

"Larel, Fritz, I would like for you both to pair off as a demonstration," Aldrik commanded.

"What about me?" Elecia whined.

"You are not even supposed to be here." Aldrik gave her a small glare, and the woman laughed. The sound made Vhalla's skin crawl. "I would also like to see where you both are at, so do not maim or kill each other, but do not hold back."

Larel and Fritz nodded, their faces sobering.

"Begin on my mark, then. And refrain from embarrassing yourselves." Aldrik lifted a hand.

Fritz and Larel took a few steps away from each other, each sinking into a very different fighting stance. Fritz was more upright, his legs wide and his hands flat and lower, near his abdomen. Larel had her knees bent and her fists near her face, ready to pounce.

Aldrik dropped his hand, and Larel charged before Vhalla could blink. She drew back a fist as though she was going to throw a right hook but, at the last moment, dropped her shoulder for a left uppercut. Fritz raised his open palm, creating a shield of ice. It hissed and shattered as Larel's fist, now swathed in flame, slammed into it.

Fritz pushed his other hand forward into her shoulder, freezing a portion of it. Larel gasped and stepped back, the ice quickly turning into a puddle around her feet. She had no time to catch her breath as he lunged. His wrist twitched, and he suddenly wielded a dagger of ice in his palm. Larel deflected by raising up her arm, and it shattered on her gauntlet.

She dropped and swept her foot on the ground, catching Fritz's ankle and sending him tumbling backwards. Larel pulled back a flaming fist and threw her momentum into it. Fritz moved his hands as if to block, but he was too slow.

Vhalla's hands rose to her mouth as she concealed a cry, fearful for her friend.

Larel's fist smashed through Fritz's face, and his body dissolved in a puff of smoke. The Western woman turned with a groan. Vhalla caught a shift in the light behind her. There was a flash of ice and Fritz faded back to sight, holding an ice dagger at Larel's throat.

"Every time!" Larel threw up her hands, and Fritz backed away with a grin, tossing the wickedly sharp icicle aside. "Every time!" she said again, kicking the ground in frustration.

Vhalla stared in wonder.

"The minister told me about you," Aldrik commented, taking a step over toward Fritz. "A gifted illusionist."

"I don't know if I'm gifted," he said bashfully, rubbing the back of his neck.

"What, what was that?" Vhalla forced out in shock when her tongue was working again.

"She's like a newborn bunny!" Elecia giggled to Aldrik, as though Vhalla wasn't even there. "She has never seen illusions before."

Aldrik shot the woman a pointed look before turning back to Vhalla, his features relaxing. "Fritz, would you like to explain it to Vhalla?" the prince ordered the Southern man, but never took his eyes off her.

"Water affinities can use the water in the air to distort

the light, to create smoke screens, fogs," Fritz started, clearly uncomfortable by the praise and attention.

"And illusions, if the sorcerer is skilled enough." Aldrik motioned to Fritz, directing Vhalla's attention back to her friend.

Fritz waved his hand in demonstration and an identical image formed next to him.

Vhalla gasped softly, taking a step toward the apparition. It looked like Fritz in every way, and Vhalla raised a hand—no one stopped her. The illusion dissipated under her fingertips, nothing more than a puff of vapor.

Vhalla's eyes widened.

She was no longer standing in that forest clearing; she was living a waking nightmare. Her twisted dreams merged with the reality before her and the horrible memories that she had pushed from her consciousness. There was wind, there was fire, there was death, and there was blood splattered across her arms and face as she watched bodies torn to shreds by howling gusts. It had been her desire. She had wanted them dead. She had wanted them more than dead, she wanted the Northerners to *suffer*.

Vhalla took a step back, shaking her head. *That wasn't who she was.*

"No," she whispered. Someone took a step toward her; all she saw were shadows from her dreams. Shadows she ripped apart by touching. "Don't come any closer," she gave a quivering warning. Vhalla brought up her hands to her ears, the screams of the people whom she had murdered filling her consciousness. She realized in horrible clarity what had been haunting her, the blood on her hands that she'd been ignoring.

She felt dizzy. Her legs buckled beneath her, and her body doubled over.

"Vhalla, what's wrong?" Fritz asked, his voice faint.

"Go," she panted. They shouldn't be near her. At the edge of her guilt-shattered conscious she could hear a wind roaring. Vhalla gripped her head tighter. She had meant to kill those Northerners on the Night of Fire and Wind, but she had not known what killing meant.

Two strong hands gripped her wrists and she lashed out, shaking her head and twisting her body. Vhalla attempted to knock the person away with a strong gust, but they didn't even seem to feel it.

"Vhalla." Aldrik's voice was strong and level, cutting through the din of the chaos in her head. "Stop. Breathe," he instructed, and she forced herself to oblige. His voice rang over the storm raging within her. "Open your eyes."

Vhalla squinted open one eye, and then the next. Even though it was almost night, the world had a hazy glow to it. Aldrik was surrounded in the golden, almost white, flame that she'd seen him in before. He burned brighter than any of the others assembled. She struggled to shift her vision back to normal, and her eyes fluttered closed.

"Look at me." Aldrik shook her.

She opened her eyes and focused on his face, slowly regaining control of her magic sight. Her breathing was ragged, and her hands trembled. Concern was written across Aldrik's furrowed brow.

"Mother save me, I really killed them," she gasped.

His mouth fell open a moment, but he recovered and relaxed his grip on her wrists. Aldrik stood, helping Vhalla to her feet. When she had her balance, Aldrik finally let go of her and took a step away. "Fritz, take her back to camp," he ordered briskly.

"Is it a good idea for me to—" Fritz was uncertain.

"Do *not* try my patience, Charem," Aldrik growled. He was every inch the Fire Lord.

It was all Fritz needed to spring to life. He scampered over to her and paused. "Can you walk? I mean, do you want help?" She shook her head. "I can do it."

Elecia stepped toward Aldrik. Her voice was low, but it was loud enough for Vhalla to hear. "She is not ready. You need to give this up now; there isn't anything you can do for her."

"Neiress," Aldrik barked out Larel's family name, ignoring Elecia. "I could use a round, if you feel up to it."

"It would be my honor, my prince." Larel gave a bow.

Fritz tugged Vhalla's attention from the scene, pulling her toward the forest that was between them and camp. She glanced back over her shoulder as a fury of flames burst out in the deepening darkness. Elecia stood, leaning against a tree. The flames lit her face, and she ran her thumb across her lips in thought. Vhalla turned forward, relieved the woman wasn't following them after Aldrik's dismissal.

Fritz and Vhalla walked in an uneasy silence as the sounds of clanking armor and bursts of flame began to fade and meld into the growing sounds of camp. Vhalla focused on the ground, letting him lead her by the hand. She chewed over her words, trying to find some kind of explanation.

"Vhalla, I'm really, *really* sorry and-and I don't know what I did but I didn't mean to upset you." Fritz broke the silence like a dam shattering. "I thought it'd be interesting for you to see, and I don't know if it messed with your magic or something, but I promise I won't do it again."

"It's not your fault." She shook her head, feeling guilty. "It reminded me of something . . . You couldn't have known. Please, don't feel bad. It really was amazing."

"If you want to talk about it," he offered, returning to her side as they began to walk again.

"No." She put an end to the notion sharply.

Fritz walked her all the way back to her tent. When she

insisted she had no appetite, he went to dinner on the promise that he would set aside a portion for her. Vhalla wasn't sure if he would be successful, but she was too tired to care. She barely found the energy to pull off her armor before collapsing in the bedroll.

Despite being overwhelmed and at the brink of exhaustion, sleep didn't come. Vhalla watched shadows from campfires dance on the walls of her tent. She closed her eyes briefly, but every time she did a new horror awaited her. Vhalla wasn't sure how much time had passed but Larel's entrance was a relief.

"Welcome back," she whispered.

"You're awake?"

"Can't sleep," Vhalla explained the obvious.

"You need to try," Larel ordered softly, putting her armor at the foot of her bedroll.

"How was the rest of the training?" Vhalla asked, changing the subject.

"Whenever the prince steps into the fray, the memory of your experience always lingers." Larel rubbed her shoulder generously as she crawled under her blanket.

Silence settled heavily between them, suppressing the words that needed to be said. It lasted so long that Vhalla was sure Larel had fallen asleep. But the other woman took a slow breath. "Vhalla."

"Yes?" she whispered back.

"I know it isn't my business . . ." Larel's uneasy start set Vhalla's heart to racing. "But you know he cares for you, right?"

Vhalla stared into the darkness at Larel's shadowy outline. She shifted, her stomach getting that strange feeling again—likely because she hadn't eaten. "He's a friend," she confessed for the first time to anyone. Vhalla thought back to the day in the chapel and her mind betrayed her by also flooding her with memories of a dance in the water gardens of the palace on the night of the gala. It all seemed like a dream from where she was now.

"A friend?" Larel mused over the notion aloud.

"A *dear* friend . . ." Vhalla felt the strange urge to qualify.

Larel clicked her tongue but withheld further comment.

Vhalla curled into a ball with a sigh and finally closed her eyes. Horrors did not greet her. A prince with a golden circlet was painted across her memories.

CHAPTER 6

"Vhal . . . Vhal." Fritz nudged her gently.

"What?" Vhalla yawned.

"You need to eat something."

This again. "I'm not hungry." She rubbed her eyes with the soft leather that covered her palms. It had been three days since the night in the forest, and none of them had mentioned training since. It made Vhalla feel all the more broken, defective.

"When was the last time you ate?" Larel was in on it now too.

"I . . ." Vhalla struggled to answer the question honestly. "I ate breakfast yesterday, and dinner the night before."

"You call that eating?" Fritz shook his head. "Those were hardly snacks."

"Let it go." Annoyance crept into her tone.

"Vhalla," a voice said sternly to her left.

Apprehension filled her at the sound of his voice. Aldrik had hardly spoken to her since the night Vhalla broke down, and she hadn't had the courage to say anything to him. It was fine to imagine that she could cut her hair and become someone strong, the monster that the Senate had every right to fear. But the moment she was presented with the beast she was, she fell apart. She was weak, so it made sense that he wanted nothing to do with her.

"You are already a risk to everyone by not being skilled in combat or having a handle on your magic. The least you can do is keep your body in good condition by eating." He gave her a long stare. "And sleeping," the prince added, as if noticing the darkening circles under her eyes for the first time.

With a sigh, Vhalla grabbed the meat Fritz held out to her and tore into it. It was cold, and slimy, and tasteless. The food on the march had quickly lost its novelty, and now it was just another reminder of where she was, of *who* she was.

"Eat it all," Aldrik instructed dryly. "It will be more graceful if you eat it yourself rather than one of us forcing it down your throat."

She took smaller bites, but managed to get—and keep—it all down. The food settled heavily in her stomach and threatened to come up with the swaying of the horse.

As if to capitalize on her sour mood, Elecia appeared out of nowhere and wedged herself between Vhalla and Aldrik.

"Good morning!" she said cheerfully.

Aldrik gave her a nod, and Fritz and Larel offered their greetings. Vhalla focused on the road ahead.

"Come now, do not be rude," Elecia said with a patronizing grin.

"Hello." Vhalla did not even make eye contact.

"My, someone woke up on the wrong side of the bed." Elecia laughed and clapped a hand over Vhalla's shoulder. "Don't be so serious!" She smiled, and Vhalla continued to ignore her. "Or not." Elecia shrugged and turned to Aldrik. "So, I don't know if you heard, but I recently began studying remedies for Channel blockers . . ."

Vhalla was forced to spend the next two hours listening to Elecia and Aldrik discuss the properties of Channels and how they could be disrupted or blocked. The discussion was over Vhalla's head, so she tried to tune them out. It annoyed her; *they* irrationally annoyed her. This woman, whom she had barely met, held a conversation with Aldrik that made Vhalla feel stupid.

Eventually her nonsensical frustration finally won and Vhalla interrupted the conversations. "So, when are we going to train again?" she asked with more conviction than she felt. All four people stared at her blankly.

"Train?" Elecia laughed. "Why would you want to?"

"Because I'm going to war," Vhalla said sharply.

"But last time—"

"Are you sure you're feeling up to it?" Larel interrupted Elecia.

"Is that a good idea?" Fritz said uncertainly.

"I can." Vhalla nodded to herself. "I will." She turned to Aldrik, searching his silence for encouragement, approval—*something*.

"Very well," he said after what seemed like forever. "We need to work on your Channeling first, so we shall focus on that tonight."

"Channeling?" Vhalla repeated.

"Wait, you mean to tell me she does not even know how to Channel?" Elecia looked between Vhalla and Aldrik. "You have hope for her, and she doesn't even—"

"It is not your decision," Aldrik barked harshly.

Vhalla was pleased by the amount Elecia was being interrupted. The sentiment was not shared, and the other woman adjusted her red bandana before riding off in a huff.

"What's Channeling?" Vhalla forced herself to ask. She hated herself for not knowing, but not asking would only exacerbate the problem. Aldrik had mentioned it months ago, but he'd never bothered to explain.

"It's how a sorcerer uses magic," Fritz began.

"I can use magic," she retorted in a defensive and tired tone.

"Yes, you can but," Fritz twirled his reins around his fingers, "but not well."

His words were like a dagger to her gut. Even he saw her as useless. Vhalla swallowed the pain of that realization, forcing it away from her eyes where it may show.

"Think of it like this," Larel started gently. "You have a pitcher and a cup. You have to get the water from the pitcher into the cup. One way you can do it is by dipping the cup into the pitcher. But this is messy and maybe it doesn't fit right and so on."

"So you pour from the pitcher instead," Vhalla finished the logic. Larel nodded and smiled. It was a welcome sight that gave Vhalla some ease.

"Exactly, we can dip into our magic to accomplish things on a whim—like you've been doing. But it's tiring, difficult, and normally inconsistent. That's why we open up a Channel for it to flow—to pour—easily into us," Larel finished.

"And, for that reason, you will be working with me tonight," Aldrik announced, loud enough that it drew Major Reale's attention.

"Thank you, my prince," Vhalla mumbled.

"I trust you will not disappoint me."

After that declaration, it was a cold silence from the normally warm man for the rest of the day. They had never had an opportunity to be talkative, not really, so Vhalla was surprised to find how much his silence bothered her. It was a weight on her shoulders until Aldrik appeared by her and Larel's tent that evening.

"Are you ready?" the prince asked.

Vhalla nodded mutely.

"Should I fetch her dinner?" Larel asked with a thoughtful glance between her awkward companions.

"Not necessary; I will make sure she eats," Aldrik replied in a particularly sharp tone. Vhalla focused on the dust covering the toes of her boots. "Come."

Vhalla's and Larel's tent wasn't far from Aldrik's. The other sorcerers had the decency to smother their looks, but a few stared in curiosity at the new woman following the prince. Behind her she heard whispering and picked out the word "Windwalker" more than once. It seemed to be the explanation that was automatically assigned when anything different or special occurred near her. It was a nice excuse to prevent rumors of anything untoward, Vhalla reasoned. But the attention still made her uncomfortable.

Aldrik ducked his head under the flap and walked into the orange glow of tent beyond. Vhalla paused, assuring herself that there was no reason to be nervous. She was only about to enter the personal quarters of the crown prince of the realm, no matter how makeshift they were. Gripping her fingers tightly, she gathered her resolve and walked in behind him.

His tent seemed more spacious on the inside. To the left of the entrance, furs and thick blankets were piled on top of chopped brush to make a sleeping pallet. Her sleepless nights must be catching up to her because the sight of it was oddly appealing. Around the perimeter hung thin disks, flames burning impossibly above the steel braziers. To the right, a large rug of great finery had been unrolled upon the bare ground, a number of pillows and a small floor table atop it.

Aldrik stood on the opposite side of the room removing his greaves and gauntlets.

"Come and help me with the plate?" he asked casually, catching her off-guard.

"M-my prince?" Vhalla stumbled over her words. It was as though the second they were out of sight she was in a different world with a different man.

"Since when are you formal in private?" Aldrik arched a dark eyebrow. "Some help?"

He turned and raised his arms. Vhalla noticed a small seam

on the back left of his plate. She crossed the room hastily and began fussing with the latches underneath.

"How, *um*, how do you get it on?" she inquired, desperate to talk over the blood rushing in her ears.

"I have help—a squire," he explained logically. Vhalla's clumsy fingers finally undid the last clasp and he unhinged it, slipping out through the side. Aldrik placed the plate on the ground and began to unfasten his scale.

"Aldrik, is this really . . ." Vhalla swallowed, taking a step back and looking away.

"Do you think me naked under my armor?" A small grin curled up the corners of his mouth as he slid off his scale, leaving just chainmail beneath.

"Your armor is the same as mine," she observed, inspecting the thin links curiously.

"Of course it is." He ran a hand through his hair, and Vhalla watched it cascade back into place around his fingers.

"Why?" She felt like she was missing something obvious.

"I made it." His eyes caught hers, and Vhalla couldn't find words between her surprise and the look he was giving her.

"Why?" Vhalla repeated again, remembering Larel telling her once about how Firebearers were jewelers or smiths due to their ability to manage flames.

"Why? Why do I make my own armor, my parrot?" Aldrik had to know that her inquiry was more than him making *his* armor. "Because I do not trust other craftsmen with something as important as my life."

There was a hidden meaning between his words, and Vhalla felt overwhelmed trying to understand its layers. Aldrik spared her from the task when he shrugged off the last of his armor—and her mind went blank. He was in a loose-fitting, long-sleeved white shirt that hung mostly open at his neck. On his lower half were a pair of well-tailored black pants that clung close to his legs. It was more casual and undressed than she'd ever seen him before, and just the sight brought a bright blush to her cheeks.

If the prince noticed her modesty, he was good enough not to comment. Aldrik sat on one of the pillows near the low table. A paper caught his eye, eliciting a small sigh.

"What is it?" she asked, still hovering.

"Oh, nothing. Just some things I need to go over with Father." He glanced back at her. "If you would like to get more comfortable," he offered with a gesture toward a seat. His gaze shifted back to the paper, and he pinched the bridge of his nose in thought.

Vhalla fidgeted with her fingers. It was armor; she'd normally worn less around him. But something about undressing *anything*, here in his tent, made her heart race. With a deep breath Vhalla reminded herself to be an adult and stop acting like an excitable girl. In the end she compromised by pulling off her boots and gloves as well as her scale, but left on her chainmail.

She sat on the pillow opposite him and crossed her legs. The pillows were comfortable, as equally fine as the rug, with tightly woven threads that seemed to be some kind of silk.

"Oh sorry." Vhalla put down the spare cushion with a nervous laugh when she felt his stare.

"What is it?" Aldrik asked, returning the paper to the stack.

"They're very nice," she said truthfully.

"You think so?" He seemed surprised, as if he was considering them for the first time.

"Well, for me they are." She smiled faintly. He forgot so easily they came from different worlds.

"In any case," he ceased his own inspection. "Channeling. It is much like Larel explained: you will tap into the source of your power, which should be easy for you, given your Affinity."

"How do I go about it?"

"Well, in a way that depends on you. I will help you understand the fundamentals of it, but ultimately it is your connection with yourself and the world." It was a cryptic explanation, and Vhalla felt her chance of success diminishing to hopelessness. "Most sorcerers have a trigger that opens and closes their Channel. This is normally physical. Many find it easier to tie it to a tangible act."

"What's yours?" she asked.

"The major told me you are capable of magical sight?" Vhalla nodded, that much she could hang her hat on. "Very well—watch." Aldrik held out his hands before her, palms open. Vhalla adjusted her vision and saw him bathed in the familiar golden flame. He clenched his hands into fists and suddenly the glow was extinguished across his body.

"Are you all right?" she gasped, looking at his now-dim form.

He chuckled and nodded. "I closed my Channel. Keep watching." He relaxed and unfurled his fingers. Aldrik snapped them closed into fists again and the white and gold flames returned.

"It's magnificent," she breathed. The complement earned her a faint smile. Vhalla looked down from his face and paused. "Aldrik . . ." She murmured as her eyes focused on a dark spot. She'd seen it before in the garden, before she even knew about magical sight. Vhalla reached out a hand to touch him, stopping herself short. She shouldn't be so forward; he was still the crown prince.

Aldrik knew what she saw. "The poison crystalized, rooting itself enough that I could not remove it. It was the best I could do."

"It's not letting your Channel work properly, is it?" Vhalla frowned, suddenly realizing what that dark spot meant.

"Exactly . . ." His voice began to grow heavy. "That is why I could not protect you as I should have that night." Aldrik paused. "Vhalla, it's my fault."

"What is?" Apprehension trailed its icy fingers up her spine.

He took her still hovering hand in both of his. "You should not have had to kill them. If I had been more capable, you would not have been forced to." Emotion burned behind his eyes and it struck her clear as day. Channeling was a side-project for him. The main goal was the Night of Fire and Wind. He was playing the puppet master again, and Larel was certainly helping.

"*I don't want to talk about it.* Teach me Channeling or we're done." She wrenched her hand from his.

"I was fourteen," he began, ignoring her. Her mouth was still twisted in annoyance. "The first time I killed a man."

Her face relaxed.

"Looking back, I didn't even have a good reason to kill him." Vhalla shifted closer to hear, his voice faint and his eyes glossy. He seemed to stare through the world around him.

"I was told that he was a bad man, that he was going to harm my family and his death would make us stronger." Aldrik chuckled bitterly. "As if death makes anyone stronger . . ."

The pressure of his gaze weighed on every inch of her body.

"I will never forget that in the end, he asked for mercy from his prince. He asked for forgiveness, and I gave him death." Aldrik's body was very still, and his eyes searched hers, yearning for something.

"Aldrik," Vhalla whispered. She didn't know what she could offer him. "I'm sorry." She initiated contact, taking his hand in her own.

He didn't pull away. "After that, the killing became easier. Soon, I forgot their faces, their cries, their stories. They merged into one communal grave in my mind, which became a gaping wound that everyone who perishes by my hand falls into. But I never forgot that first man's face. I have tried to plunge him into that hollow void and push him away, but I have *never* forgotten."

Vhalla stared at him in a mix of horror and pity. She squeezed his hand and was surprised when she felt a squeeze back.

"I see you taking steps down this path, and I don't want you be lost to that darkness." He laughed and bore the most unfiltered sorrow she had ever seen from him. "What is worse is, thanks to the extraordinary wisdom of the people's Senate, I cannot protect you from that."

"So, what do I do?" Vhalla finally sought guidance for her guilt.

"Never forget who you are, and do not let the dead define you." He spoke as if he'd been reading her thoughts for weeks. "Talk to me or Fritz or Larel. I do not think any of us are prepared to lose you to your demons."

She stared at him; she didn't want to think about the Night of Fire and Wind. She wanted it to go away. He'd lured her into his den with his pretenses, and now she was the captive of his stares and touch. Vhalla closed her eyes and took a breath.

"Every night, I see them. I hear their screams and I feel their blood on my hands, on my face." She shuddered as her voice broke and pulled her hand away from his to wrap her arms around herself. "At first I didn't know what they were, but that night, in the forest, I remembered." It seemed silly to her, to say she'd forgotten the first time she'd killed a person but her mind had been so efficient at pushing it away.

"I wish I could be better comfort to you," he murmured softly. Aldrik leaned over and, with only his fingertips, he pushed aside some stray hair. They both seemed to catch their breath as his skin lightly brushed her face. He pulled away, his hand balling into a fist.

"You are," she said quickly, earning herself a surprised stare.

"I am?" he repeated skeptically.

"I—" Vhalla stumbled over her words. "I am . . . happier . . . with you, near you." Something about him softened, but there was a sadness to it that made Vhalla feel guilty for her confession.

"In any case." He was back to avoiding her attentions. "My ear and my door are always open for you."

"Thank you." Vhalla wondered how many people he had offered that to. She couldn't imagine it was many.

"For now though, we should make sure you know how to Channel." Aldrik seemed as uncomfortable as she was and the moment—whatever it had been—vanished.

They set to work on what Vhalla discovered was the seemingly impossible task of Channeling. Vhalla saw shades of the phantom she had exchanged notes with months ago as he spoke volumes of knowledge worth of magical theory with deft ease. His silver tongue licked across her intellect, wetting her mental palate for new information.

But the willingness to learn and the practical execution were also much like he had told her months ago—it was harder to do than conceive. At her every attempt Aldrik instructed that she "only needed to find the magic within her" or "tap into her power." But Vhalla felt like she was shooting for an unknown target in the dark.

By the time he fetched food, she found herself exhausted. Their conversation turned casual and Vhalla relaxed, absentmindedly consuming the meal before her. He made her sides split with laughter by telling her a story of when he taught his younger brother to ride a horse for the first time. Vhalla shared the first time she'd gone to help in the field but had ended up just playing in the mud for most of the day. He seemed to find it as shocking as he did amusing. For that brief hour the horrors she had seen, she had committed, didn't matter.

Reality could not be escaped for long. The moment the food was finished, they returned to Channeling.

"I think it may be pointless," Vhalla sighed, dropping her

arms. She'd been waving them about like a fool trying to find the "essence of air."

"There is one more thing that we could try, since you do not have the luxury of time," Aldrik said thoughtfully after a long silence. "But it is not a conventional method. It is rather theoretical, actually."

"Oh?" He knew what to say to make her insatiably curious.

"It is more on Bonding than Channeling." He leaned forward. "Did you have a chance to read anything on Bonds before you left the Tower?"

"I couldn't find much," she replied.

"That is because there is not much," Aldrik affirmed. "Bonding is a strange occurrence and difficult to understand because, to the best of every scholar's assessments, it is the literal opening of a magic passage between two people. You opened your magic to me to save my life."

Those words soaked into both of them for a moment.

"But, as they say, doors and gates open both ways," Aldrik finished, easing that odd tension they flirted with every time they were together.

"Wait." Vhalla blinked. "You're saying I have some of your magic in me?"

"Not just some; it has the capacity to be a passage between us," he affirmed.

"That's amazing," she whispered.

"That is why I do not think your magic is as effective against me as it is on others. It will not hit me as strong. Our own magic cannot hurt us." He shook his head. "There are a number of interesting theories we could discuss and explore another time. For now, we are going to try Joining."

"What is *Joining*?" she asked, braving a parrot comment.

"It is difficult to explain. Think of the Bond as a latent Channel. Joining will activate it, widen the Bond." Aldrik leaned closer, and Vhalla's heart beat hard. "This may not even work. But for it to have a chance—do not fight me."

If Vhalla had wanted to, she couldn't have. She was so stunned by his forward advances, by the fingers that lightly touched her temples, that she could barely speak. Aldrik's eyes fluttered closed and he took a breath. She bit her lip, unsure if she was supposed to do the same. But if she didn't, she would spend the time studying his sculpted features in the firelight— and she might die of embarrassment if caught.

So Vhalla closed her eyes as well.

At first, there was nothing. She heard her breathing and felt his hands on her. His fingertips warmed and then, faintly, she heard her heartbeat. *No*, she realized, it wasn't her heartbeat, *it was his.* Her initial reaction was to panic at the sensation of another heart beating in her chest, but Vhalla forced herself to stay still and calm. Soon the chorus of sound extended to his breathing, overlaid on the noises of her own body. The din reached a crescendo that threatened to consume her awareness. But Vhalla remembered his words and she gave into it, *into him*, letting the wave crash upon her.

There was one inhale, one exhale, one heartbeat between them.

She melted into the strange warmth of the communal existence, relinquishing the last of her physical senses. It was unlike anything she had ever felt. Like life and death all bundled neatly into one moment of beauty. She tried to find where her own self ended, to find where he began, but there were no ends or beginnings anywhere. They were infinite.

She felt as he felt, and he thought as she thought.

Suddenly there was a warm breeze blowing over her metaphysical self. It was strong. Something she had known from birth, known her whole life, without ever really having words for it before. As Aldrik opened his Channel, hers opened alongside it in all its brilliance.

She felt him pulling away from her and, in her mind, she objected. There was a safety there, a reassurance, a compassion, and more she dared not give words to. It was a gentle departure, but a departure all the same. Vhalla sighed faintly as her eyes fluttered open. Aldrik stared back. His chest expanded slowly with every deep breath.

For a long time they sat unmoving. Her body felt the same, but everything had changed. His hands slowly fell away from her face, and the last connection was through their gaze.

"Vhalla, I . . ." he uttered over a thick tongue.

Some madness overwhelmed her, and she grabbed for his hands. "Aldrik," she breathed, clutching at him desperately. Vhalla searched for some validation of what she had found in their brief period of shared existence.

Aldrik stared back at her. Long before he pulled his hands from hers she saw a moment of panic, *a moment of want*—and he withdrew mentally. Vhalla realized he may be unable to hide anything from her again in the darkness of his eyes, she'd seen it all as though she was looking in a mirror. She wasn't sure if this Joining was a blessing or a curse.

"I think we have accomplished enough for tonight." Aldrik looked away, sitting straighter, more composed.

"Aldrik," she whispered. Even his minor withdrawal hurt her more deeply than it should have. It felt like a piece of her had been carved out.

"All you need to do is repeat that process, what you felt. I think you can figure that out on your own." He still didn't look at her.

"*Aldrik,*" Vhalla pleaded.

"You can ask Larel for help also. Just pick a motion and repeat it as you Channel. Repeat the action every time you try, so when you succeed you will begin to associate the act with that trigger." He turned back to the table, picking up the parchment he'd been reading earlier.

Vhalla wasn't sure what she had done wrong, but he had completely shut himself off from her. He was the one who had suggested the Joining; what was he suddenly so afraid of? She sighed and pulled herself to her feet.

Aldrik didn't look at her as she slipped back into her armor. It was a short walk but the last thing she wanted was to leave a man's tent—the crown prince's tent—less dressed than when she came in. He said nothing and made no motion toward her.

"Well," Vhalla said uncertainly, "thank you." A splash of bitterness crept into her voice. He made no motion as she turned to leave.

"I will call on you," he said abruptly, just as she was about to pull back the tent flap.

"What?" Vhalla turned, her heart racing on hope.

"Work on your Channeling, you will need it for what I'm going to ask of you," Aldrik said, turning to her. "We shall begin when I am satisfied with your progression."

Vhalla nodded and searched his guarded gaze for a long moment. She saw it there still, his turmoil. *But turmoil over what?* That was a question she had yet to answer.

"Very well. Goodnight, Aldrik." Vhalla pulled back the tent flap, making her departure.

"Goodnight, Vhalla."

CHAPTER 7

*T*HE DAY WAS *overcast and hot. There was a dry breeze, but it offered little respite from the oppressive heat. It was the kind of day that one wanted nothing more than to find a cool, shady corner to curl up into. But the sun beat down on her shoulders.*

She stood before a grave. It was in the center of a glass-covered garden. Many plants had been landscaped and most were hanging on despite the temperature. But the crimson flowers that surrounded the sculpted marker before her were wilted and shriveled. It was not the first time she had been in this garden of the dead.

The grave before her was shaped as an obelisk. Sitting at its top was the figure of a woman. She had long hair that hung perfectly straight, almost to her waist, and a soft, yet stern, visage cast in the flawless marble. Behind her was a golden and ruby sun that cast a red haze on the ground below.

Vhalla held out a hand and touched the familiar letters, as though it would connect her to her dead mother. There was nothing but stone beneath her fingers. She sighed, shifting her weight. She really hated being here.

"Stop fidgeting," came a strong voice from next to her. She turned her face upward but the sun shrouded the man towering over her.

Vhalla turned and cracked open her eyes. The back of her hand rested against her forehead. She stared at the slowly illuminating canvas above her. It was a strange dream that played more like a long-forgotten memory. Vhalla ran through it again and, despite the overwhelming nostalgia, nothing seemed familiar on a second review. She was too tired to give the dream much attention and went about her morning duties.

Joining, that was what Aldrik had called it. Vhalla fidgeted over breakfast, trying to force herself to eat. She still didn't understand the widening of the Bond, as Aldrik had put it, but it had certainly been significant. The ghost of him was still upon her. She could still feel the caress of his essence throughout her bones. Vhalla stared at her hands. Learning how to Channel seemed so unimportant in comparison.

"How did it go last night?" Fritz asked as he joined her and Larel.

"What?" Vhalla snapped herself out of her thoughts.

Larel's interest had clearly been piqued. She hadn't inquired last night when Vhalla returned, exhausted and bleary eyed, and had been silent all morning.

"With the prince," Fritz dropped his voice. "Do you have a better idea of how to Channel?"

"I think so." Vhalla nodded.

"Good, good!" Fritz beamed. "You'll get the hang of it in a few weeks, I'm sure."

Vhalla felt the magic crackling around her fingers. She didn't need a few weeks, she could do it now. Her body knew it. But she didn't have an opportunity to correct Fritz as the horns blew, summoning everyone back to their places in the host.

The soldiers moved more slowly now. A week of marching had begun to take its toll on the new recruits. Vhalla's legs were stiff and sore-ridden from her own saddle. She had no idea how the men and women who walked were managing. How would they fight when they reached the North?

Aldrik was slow as well this morning, the host was practically moving when he rode up from the outside. Even in all his bulky armor he was still full of poise atop his War-strider. Her heartbeat began to race and, as if sensing it, Aldrik's eyes found hers. Tension radiated between them, even across a dozen people.

He pulled hard on his reins and turned his mount, riding along the outside of the host to a few rows behind Vhalla. She watched the prince as he fell into line beside Elecia. Vhalla tore her eyes away before she saw more than a moment of their immediate and engaging conversation. There was an ugly emotion within her, one she wasn't used to and didn't know how to combat.

"I'm going to ride up at the front," she announced.

"Why?" Fritz seemed startled by her suddenly declaration.

"I have friends up there," Vhalla mumbled.

"You have friends here," Fritz retorted, not understanding.

Vhalla wasn't sure if she could, or should, explain it to him. From the corners of her eyes Vhalla saw Larel's attention sweep back toward Aldrik and Elecia. The Western woman was too attentive for her own good.

"It's nothing you did, Fritz." Vhalla found the strength to smile, and grab his forearm supportively. "Just some people I want to see."

There was no further protest from Fritz or Larel on the matter. As Vhalla cut through the ranks, she made sure to catch Aldrik's eyes. It was nasty to admit, but she wanted him to watch her ride away and feel that same ugly emotion that he had evoked in her.

The Golden Guard wasn't hard to find; a group of three surrounding the younger prince with golden plated bracers.

They marched at the center of the host, and Vhalla faltered at the foul looks she received from the soldiers at the edge. She was about to ride back as the whispers started when Daniel turned in her direction.

"Vhalla!" he called, almost dislocating his arm to wave her over. Soldiers parted in shock, and Vhalla had no option but to heed him. "We weren't expecting you." Daniel smiled, and Vhalla instantly felt easier.

"Not in the slightest." Prince Baldair's words deflated her.

"I hope it's no trouble." Vhalla lowered her eyes.

Daniel held his tongue for the prince.

"Don't worry yourself so much." The prince waved away her insecurities with a full bellied laugh. "I said it was fine."

"This may be the first time a sorcerer rode with the swords," Craig remarked.

Vhalla believed it from the looks the other soldiers gave her.

"Vhalla, this is Raylynn." Daniel motioned to a woman who rode at Baldair's right. She had long blonde hair, the color of a Southerner's. But it was straight, like a Westerner's would be, and her skin held an olive tan.

"Nice to meet you," Vhalla said politely.

The woman regarded her thoughtfully for a long moment. She had eyes like Aldrik, Vhalla noticed. Black and piercing, they confirmed Vhalla's suspicion of Western blood in the woman's veins—if her sun-kissed skin wasn't proof enough—and cut through Vhalla easily.

"You're the Windwalker." It was the second time the phrase wasn't posed as a question.

"I am," Vhalla affirmed.

"Ray, be nice." Daniel maneuvered his horse next to Vhalla's. Raylynn gave Vhalla one last long assessment before unleashing a series of hushed whispers to the prince. Daniel kept Vhalla from listening in. "Ray had family on the Night of Fire and Wind," he whispered.

Vhalla pulled taught the reins, ready to turn Lightning around and ride back to her place in line. A golden gauntlet quickly covered her hand. She looked up at Daniel in confusion and frustration.

"Don't go. I think it'll do her good."

"What?" Vhalla inhaled in apprehension.

"You're not the monster they think you are." His declaration cut straight to her core, and Vhalla's expression must have said it all. "I . . ." He was at a loss for words—they both were as the wave of brutal honesty crashed upon them. That moment of openness had crippled her, and Vhalla was thankful for the strong legs of the steed beneath her. "I shouldn't have said that."

"I needed to hear it." She was overcome with his truth; it was infectious, and Vhalla wanted to coat herself in it.

Daniel noticed his hand was still on hers and pulled away quickly. Judging from the sideways glances from Craig and Baldair, he was the last to notice.

Vhalla relaxed her grip on the reins. "So, I thought the Golden Guard was bigger than three."

"There's five of us in total," Daniel affirmed. He seemed just as relieved to switch the conversation.

"The other two are at the front," Craig filled in. "Head Major Jax Wendyl and Lord Erion Le'Dan."

"Head Major Jax?" Vhalla had heard the name before. "Of the Black Legion?"

"The same." Daniel nodded.

"But, he's a sorcerer," she pointed out dumbly.

"What?" Prince Baldair gasped. "He's hid this from me this whole time?"

Daniel and Craig burst out laughing, and even Vhalla cracked an embarrassed smile.

"He's a sorcerer." The prince nodded, looking northward. "But he's also a good man." The golden prince turned back to her, looking over Craig and Daniel. "You'll find I only surround myself with good men, Vhalla."

Raylynn snorted.

"And women." Prince Baldair chuckled and turned back to the swordswoman.

Vhalla spent the rest of the day learning about the history of the Golden Guard. Prince Baldair had instated it as a boy with Lord Erion Le'Dan and, at the time, it was mostly a joke between young men. But when the war on the North started, he turned to his friend to survive the front. Slowly, other men and a woman were added, those who were deemed the most skilled and valuable.

Daniel had been the most recent addition after he'd assumed command during a battle when no one else would, salvaging a brutal defeat in the North and saving the prince's life in the process. Vhalla had no idea that the Easterner she'd been musing over growing potatoes and chatting about Paca's festival with was a lord. Daniel seemed uncomfortable by the notion himself, assuring her that she should not treat him any differently.

She hadn't realized how much time had passed until the horn blew, calling for the stop. Daniel laughed as well, saying that time had gotten away from him. He invited her to dinner, which Vhalla refused due to guilt over leaving Larel and Fritz for the whole day. Before she left he invited her out to ride with him again and, upon remembering Aldrik and Elecia together, Vhalla couldn't outright refuse.

"So we found out something about Elecia today," Fritz said as they were finishing setting up their tents.

"What?" Vhalla wasn't sure if she wanted to know.

Larel had a cautionary glint to her eyes.

"We were talking with the foot soldiers," Fritz continued, missing both ladies apprehension. "And apparently they've seen Elecia before."

"They have?" Vhalla asked.

"She's been in and out of the palace since the prince was a young man, one was saying," Fritz explained.

Vhalla didn't know why that fact would fill her with such dread.

"As if common soldiers would know anything," Larel mumbled, finishing her bedroll.

"Yeah, but you have to admit that Elecia and the—"

"And who?" the woman herself finished, and all three turned in surprise.

"And, uh . . ." Fritz was a mouse in the trap of a gleeful cat.

"And the prince," Larel finished fearlessly.

To her credit, Elecia was only startled for a moment. Vhalla made a note that the outright mention of a connection between Elecia and Aldrik paused the woman. "Speaking of the prince, he said he shall train you tonight." Her eyes fell on Vhalla, speaking volumes soundlessly. "So let's get this catastrophe over with."

During the walk to meet Aldrik in the woods, Vhalla mused over Elecia and him. People were already talking about the two of them. What if there *was* history between them? What if Larel was wrong and it wasn't just camp gossip? Her mind wrapped and wandered around the ideas, only coming to a halt when Aldrik began to speak.

"Your nights will be half training your physical bodies, half training your magical prowess," he declared while walking around Vhalla, Larel, and Fritz. "If you have any hope of making it into and out of the North alive, you will need every minute of training I can give you."

Elecia hovered off to the side, exempt from Aldrik's words.

"If you talk back or refuse, I may reconsider my kindness of being your teacher."

His voice was that of a prince, not the Aldrik she knew. Vhalla glanced at Fritz, wondering if it was only for his benefit. Larel was friends with Aldrik; Elecia clearly had some connection; and Vhalla was . . .

What was she?

That question echoed in her mind while they began their physical training. It ran through her head until Vhalla focused only on not getting sick from running and jumping. Aldrik refused to let them take off their armor; their physical training required it, he said. Fritz was the first to collapse, earning his ire.

"Charem, get up." Aldrik sighed, leaning against a tree. "Or would you rather be torn limb from limb by the Northern clans? Or maybe a Noru Cat?"

Fritz struggled to his feet. Vhalla and Larel stood panting. Larel was in far better shape than Vhalla, who felt like she could collapse at any moment.

"Right, then." Aldrik shared a long look with Elecia. "Elecia, Vhalla, pair up."

"*What?*" both women exclaimed in unison.

"That is an order." Aldrik pushed away from the tree, looking down at Elecia. "I trust you to impart your knowledge and skill."

The dark-skinned woman rolled her eyes, but didn't object a second time. Aldrik didn't even look at Vhalla, giving her no say. Vhalla decided that she had done something terrible to offend the prince, but whatever it was eluded her. The only thing she could think of was the Joining. But that had been *his* idea. And of all the words Vhalla could use to describe what happened between them the night prior, none would be negative.

"Larel, can you tell me how a Firebearer fights?" Aldrik asked.

"Hand-to-hand combat with the occasional long-ranged attack," Larel responded.

"And Waterrunners?" The prince nodded and turned to Fritz.

"A mixture of offensive freezing attacks and defensive illusions," Fritz sounded like he quoted from a textbook.

"And Groundbreakers?" Aldrik turned to Elecia.

"Highly defensive magic, stone skin impenetrable to bladed and most ice or fire attacks, combined with skills in weapons." The woman rested her hands on her thighs, and Vhalla noticed the grooves in the other woman's greaves were not decorative. She'd overlooked it before, but Elecia had two short swords strapped to her legs.

"As for Windwalkers . . ." The prince's voice faltered slightly when he turned to Vhalla. Her chest was tight, waiting for him to finish his thought. "We will find out."

They spent the rest of the night going over basic punches and dodges. Elecia seemed just as displeased about having to help her as Vhalla was. The woman was curt and kept her comments short. But even through pursed lips and disapproving glares, Vhalla was learning.

The curly-haired woman was clearly experienced in combat. She moved lightly, easily, and never broke a sweat. She never made a single mistake and was never out of breath.

Everything about her seemed to get under Vhalla's skin.

It was Vhalla's turn to practice attacking and Elecia's to dodge and deflect. Elecia found everything amusing. She had this annoying manner that made her seem like she was better than everyone else. She took Aldrik's time and attention. Her motions were flawless. She had an elegant ease about everything, something that Vhalla had only ever seen royalty exude. Vhalla swung wide, and Elecia gave a small jab to her open shoulder. She took a step back and stared at Elecia.

Vhalla blinked in shock that she hadn't put it together sooner. She had no proof, but something in her gut told her she was not wrong. The rumors of her being in the palace, the casual attitude toward royalty, it all made sense. Only people who came from wealth and affluence acted the way Elecia did. As if the world was a toy for her entertainment.

"What is it?" Elecia asked. "Giving up already?"

Vhalla returned to her assault. "Elecia." She threw a punch, the other woman dodged. "Tell me—how old—were you—when you—first came—to the palace?" Her words were punctuated with her fists.

Elecia took a step back and paused. "What are you talking about?" The woman arched an eyebrow.

"Was it for a gala? Or was your father or mother on official business?"

Elecia's eyes widened, and Vhalla resumed the attack. The woman recovered slowly and her blocks were suddenly sloppy. "Did you sleep in a guest suite?" She threw right. "Or did your family stay somewhere else in the upper part of town?"

An annoyed frown crossed Elecia's lips. "I don't know what you're talking about."

"And you're an awful liar," Vhalla spat back.

Elecia looked at her in shock. "What about you, *Vhalla Yarl*? How exactly did you, less than a slip of a common girl, catch the eye of the crown prince? A nothing like you fraternizing with him!"

That got Aldrik's attention. He quickly approached from where Larel and Fritz sparred.

"You have to know that you don't deserve even—"

Vhalla lunged with a shout, not letting Elecia finish another wounding word. Elecia dodged easily and put a fist in Vhalla's stomach. The woman's arm felt like a rock sinking into her abdomen, and Vhalla wheezed for air instead of crying out.

"Elecia!" Aldrik shouted as Vhalla doubled over, holding her stomach and coughing. He quickly crossed the remaining gap, standing between the two women.

"You think *that*—" Elecia cast a finger in Vhalla's direction, "—will ever be anything?" She threw her head back and laughed.

"Elecia, *stop this*," Aldrik growled.

"Oh yes, defend your pet," she sneered back.

Larel and Fritz stared in shock.

"Elecia," he ground out through grit teeth, his hands balled into fists.

"Are you finally going to fight me? I've been waiting for a real challenge." The dark-skinned woman said, putting her fists up. "It's been far too long since we last went a round."

Vhalla managed to tilt back onto her feet, still holding her stomach as it spasmed in pain.

Aldrik stomped over to Elecia and grabbed her by the collar of her plate. He jerked her to him and leaned in to place his face right in front of hers. "If you want me to spar with you like an adult, acting like a petulant child is not going to yield results, 'Cia."

Elecia pushed him away with a frown and a shake of her head. "Fine," she said with a glint in her eye. "You continue to play your games with them, Aldrik," she spat back.

Vhalla felt her mouth drop open in shock at the other woman's use of Aldrik's name.

"But—I will tell you again—that lowborn bitch isn't worth an ounce of what you give her." Elecia turned and stomped through the forest noisily. The brush and trees shrunk around her before curling back even more overgrown and thorny than before.

Aldrik sighed and pinched the bridge of his nose, giving himself a moment before turning and kneeling in front of Vhalla. "Are you all right?" he asked.

She nodded. Her stomach still felt like it was turned inside-out. Fritz and Larel hovered a few feet away from them in obvious uncertainty.

"Let me see." The prince reached out, and Vhalla removed her hand. It hurt to straighten her back. "Take off your armor," Aldrik ordered, and she began to fuss with the latches up the front. "Here," he said softly and reached out, helping her from the bottom. Vhalla hunched her shoulders, let her hair fall in front of her face, and hid her shame.

Aldrik took her scale from her; a few of the small plates were dented around the abdomen.

He sighed audibly. "I will fix this tonight, and have it to you by morning."

She looked down at her chain; it appeared to be undamaged. There was a moment of silence and a soft night breeze ruffled her hair. Aldrik reached out and clasped a hand over her shoulder. "She is . . ." He sighed. "Do not pay what she says any mind."

Vhalla nodded silently. It was a nice sentiment. But once some things were said they could never be unheard, and the brief exchange was already repeating in her ears.

Aldrik nodded back at her before standing, turning to a shocked silent Larel and Fritz. "Larel, take her back to your tent. You may have to burn through one or two of those altered shrubs." He glanced at Elecia's path out. "Fritz, come with me. I am sure Vhalla has internal bleeding from a hit like that, and I will not have her riding a horse tomorrow without getting a potion in her tonight."

They both nodded, and Larel slipped Vhalla's arm around her neck, helping her to her feet.

"It's not that bad," Vhalla insisted softly, not wanting to make any more of a scene.

"There's no shame in accepting help. This march is too long to justify acting too strong now," Larel told her sternly, yet gently.

"Listen to that one, Vhalla. She has a good head on her shoulders." Aldrik pointed to Larel, and Vhalla saw the Western woman's face turn up to a small smile. "Fritz, come," he ordered briskly, and the two walked off in a different direction.

Just as Aldrik had said, the brush needed to be burnt away in some places. It was riddled with vines almost as thick as Vhalla's wrist, blocking the most direct route back to camp. Larel used intense firebursts to incinerate a clear path.

"Groundbreakers can alter trees and plants?" Vhalla asked.

"Some can." Larel nodded.

They didn't speak again during the rest of the walk back to their tent. Larel offered to help Vhalla change into her sleeping clothes, but Vhalla insisted she could do it on her own. Elecia's words ran through her head. The conversation had yielded too much information to dissect now. A sickeningly purple bruise had already formed on her stomach.

Vhalla only barely finished pulling on a long-sleeved nightshirt when there was a tap on their tent pole.

"Vhal? Larel?" Fritz asked uncertainly.

"It's fine, Fritz," Vhalla called, and he poked his head in. Larel shifted to make enough room for him to sit. It was crowded with three.

"Here, the prince told me to give it to you." He handed her a small wooden vial.

"Thank you," she said softly, taking it from him and downing it quickly. She recognized the fiery feeling of this particular potion and winced slightly. Vhalla was beginning to suspect the clerics healed everything with this one magic liquid. "Sorry to be trouble."

"It's fine," Larel consoled. "This was hardly your fault."

"What exactly happened?" Fritz asked.

Larel elbowed him in the side. "Not our business," she scolded.

Vhalla fidgeted with her fingers.

"Fine, fine. I hope you feel better soon." He reached out, ruffled Vhalla's hair, and turned on his knees to crawl out of the tent.

"Wait," Vhalla stopped him. There was a sick feeling in her stomach, but Vhalla thought it had more to do with nerves. "Wait," she repeated again as he sat down. Vhalla passed the vial from hand to hand, unsure of her next words. But Fritz and Larel had already proven to be kind and loyal. She took a breath.

"Vhalla, you don't have to—" Larel seemed to sense her trepidation.

"We're Bonded," Vhalla said directly, getting it out before she lost her resolve.

Both stared at her in shock and confusion.

"Wait, what?" Fritz had a dumb look on his face.

"You and . . ." Larel whispered, her voice leaving her before she could finish the sentence.

"Aldrik." Vhalla cursed aloud. "*The prince.*" She shook her head; it was too late and she was in too deep. "Aldrik and I are Bonded." Vhalla looked away from them. She barely understood what being Bonded meant so how they would react was up in the air. They both stared at her with their mouths open, shocked into silence. "Well, say something," she sighed.

"You're sure?" Larel asked.

"Very," she affirmed, recalling her Channeling lesson.

"Does he know?" Fritz asked.

Larel cuffed him on the back of the head. "Of course he does," she chided.

"How?" Fritz asked. The Western woman shot him a sharp glance. "I know how, as in I know how Bonding works *in theory*. But how did you become Bonded with the prince, of all people?"

"I don't really understand it all myself." Vhalla thought back to a night in the library, a night that seemed forever ago. "It was when he came back."

"From the front? In the summer?" Larel seemed to be already piecing it together.

Vhalla nodded. "I was working in the library and I—" Vhalla paused, leaving out the truth that she had thought she was saving a different prince. "I wanted to save him, I wanted to give anything to save him. He said I wrote magic, or made vessels— I'm not sure. Something about it opened a link and that was a Bonding." She shifted, trying not to allow the conversation she'd started make her uncomfortable.

"That's amazing," Fritz breathed.

"So, that's—that's why things are different with us." She wasn't sure anymore why she had confided this to her friends.

"What is it like being Bonded?" Fritz asked.

"It's hard to tell," Vhalla confessed. "I've never known magic and not been Bonded. So it's normal for me."

"You Manifested quickly," Larel pointed out. "Even the minister was shocked, but it would make sense if you had a Bond with someone like Prince Aldrik."

"It was also how . . ." Vhalla hesitated about sharing the previous night with them, but she was in too deep to stop herself now. "During our Channeling lesson, he showed me how to Channel."

"Well, of course." Fritz clearly didn't understand.

"No." Vhalla shook her head. "He *showed* me. While we were Joined."

If Vhalla had not understood the gravity of a Joining before, she understood it then. Fritz and Larel looked at her with a combination of shock, amazement, and—what was most unnerving—a touch of fear. Vhalla brought her hands together, wringing them roughly.

"It's . . . *possible?*" Fritz asked, finally.

"I suppose so? I only have what Aldrik said to go off of." Vhalla's eyes darted between them, desperate to spark some more conversation so they'd stop looking at her like she had sprouted a second head. "What does it mean?"

"I've only read about it." Asking Fritz to recite things from books had the same effect as it did on Vhalla. His mind began churning once more. "Literature on Bonding is very few and far between because most people who try to create a Bond fail, and one person dies in the process. But Joining is supposedly a state of merged consciousness or awareness."

"That sounds right." Vhalla nodded in affirmation.

"I can't believe he did that." Fritz stroked the stubble on his jaw. "It's supposed to be a risky process."

"Risky?" Vhalla asked.

"Again, I've only read . . . But if the Bond isn't solid, complete, if the two people are Bonded but not compatible, or if—" He paused, censoring himself. "Well there are other things that can help or hurt it. But I've heard it could result in one person losing himself in the other. You end up with one being mindless, while the other goes mad with the noise in his head."

Vhalla stared in shock and then started laughing. "Risks are something the prince has no qualms taking," she assured them—it seemed to adequately sum up their entire relationship.

"Why did you tell us this?" Larel asked. "I can't imagine the prince would be pleased."

Vhalla honestly hadn't considered that. "Because you both are my friends. I trust you, and I want you to know I do. What are friends if you cannot share your secrets with them?"

"I won't tell a soul." Fritz grabbed her hand, and she smiled at his kind eyes.

"You know you have my silence," Larel affirmed with a nod.

"But you know I'm going to be asking you about it, right?" Fritz grinned his goofy toothy grin.

Vhalla couldn't help but smile back. "I'll answer as best I can," Vhalla promised. "Talking about it may even be nice."

Fritz left shortly after. He squeezed Vhalla and Larel both tightly, and Vhalla wished he could stay with them. She selfishly wanted to spend the night tucked between him and Larel. But Vhalla didn't make any demands. At best she'd just wake him with thrashing from nightmares.

CHAPTER 8

FRITZ RETURNED VHALLA'S armor the next morning, leaving Vhalla conflicted and uncertain once more. The prince was a strange creature. At times, he seemed like he worried for her above all else, like when Elecia made her cheap shot. Other times, like the entire day's ride, it seemed as though he didn't even want her around.

If he was trying to avoid her, then he was destined for failure. Aldrik saw her each night when they trained together and maybe that fact frustrated him, because the prince pushed his three pupils beyond tired and into levels of exhaustion that Vhalla had never known before. The second day of training was harder than the first, and the third was harder than the second. The fourth morning Vhalla was certain that she couldn't get out of bed; it took almost being late for her to be coaxed into the saddle.

Aldrik had the sense to not pair Vhalla and Elecia together again; they were kept at other ends of the makeshift rings they worked in. Vhalla was thankful that she had the opportunity to work with Fritz, but felt sorry for Larel for having to endure the other Western woman's jabs and sneers. If Aldrik was upset with Elecia, he didn't show it. He still rode with her during the day and never sent her away from the training.

In all, it made Vhalla feel worse. She still remembered what Elecia had said about her birth, her questions of why Aldrik was spending any time with Vhalla. It made Vhalla doubt everything, and then she felt guilty for second-guessing Aldrik after all he had done for her. But she didn't know how to feel, and Aldrik wasn't helping her sort it out.

So during the day she'd taken to riding with the Golden Guard. Daniel and Craig were always welcoming, and even Prince Baldair seemed to be more amused than put off by Vhalla's persistence around them. Raylynn was even beginning to thaw. It was an odd routine that Vhalla fell into; she wouldn't call it peaceful, but with time everything became easier. Even her dreams had begun to lose their edge.

Or so she had thought.

A month into the march, Vhalla woke up one night shivering and shaking, despite the warming temperatures as the host grew closer to the Western Waste. Fear clawed and bit its way through her, but she had somehow not woken Larel. Vhalla quickly gulped in breaths of air. She stared down at her wrists.

The dream was just as vivid as her memories of the Night of Fire and Wind. Her mind told her she had felt these feelings before. The noises, smells, and touch were all familiar. And yet, Vhalla had never seen or done anything like it.

She'd stood in an opulent room, dark with oppressive gloom. A thunderstorm raged against the glass windows, and she'd been soaking wet. Vhalla shivered, grabbing her arms to ward against the phantom chill. And then she'd taken a knife to her own flesh.

Vhalla was looking at her forearms again.

The crimson blood that had stained pale skin and white carpeting was not what was most prominent in her memory. It was the fear, the overwhelming guilt she had felt and—most notably—when she had caught her eyes in the reflection of the blade—*they had not been her eyes.*

Vhalla covered her face with her palms. *It was just a dream,* she repeated over and over again. But she could still feel the blade cutting into the pale skin. She could see the palace handmaiden rushing in, horrified and desperate.

Vhalla was up and out of the tent.

It was still a good hour before dawn and the world was yet dark. Vhalla ran through the silent camp, barefoot and in sweat-damp clothes. Her heart raced, and her mind didn't allow her to calm, not until she knew he was all right. She didn't care if Aldrik was still cross with her. *She had to see him.*

Knocking on the crown prince's tent pole before dawn had to be foolish, but that didn't stop her. Vhalla brought her hands together, fidgeting in the eternity that seemed to follow as she waited. "My prince?" Her voice was strained with tension. Vhalla fought down a whimper. "*Aldrik?*"

To her relief, she heard a faint stirring come from inside the tent. The canvas shifted as ties on the inside were undone. Aldrik opened the flap in annoyance. With his other hand he pulled on the hem of a shirt, situating it over his chest.

"Vhalla?" He rubbed the sleep from his eyes as if he wasn't seeing properly, his temper quickly vanishing.

She felt something in her break with relief and she covered her mouth with her hands to muffle a small cry. Aldrik took one look at her panic-stricken face and, with a quick glance to ensure there were no observers, he grabbed her hand and pulled her into the tent.

The moment he released the heavy canvas flap, they were plunged into near-darkness. She blinked in the dim light. His bed was a mess of blankets; papers and empty bottles cluttered his table.

Aldrik quickly rounded her and placed his palms on her

shoulders. He inspected her from toe to head. "What is it?" His voice was tense. "Are you hurt?" Aldrik moved a hand to her forehead and ran it down her face to tilt Vhalla's chin up to look at him.

The feeling of relief was still too strong for her to feel embarrassed. "I'm okay," she finally managed weakly. Vhalla reached up and grabbed both his wrists. She let out a noise between a laugh and a sigh when she saw the sleeves of his shirt showed no signs of blood. "I'm okay." Vhalla breathed. "I thought, you . . ."

"I what?" he asked. Aldrik was clearly confused, but the prince made no motion away from her.

"It doesn't matter." She laughed uneasily. "It was a dream. Something bad . . . I thought you were hurt. But it was just a dream."

Aldrik paused before moving his hands to cup her face. He ran his thumbs over her tearstained cheeks, and she relished his eyes on her for the first time in what felt like forever. "I'm fine," he whispered. "See, I am fine."

His tenderness set free a small hiccup in her throat, and she squeezed his forearms. "I was afraid," she admitted. His eyes widened. "I thought . . ." She choked on her words.

"What? Thought what?"

Vhalla searched his questioning gaze. "Nothing," she said with a shake of her head. "It doesn't matter; you're well."

"Vhalla," he insisted, his hands on her face preventing her from looking away.

"I was afraid I'd lost you." The words were an arrow into the heart of the silence that had been flourishing between them. And words, like arrows, once let go, could not be taken back. Vhalla had confessed as much to him as she did to herself. The truth of her admission slowly dawned on them both. She felt her jaw quiver. "I'm sorry, I shouldn't have bothered you."

She released his arms and stepped away to leave. Vhalla's ears burned with embarrassment, and she dipped her head. What had overcome her? *Why had she come?* He'd made it clear for days that she'd done something to offend him. That he didn't want her presence.

Aldrik closed the gap between them. Bending over slightly, he curled an arm around her upper waist and wrapped the other around her shoulders. Vhalla gasped and got a breath of his shirt as her face pressed against his chest.

He held her there and took a few deep breaths. Vhalla felt his chest move under her cheek, and she heard his heartbeat run fast. Uncertainly, she raised her hands and grabbed the back of Aldrik's shirt. He didn't pull away.

"I told you, you foolish woman," he whispered, his breath washing away the scalding embarrassment. "You have to tell me if you want to lose me."

Vhalla tightened her arms around him and closed her eyes. His contact calmed her, and she felt her heartbeat slow with his. Aldrik's hand shifted, and she felt his fingers lose themselves in her tangled morning hair.

"I thought you were hurt." He laughed dryly. "I'd just been . . ." Aldrik seemed at a loss for words. "I had my own dream, I suppose."

Vhalla inhaled deeply. He smelled like smoke, sweat, metal, leather, and something distinctly Aldrik. She felt him shake his head, and they continued to stand in silence. He was warm through the thin fabric of his shirt, and she pressed herself closer.

She wasn't sure how long they stood there, but eventually she felt his arms loosen around her. Vhalla wanted to protest, but her grip relaxed. Aldrik straightened, but an arm remained around her waist. His other hand curled around the back of her neck.

"Tonight, come to me."

Vhalla felt the pads of his fingers indenting the nape of her neck. "Tonight?" she squeaked, her throat suddenly dry.

Aldrik was suddenly as startled as she was. His eyes lost some of their intensity to surprise and confusion, as if his mouth had spoken before his brain could process his previous demand of her. "I told you there were things I wanted to work on with you."

"Right." Vhalla nodded. He'd been so distant she'd almost forgotten.

"You should go," he murmured as his hands relaxed their hold on her. Aldrik stepped away. "Before too many wake up."

Vhalla nodded. "Again, I'm sorry for disturbing you," she said softly, shock at their actions beginning to settle in.

"It is fine," he said gently. "We can speak properly later."

Vhalla nodded. Aldrik walked over to the flap of his tent and looked about. "It seems clear." He stepped aside and she stepped out.

Vhalla heard the canvas close abruptly behind her, and she walked away, only looking forward. There were a few more people up and moving about, but none paid her any mind. The sky was painted with oranges and blues; dawn drew close.

She dressed in her armor outside of her tent, so as not to wake Larel. Her skin tingled as she slipped the chainmail over her woolen clothes, and Vhalla reminded herself to breathe. A dream had sent her into a blind panic, running to the crown prince.

Why?

Vhalla's fingers faltered on the latches of her armor. The memory of their dance at the gala rushed back to her with stunning clarity. He'd held her then also and, like this morning, she'd never wanted it to end. She pressed a hand over her eyes, blocking out the dawn with a groan.

She came from nothing, and *she was no one*. She had no

business spending any time with the crown prince, the man who would be her future Emperor. He didn't have time to waste on people like her. Elecia's words cemented themselves further in her consciousness.

"Vhalla?"

She hadn't even heard Larel stir.

"Morning." Vhalla finished dressing quickly.

"Are you all right?"

It was annoying how Larel missed nothing. "I'm fine." Vhalla began breaking down the tent.

"Was it another dream?" Larel asked.

"Enough, Larel," Vhalla sighed and straightened. The Western woman was silent. Vhalla should've been too, but there was an aching feeling in Vhalla's stomach that put nastiness in her blood. "Why are you always pestering me? It's none of your concern what I dream or don't dream, what I eat or what I don't eat."

Larel's face was expressionless.

"Just leave me alone for once." Vhalla grabbed her pack and stormed off, leaving the rest of the tent for Larel.

She hated herself for those words. It wasn't Larel's fault. The class Vhalla was born into, the Night of Fire and Wind, the prince's confusing and frustrating hot and cold attitude toward Vhalla. Larel had no control over any of it. Vhalla had just taken her frustrations out on someone who wasn't expecting it.

Vhalla marched alone. She found a random corner of the host to fall in with away from Elecia, Aldrik, Fritz, Larel, and the Golden Guard. Fritz noticed instantly and was about to ride over to her when Larel stopped him. They found themselves engaged in a heated conversation that Vhalla tried to ignore. They were clearly talking about her.

When the march finished for the day, Vhalla had imagined every possible thing Larel, Fritz, and Aldrik could've said about her. Some of the things she felt guilty for even thinking they would utter, but somehow it still seemed plausible. Vhalla's shoulders hunched, and her head dipped. She suddenly felt so tired.

"Vhalla." Her head snapped up, turning to look up at the dark prince who had materialized at her side. "After everyone is settled, come and we'll begin work."

He still didn't specify what work, and Vhalla felt odd under his studying assessment. After drifting through camp, waiting for Larel and Fritz to be away to strip her armor so she could avoid any odd confrontations, Vhalla finally dragged her feet to Aldrik's tent. She came in the same woolen clothing she'd worn in the morning—that she'd been wearing for days.

The flap of his tent was open, and Vhalla paused politely in the entryway.

"My prince?" she asked softly. "Am I too early?"

He was sitting at the small table marking a piece of paper before him. His armor was propped on its stand opposite the entry, and he sat in tan pants and a white cotton shirt. "No, you are fine, Vhalla." He glanced at her briefly. "Close it behind you." He motioned to a tie on the inside that held up the flap, and she obliged.

Vhalla was momentarily overcome from the last time she had been in his space. She quickly crossed and situated herself on a pillow opposite him. Tilting her head, Vhalla assessed the prince, trying to figure out what was different.

"What is it?" he asked without looking up from whatever he was doing.

"You're not wearing any black," she realized.

Aldrik paused and considered his attire. "I suppose I am not." He finished what he was working on and folded it twice, placing it aside.

"It's strange," she said thoughtfully.

"Is it?" Aldrik rested his elbow on the table, his cheek on his fist.

"You're always in black," she explained.

"Not true." He shook his head.

"Yes, you are," Vhalla insisted.

"I wear black in public."

"Why?"

"I will tell you, perhaps, if you tell me what cloud situated itself over your head." Clearly her day of sulking had not been lost on him.

"I'd rather not talk about it," she mumbled.

"I would rather you did." He leaned forward. "Was it the dream?"

"Why is everyone so obsessed with my dreams?" Vhalla shrunk away.

"Because we care about you," Aldrik explained.

"We?" she repeated.

"Fritz, Larel, and I."

"Why . . ." *Why did he insist on caring about her?* "Well, you should stop."

"That is not—"

"I thought I came here to work on something with you." Vhalla was on her feet. "I'm not doing this again, Aldrik. I won't be your project."

"Yes, yes, of course, my lady." He waved a hand.

"Don't patronize me." It struck a chord with her.

"Are you not a lady?" he asked.

"I am a *woman,*" Vhalla said with a roll of her eyes. "But I am not a *lady.*"

"Fine then, my princess." He smirked.

"Stop," Vhalla cautioned.

"Why, my queen?"

She'd had enough and was halfway to the door when Aldrik snatched up her wrist. Vhalla didn't even turn and look at him.

"They're just words." The timbre of his voice had gone low and deep.

"They're *not*." She thought of all the lords and ladies she'd seen in the palace, how different she felt on the night of the gala. Titles were more than just words. They were walls and barriers and parapets to lift up some and keep others out.

"Look at me." He commanded and she obliged. "I could give you any of them."

"It doesn't work that way."

"It does." She made the mistake of giving him her focus, and Aldrik's serious gaze consumed it whole. "One day, I will be Emperor. I could make you anything you pleased."

"Why?" Vhalla whispered.

"Because . . ." He was at a momentary loss for words. Then the prince did something he had a reputation for avoiding. He met her gaze and showed her the truth from which he spoke. "I would do it *because* it would please you."

Vhalla turned to face him, searching the prince with skepticism. She opened her mouth and closed it again, unsure how to reply. She didn't know if she was brave enough to be so bold.

He relaxed his grip on her wrist, and his hand shifted to hers. "I realized something this morning, these past days," Aldrik murmured. "I am a spoiled prince. No matter how unfair it may be, I do not do well being denied something I want, even if it's self-inflicted. I have hurt you, I have put you in harm's way, and I will continue to ask this and more of you the longer you stay near me. Yet knowing this, I seem to want you closer even when sense tells me the opposite."

"Aldrik." All words but his name failed her.

"You asked me before for honesty; there it is." It was his turn to search her features for her reaction.

Vhalla felt dizzy, and all she could manage was a nod. He led her back to the small sitting area and sat with her. Vhalla felt the warmth of his skin under her fingertips, and she did nothing to break their contact. "So, if it involves my feelings, trust me above all others."

"Above Elecia, you mean." Vhalla didn't leave things to chance.

"Above Elecia," Aldrik agreed with a nod.

"So then, you're not upset with me?" If they were clearing the air, Vhalla wanted to get everything out.

"Not in the slightest." Aldrik's thumb ghosted over the back of her hand. "If anything, you should be upset with me for . . ." He sighed and ran a hand through his hair.

"Let's call it even." Vhalla didn't want to dwell. She had done enough of that all day, and she felt at ease finally knowing more or less where she stood with Aldrik. "So what are we actually supposed to be working on?"

Aldrik shared a brief smile with her before his face quickly turned somber. "I have a plan to take the North." His eyes bore into her. "But I will need you."

"What could I do?" She hadn't mastered any type of combat.

"It will depend on if you are able to become proficient at Projection. I believe I am able to see you when you are Projected because of our Bond, but no one else should be able to. If you can Project, you can infiltrate the Northern stronghold undetected. Learn its passages and its weaknesses. The information you could give might make them fall in one night."

Vhalla instantly felt uneasy at the idea. "But last time I became stuck."

"I will help you, I will be here." Aldrik squeezed her hand lightly. "If you are willing, we will begin practice tonight."

After some internal debate, Vhalla finally decided. "I will." Perhaps this would be the one thing she could do that would give meaning to her conscription into the military. "What do I need to do?"

"Well, have you worked on Channeling?" Aldrik finally straightened, pulling his hand from hers. The distance he'd previously placed between them didn't come rushing to fill the space. It didn't feel like he was planning for it to be the last time they touched.

"Not really." Vhalla glanced away.

"I didn't see you using magic when we practiced either." Aldrik gave her a knowing grin. "So, let us practice that first."

Vhalla nodded and thought back to the last time they had worked together. It was an easy memory to recall, given the impact the Joining had on her. Vhalla extended her hands, focusing on them. She'd seen Aldrik repeat the movement countless times.

She clenched her hands into fists, and felt a rush of power. It was the same feeling he had imparted upon her during their Joining, and it made Vhalla wonder why she'd been so fearful to attempt it. Her eyes darted back to him. "I think I did it."

"Really?" He seemed both surprised and skeptical.

"Check," she suggested.

Aldrik looked askance. "I cannot."

"What?"

"I cannot use magic sight." Aldrik seemed embarrassed to admit the fact.

Vhalla stared in shock. *He couldn't do something?* More notably, he couldn't do something that she could. His eyes failed to meet hers, and Vhalla cleared the look from her face. He'd been helpful to her when she had no idea what magic was. She'd not chastise him now.

"Well, let's just assume I can." Vhalla gave a small grin.

"Truly? So easily?" He was surprised.

"I have a good teacher." She flashed him a wide smile, and his mouth curled upward in reply before he could give it thought.

"Do you remember how you Projected?" he asked.

"Vaguely," she confessed. She remembered trying to be near him when the Emperor had returned to the capital, and Vhalla remembered stretching her mind toward the rose garden. She thought it'd been a dream then, but perhaps it made more sense as a Projection.

"Try to repeat that process." Aldrik seemed as uncertain as she felt.

Vhalla nodded, willing to let his confidence in her give life to her attempt. She closed her eyes, thinking back to the process she had used long ago. *Visualize*, she instructed to herself. In her mind's eye the room began to rebuild with a magically sharp clarity.

Vhalla allowed the world to slow and still. Farther, she needed to stretch farther. Now able to maintain an open Channel, Vhalla found it easier to construct a magical world for her to walk within. She was the air; it beckoned endlessly to Vhalla, asking for her to fill the space. Soon sound disappeared, and she stood.

Her senses rushed back to her, but they were different than before. She heard by feeling the air move; she saw by how the shimmering currents of air circled around objects. Vhalla watched her body slump limply.

Aldrik caught her physical form and shifted it to rest in his arm. A smile curled his lips at the sight of her.

"Excellent," he enthused.

Can you see me? she asked.

He nodded. "Try walking."

She turned in place. It was easy to cross the room, and his eyes followed her the whole time. She walked over to his armor and reached out a hand. Vhalla studied it uncertainly.

What do I look like? she asked, wondering if the ghost-like appearance of her hand was the same for him.

"Fuzzy, as though you are in a fog. How a mirage looks in the desert," Aldrik replied.

Vhalla tried to touch the plate and found her hand passed right through it. *I can't touch things,* she observed.

"Try to use your magic," he suggested.

Vhalla held out her hand, attempting to manipulate the wind around her. It was suddenly slippery and formless, like a vat of snakes and oil. Vhalla demanded it oblige her, focusing harder.

"Vhalla, stop," Aldrik warned.

She didn't even look back at him. Vhalla tried to take a deep breath, to feel the air, but found she couldn't in this form. She would just have to force it. Immersing herself in her Channel, she insisted the armor move. Her vision shifted, the world phased between light and dark.

Aldrik? she called.

"Vhalla, stop!" He sounded distant and far.

Aldrik! she cried. Vhalla stood in a world of blinding light.

"Vhalla." Aldrik's voice was faint. "Come back to me." She turned in the white emptiness but couldn't find where he was. "Listen, find your heartbeat. Find mine. Come back." He sounded strung out, which only caused her to feel more distraught.

Aldrik? she asked into the emptiness. There was no reply. Vhalla closed her eyes, only to find more light. She listened, there was nothing. Vhalla walked for a bit, but couldn't make anything appear before her. Time seemed to have stopped, and she wasn't sure how long she wandered. Finally, she sat and simply listened.

Slowly, painfully slowly, she began to hear a distant drumming. It was a familiar rhythm, and it called to her. Vhalla allowed it to flow back into her, it resonating through every aspect of her consciousness. It was a slow transition as the world faded into blackness.

Her eyes fluttered open. Aldrik's face hovered above her, and he let out a small relieved laugh. For the second time in one day she found herself pressed against his chest. Vhalla sighed softly. It was a trend she could learn to live with.

"You scared me again," he muttered. "That'll be the last time we do that."

"No," Vhalla insisted with a shake of her head. "I'll get it, I just need more practice. I pushed too hard."

He studied her carefully, and she yawned, suddenly feeling exhausted. She made no motion to get up, and he made no motion to remove her from his person. Vhalla's eyelids drooped closed.

"Rest," the prince instructed.

She shifted slightly, her ear against his chest. "Aldrik?" she inquired with another yawn.

"Vhalla?"

She struggled to find the right words. "*This* is a really, really awful idea."

Vhalla felt him stiffen a moment, and he let out a small sigh. "I know." His voice was barely audible. "I know. Now rest."

Vhalla felt her consciousness fade as she was swathed in a comfortable warmth that only he could exude.

CHAPTER 9

VHALLA WAS ONE of those perpetually cold people. With a small amount of body fat, likely due to her spotty eating habits when wrapped up in something, she was usually the first to complain about a chill. She had long since accepted it as part of her lot in life and dressed as warmly as possible to make up for it.

However, at this particular moment she was pleasantly warm. It was a surreal feeling and, in her half-sleep haze, she shifted, pressing herself closer to the source. That source adjusted itself beneath her before settling again. The unfamiliar sensation brought Vhalla back to awareness. Her mind was sluggish with sleep, and she struggled to make sense of it.

His heartbeat was the first thing she heard. Slow and strong against her right ear. The second thing she heard was the scratching of quill on paper. Vhalla cracked open her eyes and saw she rested in the crook of Aldrik's left arm, which wrapped around her side. She was halfway onto his lap as he sat cross legged on the floor. Stretched across her was his right hand as he marked papers on the table.

The previous events came back in pieces, punctuated with a yawn.

"You're up." Aldrik placed the quill on the table and ran a hand through his hair. "How do you feel?"

"Tired," she responded groggily.

"I could tell." His tone was flat but his posture had no heaviness to it. "I'm fairly certain you depleted most of your magic and fell into your Channel."

Vhalla made a note to ask him, Fritz, or Larel about that later when she didn't feel so sleepy. "How late is it?"

He shifted and reached out to the edge of the table. It had parchments strewn across it with all manner of scribbles on their surface. Aldrik pushed some pages aside, and a glint of silver caught her eye.

"Let's see, eight-thirty." He inspected the pocket watch.

"Can I see it?" Vhalla held out a hand.

He looked at her curiously but obliged. Vhalla turned the watch over in her fingers. The back was polished to a mirror finish, the front held the blazing sun of the Empire. Time pieces were rare because those who understood their strange mechanics were few and far between. Vhalla stared past her reflection in the glass that covered the obsidian and alabaster face of the watch. "It's beautiful."

"Thank you," Aldrik replied awkwardly.

"I've never held one before," Vhalla mused aloud. The few clocks she had ever seen were large, like one at the circulation desk in the library. "It's like holding time itself, isn't it?"

"I suppose."

"I wish I could make it stop," she breathed.

His hands closed over hers and the watch, shutting the front latch closed. "If you could, what would you do?"

Aldrik's breath was warm on her cheeks, and Vhalla was keenly aware of how close they were. He held her in one arm, the other hand holding both of hers, her side pressed along his chest. *What were they doing?*

"I . . ." She would be lost in those black eyes if she wasn't careful. Vhalla straightened. "What're you working on?"

"This?" Aldrik motioned to the parchment, allowing her to save them both from themselves. "There is the exciting job of checking our stock, making sure we have enough supplies to make it to the Crossroads. There were one or two discipline reports; I screen them for Father." He paused; she followed his stare to one piece of paper that was completely full of his slanted scribbles. "I also began taking some notes on our Bonding."

"On us?" Vhalla glanced at the paper.

"There is not much information on Bonding. I wanted a record I can look back on later if anything strange happens."

She bit her lip, unsure how she felt about her experiences with Aldrik potentially being read by someone else. "I suppose it makes sense. If you need any insights from me, let me know." Vhalla offered, and he nodded. "Does your brother help you with the other things?"

"Baldair?" Aldrik pushed his hair back with both hands. For a moment he looked like the man she'd met back at the palace; at least until the hair fell back messily around his face. "He is not really the type for official business." Aldrik's voice was cool.

"He said you two had a strange relationship." Aldrik raised an eyebrow at her statement. "When he came to my cell, during the trial."

"Did he?" Aldrik chuckled darkly. "That is one way to describe it."

"You don't get along." Vhalla didn't need to have siblings to see it.

"Our relationship works when we need it to, how we need it to. We normally have an understanding." His guarded words and tone made it clear she wouldn't get any more out of him.

Vhalla yawned again despite herself. "I should go, I suppose." She glanced away. In truth, she had no interest in leaving.

"You have not eaten yet." The sentiment seemed to be mutual.
"I could get us some food."

"All right." It was easy to agree.

Aldrik stood and stretched. He grabbed his chainmail from where it hung on a peg by his other armor and pulled it over his head.

Vhalla leaned back, studying the subtle grace to his movements. "Is chainmail really necessary in camp?"

Aldrik paused, and she watched his face become pained. "You can never be too careful," he murmured. His demeanor changed back before Vhalla could comment on it. "Wait here, I will return shortly." She nodded and he slipped out of the flap.

Vhalla dropped back onto the pillows strewn about rug. The whole evening, the past day, had been completely surreal, and she didn't want it to end. He wanted her closer, or so he had said. It put butterflies in her stomach as much as it put alarms in her head.

She groaned, covering her eyes with the back of her forearm. The smart thing to do would be to end this now, whatever *this* was. It would be best to apologize, refuse, leave, and prevent anything further from happening. Vhalla tilted her head back and watched the flames dance in one of his hanging braziers. That would have been the smart thing to do, but what she actually did was lay there until he returned.

"My, you look comfortable." Aldrik wore a lazy smirk.

"I've not had a real pillow to sleep on in over a month," she reminded him, sitting.

"So take one." He shrugged, placing a small sack on the table.

"I cannot take your pillow." Vhalla accepted a roll he handed her.

"Why not?"

"Oh yes, by the way, the Crown Prince Aldrik gave me a pillow. That's normal right?" Vhalla rolled her eyes.

"I hear it is all the rage for ladies' gift-giving in the East. You mean to tell me my sources are incorrect?" Aldrik grinned.

"Oh cute."

Vhalla grabbed one of the pillows in question and threw it in his face. It hit him square and the prince stared at her. For a moment Vhalla felt her nerves take over.

"You just assaulted the crown prince." He glared, but she saw the tell-tale glimmer of mischief in his eyes. "Vhalla, I think that violates the terms of your probation."

"Oh? Tell me what will you do to me?" She did her best to imitate one of his trademark smirks, and she was rewarded by the spark turning to a fire in his eyes.

"I could think of *quite a few* things to do to you." His voice was gravely and deep, and Vhalla felt a flush rise to her cheeks.

Not having a good response, she took a bite of her bread and filled the silence with chewing. He chuckled and shook his head. Vhalla finished her roll, and he passed her a bladder of water. Vhalla wiped her mouth with the back of her hand, considering the prince.

"You're really nothing like they said," she mused. He raised an eyebrow, prompting her to continue. Vhalla grabbed one of the smaller scraps of meat from the bag and chewed thoughtfully. "Everyone, who ever said anything about you. It was warnings, caution." Vhalla tilted her head, thinking back. "When I had lunch with your brother, he said he saved me from you, that you'd eat me alive." She gave a small laugh and a grin, but it quickly fell from her face as she saw him tense.

"I am sure my brother would be more than happy to save anyone from me." Aldrik balled a hand into a fist.

"I don't believe them." Vhalla hoped that much was obvious.

"I know." His voice was faint, and Aldrik avoided her gaze. "But they are right, you know. I'm not a good person to be around."

Vhalla frowned, quickly gulping down the last of her food. She shifted closer to him, leaning over to put her face in front of his, searching his features thoughtfully. "No more of that, okay?" she whispered. "I'm not going anywhere, unless you say the word."

His lips parted slightly as his jaw went slack. "It's late."

"It is," she agreed.

The silence that settled over them was an odd mix of comfortable and painful. Vhalla found her heart trying hard to escape her chest. Hesitantly, she reached out. Her fingertips brushed lightly against his knuckles. He held her gaze, and she closed her fingers around his.

"You should go," he breathed. There was a tension there that Vhalla had never heard before.

"I *should*," she agreed.

Neither of them moved.

"Vhalla," Aldrik whispered. Her name strained against his lips, and she found some part of her relishing the sound.

"Aldrik?" she replied in kind.

He squeezed her hand fiercely a moment, and she held her breath. But as he relinquished his hold, she felt the insanity that had overcome them in that brief exchange dissipating into the air. "I will ride with you tomorrow," he promised. "Don't ride with anyone else. Stay by my side."

Vhalla nodded. "I will. I promise."

Aldrik helped her to her feet, and she stood facing him, her fingers still in his. Slowly he raised her knuckles to his face and gently pressed his lips against them. His mouth was soft and the heat of his breath sent a small shiver down her spine.

Vhalla put on her boots and crossed the few steps to the entrance of the tent and stopped, turning. "Aldrik, tomorrow." Vhalla paused, the words sticking to the inside of her throat, she swallowed hard to free them. "Will all this be a dream?" His brow furrowed a moment. "The next time we meet, will it be as though none of this happened?"

"Of course it will be," he said very matter of fact. Vhalla felt her chest tighten. Aldrik crossed the distance between them and placed his palm under her ear, his fingers wrapping around the back of her neck. He leaned in close and she saw a flash of amusement in his eyes. "To *everyone else*, of course it will be."

"To us?" Vhalla didn't know how a begging tone had slipped into her voice.

"For us, it is waiting four more days until we practice your Projection again."

She smiled faintly in relief, hoping she understood his meaning correctly. "Until then."

"Until then." He straightened and pulled back the tent flap to allow Vhalla to disappear into the cool night.

Her stomach was nothing but butterflies, and she suppressed a strange noise of elation as she walked back to her tent. Vhalla had never known a feeling quite like this before, and she found she enjoyed the bubbles it put in her blood. Four more days; it was far better than a month. Vhalla cupped one hand over the other, feeling phantom lips upon her skin.

Aldrik had been right, it was late. Most of the fires burned low and were located toward the center of camp. Along the edge there were few people. She made it far enough away from Aldrik's tent before someone noticed that her presence could have been a result of any number of reasons. The quiet night began to subdue her as she neared her tent with every step. She needed to apologize to Larel.

Larel was curled up in her bedroll, and she made no motion as Vhalla changed silently. The air was cool against Vhalla's bare skin as she undid the bindings she had begun to wear over her breasts to prevent uncomfortable chaffing in her armor. Vhalla's mind instantly thought back to the prince's warmth, and it sent a chill of a different kind through her. She sighed as she crawled into the scratchy wool of her blanket.

Vhalla had been content to let things with Larel go until the morning. But the Western woman had only been feigning sleep, and Vhalla was quickly locked into a staring contest. Larel regarded her thoughtfully and allowed the silence to stretch on until it was clear that she was waiting on Vhalla.

"I'm sorry for making you set up the tent alone today." Vhalla's ears burned with embarrassment.

"*That* was no trouble."

That wasn't, but how Vhalla had acted was. "I'm sorry also for snapping at you." She did her best to keep eye contact with Larel, but shame eventually won out and Vhalla avoided the other woman's gaze. "I didn't mean it, I was just, I was exhausted and—" Vhalla swallowed her stalling "—Larel, you're my friend. I couldn't have done this without you. I wouldn't have survived this long without you."

Vhalla choked on emotion. It was true. If it weren't for everything Larel had done and was continuing to do for her, Vhalla would have been alone. Sure, Aldrik was helping her and he could bring Vhalla as much joy as he could frustration. But things were strange there, because of their own hesitations and the world's expectations. In comparison, the bond Larel had built with Vhalla was perfectly simple.

Larel's hand closed around Vhalla's tightly. "Don't think on it any longer," Larel said finally. "I forgive you."

Vhalla took a shaky breath, clinging to Larel's palm.

"You are more than a protégé to me, you know. You are a dear friend." The Western woman ran a hand through Vhalla's hair lovingly. "I don't have many friends."

"I never did either," Vhalla laughed weakly.

"Aldrik was one of my first friends." The prince's name from anyone's mouth gained Vhalla's attention, and Larel said it even more easily than Vhalla could. "You shared your secret with the prince. I'll share mine."

"You don't have to." Vhalla could sense an unfamiliar aura around Larel, one of discomfort.

"I know." The woman smiled. "But I want you to know I trust you as you trust me." Larel shifted, her eyes growing distant. "I suppose nothing will make sense unless I start at the very beginning. I came from a very poor family in a small town called Qui."

"I don't know it," Vhalla confessed.

"You wouldn't, not unless you've studied Western mining. Qui is a town around halfway to Norin. At least, if you took the old routes before the Great Imperial Way was extended. Back then many would stop through for supplies or to rest horses." Larel rolled onto her back, her fingers only lightly entwined with Vhalla's.

"It's a town that's full of more shit than a cow pie." The woman was uncharacteristically bitter. "My father was a miner who never amounted to anything other than turning alcohol to piss. My mother was a broken woman, and all I think she could do was stare into space, especially after my father hit her."

Vhalla blinked in a stunned silence.

"There was no money, no future, and no joy there. Mother help me, I hated that shack they called home. One day, I was five, maybe six? My father brought home a man I'd never seen. He said that the man would give us all the money we needed and all I had to do was be a good girl and do as I was told." Larel placed her forearm on her forehead, staring at something far beyond the canvas above them.

"I didn't understand until I was alone with that man. I screamed, I cried, and no one came. In that moment, I just wanted them all to die." Larel sighed softly. Vhalla could hardly process what the woman was implying. "They found me sitting among the ashen remains of that home. I don't think I mourned once." She turned back to face Vhalla. "That was when I first Manifested. I was just a child, and a sorceress at that. So I was given to the mines. Every day I was lowered into a hole. I dug *and dug*. Or made fires, melted things away, or whatever else I could do."

"I'm sorry," Vhalla whispered. Those two words didn't seem to even come close to enough.

"This was a different life, Vhalla." Larel shrugged. "Honestly, the mines paid me a copper for every day I worked. It was enough to buy dinner, and I slept in empty storage sheds." Larel returned onto her back, her eyes glassed over with memories. "Then one day there was an Imperial company riding through. The Emperor himself was there, and they made a stop to rest their mounts and resupply their stock. I'd never seen anything as amazing as the gilded carriages and horses covered in dyed leathers.

"The Emperor said he wanted a tour of the mines. They were headed to Norin but Emperor Solaris knew our mine was one of the West's primary silver veins and he was kind enough to at least feign an interest. Aldrik was there."

Vhalla struggled to envision what a child-Aldrik would look like without his adult demeanor and presence.

"He was twelve and every inch the prince—even then. He followed his father around the mines dutifully. But he was still a child, and eventually he wandered on his own, well, with a guard. Though no one in the West would ever hurt him. He's one of the West's own, after all. I saw him making some fires to play with. I'd never seen another person like me." Larel laughed softly.

"I was such a grubby little thing, Vhalla. I had no business approaching the crown prince. But he smiled kindly and let me show him what I could do. He told me there was a place in the castle, a Tower, where people like us were special—where

I wouldn't have to live in the dark. I remember crying; I cried because it sounded so perfect, I cried because I knew I would never go.

"He looked at me strangely. He didn't understand why I wouldn't. His guard explained it to him, and Aldrik just said he would take me." Larel fussed with her blanket. "He took me to his father and told him, in front of everyone there, that I was coming back to join the Tower. At first the foreman objected, saying I was property of the mines. But Aldrik wouldn't hear it. In the end, I was bought with seven gold pieces and an Imperial thank you. I was eleven when I finally left that town, and I never went back."

Vhalla stared in awe, but Larel seemed to only be half-finished.

"I joined the Imperial caravan to Norin, and then back to the Southern palace. Aldrik and I were inseparable the whole time. We were kids—and, well—kids don't understand the world and all the reasons that keep people apart. Right from the start he didn't want me to call him "prince", said it made him feel strange. I was happy to oblige. When I joined the Tower, he insisted we trained together. Minister Egmun didn't—"

"Egmun?" Vhalla interrupted in shock.

Larel knew there was something more to Vhalla's tone. "Egmun was the Minister of Sorcery before Victor."

Vhalla sat up. "*No*, not the same Head Elect Senator Egmun?" It had to be a mistake.

"Yes, he stepped down from his minister position to join the Senate," Larel explained.

"He-he—" Vhalla seethed and sputtered remembering the man who tried to beat her into a submission that would mean accepting death as an alternative to the pain.

Larel let Vhalla's words fall away. "I hear Egmun changed a lot during his transition to senator."

"Sorry, continue." Vhalla shook her head, pushing away the senator whom she considered evil incarnate.

"Anyway, they didn't think it proper I trained with the crown prince, but Aldrik is Aldrik. So we trained together anyways. Every day I got to spend with him was better than the last. Even the times he was angry or sad, I just enjoyed being with him, seeing him . . ." Larel trailed away into nostalgia with a soft, sad smile.

Vhalla's eyes widened. "Did you love him?"

It would make sense if she had. He saved her, he brought her to a new life, and he stayed by her side as he showed her an amazing new world. Who couldn't love someone under those circumstances when they were as amazing as Aldrik was?

"Well . . ." Even in the dim light Larel's cheeks were slightly flushed. Vhalla had never seen her blush before and it made her insides clench. "There was a summer, he was barely fourteen and I was thirteen. It was that age when you first start wondering what love is. We had a moment; he was the first boy I kissed." Vhalla shifted her blankets. "But, it faded just as fast as it came on. We both realized we were kids playing at love and laughed it off."

Larel sighed softly.

"Right at the start of the war in the Crystal Caverns, he hit a really dark point. I tried to get to him, and he pushed me away. We had a fight, and we both said things we regretted." She looked pained. "I was proud, I was hurt, and I walked away. I know he needed me—needed *someone*—more than ever, and I withdrew." Larel's attention was back on Vhalla, the haze of the past lifting for a moment. "I promised then that I'd never abandon someone in need, if I had the chance again. I'd never ignore a friend because of the foolish things pain could make them do."

Vhalla quickly realized Larel was speaking about her.

"After that, for many years, things were awkward and cold between us." Larel was back to her story. "But time heals all wounds, and we found our friendship again. It'll never be what it was, but what we had created a strong foundation. He knows he can trust me implicitly, and I can trust him."

Silence filled the air as Vhalla digested Larel's story. It made her feel heavy, and it put her stomach in a knot. She felt sorrow for her friend; joy, excitement, and a touch of jealousy. She felt like a child when she wondered what it was like to kiss the prince and kept her questions at bay.

"So that's why you're my mentor." Vhalla saw it with a new light.

"Yes. During your Awakening, Aldrik was obsessive with worry over you. We had to practically remove him by force. He wanted to screen everyone who was allowed to even see you, more or less touch you. Because Victor kept pushing him away, he appointed me to the task. He asked a favor. Of course, now I know why he was frantic. If you're Bonded."

Vhalla twisted her blankets between her fingers. It was not the first time she'd been told he called in favors for her. Vhalla tilted her head. "The Bond?"

"You know how a Bond is made," Larel said delicately. "You are both a part of each other. There are records of people going mad because they lost their Bonded. Some theorize that, depending on the depth of the Bond, should one die the other will as well."

Vhalla sat upright, resting her forehead in her palm. *It was self-preservation for him.* "He's keeping me safe because if he doesn't—"

"He's keeping you safe because he *wants* to keep you safe," Larel interrupted.

Vhalla looked over at the other woman, who was now also sitting. Larel wrapped an arm around her friend's shoulders, pulling Vhalla back, and engulfing Vhalla in her warm safety.

Larel's voice was sad and sincere. "Aldrik's been through a good deal, much of which he's never even imparted to me. But I've seen the edges of the darkness he shoulders. I don't think he worries for his sanity or his mortality. He doesn't want you to die because he's afraid that it would mean he'd have to live without you." Larel stroked the top of Vhalla's head.

"Listen close. I've known him for twelve years. And a good many of those were spent, dare I say it, as his best friend. I know Aldrik—the good and bad." Larel sighed. "I don't want to say anything he hasn't said himself. But he *cares* for you, Vhalla. In a way that I've never seen him really care for anyone before."

Vhalla pressed her eyes closed, imagining she was back in the palace. "Thank you for telling me all this, Larel."

"Sweet Vhalla, you know I will always be here for you." Larel squeezed her tightly, and Vhalla slept peacefully for the first time in what seemed like years.

CHAPTER 10

THE NEXT MORNING Aldrik kept his promise and rode at her side. They talked the day away, almost exclusively with each other. He asked about her life in the East, her farm, her family. Vhalla probed him for magical knowledge that she had no other way of learning. The man was practically a walking library.

There were no remnants of tensions between her, Fritz, and Larel either. Fritz had caught on quickly that whatever oddities had been going on were resolved, and the Southerner had enough sense not to linger. Armed with her friends at her side and secure in the knowledge of the stability of her and Aldrik's relationship, Vhalla ignored Elecia throughout training—much to the other woman's frustration.

Vhalla used her Channeling liberally, to the surprise of everyone but Aldrik. Fritz and Larel were expectedly encouraging. Elecia was obviously perturbed and avoided her for the next three days.

Vhalla was amazed at how easily control came following those first few days of Channeling without hesitation or fear. Supported by her friends and Aldrik, Vhalla found herself finally relishing her magic. The wind slipped easily between her fingers, heeding her will, and Vhalla was quickly surpassing the basic introductions to magic Aldrik had given her months ago. Magic, she was discovering, was like poetry. Once you understood the logic, the meter, the rhyme behind it, you could embellish upon it and make it your own.

On the third night, she was setting up Larel's and her tent with just her magic alone. That was the first time Vhalla felt eyes on her for her sorcery, eyes that weren't daunting or scared. The Black Legion began to pay attention to their Windwalker once more, not for the Night of Fire and Wind, but for the daily feats she was beginning to be able to perform. It was a sanity-supporting confidence-booster for Vhalla.

She was in such a high place with it all that when Aldrik paired her with Elecia during training—at the other woman's request—Vhalla didn't even blink. She accepted the other woman's presence opposite her. If it was an actual competition for Aldrik's attention, it was one Vhalla was winning. The crown prince had rode at her side without stop, and tomorrow they would practice Projection again.

Aldrik had been intent on working toward more hand-to-hand combat, and Vhalla was happy to oblige. The Northern-looking woman needed to be knocked off her high horse and tonight was *Vhalla's* night, Vhalla assured herself. She'd been feeling stronger with every passing week, less sore, more capable.

"You sure you want to do this, Yarl?" Elecia smirked, her eyes darting toward Aldrik.

"It's just practice, right?" Vhalla sunk into her preferred fighting stance, one arm up and the other at chest-height.

"Oh, of course." Elecia balled her right hand into a fist, clasping her left overtop.

Vhalla clenched her hands into fists and welcomed her magic as well. "Your mark, or mine?"

"Mine—don't want you cheating." Elecia laced her voice with

sarcasm, but Vhalla knew it was a thin veil for sincerity, and her eye twitched.

Elecia moved, and Vhalla instantly went on the offensive. The dark-skinned woman dodged and ducked ably. She narrowly avoided Vhalla's hooks and jabs. But Vhalla's punches were missing by a narrower margin than she would've expected. Vhalla took a breath and focused. She began to feel the ripples in the currents of air as the other woman's muscles tensed and pulsed before she threw a punch or kick. Vhalla's body knew before her eyes could see. Vhalla's heart began to race. She could do this: *she could fight.*

A pulse began to fill Vhalla's ears, and she allowed herself to rely on instinct. Vhalla moved like the wind, fast and precise. Her hands swung in exact arcs, hitting their target almost every time. The constant offense had Elecia beginning to panic, and panic made the other woman sloppy. Vhalla heard nothing other than the heartbeat.

Elecia threw a fist at Vhalla's face; knowing it was coming, Vhalla dodged at the last second. She clamped her hand around Elecia's wrist and savored the look of pure shock as her foot kicked the other woman's feet from beneath her. Elecia fell to her knees, and Vhalla reached for the woman's face with her free hand, clamping it over Elecia's mouth.

The dark-haired woman's eyes went wide with terror.

"That's enough," Aldrik barked from their right. "Vhalla, *let her go.*"

The heartbeat in Vhalla's ears began to fade: it was almost like coming out of a trance. As if seeing the other woman for the first time, Vhalla quickly pulled her hand away, staring at the appendage that had found a mind of its own.

"What in the Mother's name was that?" Elecia sprang to her feet.

"Just a spar," Vhalla said curtly. She wasn't about to let

shock give Elecia leeway to ignore the fact that she'd been outperformed. "A spar you were bested in."

"Right," Elecia mumbled, her eyes swung to Aldrik. "Bested by an *awfully familiar* fighting style."

"I think that's enough for the night." Aldrik's tone was clear: he didn't want any further discussion on it.

"Why?" Elecia took a step forward. "So you can continue to train her in secret?" *Was that hurt in the other woman's voice?* "What do you do those nights you call her to your tent?"

"That is not your concern." Vhalla had never heard Aldrik so sharp with Elecia.

"It is, because you are my—"

"Just *go*, Elecia." Aldrik pinched the bridge of his nose with a sigh.

He was her what? Vhalla wanted to scream the question, but she was barely finding enough air to breathe through the whole exchange.

"Fine, Aldrik. If you want to train her in secret, go right ahead. But don't think your favor heaped upon the undeserving lowborn will go unnoticed or unquestioned." Elecia was at the insults again, and Vhalla wished they would dull just a little more instead of still feeling like daggers to her gut.

"All of you, go back," Aldrik commanded as Elecia stormed away.

"Aldrik," Vhalla said softly as Fritz and Larel got a few steps ahead.

"Where did you learn how to do that?" The prince stared down the bridge of his nose at her.

"Where else could I learn?" She didn't understand why she was being given his displeasure. "You, Elecia, Larel, Fritz, Major Reale, you know everyone who's ever taught me."

"The way you moved. None of *them* could have taught you that." He was somber.

"Well, I have a good teacher." Vhalla attempted a smile that she quickly abandoned. Aldrik's eyes were dark with a tempest of emotion, none of which good. "It was more than that, Vhalla," he pressed.

"I don't know what else you think I've done." She took a step away, crossing her arms. "If you remember, my life hasn't been mine for the past few weeks. I'm *owned* by the crown, my prince."

"Is that it? You're just owned by the crown? There is nothing more?" Aldrik shortened the gap between them with two steps. "What else more would there be?" *Why else would she be headed to war?*

His eyes widened by a fraction, and Vhalla realized that they weren't talking about her presence in the military or combat. Aldrik stormed past her, his shoulder hitting hers lightly.

"Aldrik, you know that wasn't what I meant," she called after him.

He froze and looked back at her. *Was that appreciation on his face?* Was he impressed that she recognized the subtle shifts in their conversation?

The moment was fleeting, and he left her without another word.

Vhalla wanted to scream. The wind tickled under her palm, responding to her frustrations. For the first time Vhalla considered running and abandoning her duty.

Later, in their tent, Vhalla vented to Larel about it all. "I don't even know what I did!" The other woman was silent. "I thought he would've been pleased I'm not utterly useless."

"You were never useless," Larel corrected unhelpfully.

"I bested Elecia!" Vhalla flopped back onto her bedroll. "I thought he'd be proud."

Larel paused a long moment, lying on her side next to Vhalla. They set up their bedrolls against each other to give more room for their armor and things in the small tent. It seemed a much better use of space, and Vhalla had already shattered any contact barriers from the nights she'd spent shaking and sobbing in Larel's arms.

"The way you fought, Vhalla," Larel began delicately.

"Not you too," she groaned.

"Well, you moved very differently than ever before," Larel pointed out. "What happened?"

"We've been training for *weeks*," Vhalla stressed. "I hope I'm getting better."

"Neither Fritz nor I could best Elecia."

"But you two weren't really sparring." Vhalla turned on her side to face Larel.

"We were." Larel nodded. "How did you do it?"

Vhalla paused, trying to put her defensiveness aside and think. "I don't know, I just moved."

"You 'just moved?' " Larel quickly dropped the skepticism when she saw Vhalla's face.

"I didn't even think," Vhalla added softly, attempting to analyze what had happened. "It was as though my body knew what to do, and I just had to trust it."

"You fought like Aldrik." Larel continued before Vhalla could point out that the prince had been training her, "No, Vhalla, you fought *exactly* like Aldrik."

"But—"

Larel shook her head. "You could have been his mirror. I've sparred enough times with the prince to know how he moves. Down to how you turned your feet, Vhalla. And then, when you grabbed Elecia's face . . . That's how Aldrik executes his enemy."

Vhalla remembered the Northerner on the Night of Fire and Wind, the one Aldrik had killed before her. He'd grabbed the swordswoman's face and burned her alive from the inside out. Vhalla shivered. "I don't know how . . ."

"The Joining would be my suspicion." Larel arrived at the obvious conclusion.

"I have to go talk to him." Vhalla was kept from scrambling to her feet by an arm around her shoulders.

"Tomorrow," Larel said thoughtfully. "I think Aldrik was very surprised by this turn of events. Give him some space to cool and process this."

Vhalla frowned but obliged her friend. Larel gave the best council and had the wisdom of years with Aldrik behind her. And the dawn wasn't that far.

But when the dawn came, Aldrik was nowhere to be seen. Vhalla scanned the campfires; the tents that were being torn down but she couldn't find his tall shadow anywhere. She didn't see him until she was falling in line with Fritz and Larel.

He ignored the space Vhalla had left for him, the space that had been constantly filled for days, and went directly to Elecia. Vhalla said her goodbye to Fritz and Larel and made a quick trot to the front of the line. His moods and his uncomfortable distances were beginning to wear down Vhalla's patience. She didn't care that by day their closeness had to be a secret— whatever that closeness even meant. She was tired of everything being on *his* terms and what *he* needed.

"Well, look who it is." Craig was the first to notice her, and Daniel beamed from ear to ear as she approached. "We thought you had forsaken us, Miss Windwalker."

"My favorite boys in gold?" Vhalla laughed away the tension of the Black Legion, falling in between Craig and Daniel. "How could I ever forsake you?"

"Good morning, Vhalla." Prince Baldair gave her a smile across Daniel.

"Good morning, my prince." Vhalla lowered her eyes respectfully. When she raised them again, they caught Raylynn's and the Southern woman gave her a small nod. Things had dramatically improved between them. "How are the swords this day?"

"Sharp as ever," Craig announced proudly. "Especially this one over here." He pointed toward Daniel, and the Easterner was overcome with sudden modestly. "He's been undefeated in the ring for two weeks now."

"The ring?" Vhalla asked. "Sparring?"

"We must keep the reflexes sharp." Baldair gave her a sideways glance. "Surely you have some kind of practice in the Black Legion as well."

"We do." Vhalla passed her reins uncomfortably from hand to hand.

"It's strange to imagine you fighting," Daniel thought aloud. "Not that I want to say you couldn't or shouldn't. When you were on trial, you didn't seem like a combatant," he added hastily.

"I wasn't." Vhalla stared forward toward the barren horizon. She'd picked the right day to ride at the front of the host. The remaining shrub trees and grasses of the forest were dissolving into the sands of the Western Waste. The Great Imperial Way cut through the pale yellow dunes like an alabaster snake, and there was nothing else for as far as she could see ahead of them.

"Would you spar with me?" Daniel asked. "I've never had much of an opportunity to spar with sorcerers; Jax is usually busy with the Black Legion. I'd love to have the practice." He smiled and pushed his sweat-slicked hair away from his face.

"Sure." Vhalla nodded and adjusted the chainmail hood Aldrik had made for her, keeping the sun off her cheeks.

"When we stop, then." Daniel seemed genuinely excited.

As a result of her decision to enter the fray, their talk settled on the history of the Black Legion and Tower of Sorcerers. Unsurprisingly, the rift between sorcerers and Commons ran deeply, and what Craig and Daniel said about it being worse in the military proved true. When the host broke for the day, the swordsmen and women regarded Vhalla cautiously as she lingered. She'd ridden with Craig and Daniel enough times to no longer receive looks or whispers, but staying with them after they stopped seemed to cross a new line.

"Are you sure you want to do this?" Vhalla asked after they tied off their mounts.

"Yes, Danny, are you sure you want to do this?" Raylynn gave Vhalla a sideways glance. Things may have improved between them, but the improvement was marginal.

"I am," Daniel laughed. "I know Vhalla won't hurt me."

Raylynn clearly didn't share the same sentiment, but Vhalla found Daniel's trust and confidence refreshing. He seemed to always give her the benefit of the doubt, to trust her without needing a reason. It had quickly devolved into a foreign feeling since becoming a sorcerer.

Vhalla and Daniel squaring off attracted the attention of more than one person, and the other soldiers began to gather, curiously gawking at the sorcerer in black plate opposite a Golden Guard.

"An easy round, then?" Daniel drew his sword. It was a beautiful blade with a golden pommel in the shape of wheat. Vhalla had admired it on many occasions as they had spoken of their homes in the East. "To forfeit?"

"To forfeit." Vhalla nodded, clenching her fists. She was almost dizzy with power. The winds of the desert were swift, unblocked, and strong.

"Craig, if you'll do the honors." Daniel glanced at their friend.

"On my mark." Craig stepped between them, raising his hand. "Mark!" He dropped his palm through the air, jumping back at the same time.

Vhalla acted on Craig's breath and was a whole step ahead of Daniel by the time Craig was even moving. She drew an arm across her chest, sending a gust of sandy wind into Daniel's face.

Daniel, to his credit, did not falter over such a probing attack and twirled his sword in his palm for a backhanded swing.

Ducking under the blade, Vhalla spun around Daniel like a dancer. She placed a palm to the center of his back, sending him falling with a gust of wind. She was disappointed; Vhalla had expected more of a challenge from such an esteemed member of Prince Baldair's guard.

But Daniel was prepared to show her how he had earned his golden bracer. As he fell he dug his sword into the sand, spinning around it to sweep her feet out from under her. In her surprise, Vhalla barely had time to catch herself and, when she did, the tip of a blade was at her throat.

"You're not bad," Daniel panted.

"Neither are you," she replied with a sly smile.

Daniel's face turned up into a grin as though they shared a wild secret now with each other. Vhalla would've never guessed it, but there was something about sparring with a person that was almost intimate.

The moment was quickly ruined as a man stepped forward from the observers. "*By the Mother*, what do you think you're doing, Lord Taffl?"

Vhalla recognized the hulking form of a man. He was the one who had confronted her at the start of the march. The one Daniel and Craig had coaxed out of accosting her.

"Getting in some practice," Daniel spoke to Grun, but he paid attention to Vhalla, helping her to her feet.

"With *that*?" Grun pointed at her.

"The *lady* graciously agreed to give me some experience against a sorcerer," Daniel bristled.

No one spoke; it was eerily quiet as every onlooker seemed to hold their breath. All seemed equally fearful of what the pieces would look like if the tension broke between the two men, Vhalla included.

"I should go, I think."

"Vhalla, no—" Daniel turned quickly.

"No, I should. Larel's likely setting up the tent without me." Vhalla smiled in an attempt to sell the poor excuse.

"I want to practice against a sorcerer," Grun said before Vhalla could walk away from the makeshift ring. "Spar with me."

Vhalla regarded him cautiously. She didn't think for a minute he'd suddenly accepted her. But maybe she could show him she wasn't dangerous, that she meant him no harm. "Very well," she said before Daniel could object.

"Vhalla, you don't have to." The Eastern man took a step closer to her, dropping his voice. "Don't feel pressured into this."

"I don't." She shook her head, whispering, "Maybe it'll be good to show him."

"Well . . ."

"Are you two done whispering your sweet nothings?" Grun asked dryly, drawing his sword opposite Vhalla.

Daniel stepped away quickly, his movements jerky and nervous. Was it the heat of the desert or was there a blush across his cheeks? Daniel lifted his palm; their mark to begin sparring would be when he lowered it.

She noticed how his dark brown hair moved as his hand cut through the air, his hazel eyes darting toward hers.

Distracted, Vhalla didn't hear Grun move until he was upon her. She turned back at the last second, making a weak attempt to dodge. He smashed the pommel of his blade against her cheek in a back-handed swing, sending Vhalla flying into the sand.

"Grun!" Daniel and Craig both called.

"Just a spar." The mountain of a man laughed. "If she wants to forfeit, she can."

Vhalla coughed blood onto the sand. Her lip was split, and her face already felt swollen. She blinked away stars, trying to get her feet back under her.

Grun's boot connected with her side, echoing against her plate as he kicked her. Vhalla rolled across the sand, the wind knocked from her. She curled in on herself, phantom blows attacking her body. Gasping, she tried to push the memories of Rat and Mole's assault out of her mind.

"Really, this is it?" Grun laughed, goading some of the onlookers into cheers. "This is the fearsome Windwalker?"

"Vhalla, forfeit." Daniel ran over to her side.

"Don't touch me," she hissed, holding out a palm. Something in her eyes froze Daniel in place as Vhalla pushed herself to her feet. Vhalla turned to Grun, feeling the wind at her back. Her heart began to race just by looking at him.

"Oh, still have some fight in you?" Grun chuckled as Vhalla stood. "Well, at least our Black Legion makes good punching bags. We should thank the Fire Lord for the only thing he's ever given us."

"*Take it back.*" Vhalla could barely hear herself over the racing heartbeat in her ears.

"Or wha—" Grun didn't finish his sentence as Vhalla's fist met the side of his face.

The man was built like a rock, and Vhalla could feel the bones in her arm compress through her shoulder as she punched his cheek. Her hand stung but she ignored it, quickly landing from her leaping punch and darting back.

Grun let out a cry of rage and swung his sword at her.

"Why do you hate me? Why do you hate us?" she cried, her body deftly dodging the swings of his blade.

"Because you're abominations!" Grun shouted, attempting to grab her plate.

Vhalla was too fast and batted his hand out of the way, spinning around his side. "We are your comrades! We don't want to fight you!"

"Says the woman who killed countless people on the Night

of Fire and Wind!" Grun raised his blade over her head and brought it down on Vhalla's shoulder. The clang of metal on metal was sharp and set her ear to ringing as she crumpled.

They thought she was a murderer.

"I didn't kill them," Vhalla whispered.

"Liar!" Grun raised his blade again. "They should've killed you that night!" The goliath swung, straight for her head.

Vhalla stared at the blade as the world devolved into chaos at Grun's clearly murderous intentions. This was not a spar; the man intended it to be an execution.

Vhalla raised her hand and the wind ripped Grun's blade from his fingers, sending it far off into the sand in the distance. She swept her palm in front of her body and a secondary gust knocked Grun on his side. As Vhalla stood, she pressed her hand downward, holding the man to the ground despite his struggles.

"I am not your enemy," she whispered in a disturbingly calm voice. "So I cannot die this day. I *will not* die until you see the truth."

"What's going on here?" a voice bellowed. Prince Baldair stomped through the crowd that had gathered, Raylynn at his side.

Vhalla relaxed her hand, allowing Grun to spring to his feet.

"She attacked me!" The man made his accusation to the prince.

"Liar!" Daniel shouted. "My prince, Vhalla was gracious enough to spar, and Grun took advantage of the situation. He made an attempt on her life."

Grun shot the Eastern lord daggers with his eyes. "It was just a spar," Grun countered with an annoyingly loud laugh. "She was the one who threw the first punch; look at my face."

Grun indeed had a bruise forming where Vhalla had hit him, but she could lick her lips and taste blood.

"She's a monster, and if she could've she would've killed me—it was self-defense," Grun continued.

Vhalla saw shades of the Senate as a few soldiers began to nod.

"That's not true!" Daniel drew his blade, his voice coarse. "Continue to lie and I will cut out your tongue."

"Defend your freak." Grun reached for his own sword, forgetting Vhalla had disarmed him completely.

"Enough!" Prince Baldair yelled. The men fumed but were silenced. The prince turned to Vhalla. "Do you have anything to say on your behalf?"

Vhalla met the prince's endless blue eyes, considering his question. Her side throbbed where Grun had kicked it, where Rat and Mole had kicked it. She clenched her fists, letting go of her magical Channel—and with it her fight. "No."

"No?" The prince was startled.

"I've learned the Empire," Vhalla turned, staring down the soldiers, "the *people*, have no interest in the truth." Vhalla met Prince Baldair's eyes coldly. "I am property of the crown, and property doesn't talk back."

The spite surprised even her, and everyone stood in a stunned silence. It was the first time she'd said it in a public place, the first time she'd assumed her new identity. They would think what they would about her—words would not change her reality. So why fight that battle? She had enough to worry about just surviving.

"Come with me, sorcerer." The prince had clearly taken offense with her directness. "Grun, Daniel, I'll deal with you later."

"Baldair—" Daniel took a half step between Vhalla and the prince.

"Silence, soldier!"

Vhalla had never seen Prince Baldair so harsh. Daniel looked at her hopelessly as she followed the prince into camp. She knew she should feel guilty, but she didn't. And her mood soured up until the point that Prince Baldair ushered her into his tent.

His tent was completely unlike Aldrik's on the inside. He had an actual table and three chairs positioned around it. A single brazier made of bronze hung from the center of the tent and lit the room. Prince Baldair's bed was larger—for reasons Vhalla could guess, given his reputation with women—and it appeared to be an actual mattress. She wondered how difficult it was for the horses to carry it all.

The prince closed the tent flap behind him and did a short circle around her, assessing Vhalla from head to toe. "Sit." He motioned to a chair. "Or perhaps you'd rather I threw some pillows on the floor?"

Vhalla's eyes widened, hearing the meaning between his words.

"You look uncomfortable." The prince paused, his eyes reading hers. "I would think you'd be more at ease in a prince's tent. Or is it just my brother's?"

"What do you want?" she demanded.

"Today, I saw him in you." Baldair squinted his eyes, as if he was trying to imagine Aldrik imposed atop her. "The way you moved, the way you were rushed by the fight. Tell me, is that the only way he's been *in you*?"

"I don't know what you're talking about," Vhalla hissed.

"I can't recall the last time I saw Aldrik with a woman, at least one who wasn't bought or given to him by our father as an attempt at finding a future Empress." Baldair took a step closer to her. She didn't know *this* prince. There was something turning him sour. He grimaced as he spoke, as if instantly regretting his words.

"Not another word," Vhalla cautioned.

"Oh? Did you think he was some paragon of purity? I've seen

him kill girls younger than you. I've seen him wind women up to crawl to his bed." Prince Baldair frowned.

The tension in her muscles became so great that Vhalla feared it would snap her bones. "Speak about him again and I'll—"

"You'll what?" Prince Baldair's expression clashed darkly with his usually handsome exterior. "Get yourself together, Vhalla. Have you forgotten the terms the Senate gave you? Have you considered that your actions may force his hand?"

Horror stilled her, and her hands relaxed. *He wouldn't.* "What do you want from me?" she whispered.

The prince leaned toward her to whisper in her ear. "Whatever you have with him, *end it now.*" His voice was quiet and it sounded sincere and pained. "If not for your sake, then for his."

Vhalla's chest tightened, but she didn't have an opportunity to ask him what he meant. The rumble of a single horse and the whinny of an abrupt halt could be heard from outside the tent.

Prince Baldair straightened as the tent flap was thrown open. Vhalla turned and a wave of relief crashed over her as she saw the dark figure step inside.

"Ah, brother." Prince Baldair rested his palms on his hips. "We were just talking about you."

CHAPTER 11

ALDRIK'S EYES FLICKED from Vhalla to his brother. Vhalla met his gaze and pleaded with him silently to get her out of there as fast as possible. She saw him collect his emotions as he folded his hands behind his back.

"What is going on here?" His voice held a deathly stillness.

"She was caught in a brawl." Prince Baldair glanced at Vhalla. "I was administering discipline."

Vhalla's head snapped back to the younger prince with a glare. *Is that what he called it?*

"I believe discipline falls to the subordinate's leader." She could hear the stress under Aldrik's cool voice.

"Normally, yes," Prince Baldair agreed. "But I think her leader is rather biased, don't you?"

"Baldair . . ." Aldrik didn't even try to hide the threat in the depths of his voice.

"I think you're confusing the woman, Aldrik. We both know how a man's needs must be met, but she's too young for you and your games." Prince Baldair crossed his arms over his chest.

Vhalla refrained from pointing out that she wasn't *that* much younger than Baldair himself.

"What is this?" Aldrik crossed over to his brother, stopping just short to stare his brother down. "Misplaced jealousy?" Aldrik sneered. "That a woman may prefer me over you?"

"Don't flatter yourself," the blue-eyed prince scoffed. Prince Baldair drew his height and still came up a hand shorter than his brother. "This isn't about me or you, this is about *her*." His eyes shifted to Vhalla. "She was kind, shy, and sweet the first time I met her. Less than a year with you and look at what you've done to her Aldrik. She's in black—"

"Baldair—" Aldrik snarled.

"—she's fighting and liking it," the younger prince continued.

"Baldair!" Aldrik's hand balled into a fist.

"She has blood on her hands!" Prince Baldair's face jerked back to Aldrik's. "Do you have the audacity not to feel guilty?"

Aldrik's jaw tightened, but he said nothing.

The younger prince shook his head. "At least you do." He turned back to her with a sorrowful expression. "Vhalla, you don't need him to shine. I tried to tell you that before the gala. Especially now, you don't have to force yourself to stomach his presence after what he—"

Vhalla had heard enough, she briskly took the three steps between them, raised her hand and brought her open palm hard across the younger prince's face.

Vhalla had never slapped anyone before. Perhaps Prince Baldair was right that she had changed significantly these past few months. If it was a change, she decided it was for the better as she felt a deep satisfaction course through her.

His hand went up to the red mark on his cheek, and he stared at her wide-eyed and open-mouthed. Even Aldrik was shocked into a gaping silence.

"Enough!" Vhalla fumbled over her words, her emotions running high. "Don't you *ever* make him feel, or suggest that he should, feel guilty for me or on my behalf." She glared at the golden prince. "And don't pretend like you somehow know,

know how . . ." Vhalla felt her insides twist, the currents in her mind cloud. "How I, or, how he . . . How we . . ." She heard her voice crack, she didn't want to confront this here.

Prince Baldair's face fell.

Aldrik spared a glare for his brother before turning his back on him to face Vhalla. He placed one hand on her shoulder, the other gingerly atop her wounded cheek. Aldrik tilted her face to his, and she met his eyes shakily.

"Vhalla," he whispered, stroking her cheek with his thumb. "It's all right, that's enough." She relaxed under the familiar warmth of his gaze, and Aldrik gave her a small smile that was weakly returned.

"It's true, isn't it?" Prince Baldair murmured.

Aldrik's hand dropped from her face, but his left remained on her shoulder as he turned to assess his brother.

The younger prince stared at the scene before him with wide eyes. "You really do care for her."

She felt Aldrik tense at the statement, but he made no motion to move away; if anything, his hand tightened slightly. Vhalla's heart beat hard. She desperately wanted to leave, to get away as fast as possible. As much as she wanted to hear the bare truth of the answer to that accusation, she didn't want it to be like this.

"And you . . ." Prince Baldair stared at her.

Vhalla mustered the last of her courage to look at him unfaltering. She succeeded well enough—the prince was the first to look away with a shake of his head. He walked heavily over to a chair and slumped into it. The prince rested his temple on his fingertips, staring in disbelief at Aldrik.

"I'd only meant to help her. I thought you were—Aldrik, you're too smart for this."

"I know," Aldrik replied quietly, the tension seemed to have vanished, and sorrow filled his eyes in its place.

"And here I thought, thought you . . ." Prince Baldair chuckled and shook his head again. "Ah, never mind."

"Prince Baldair." Vhalla took a step forward, and Aldrik's hand fell from her person. "I'm sorry for my actions today. More importantly, I am sorry for striking you." She took a breath. "I would appreciate it if-if it isn't used as a reason to end my life."

The prince began to laugh; he placed a palm on his stomach and let the melodic sound break the tension in the air.

"No, I rather deserved it, didn't I?" Vhalla stared at him, stunned. The prince turned to his brother. "It wasn't her fault today, Aldrik. I think some of what she said actually may have gotten through to the men. You would've been proud if you'd seen it, I think." Prince Baldair shifted to rest his cheek in his hand. "And Vhalla, I'm sorry. That was not a princely way to act."

Vhalla studied him carefully. On the whole, this man had done more good by her than ill, and he had earned credit while she was on trial that he was spending now. He may be an emotional fool, but Vhalla wasn't certain he was malicious.

"I forgive you, my prince," she said. His words still stung but Vhalla put it out of her mind, at least for now.

Vhalla turned back to Aldrik—her tall, wonderful, dark prince—and gave him a relieved smile. His eyes fell softly on her, and it felt as though the tension that had been building between them was close to breaking. It was not an unwelcome feeling.

"Let's go?" she asked.

He nodded, shooting a final glare at his brother before stalking out.

Vhalla paused briefly, turning. She assessed the fair-haired prince who stared curiously back. "What you wanted from me, I'm afraid I cannot give it." Vhalla had come to accept that whatever happened, whatever they were, she would not be the one to end it between her and Aldrik.

"Tread carefully, Vhalla," Prince Baldair cautioned. "I know a lot more about my brother than you. I may seem like an ass."

She raised her eyebrows.

"I *am* an ass at times," he corrected with a chuckle. "But I am exactly what you see. He's not. There are things about him you still don't know."

Vhalla pulled back the tent flap. Even if there were things, Vhalla wasn't going to hear them from Baldair. Aldrik would tell her, in time.

"And Vhalla?" The prince stood. "Ride up at the front again. Don't let this dissuade you."

"Why?" she asked skeptically.

"Because I think it does the men good to see you with me." He sensed her confusion and continued, "You are a symbol, Vhalla. And, despite what some may have you believe, you have more control over what you symbolize than anyone else."

"I am no one," she muttered, hearing Aldrik mounting his War-strider.

"Even something very small can cast a large shadow when it is close to the sun."

Vhalla considered this for a long moment, searching the prince's face for a hint of insincerity. She could find none and left him behind her before he had a chance to say something else that could potentially throw the fragile peace into disarray. For everything Prince Baldair was, and had been, somehow he didn't feel like her enemy.

Aldrik took a foot out of his stirrup for her to use, offering her a hand to mount his horse. Vhalla's cheeks grew hot as she swung up behind him in the saddle. Her hands fell lightly on his armored waist for balance.

"Where's Lightning?" she asked.

"My brother's Easterner rode him back when he went to get Fritznangle." Aldrik spurred the mount forward.

The wind was fresh and warm on her cheeks after the oppressive atmosphere in the tent.

"Daniel?"

Aldrik nodded mutely.

"Is it a good idea to ride like this?" Vhalla asked softly, noticing the glances from the soldiers.

"I want them to see you with me." He responded so quickly that there couldn't have been any thoughts into his words.

"Why?" she breathed.

"Because I want them to know that if they lay a hand on you again, they will deal with me directly." Aldrik's voice was deep and harsh, and it made her want to grab onto him and never let him go.

He took them directly to his tent. Black Legion soldiers who had just finished setting it up were beginning to dissipate, and they all peered at her curiously as Aldrik ushered Vhalla within. Getting away from the world's prying eyes was a relief, but it was equally nerve-wracking to have those prying eyes watch her being led with the prince's palm on the small of her back.

The moment the tent flap closed, the braziers lined along the perimeter lit with flames. Aldrik didn't seem to even think about using his magic. "Take this off, I'll fix it." He placed a palm on her wounded shoulder.

Vhalla nodded, beginning to unclasp the scale mail as Aldrik did the same. She felt comfortable and nervous at the same time. Aldrik took the plate from her as Vhalla shed her chainmail.

"So what happened?" Aldrik asked.

"Well . . ." Vhalla sighed and recounted the events leading up to Baldair's tent.

"You bested him in the end, though?" he asked after she had finished her story.

"I did." Vhalla nodded.

"How?"

"I just moved . . ." She wasn't sure what answer he was looking for with such a question.

"Like with Elecia?" Aldrik glanced up from his work on the plate. His thumbs ran over the red hot metal.

"Yes . . ." Vhalla trailed off, waiting for him to fill in the blanks. He didn't, and frustration snuck up on her. "You can't keep doing this."

"Keep doing what?" He seemed startled by her tone.

"You can't keep asking cryptic questions and storming off to sulk without giving me answers that I know you have." Vhalla was no one, and yet she fearlessly made demands of the crown prince.

Aldrik just sighed and let her. "Fine, stubborn woman." He placed her repaired armor off to the side. "Do you not think it strange that you are suddenly capable of besting soldiers with *years* of practice?"

"We've been training." It was a cringe-worthy excuse when Vhalla actually thought about it.

"You were sloppy, at best." When Aldrik was honest, he held back nothing. "I was beginning to fear for what we would need to do to keep you alive when we reached the North."

"So, what happened?" Vhalla pressed.

"You fight as I do." Aldrik met her eyes.

"Of course I do."

"No, Vhalla." He shook his head. "You fight *exactly* as I do."

"Why?" she whispered.

"I can only assume it to be the Joining," Aldrik mused.

"But, we're not Joined anymore." They had not attempted it either since that first night weeks ago.

"No, but the Bond was widened, our minds were—" Aldrik paused, closing his eyes with a soft sigh. "Our minds were linked. It was a reckless thing to do on my part given how little is known about its effects."

"So, then," she fumbled, her words struggling to find the source of his discomfort. "Why don't we close it?"

"Even if we could, I would not."

"But . . ." It seemed to be causing him so much distress, *why not end it?*

"Because now I can have some measure of security that you will make it through this war alive."

Vhalla was stunned into silence. She couldn't take the weight of his gaze and engaged in a quick staring contest with his table. "I know," she began her confession. "Larel told me about Bonds. That, if I die, you'll die."

"That's just a theory." Aldrik brushed away the thought easily. "And not by any reputable scholars."

"But—"

"I want you to worry about yourself." He sensed the remaining fight in her. "Vhalla, *please*, promise me that."

The firelight played tricks on her eyes. It made the man who was nearly seven years her senior look like nothing more than a frightened child. Vhalla moved without thought, taking his hand in hers. Aldrik gripped her fingers tightly, and she erased all thoughts of doubt.

"I will promise you, if you promise me that you will stop running away and hiding these things. I don't want to feel shut out from you." Vhalla's voice had dropped to a whisper, and Aldrik nodded silently, sparing her any further explanation.

"We should practice your Projection." He broke them out of their trance.

"Oh, right." Vhalla had completely forgotten they'd actually planned to work together that evening.

"Let's put magic aside, for now, and focus on seeing how far you can go." Aldrik situated himself before the table, adjusting his papers.

"Sure," she closed her eyes.

"Would you care to lay down first?" Aldrik reminded her that her physical body went limp the last time. He grabbed one of the pillows and propped it against his leg.

Vhalla hesitated, the invitation clear. The prince feigned attentiveness to his paperwork, clearly apprehensive of whether she would accept or reject him. Prince Baldair's words of caution frustratingly replayed themselves in Vhalla's mind and she lay down quickly, her head resting on his leg. She would not let the younger prince and his games get in her way.

Vhalla slipped out of her body shortly after closing her eyes. It was surreal to see her physical form so still, as if barely breathing. Aldrik watched her closely, waiting for any signs of trouble.

I think it's easier, Vhalla said with a thought.

"It seems so," he agreed.

Can you hear me even if I'm far away?

"One way to find out. Go slowly," he cautioned, but didn't tell her to stop.

Vhalla passed through the canvas of the tent flap. There was some resistance, but nothing unmanageable. People walked about from one campfire to the next, but no one noticed her.

Can you still hear me?

"Without a problem." Aldrik seemed excited by her progress, and it encouraged her onward.

She progressed forward in a straight line and discovered that it was only uncomfortable when someone walked through her. It was a strange chill, and the world became disoriented for a moment. But after the third time, Vhalla was beginning to adjust her magic accordingly, recovering faster.

"Are you all right?"

Yes. I'm on the edge of camp now.

"Go a little farther."

Vhalla walked into the desert until the sun had dipped below the horizon. She called out to him regularly, but the link was consistent and strong. By the time she returned back to her body, there was little question that she'd begun to master the art of Projection.

Returning was simple; she listened for the pulse that had guided her back the first time and let go of her magical hold. But when her real eyes fluttered open Vhalla let out a soft groan at how the world spun.

Aldrik shifted, leaning over her. "What is it?"

"I think my brain is just-just returning slower from the distance." She wasn't sure if it made sense. There was a scratching noise, and she saw he was back to making notes. Vhalla struggled to sit.

"Lie down, Vhalla," he scolded. She returned to her former position, his left hand ran over her hair gently. "You are amazing." Aldrik's voice was breathy and he focused on the papers instead of her. Vhalla stared up at him but he seemed to be talking more to himself. "Atop everything else, you will be the key to ending this war."

"Do you think so?" Vhalla mumbled tiredly.

"I do." There wasn't a trace of doubt. "Now rest."

Vhalla obliged and closed her eyes.

The weeks slipped by like the sand across the dunes. The desert was bleak and empty, but Vhalla's days were full. Be it at her request or of his own accord, Aldrik recovered quickly from the shock of the effects of their Joining. Privately, he encouraged her to liberally rely on her link with him. He assured her that it did not affect him in any way.

Vhalla was cautious—at first. But the more she allowed that

pulsing beat to take over her ears, the stronger and faster she became. It was as though her body was re-learning what it already knew, making every movement sharper and more precise. Aldrik still rode with Elecia some days, and Vhalla up with the Golden Guard. Prince Baldair seemed pleased by her presence. The more time she spent with the younger prince, the more time she wanted with him in private. She had questions for his cryptic messages and sloppily veiled warnings. She wanted to ask him outright what he knew, what he meant. But their time together never extended beyond the march.

Vhalla's evenings were spent sweating and pushing her body past its limits at the demands of the elder prince. Vhalla was thankful for the mix of gentle and forceful encouragement from Aldrik and her friends. Her body was beginning to fill out once more, muscle defining in places she had never known it could.

The atmosphere on the march began to shift as they neared the Crossroads. There was a palpable relief among the road-weary and sunburnt soldiers to be close to a resting point.

"How much longer do you think it will be?" Vhalla asked her companions.

"Perhaps a day, maybe two," Aldrik answered. His attention on her was now a regular occurrence.

"A bed," Fritz said wistfully.

"A bath," Vhalla sighed happily at the thought. "There *will* be water at the Crossroads, right?" The host had been reduced to water rations from the wells that lined the Great Imperial Way in long intervals. None of them had washed for weeks, and Vhalla couldn't imagine how badly they all smelled to someone who wasn't accustomed to the stink.

"Of course there will be water," Larel laughed. "The Crossroads is a magic place, Vhalla. It's the middle of the world."

"I can't wait." She was genuinely excited after being on the road for so long. "What will you all do first?"

"The first thing I am going to do is drink a Crimson Dragon," Fritz proclaimed.

"You're such a drunk," Larel teased.

"A what?" Vhalla asked.

"A Crimson Dragon is a type of drink," Aldrik answered from her left. "It is made with Western spiced alcohol, has a sharp taste, and is very strong."

"I want to try one too, then." She smiled back at Fritz and the messy-haired Southerner went off planning a grand adventure for the three of them to have. Larel tried to wrangle in his grandiose dreams and the two were bantering back and forth within minutes.

"Vhalla," Aldrik said in a voice that was meant only for her. She swung her eyes up to him. "There's something I want to tell you."

"Yes?" His tone made her pulse race.

"At the Crossroads, I have some . . . business I will attend to with Elecia."

Vhalla was more worried at how delicate he was being with the subject than the words themselves. *What had him looking so uncomfortable?* "What is it?"

"You do not need to worry about it." His eyes were guarded.

"Aldrik, you promised me—"

"*Vhalla,*" he hissed. She brought a hand to her mouth glancing around quickly to see if anyone noticed her slip in forgetting his title. "I will tell you, I promise. But only when the time is right."

"When will the time be right?" she pressed.

"When it is over and sorted." His tone told her she'd get no more information on the matter. Vhalla sighed softly. "It should only be two days, three at most. I will find you after and tell you everything."

"All right." Vhalla nodded and put on a brave face for the rest of the day. But his words rattled in her brain with every step, echoing into the night.

CHAPTER 12

*T*HE DAY WAS *sticky, and her hair clung to her face and neck with sweat as she pulled off the helm. She looked up at the dense trees overhead, gnarled and thick with brush and vines. Her mind lamented over the last time she had seen the unbroken sky. A bird darted between the foliage before breaking through to the heavens above. She found herself wishing she could do the same.*

The smell of ash and fire filled her nose, an all too familiar scent that she barely noticed anymore. Her gaze returned to the earth, and back over the destruction that had been wrought. The last of the survivors were being put to the sword. Blood was splattered over her own armor, the crimson turning dark against the black of the scale and plate.

Vhalla vaguely recognized something being distinctly off. The edge of awareness of something amiss crept upon her.

She walked back to her tent. No, not hers; or was it? Trying to think was too difficult, like she was fighting the obvious.

Inside was the same familiar area on the floor with pillows and a small table, though this time it was near the bed. A large rectangular table and chairs dominated the other space. It was messy with papers that spilled onto the floor, and she pulled off her large gauntlets, dropping them haphazardly.

Her breath became ragged and she turned. With a sweep of her arms she pushed all the papers and documents onto the floor with a grunt. She slammed her hands down on the table and felt her shoulders shake.

This town had not been part of the militia. Perhaps a few had joined the resistance, but all had been put to flame and steel. Her nails dug into the wood of the table as she muffled a frustrated cry. No one could hear her pain. She couldn't let the soldiers catch wind of her turmoil. She never could.

The eyes of the dead lingered with her, their pleading, fearful eyes as she rounded them up in flames and burned them alive. It never got easier with time. The memories were never lighter to bear.

Regaining control, she began to pull off her armor. She really needed someone's help for the larger plate but she couldn't be bothered as she burned through the leather clasps hidden beneath it. She'd fix it later.

If her sins were as easy to remove as her armor, she may be able to sleep at night. She rubbed her eyes tiredly. With a sigh she began to rummage through a bag hidden by her bed, fishing for the only thing that could wash away her pain and drown their cries. A call halted her actions.

"My prince." *The voice was familiar,* one of Baldair's men.

"Enter." *Her voice was deep. A man with dark hair and eyes entered the tent, and she assessed him viciously, uninterested in entertaining company and fully hoping he would realize this.* "How may I be of assistance?" *she asked briskly.*

"Today," *he took a step forward, his movements jerky; she wondered if he had beaten her to the bottle.* "Today you led the assault, did you not?" *He was still in his armor, covered to his elbows in blood and ash.*

"I did." *She was already annoyed with this discussion. Despite what the soldiers thought of her, the last thing that she wanted* to do was re-hash her murders. "If there is nothing else . . ." She turned her back on the man, pretending to be interested in picking up the scattered papers. Just the limited words he said had brought the horrified faces back to her mind.

"H-he would've been twenty-two," the man rambled. "He had dark hair, like us; he was of the West."

She picked up a paper, continuing to ignore him; the man didn't seem to get the hint.

"He married when he was young, a Northern bride." Something twisted in his voice.

"I am afraid I do not know who you are talking about," she said, returning a handful of papers to the table.

"My son." The man gave a twisted cry and lunged for her. The dagger dug into her side, just above her hip.

There was a man's cry that was one of the most horrifying awful sounds Vhalla had ever been forced to hear, and she screamed with him. She began to fight against the mental prison which confined her. She didn't want to see anymore.

She felt the poison, a sickening dizzying feeling washed over her almost immediately. She looked at the man in shock as he took a step back. Her hand reached out for his face and soon he was aflame, his features twisting before they burned away.

Her feet began to stumble and give out. She placed her hand on the dagger. Removing it would prompt blood loss, keeping it in continued to inject more of the searing poison into her veins. She cried out, leaning against the table. With a shaky hand, she grabbed for the dagger, making her decision as she pulled out the wavy blade. It bit into the flesh again as she ripped it from her side.

Her hand was pressed against the gaping wound. A soldier rushed in. "About time," she wanted to say, but her jaw was clenched taut, blood soaking through the thin shirt she wore and oozing between her fingers. Her vision began to blur and she *shifted her power inward, feeling the fire burn through her veins as she tried to purge the poison.*

Vhalla woke with a cry, her hand on her hip. She tossed aside the blankets, looking at her body. Vhalla lifted her tunic, seeing only smooth unmarred skin where she expected blood. She raised her hand to her forehead and wiped away cold sweat.

She felt sick. Her brain eased itself back into place as she struggled to find her breath. Vhalla tried to tell herself that it was just a dream, that it had *only* been a dream. But she had felt every minute of it. She had heard Aldrik's voice.

Suddenly a memory of a night long ago returned to her. She wondered how she could have forgotten. It had simply vanished from her mind into the chaos that her life had unraveled into.

Echoing through her mind were the Northerner's words during the Night of Fire and Wind.

"Of course, we also hoped that if the poison failed to kill you, the shame of one of your dear sweet brother's men stabbing you in the back would be enough."

It hadn't made sense. *It didn't make sense,* she reminded herself. Her mind had dredged up an explanation for that confusing moment and played it for her. Vhalla wrapped her arms around herself. The alternative explanation was too impossible. Like the last fractured dream, she wanted to go to him. Every heartbeat made her struggle with the distance between them.

"Vhalla, what is it?" Larel rubbed sleep from her eyes.

"Nothing," she panted.

"Are the dreams returning?" The Western woman sat also.

"No." Vhalla shook her head. "It was a dream, but not *that* dream. Just a random nightmare." She began pulling on her armor, hasty to get the day started and shake off the remnants of the vision.

She was so relieved to see Aldrik later that she wasn't even bothered when Elecia rode up and wedged herself between them. The sight of the prince soothed her nerves and fears, reassuring her that her dreams were nothing more than night terrors. They spoke about some Western holiday, and Vhalla savored the sound of his rare laughter. Much to Elecia's annoyance, Aldrik worked to include Vhalla in the conversation.

"You have never been to the West before, correct?" he asked across Elecia.

"I have not." She shook her head.

"A shame we cannot make it to Norin," he said thoughtfully.

"I would like to see it someday." Aldrik smiled at Vhalla's statement. "What is Norin like?"

"Norin is settled in—" Elecia began arrogantly.

"The great oasis by the Western Sea," Vhalla interjected. "The sea breeze helps keep the city cool despite the desert heats, and the castle of Norin is one of the oldest in the world. Or so I read." Vhalla savored the look of satisfactory pride the prince was giving her.

"Well, much of Norin is the oldest in the world. There's a reason why it took ten years for it to fall to the Empire." Only Elecia could turn a defeat into a point of pride and she turned up her nose at Vhalla.

Vhalla paid Elecia no mind, her attention only on Aldrik. His mother had lived in that castle as one of Mhashan's princesses. *He was a prince of two worlds.* "What is the food like?" she asked, deciding to stay involved in the conversation.

"Western food is cleaner than the things you have in the South. We use less butters and oils," Elecia proclaimed haughtily.

Vhalla barely refrained from rolling her eyes.

"There is a dish I think you would like, actually," Aldrik hummed. "They take the peel of lemons and candy them with sugar."

"That does sound delicious." Vhalla smiled conspiratorially, remembering the lemon cake they shared in Aldrik's garden.

"Perhaps we can find some at the Crossroads." The prince removed his helm a moment to run a hand through his hair. Sweat made it stick to his head and Vhalla debated which style was better.

"And what about Eastern food?" Elecia asked, interrupting Vhalla's admiration of the prince.

"It's simple, I suppose." In truth, Vhalla's family had never had money for expensive or fancy foods. "I've never had a better bread than from home around harvest time. But I grew up mostly in the South."

"Oh yes, library apprentice," Elecia said matter-of-factly.

It annoyed Vhalla that this other woman just happened to know things about her and never explained how.

Vhalla opened her mouth to speak when a horn blew out from the south of the column. They were not more than a few hours into the march; surely it could not be time to stop. Everyone turned when the horn blew again in warning.

Vhalla heard Aldrik curse loudly before his horse broke into a run, sprinting through the ranks toward his father in the legion ahead of them. Elecia squinted at the horizon. Vhalla looked also.

"What is it?" she asked, trying to discern the reason for the sudden change in mood.

"It looks like a sandstorm. Mother save us." Elecia's head turned forward and back again. "There're too many on foot . . ." she mumbled and her head snapped to the right. "Larel!" Elecia called. Larel caught the other woman's eyes. "How far out is the first barrier wall of the Crossroads?"

"An hour, maybe, of hard riding," Larel replied, squinting over her shoulder.

"A closer town?" Elecia gripped her reigns.

"None that I know of." Larel frowned, her face pulled taut.

"We'll have to make a run then." Elecia cursed and sped forward toward the Imperial family.

"What's going on?" Vhalla was confused.

"It's a sandstorm, Vhal." Fritz looked back again uncertainly. "It's far off, but we don't want to be tangled up in one of those. They're temperamental and fast. If we can make it to shelter, it may only kill a few from suffocation. There's a lot here the wind could pick up and turn into projectile nightmares."

"Is it that bad?" she asked in shock.

"The Western winds are known to be strong enough to rip trees from their roots and sweep grown men off their feet like ragdolls. They normally blow with the summer air. It's abnormal for a winter one. We're not prepared," Fritz replied gravely.

Vhalla twisted in her saddle, looking at the dark point on the horizon. *At best it may kill?* That didn't sound like a best case scenario to her. She wondered if she imagined it growing in the southern skyline. Another horn blew out, a series of blasts and others picked up its call. Aldrik and Elecia rode back together.

"We make haste for the Crossroads!" the prince shouted, calling attention of all the soldiers in the Black Legion. "Speak not another word and listen for orders."

It seemed as though everyone understood at once what was happening and the host picked up its pace. But with so many soldiers on foot, they were severely limited in speed. Vhalla glanced over her shoulder. It seemed like they were making headway against it, or it wasn't coming their way.

Then the wind shifted.

She felt it there, the raging angry mass behind them. It was a fury unlike any Vhalla had ever felt before. It was pure power and wind that pushed forward to consume every last person in their host. Vhalla turned back and saw it again. It appeared no bigger, but she knew better.

"How much longer until the Crossroads?" she hissed to Fritz and Larel.

"I don't know. I've only been this way once before," Larel whispered back. Her voice was barely audible over the horses' hooves on the stone road.

"How much longer?" Vhalla tried Elecia, the other woman glanced at her in annoyance but Vhalla gave her an unwavering stare. She'd have none of it.

"Maybe less than thirty minutes?" Elecia said.

Vhalla cursed. They wouldn't make it. *She felt it.*

"My prince!" Vhalla called. Aldrik glared at her sharply for speaking out of turn, she ignored it. "We're not going to make it if we don't go faster."

Seriousness furrowed his brow. "You're sure?" he asked gravely.

Vhalla ripped off her gauntlets and stuffed them into her saddlebag. Clenching her hands into fists, she let go of the reins completely and held them in the air. Closing her eyes, Vhalla unfurled her fingers, not caring how silly it may look. The wind pushed through and around her hands, she felt the storm's power at the end of every gust.

Her eyes snapped open. "We won't make it!"

Elecia's attention darted from her to Aldrik. "Aldrik, there's no other cover but the barrier walls for the Crossroads." Tension brought Elecia's voice to a tremble.

Vhalla scanned the landscape around them. It was true. Sand and sand as far as the eye could see. She glanced over her shoulder. The dark spot had turned to a wall on the horizon.

"Damn it!" Aldrik spurred his horse forward again and Vhalla saw him race back to his father. For just a brief moment she saw the Emperor look back in her direction. Aldrik's horse dropped its pace and the host sped around him as he returned to his place. Another horn blew out followed by more.

The Imperial army was in a run along the Great Imperial Way. The rumble of horses and the chorus of armor cut through the slowly increasing volume of the wind. Vhalla looked back at the sections of carts, those horses couldn't be pushed any faster without losing their load. Foot soldiers were already being left behind as those who were mounted began to panic and push faster. She saw the roaring wall behind them, blotting out the sun ominously.

A heavy realization pulsed through her. *They still weren't going to make it.* Horses wouldn't outrun this wind. Even for a single rider it was too large and too fast. Vhalla absorbed the panicked faces of the people around her, the strained expressions of her friends.

Not a single word was said among any of the soldiers. It seemed as though she wasn't the only one to come to the sobering awareness of their plight. It didn't require magic to feel the ever increasing gusts that began to make men and women stumble and mounts falter. A horn blew out, a frantic pulsing sound. Everyone turned. Vhalla's heart beat in her throat.

A swirling mass of sand and death cut from earth to sky. The wind howled and consumed everything in its path, plunging the world into darkness. It stretched out on either side of them. The storm meant to swallow them whole and was about to begin its meal with the last rider at the end of the host.

Vhalla's saw the faces of those around her as they confronted their own mortality. Her gaze swept back until it fell on Aldrik. He had a tormented expression of frustration and desperation. Vhalla felt something pulse through her frantically; *she would not let him die.*

As if feeling the intensity of her attention, Aldrik's head snapped back at her; something on her face made panic overcome him. She barely saw the movement of his lips as he was going to say something. Vhalla turned Lightning hard to the right, cutting between the legions.

They could do nothing; none of them could do anything. If she didn't try, then it was over. Vhalla dug her heels into Lightning's sides as she cut through the shocked expressions to the outside of the column. Somewhere, someone was calling her name.

Vhalla didn't look back.

The wind was in her ears, it flowed through her and, despite all her fears, she did nothing to suppress it. This would not be like the last time. She would find the wind and use it to save, not to kill.

Vhalla snapped the reins. "Faster," she demanded. "*Faster!*" she cried, watching the sandstorm creep toward the end of the column. Her heart threatened to burst from her chest, and Vhalla blinked the sand from her eyes.

The solders of the rear legions stared at her in shock as she ran headfirst toward the storm. There was more shouting now from behind her. Vhalla glanced back. The Black Legion was a roar calling for her. She turned her head away from them, almost at the end of the host.

The wind whipped her hair, and soon Lightning began to spook and fight her pushes to advance. Vhalla cursed at the beast, begging it to carry her just a little farther. Through her words or her heels at his sides, Lightning obliged. She cut back onto the road when the last of the legion sprinted past her in the opposite direction. Their horrified expressions were all they could give her.

Vhalla pulled hard and dismounted ungracefully, stumbling and recovering. Turning Lightning back to the host she gave him a slap on his rear—the horse needed no further urging to run from the swirling sands. The soldiers kept going.

She breathed a small sigh of relief. They needed every chance they could get. If she should fail, they needed to keep pressing on. At the very least she would buy them time. Vhalla turned and looked up at the titan of wind and sand.

And she felt very small.

Vhalla spread out her feet and planted them, bracing herself. She held out her bare hands into the wind. If she could make a storm, she could end one. Vhalla felt the wind through her fingers, she felt the currents, they were part of her—and they would answer to her.

Nothing prepared her for the impact of the storm. It was as though she was thrown from another roof and Vhalla felt her shoulders pop from the strain. Her whole body was pressed down, and her knees trembled.

Vhalla closed her eyes and grit her teeth. There was sand all around her, in her hair, in her ears, and in her nose. But it would end here, with her. She leaned into the storm, pushing back with all the force she had. In the chaos of the sand and the roar of the wind, she couldn't open her eyes. Vhalla tried to reach outward to see if she had even managed to stop or slow the storm, but her senses were jumbled with the raw power she was trying to draw from.

The first time she cried out was when one of her fingers snapped back. The sharp and sudden pain of her bones being pulled from their joints made her focus falter—she felt the wind collapse in on her, almost losing her balance. Vhalla forced her legs to straighten, straining against the pain. Another finger went, and then her shoulder threatened to give out.

Her hands trembled and Vhalla felt herself at the edge of exhaustion. With a cry she did everything Aldrik had cautioned her against since her very first lesson with him. Vhalla threw herself into her Channel with the singular thought that this storm ended here, that it would not reach her friends—*it would not reach him.*

The moments that followed were a strange dichotomy of feeling, like her body was dying and her mind was being born again. Light seared at the edges of her closed eyes and flooded her senses. With an almost audible click she felt herself connect to the storm through her Channel. She felt every edge of it, understood its violent gales. It was hers now, an extension of her magic that she possessed a fragile measure of control over.

She struggled to move her arms. Vhalla felt the connection with her physical body wavering. She cried mentally, straining against the impending failure of her systems. *A little more*—it was both a prayer and a rally—*a little more*. Her arms out at her sides, Vhalla took a deep breath and felt the sand fill her lungs. She gave one last push to make the storm a part of her. And then turned that power inward, pushing it down into her Channel and smothering it.

The winds died and silence filled her ears. Vhalla's legs gave out, and she collapsed to her knees, her arms dropping to her sides. Cracking her eyes open she saw the blazing brightness of the sun against a blue sky. A small sob escaped her mouth and she coughed, her lungs on fire. There was still a strange blur of light and dark playing at the edge of her vision. Vhalla felt her shoulder hit the stone of the road, then her temple—and the world went black.

CHAPTER 13

A SINGLE FLAME DANCED at her bedside and the moon shifted through foreign curtains as Vhalla drifted in and out of consciousness. She shifted restlessly, trying to free herself from the prison of exhaustion and the twilight state of dreams.

A warm palm touched her cheek, followed by the whispering of soothing words. She stirred at the rustle of the blanket being pulled over her. Vhalla cracked her eyes open.

The room came slowly into focus. Vhalla didn't recognize the tasteful decoration or sumptuous décor. But she did recognize the woman tending her bedside.

"This is getting old," Vhalla whispered weakly, nearly startling Larel out of her skin.

"You're awake," the Western woman breathed with a sigh of relief. "This *is* getting old. Stop beating yourself up." The levity was not lost on Larel, and the woman was joyous just at the sight of Vhalla's open eyes.

"Where are we?" Vhalla asked between a fit of coughing. It felt as though her insides had been shredded.

"The Crossroads." Larel held a cup of water to Vhalla's parched lips.

"We made it?" she sputtered in surprise.

"We did." Larel passed the cup to Vhalla's eager hands, standing from her place at the bedside. "And there's someone who has been *very* eager to see you."

Larel left the room without further explanation, but Vhalla wasn't surprised when a raven-haired prince silently slipped through the door a short time later. He turned and Vhalla's breath hitched. His hair was fixed in place, and he was swathed in finery, not armor. He was every inch the prince she'd met months ago. Every inch the prince she had risked her life to save.

"Vhalla . . ." Aldrik croaked.

She saw dark circles beneath his eyes as he staggered toward her. Vhalla sat straighter, wincing slightly at the pain in her back and shoulders as she placed the mostly empty cup on the bedside table. Two obsidian eyes consumed her hungrily, though Vhalla knew she looked a mess.

As Vhalla opened her mouth to speak, the prince collapsed to his knees at her bedside. She was stunned into silence, and Aldrik buried his face in his forearms. She watched his shoulders tremble for a moment and heard ragged breathing. Unable to bear his meaningless pain, Vhalla reached out a bandaged hand, placing it on his hair.

The prince's face jolted upward, startled by her touch.

"What happened?" she whispered, unable to logically piece it together.

"You foolish idiot," he suddenly rasped, drawing himself to his feet. "You went without orders from your superior. You ignored the call. You could have killed yourself, you dumb girl."

Vhalla shrunk back as though he'd slapped her.

"And you stopped the storm." He sat heavily on the edge of her bed. Without hesitation, Aldrik reached up and cupped her cheek gently. "You foolish, amazing, astounding woman, you saved us all."

Vhalla let out a small sob of relief. That truth could be assumed by his presence, but hearing him say it made it all the more real. She hung her head and covered her mouth with her palm, trying to restrain her emotions. Aldrik shifted and wrapped his arms around her, pulling her to him. It hurt to move her body in some places, but Vhalla ignored it easily as she pressed her face into his shoulder.

"You were wondrous, Vhalla," he breathed deeply into her hair. "And I swear, if you ever do something like that again."

Vhalla pulled her face away in surprise, his hands wrapping themselves around her shoulders.

"When you ran off, I couldn't follow you; I couldn't send anyone for you—I should have. I'm sorry, Gods I wanted to . . ." Aldrik breathed deeply and fought for his composure.

"Aldrik," she said, moving his hands from her shoulders into her grasp, barely containing a small wince. "I didn't want you to follow me." Hesitantly she reached out a bandaged hand and caressed his face. It was the first time she could remember touching his cheek and instantly regretted that half her hand was wrapped. Vhalla gave him a small smile. "I wanted to keep you safe. That's my job right? Keeping you alive?"

Aldrik let out a chuckle and shook his head. He shifted, leaning toward her. Her fingers fell from his face into both of his hands. Vhalla felt lightheaded from sitting as she became aware of his proximity.

"Vhalla," he murmured softly, tightening his grip. "I thought I might never have another opportunity to see you, to talk to you." Aldrik stared at their laced fingers; his thumbs stroked the backs of her bandages. "I thought you would ride away and I would never . . ." His voice trailed off to barely more than a whisper. He braved giving her his attention once more, and Vhalla felt something flutter frantically. "I would never have the opportunity to tell you that . . ."

Vhalla leaned closer to him, savoring every word. She could almost feel his breath on her face when he spoke.

"That I . . ." Aldrik was suddenly keenly aware of her attentiveness and there was something that resembled fear at the realization. Aldrik's lips parted.

Vhalla held her breath.

He promptly closed his mouth and looked away as the rumble of heavy footsteps drew closer. Vhalla followed his eyes to the doorframe.

"Lie back down," Aldrik mumbled with resignation.

Vhalla obliged and stared upward, hoping she'd feel less dizzy soon. Aldrik sighed and stood, moving to a cleric's chest that sat open on a nearby dresser. He was picking out a bottle filled with a clear-syrup when the golden prince burst in without a knock.

"Vhalla, the hero!" he enthused. "I heard you had woken!"

"Word travels too quickly," Aldrik cursed under his breath.

"How do you feel?" The younger prince walked over, ignoring his brother.

"Tired," she said simply, truthfully.

"Yes," Aldrik crossed the room to hand her the vial, and she took it without question in one gulp. "She should not be entertaining company right now."

"Oh?" Prince Baldair cocked an eyebrow. "What are *you* then?"

Aldrik glared at his brother.

"Boys, don't fight," Vhalla muttered; she was too tired for their nonsense. Aldrik blinked at her in surprise and Prince Baldair chuckled. "How can I help you, my prince?"

"Our father would like to host you for breakfast."

Vhalla blinked at the prince, fairly certain she heard him wrong. "Wh-why?" She stared in shock. The last time Vhalla had seen the Emperor up close he was passing judgment on her for an attempt on his son's life. Vhalla sought silent guidance from Aldrik, but he had that stony walled-off glare he got around his brother.

"To thank you, I am sure," Prince Baldair answered.

"She needs her rest," Aldrik objected.

"Surely she has to eat?" the younger prince protested.

"I'm not in a state that is fit to see—" Vhalla paused; she couldn't say "royalty" as half of the Imperial family was before her. "—to see the Emperor," she finished.

"Father understands your situation. Don't fret over decorum," the golden prince countered with a smile.

Vhalla picked at the bandages around her fingers. "I suppose I cannot refuse my Emperor," she said softly.

Aldrik looked at her with marked concern. "I will speak to my father."

"It's just breakfast." Vhalla tried to reassure herself more than anyone else. Aldrik stared hopelessly at her, and she gave him an apologetic look.

"Excellent! An hour then." Baldair clapped his hands together and left.

Aldrik shifted, pulling a chain that ran from a button to his pocket. He glanced at the silver pocket watch she'd admired on more than one night after their Projection practice. "You shouldn't have agreed," he murmured and returned to his prior position.

"Aldrik, when will you understand?" She struggled to sit again, pressing the heel of her palm to her forehead with a sigh. "I am *never* in a position to refuse your family."

"What?" He seemed honestly confused.

Vhalla smiled tiredly, it was cute how clueless he was at times. "I am nothing, no rank or title. More so, I'm property of the crown. You or any of your family could order anything of me, and I would be forced to oblige." Vhalla ran a hand up his forearm, but he pulled away briskly.

"Do you just oblige me?" Aldrik asked coolly.

Vhalla laughed. "Of course not. I enjoy being near you, hearing your thoughts, spending time with you. You're one of the best things that have ever happened to me." Vhalla smiled at him, and she saw the prince relax. How had she never realized how insecure he was?

"You're so funny. Do I oblige you? Aldrik, I—" Vhalla stopped herself, her smile slipping in the wake of a revelation. "—I—"

Love you.

That's what her mind wanted to say, and it hit her harder than the sandstorm.

"You?" He let the word hang expectantly.

Vhalla inhaled sharply. "I . . ."

It was hopeless; *she* was hopeless. She loved him, and she couldn't deny it anymore. One look had spurred her to race to a likely death on the notion of saving him. Now that she realized it, she realized how long she'd been hopelessly falling for this infuriating, charming, enigma of a man.

"Well, I . . ." Vhalla met those dark black eyes. All the moments of his gaze came back to her in a flood of emotion. She remembered a night forever ago when he had held her with his stare alone in the library, pulling her from a dream. Vhalla remembered gazing into them as he'd held her during the gala, how she'd wanted him. She remembered waking up to them, more than once now, and wanting to see nothing more every time she roused.

"I really, truly . . ." Vhalla reached out and touched his cheek lightly. His gaze had turned serious, and his breathing was shallower. Her stomach twisted in a knot. She could never, she would never, *should never*, have this man. And, for once, Vhalla gave into the alarms in her head.

"I love to be someone you consider your friend."

Aldrik considered her for a long moment. His lips parted

slightly and his eyes scanned her face. Vhalla wasn't sure what he was looking for. Aldrik inhaled sharply, opened his mouth. Vhalla's heart skipped two beats. He deflated and avoided her expectant stare.

"You should get ready to meet Father," he said softly. Aldrik stood and adjusted his double-breasted coat without so much as a glance back at her. "I will return in thirty minutes."

Vhalla tried to get in another word but the door had already closed behind him. She drew a quivering breath. "I love you, Aldrik," she whispered into the silent air. The next breath was shakier than the last, the breath after was stuck in her throat with a pained whimper that she could only dislodge by releasing the tears.

Vhalla balled her hands into fists and buried her eyes in them. She had to compose herself; this was not the place or time to lose her wits over being in love with the crown prince.

First, she attempted denial. *It wasn't possibly love.* She'd almost died, and he'd held her, he'd given her comfort. She was just clinging to him in an emotional state. Vhalla laughed with a hiccup and a rasp. She wasn't sure if she had ever loved before, but she knew that this was it.

Then she tried to blame it on the Bond or the Joining. Clearly, it had affected both of them in multiple ways that was barely understood. It was creating something out of nothing. It had always been there as long as she had known him.

No, for as little she knew about the Bond academically, Vhalla was confident in her feeling of it. She felt the extension of herself into him, the calm his proximity brought from having that piece near her again. The Bond was a door, a window, a Channel; it didn't alter them, it just gave them access to what lay beyond in the other. It let the truths they tried to keep hidden be exposed.

Finally, she attempted reason. Vhalla assured herself that it was simply a result of spending so much time with him on the march. Even Prince Baldair mentioned the *needs* one will have naturally. She saw him every day, he was her teacher, and it was easy to develop feelings for someone in such a position. Vhalla looked down at her palms. *It wasn't just the march.*

Vhalla sighed, reclining onto the bed. She wasn't sure when it had happened. Closing her eyes, she let the memories come in a painful flood of quiet sobs, looking at them in a way she never had before. Was it the moment he dropped those papers everywhere, when she stayed in that rose garden a minute longer than she had planned, his apology? Perhaps it was the moment he had run to her side, casting away whatever official duty he had when his brother and father returned South. Was it the minute her heart fluttered when he confessed he wanted to see her again? Or knowing he had begun to go out of his way for her? Could it have even started before she knew who he was but relished his mind through that beautifully curved script?

She realized that whenever it had happened, she had loved him before the moment he had seen her with Sareem. When her heart tightened with worry that he would think she was someone else's. She had loved him when she had chosen to wear the black gala gown rather than an appropriately colored one. She loved him when she wanted nothing more than for him to stay by her side in the palace and never go off to war again.

Everything after had just been denial.

Vhalla opened her eyes and placed a hand over her mouth, muffling her tears. Now she knew. She knew that she was hopelessly in love with a man who would eventually leave her life. It was an earth-shattering revelation. Even if somehow they managed to stay near to each other by living in the palace, he would someday be the Emperor. He would marry someone befitting of his station, and she'd have to kneel before him and the woman who would be her Empress and mother of his children.

He had said titles didn't matter, that he could give her any he wanted as the prince or Emperor. She'd believed him because she wanted to. She wanted to think it could be simple and beautiful. Vhalla had never told him why she was so wounded by Elecia's words. That she wished for nobility to make it acceptable in the eyes of society for her to be around him. Not just as a friend, but as a lover. If he knew, he likely would've never said anything of granting her whatever title she wished.

The door opened suddenly, startling her. Snapping her head to the entry she saw Larel holding a small bundle of clothes. Vhalla tried to smile, she tried to be strong, but she only found herself crumbling again.

"Larel," she choked out weakly. The other woman ran over, dropping the clothes on the foot of the bed and placing her hands on Vhalla's shoulders.

"Vhalla, what is it? What hurts?" Larel inspected her bandages quickly.

Vhalla shook her head, dropping it into her hands. She couldn't handle the concern; she couldn't handle the shame for why she was breaking apart.

"Vhalla, please," Larel pleaded.

"I love him," she whispered through a ragged breath.

"What?" Larel asked, leaning closer.

"I love Aldrik." Vhalla searched the other woman's expression for something, anything.

"Oh, Vhalla," Larel enfolded her into a warm hug. The motion shattered her control and Vhalla openly sobbed into Larel's shirt. "Hush, hush . . . What's so awful about that?" Larel leaned back slightly, tilting her head to look at her.

"Because, because he will never want someone like me. Because I am not good enough to even deserve half of what he's given me. Because, at the end of everything, no matter what we are, he will leave. Because I think he's wonderful, and everything

I will never have. Because . . ." Vhalla took a shuddering breath. "Because, I don't know if I've ever loved like this before and it *terrifies* me."

Larel gave her a kind, tired smile. She ran her hand through Vhalla's hair and pulled her close again. Larel stroked her back, and Vhalla allowed herself to shamelessly take in every comfort the other woman offered and then some. Eventually her initial panic—compounded through fear and despair—weakened and her tears returned to the realm of control.

"Vhalla," Larel finally said. "I will not tell you what way is best. I cannot even pretend to know." She sighed. "I will tell you that once something is broken with Aldrik, it is very difficult to fix it." There was a sincere sorrow in the softness of Larel's voice. "I will also tell you that you're right, in this way it's likely impossible for you to be anything permanent in his life. That if you try, you're probably going to be met with heartbreak. You have to decide if the moment, however long it lasts, is worth overcoming that fear. Is worth him."

Vhalla sighed, sitting up and rubbing her eyes. She wondered when Larel became so insightful and wished that the wisdom had been in her life much earlier than just the past year.

"To him, I'm just a—" Vhalla wasn't sure what she was to the crown prince. She was more than his subject. Student didn't seem to quite cover the extent of their relationship. *A friend?* Even that seemed laughable; she couldn't ever recall holding her friends as she had held him before. "A . . ." Vhalla paused, she didn't have a good answer.

"I wouldn't say *just* anything about you, Vhalla. I think you're a lot more than you give yourself credit for. Especially to him." Larel met her eyes with an unwavering stare. When it became clear she had no more words, Larel shifted, picking up the clothes.

"You're going to meet the Emperor soon. I figured you'd

want a change of clothes; I hope I chose all right, half isn't dry yet."

Vhalla considered Larel's choice. Tan leather leggings with a gray woolen long-sleeved tunic. They smelled like crisp morning air, and the lack of grime further confirmed that they had been washed.

"How did you know?"

"Aldrik found me." Larel smiled softly, and Vhalla gave a weak laugh. "Do you want help changing?" the older woman asked.

Vhalla shook her head. "Compared to some other experiences I've had when I've used that much magic, this isn't that bad." She could already feel the potion Aldrik had given her working.

Larel nodded. "All right, I'll leave you to it then. I'd recommend this one before you go." Larel pulled a vial of purple liquid and placed it by the chest of medicinal items. "It'll numb things a bit and should level your head, if you need."

"Thank you," Vhalla said earnestly.

"Of course, Vhalla. Fritz and I are staying in this inn also. Your friends in the Golden Guard as well. We'll be here when you get back. Good luck." The woman smiled and departed.

Vhalla wondered what she was really being wished luck for.

She dressed as quickly as possible but it was also an opportunity to take stock of the condition of her body. Her shoulders were stiff and felt swollen; her elbows also reminded her of the pressure she had placed them under. Her hands were a bit of a mess, but on a positive side, nothing seemed broken.

There was a mirror in the room that instantly caught Vhalla's attention. It was full-length, and she saw herself for the first time in months. Her hair had grown, down to somewhere around her shoulders, falling in tangled brown waves. Her face had thinned and her eyes seemed to have sunken slightly, the shadow of her brow bringing out the flecks of gold around her pupils. Muscles she didn't even know she possessed were beginning to take form beneath taught skin. Even bandaged, she had a sharp and strong appearance, more confident than she felt.

Aldrik returned as she was taking an assessment of her condition. An odd mix of emotions overtook him the moment he saw her, and Vhalla's heart instantly raced. She took a step toward him, swaying slightly at the pain in her knees. He was there in an instant, his arms supporting hers for balance.

"This is a bad idea." His voice was low and it rumbled through his chest.

"I have a lot of those lately," she said softly. Vhalla regained her footing and stepped away. She was afraid of what those dark eyes might see if she lingered too closely for too long. "Shall we?"

He pursed his lips together for a tentative breath but said nothing.

Aldrik walked first, holding the door open for her and leading her down a short flight of stairs. He wrapped an arm around her waist and held one of her hands in his as she hobbled downward. Daniel, Craig, Fritz, and Larel were milling about in an upscale lobby, clearly waiting for her. Aldrik made no haste in dropping his hands from her person.

"You really are alive," Daniel whispered, as though she was a ghost.

"Vhal!" Fritz threw his arms around her shoulders, nearly knocking her off her feet.

"Fritznangle," Aldrik cautioned, taking a step toward the Southerner.

"Vhal, you were stunning! It was like the Mother banishing the night. Just this tiny little thing against that huge, massive, gigantic, storm!" Fritz babbled like a madman.

Another walked from a corner of the room, someone that

Vhalla had not noticed before. Two emerald eyes assessed Vhalla thoughtfully.

"You're one of the craziest people I've ever met." Elecia placed a hand on her hip and shifted her weight to extend the other to Vhalla. "And because of that, I owe you my life."

Vhalla reached out, clasping her bandaged palm against Elecia's.

"Thank you, Vhalla Yarl," Elecia uttered the most sincere words Vhalla had ever heard from her.

Vhalla was in a daze as she headed for the door. Aldrik held it open for her and she stepped out into the dawn. Red streaked across the horizon, washing a crowded square in oranges and pinks. Large buildings constructed of marble and sandstone glittered in the twilight. They sported proportionally sized pennons, reds and blacks of the West and whites and golds of the Empire. The ground beneath her was polished stone, and Vhalla looked upon the center of the world in wonder.

"That one." Aldrik pointed to a building on the other side of the square with three large, circular stained glass windows upon its front. "Do you need me to help you?"

"No." Vhalla shook her head. "Just knowing you're here is enough." She allowed him to read into it as he liked.

Vhalla had taken no more than three steps when the first member of the Black Legion noticed her. He walked over, giving her the salute of the Broken Moon. This inspired the next to come up and offer her thanks and praise. Her eyes caught Aldrik's in confusion and wonder. He heaped silent admiration upon her, and Vhalla felt a flush rise to her cheeks.

It was slow going due to being stopped at every step. The Black Legion had been waiting at the door, but Vhalla noticed that the majority of the people in the square were soldiers. They paused what they were doing, stopping at the sight of her.

A man of rank drew the sword that was strapped to his hip.

She glanced at Aldrik nervously, remembering the last time she'd encountered the swordsmen. The man brought his feet together and stood tall. His left hand went to the small of his back as he raised his sword over his chest and face in a pristine salute with his right.

She wasn't certain what he wanted from her, and Vhalla nervously took another step. An older woman repeated the motion. Swordless, she brought her right fist to her chest in salute.

Vhalla took another step. Two more stepped forward in salute.

Every step Vhalla took there was another, and another, and another. They began to line her path, holding their salutes in reverence even after she'd moved on. Vhalla turned as the entire square—man, woman, child, soldier, and citizen—showed their own display of reverence.

"Do they always do this for you here?" Vhalla whispered to Aldrik. The attention made her nervous.

He stared at her, bewildered. "Vhalla," Aldrik leaned close to her ear. "They are not saluting me, they are saluting *you*."

No one said a word; they held their honors quietly, and their silence spoke so loudly in her ears that Vhalla wanted to cry. For the first time since becoming a sorcerer she felt a mass looking at her with respect, with praise. As much as it hurt her body, she held herself taller.

The Emperor and Prince Baldair were waiting on the outside the building Aldrik was leading her toward. Emperor Solaris surveyed the scene with his ocean-blue eyes, landing on the woman who was being led by his eldest son and saluted by his people. He folded his hands behind his back in a position that struck Vhalla as very Aldrik.

"If it is not the hero of the day." The Emperor spoke loud enough that most of the square heard.

Vhalla dropped into a clumsy kneel, her knees popping and aching.

"My lord, thank you for your invitation," she said respectfully, lowering her eyes.

"Stand, Vhalla Yarl. You are the most welcome savior of my army," he commanded lightly.

Vhalla put both hands on her upward knee and struggled to stand, grimacing at the creaking in her legs. She felt much older than her eighteen years and could feel the tension radiating off Aldrik at her pain, but he made no motion. Vhalla was thankful he allowed her to do it on her own before his father and all those who had assembled.

"Come, I wish to bestow my thanks upon you." The Emperor took a step back, and Prince Baldair held open the doors for them.

CHAPTER 14

T HE BUILDING SHE entered was like a small palace. Alabaster, marble, silver, gold, and gemstones glittered everywhere. As the sun rose, it was piped in through portholes in the walls, giving the opulence new life. The Emperor led her into a side sitting room. There were couches and a table to eat at, opposite a tall, standing table cluttered with papers.

To her surprise the Emperor walked over to the table that did not hold the food. Prince Baldair walked around to his father's right side, Aldrik hovered near her. He didn't move until she did, her silent shadow.

"I would like to show you something." Emperor Solaris motioned to her.

Vhalla walked over, Aldrik stood on her other side, leaving her right open to the Emperor. She assessed a large map and the Emperor pointed to a spot on the Great Imperial Way, just south of the Crossroads.

"This is where we were, when the sandstorm was upon us." Vhalla's eyes swung back to the Crossroads; *they had been so close.* As if reading her thoughts the Emperor continued, "The men at the front of the host were less than five minutes to the storm break walls."

Vhalla stared at the map. She remembered the column running, but so many wouldn't have made it.

"Tell me," the Emperor asked as he stroked his beard and assessed her, "what orders would you have made?"

"Orders for?" she asked, not sure if she understood his question.

"If you were in my position, what call would you have made?"

She looked up at the man and then back to the map, taking a breath that was followed by an annoying cough at the feeling of sand in her lungs.

"Excuse me," she mumbled. Keeping her face toward the table Vhalla tilted her head to the side. "I would have split the line."

"Split the line?" It was Prince Baldair who asked.

Vhalla nodded. "One," she pointed to the younger prince. "Two," she turned to the Emperor. "Three," she pointed to Aldrik. "Split it three ways. Keeping you central may make sense for a march; perhaps even in combat settings for protection, but for this, we'd be playing odds."

"What odds are those?" The Emperor rested his hands on the table. Vhalla felt very short as the tabletop came up to her waist rather than her hips or lower like the taller men.

"Your lives," she said matter-of-factly, surprised at the coolness her logic created in her voice. Prince Baldair actually had a somewhat horrified expression. Vhalla met the Emperor's eyes. "If you three stayed at the center, you would have been in the middle of the storm, little more than a dozen horse lengths apart. If one of you died there is a great chance that whatever killed that person would kill those near him; the closer the proximity, the greater the odds of death. You three die, we all lose. If the Emperor and all heirs were suddenly lost, this realm has more than one battlefront."

The Emperor rubbed his chin. "Go on."

"You would all run in different directions with the fastest riders prepared to give their lives for you. It would be the best chance for survival," Vhalla explained simply.

"You know that means half the host would be left behind on foot." The Emperor regarded her thoughtfully.

"I know that." She nodded. "They would be left to chance." The word *chance* sounded nicer than *death.*

The younger prince seemed horrified, and Vhalla would have to turn to see Aldrik's expression. The Emperor was almost too analytical in the way he seemed to calculate her words against an invisible tally. Vhalla brought her hands together, wringing them.

"You do have some intelligence to you," the Emperor said lightly.

"My lord, if I am intelligent it is because you have filled your castle with good teachers." She thought back to Mohned with a pang of homesickness.

"Ah, Vhalla, do not be so modest. Knowledge and power are a dangerous combination, and you appear to have both in quantity." The Emperor turned and motioned toward the table that had been set with food.

Each person sat in turn. Aldrik pulled out her chair for her, though he didn't offer her so much as a glance. Vhalla wondered what exactly had changed his demeanor. Clearly, whatever his concerns were they factored in calculated restraint. Aldrik sat to her right, Prince Baldair to her left, and the Emperor across.

Vhalla had not seen food so fine or a table so cluttered with silverware, glasses, and plates since she had dined with Prince Baldair back at the palace. The meal was hot and fresh and she barely managed to contain a particularly loud stomach grumble by placing a hand over her abdomen. She was careful to eat after the three royals had served themselves. Propriety was a convenient excuse. Vhalla had no idea which forks were meant to be used when or why they used a different fork for every dish—she just followed.

"This is an incredibly peculiar situation, don't you think, Miss Yarl?" the Emperor started.

"Vhalla is fine," she said, unsure if it was appropriate to offer. It felt weird having both of his sons call her by her first name and to have the man who sat above both of them be more formal.

He ignored her and continued, "It is not normal for someone to sit on trial for murder and treason and then dine with the Emperor only a couple months later."

"Very few things I find in my world are what I would call *normal* at this moment, my lord." She nibbled on bread, her brain continuing to obsess over being in love with the crown prince.

The Emperor chuckled. "Yet you rebound and become stronger. I knew you had strength in you when I saw you in that cage."

Vhalla continued to try to eat politely, struggling with her bandaged fingers. She didn't want to think of her trial. She didn't even really want to be sitting at this table.

"I am prepared to pardon you for your crimes," the Emperor mused, sipping his wine.

She stared in shock. *A pardon?* Someone needed to pinch her, she was dreaming. "My lord?"

"You earned sufficient trust for a second chance by saving the life of one prince. I think potentially saving the life of the Imperial family, perhaps the Emperor himself, earns you a clean slate." He wore a smile beneath his beard but his eyes were detached from any levity.

Vhalla paused. *Saving the life of one prince?* Did that mean Aldrik had told him what had really happened on the Night of Fire and Wind? She refrained from looking over to the crown prince.

"Thank you, my lord." Vhalla lowered her eyes.

"But you see, my hands are tied." The Emperor chewed thoughtfully on a piece of dark meat, before dabbing his mouth with his napkin and continuing. "The Senate, the voice of the people, they saw your military service as the fitting punishment, and I would not want to betray the trust of my loyal subjects."

"Of course not . . ." Vhalla said numbly, the word *pardon* echoed over and over again in her head.

"Don't be fooled, Vhalla. They're as hungry as ever, and if I pardoned you now those same people out there who were saluting you would turn again." The Emperor glanced up at her.

From the corners of her eyes she could see Aldrik shifting uncomfortably in his seat.

"But if you were to give us victory." The man chuckled. "Now *that* would be something worth reward."

"Victory? I don't know how I could . . ." Vhalla fumbled. Her sentence seemed to be increasing, not diminishing. Before she was only meant to serve in the war; now she had to bring victory? *Had they ever planned on freeing her?*

The Emperor's icy blue eyes flicked over to Aldrik. The eldest prince took a very long dreg of his wine. "My son tells me he's been working with you on something important."

Vhalla said nothing for fear of incriminating her and Aldrik with something he'd yet to mention to his father. But there were things she couldn't imagine him ever saying. Despite herself, she glanced at the dark prince.

"He tells me you can give me the North with your powers as a Windwalker." The Emperor leaned forward, placing his elbows on the table.

"I am still learning most of my own abilities myself," she hedged carefully.

"I have been made aware." The Emperor waved the concerns

away. "Aldrik has sent me detailed reports of your investigations into them."

"I see . . ." Vhalla murmured, looking at the man in question curiously. Aldrik did not seem to stop occupying his mouth with his wine glass.

The notes Aldrik had been taking on their Bonding flashed in her mind. He said he was going to use them for reference. He had told her that he had a plan to take the North using her power. *So why did she suddenly feel betrayed?*

"While I am extensively impressed with your abilities to command wind and storms, what I am most intrigued by, Vhalla, is this ability to place your mind beyond your body. It seems too astounding to be real. How confident are you in your control?" The Emperor finally reached his point.

Vhalla swallowed hard and reached for her glass of water, ignoring the alcohol. This was not a polite call to thank her for saving his army. That was a pleasant excuse for him to sit her down and formulate battle strategy.

"I suppose the crown prince would have a better judge of my control, he is far more experienced than I." Vhalla muttered as she stabbed at some food on her plate, chewing through the silence that followed.

"You think she will be ready?" The Emperor turned to Aldrik.

Vhalla's eyes drifted upward just in time to catch his as they fell on her with a frown.

"I think she will be," Aldrik replied, turning to his father.

"Then I'd like a demonstration before we leave the Crossroads." The Emperor sat back in his chair and folded his hands.

"A demonstration? Why?" Aldrik asked, bolder than Vhalla could ever be.

"I need assurance." The Emperor did not look pleased at being questioned by his son.

"In light of recent events, I'm not sure if magically that's—" Aldrik started.

"You will have your demonstration." Vhalla focused on the Emperor, ignoring Aldrik and the fact that she had interrupted him.

"*Ah*, there is the fire I saw at the trial." The Emperor smiled. She glanced at Aldrik, he barely constrained his frustration. "There are opportunities in your future, Vhalla Yarl. Obedience is rewarded."

"Thank you, my lord." Vhalla was suddenly ambivalent to it all. She felt maneuvered and played, but she wasn't sure by whom.

Aldrik had been honest with her about their meetings. *So why did it hurt so much?* Vhalla wrung her hands in her lap.

The second the food cleared Vhalla was eager to make her escape. "Please, forgive me my lords, I feel quite exhausted."

"Certainly. Recover quickly, Vhalla Yarl." The Emperor and his sons stood as well. "We shall reconvene in a few days."

Vhalla nodded mutely, gave a small bow, and turned to the door.

She felt him before Aldrik even moved.

"I will make sure she returns to the inn," the crown prince declared.

"Aldrik, I would like you to go over a few plans for managing the troop additions. They will arrive within the next few days, and you have your matters with Elecia." The Emperor's voice was definite.

Vhalla bristled at the other woman's name. She'd all but forgotten Aldrik's *business*.

"I shall just be a moment," the eldest prince protested.

"It is not necessary, my prince. The walk is not far and I don't mind being alone for it," Vhalla countered.

Aldrik's eyes squinted slightly in confusion or agitation. "I would much prefer to leave nothing to chance," he said tensely. "The Crossroads can be full of unsavory characters."

"My brother, ever concerned for the well-being of his subjects." Prince Baldair strolled to her side. "Luckily, you have two sons, Father. I would be happy to make sure our little Windwalker makes it home safe and sound."

Vhalla looked up at the golden prince in confusion. She was fairly certain she'd just said that she would walk alone.

"Excellent suggestion, Baldair." The Emperor walked over to the large table and motioned for Aldrik to follow. "I look forward to your demonstration, Miss Yarl," the Emperor said before turning his attention to the maps and papers on his table.

Aldrik stared at her hopelessly, then glared at his brother, but he went obediently to his father's side.

Vhalla felt Aldrik's eyes on her as Prince Baldair's hand fell lightly on her hip, and he led her out of the room into the morning sun.

"Please remove your hand from my person," Vhalla mumbled to the Heartbreaker Prince.

He flashed her a toothy grin. "Now, now, be more gracious," he said charmingly. "People are watching you." He smiled at a few soldiers as he began leading her back across the square.

"Exactly," she replied. People watching was precisely what she was worried about.

"Oh? Don't want them to think that you're involved with me?" Prince Baldair returned a wave. "Just my brother?"

Vhalla glared at him. "Let it drop," she cautioned. Her pace quickened to cross the distance faster.

"Not until you realize he's playing you." All jest, all joy was gone from his voice, and Prince Baldair's face had turned serious.

"It's not your business," Vhalla argued.

"I thought he wasn't. I thought maybe he had changed." The

prince held the door of the inn open for her, and Vhalla all but flew up the stairs. "But from what I saw, *what I've heard*, this past day—that's not the case."

Vhalla bit her tongue and swung open her door, hoping Larel would be waiting and would save her. She was not. The prince caught the closing door with a hand, and Vhalla turned sharply. "I am still recovering, my prince, and would like to rest. Please, excuse me." She mustered the last of her polite decorum.

"I am trying to help," he said.

Vhalla saw concern marked across his pained expression. "Oh?" Her patience ran thin. "Like you helped the last time we had a little *chat?*"

"Everything I told you then was true." Something in his tone gave Vhalla pause, she swayed slightly. "Vhalla, please sit. My brother and Father will give me hell if something ill befalls you on my watch."

Vhalla eased herself onto the bed, pulling off her boots and lying down. She rolled on her side, her back to the prince. Everything hurt the moment she began to relax, but there was not much opportunity to do so as the prince rounded to sit on the edge of the bed, facing her. Vhalla glared at him.

"Vhalla, please listen. I want to tell you something," Prince Baldair implored.

She sighed. "If I listen, will you go?"

He nodded, and Vhalla waited expectantly. "My brother and I are three years apart, which is a significant gap when you are five and eight, or twelve and fifteen, but at fifteen and eighteen and up it becomes less and less significant." She wondered why he was exhausting her with trivia about their birthdays. "Not long after my ceremony of manhood there was a year where my brother and I decided to engage in some *friendly competition*."

"Friendly competition?" Vhalla braced herself for what that meant between these men.

"I've always been . . . charming." Prince Baldair smiled at her, and she didn't even refrain from rolling her eyes. At least he laughed. "My brother grew as a strange, sad child. At one point it seemed as though he hit a new low and just gave into the darkness and distance surrounding him. To be honest, I never saw him leave it."

Vhalla found it interesting how Prince Baldair's and Larel's descriptions could be both similar and different.

"At some point we had a row, and doesn't really matter about what, he was eighteen and I was at the ever hot-headed age of fifteen. I said he could not even get a woman to so much as glance at him because of how he was." Vhalla stilled, beginning to listen intently. "For whatever reason, my brother took the challenge."

"Challenge?" she repeated softly.

"For one year, it was a challenge for who could have the most women agree to share their bed."

Vhalla's eyes widened. "That's . . . awful."

"It is certainly not the worst thing either of us have done to pass the time. Nor the worst thing young princes have ever, or will ever, do." Vhalla saw the likely truth of his words with horror. "At first, I was an *overnight* favorite. But I underestimated my brother. One by one, like flies in a web, they began to offer themselves to him. I didn't understand and it frustrated me daily. How my lanky, awkward, depressing shell of a brother managed to reclaim a solid lead."

"Enough, I get it." She pressed her face into her pillow.

"No, we haven't gotten to the point yet." He had a grim expression and Vhalla obliged silently. "I thought it was simply because he was the crown prince. But that wasn't the case as the ladies seemed to call long after their turn was up, ever hopeful. Eventually I found he was not actually taking them to bed. They agreed to it, which given the wording of our bet placed him in the lead. But he never actually *took* one of them."

Vhalla's brow furrowed. "Why not?" Of course, she felt happy hearing that he hadn't slept with a host of women, though luring them in like cattle seemed bad enough.

"I finally asked him once when I confronted him about the terms of the challenge. I'll never forget what he told me." Prince Baldair looked away. "He told me that it was the hunt that he relished. That none of them were good enough to merit his touch. That he did not have to kill the prey to have the satisfaction of the win. It was amusing; it was sport to watch them fall. For the next six months after, I watched him skillfully play every eligible woman he met. Somehow he knew what they wanted to hear, how they wanted to be led, and he did it with a complete mask of sincerity. He took things from them, but not their bodies. Their dignity, their time, their dreams . . ."

"Please, I understand," Vhalla breathed and was too tired to be as strong as she wanted to be.

Prince Baldair sighed and reached out, placing a large palm on the top of her head. Vhalla tensed at the momentary foreign touch.

"I thought maybe he'd changed." The prince's voice was soft. "But then I overheard a conversation between him and Father. Aldrik swore that he would be the one to make you obligated to gain victory. That you would be mindlessly obedient to him above all else and that he had you under his command without question. That the sandstorm was an example of this—and I realized he'd never relinquish the control he has on people."

"Prince Baldair, I am very tired," she whispered. The notes on the Emperor's table returned to her, the mention of reports being given. Had she been a puppet for Aldrik and his father the whole time? Paying the greatest actor in the world with her emotions?

"I do agree with them—Aldrik and my father. You are smart,

Vhalla. Please, just see him for what he is?" Prince Baldair searched her.

Vhalla closed her eyes, wanting nothing more than to cower. "I appreciate your concern, my prince." It was all she could say in the end.

He sighed heavily. "Rest well, Vhalla." Prince Baldair stood. She relied only on the sounds of his departure.

Vhalla shivered, despite the room being warm. Of course, the day she realized she was hopelessly in love with a man was also the day she would be given additional proof of his being a rather twisted ass. At least, if one considered Prince Baldair's word as proof. Vhalla laughed, and coughed from the state of her lungs.

Had Aldrik not warned her of all this? Hadn't he said on multiple occasions that he was not a good man? Vhalla sighed again and wondered if it was even fair of her to hold it against him. All their meetings had been an excuse to test her abilities. She was foolish for thinking they—she—meant otherwise. Vhalla took a delicate breath and fought against tears until exhaustion claimed her.

CHAPTER 15

"VHAAAAAAAL . . ." Fritz sung softly. "Vhaaaaaaal-laaaaaaaaa."

A finger poked at her cheek. She groaned, rolling away from the source.

"Let her sleep," Larel scolded.

"But she's slept the *whole day*, and it's our first real night in the Crossroads," Fritz whined.

"You two are so loud," Vhalla cursed softly.

"*One* of us is," Larel corrected with an offended note.

"Vhal, don't you want to wake up?" Fritz crawled into bed with her.

"No." She didn't feel like it in the slightest. After Aldrik and Prince Baldair that morning, and the Emperor's proclamations and demands, she had half a mind to spend the rest of her life in bed.

"What's wrong, Vhal? The world is celebrating you right now, you need to celebrate with them." Fritz grabbed her with both arms, sitting her up.

Larel took the opportunity of Vhalla being upright to coax two elixirs down Vhalla's throat.

"So, we're all going out." Fritz crawled around the bed, situating himself in front of her.

"Out?"

"He got the idea from your friends in the Golden Guard."
Larel sat on the edge of the bed. It wasn't a large piece of furniture, and they were all crowded around each other. "They're going out to celebrate their first full night in the Crossroads. Apparently there's to be some celebration in the Windwalker's honor."

"In my honor?" Vhalla blinked.

"Yes, in yours." Larel beamed. "You saved hundreds of lives—understand that."

Vhalla nodded mutely.

"We want you to come." Fritz grabbed her hands.

"We?" Vhalla looked to Larel. She couldn't imagine Larel partying in the streets.

"I've nothing else to do," the woman laughed lightly. "And the Windwalker they are honoring happens to be my protégé. It'd be a shame if I didn't at least have one drink in her honor."

"Will you come with us?" Fritz asked again.

"I . . ." Vhalla sighed, looking at the setting sun through her curtains. She thought of Aldrik and the Emperor once more, conspiring in that opulent palace of a building. A small spark of anger flared in her, and Vhalla gripped Fritz's fingers. "I'd love to."

"Are you sure you feel well enough?" Larel sensed something was wrong, but the other woman seemed to be mistaking Vhalla's wild emotions over the prince for physical pain caused by her injuries.

"I've felt worse." Vhalla put on a brave smile. "Who knows, perhaps the company could do me good?"

It would have been more convincing if she didn't dissolve into a coughing fit. But Fritz was her champion for the evening, linking elbows with her and helping Vhalla into the hall and down the stairs. Larel must have agreed with the assessment because she didn't object.

Once her body was moving, Vhalla found she felt better, proving her physical wounds were superficial. They likely had refrained from forcing any potions down her throat when she was unconscious; but now that the clerics' concoctions were working, her body was rebounding quickly. No one was waiting for her outside the inn this time, and for that she was thankful. Vhalla didn't want any more attention.

The Crossroads was a place unlike any Vhalla had ever seen. The capital was crowded, but not like this. It seemed like every person of every shape, shade, and size was crowded into the streets, and the streets were packed with tempting markets that didn't seem to know what closing meant. The three went down a small side road, following the instruction Craig and Daniel had given Fritz.

The bar was noisy, and the sounds of men and women singing, laughing, and talking drowned out any of Vhalla's thoughts and doubts. She was in a foreign land as a celebrated hero. And, if Fritz and Larel were to be believed, the source of all these people's joy was she. Even if that was only half true, Vhalla had vowed to live in spite of the Senate, and she now vowed to be happy in spite of whatever game the Imperial family was playing.

"You guys made it!" Craig waved them over.

Daniel was out of his chair the moment he saw them. He crossed to Vhalla in a step. "How do you feel?"

"Better," she answered sincerely.

"I didn't expect to see you out." He somehow wedged himself between her and Fritz.

"Well, Larel and Fritz tell me that this is *my* party," she said with sarcastic haughtiness.

"It is indeed!" Craig laughed loudly. He quickly downed the contents of his metal flagon, and slammed it against the table a few times for the bar's attention. The Southerner jumped up onto his chair, swaying alarmingly for a moment. Raylynn was on her feet, ready to catch him. "Good people, fellow soldiers! It is our honor tonight to drink with the Windwalker herself!" Vhalla's cheeks burned scarlet as the room recovered from its stunned silence and burst into cheers.

"But, I regret to say, she does not yet have a drink!" Craig laughed.

Like magic, there were three glasses of varying shapes and sizes before her.

"Try this one." Daniel placed a fourth glass in front of her; it was only the height of her fist and filled with a syrupy red liquid.

"What is it?" she asked.

"A Crimson Dragon." He tapped his nose. "The West is known for them."

Vhalla recognized the name and took a timid sip. It was icy cold and burned the back of her throat. She blinked away tears and held in a cough.

"Not a drinker?" Craig laughed.

"Nope!" Vhalla took another sip for good measure.

The Crimson Dragon was gone and the alcohol in two other glasses went quickly after. She and Daniel had found themselves engaged in an intense argument over the weight of a prize pig at one of Paca's infamous festivals. Vhalla leaned on the table for support as she turned to face him.

"No, *hundred*," she insisted. "I swear, *I swear*, that pig was a hundred stone."

"Vhalla, you crazy Leoulian," Daniel laughed and took another long gulp from his flagon. She watched the bump on his neck move as he swallowed. "No pig weighs anything close to a hundred stones." He pointed a finger at her.

"Don't you point at me." She grabbed his index finger, a fit of the giggles overtaking her. "It is *so rude*."

"Unhand me, woman." Daniel tried to make his face serious,

and Vhalla laughed at the way he pursed his lips together. Somehow everything was awfully funny right now.

"Fine. Fine. But you're wrong, and you know it." She leaned back into her chair.

"Vhalla, Daniel, we're going." Craig shook her shoulder.

Vhalla blinked, wondering when the rest of the table had stood. She'd only just started talking to Daniel.

"Where?" Her fellow Easterner was as confused as she was.

"Dancing!" Fritz twirled.

Vhalla burst out with uncontrollable laughter, almost spilling drink number . . . something, everywhere.

"Do you want to go?" Larel laughed. The Western woman was looking out for Vhalla even when she had a flush to her cheeks. The big sister Vhalla never had.

"Of course!" Vhalla chirped cheerfully.

She attempted to jump to her feet and almost fell. A muscular arm quickly wrapped itself around her shoulder. Vhalla caught Daniel's eyes in surprise. He was a lot sturdier than he looked.

"This is a bad idea," he laughed.

"You—you will learn this the longer you're around me: I am the queen of bad ideas." Vhalla barely suppressed commenting about Prince Aldrik.

Daniel led her out into the night behind Fritz, Larel, Craig, Raylynn, and others Vhalla couldn't even name.

The dance hall they ended up in was hot and hazy. Even though all the large doors on the ground floor were open to the cool night breezes, steam from sweat hovered in the room. It was a large, open, wooden space with a stage on one wall, a bar on the other, and benches lining the border—a place to rest exhausted feet.

Vhalla collapsed with a fit of laughter onto one said bench. The mass of people continued to move to the music before her. Somewhere in there Fritz was making a fool of himself with his third or fourth boy, and Larel, Craig, and Raylynn were nowhere to be found. Western dancing had loud drums, brass horns, and favored a strong rhythm. As such the steps were faster compared to the Southern style, people twisted and turned, kicked and spun around each other.

Daniel sat heavily next to her, his thigh touched hers, and he wiped sweat from his brow. He passed her a mug. Vhalla took a long drink and peered at him.

"*Water?*" She frowned.

"For your head, tomorrow. Start now," he panted.

"I don't want water." She stuck her tongue out at him and he laughed.

"Fine, but don't cry to me in the morning." He handed her his ale, and she took a sip before passing it back to him.

"It's hot." Vhalla swayed back and forth.

"Want to get some air?" he asked.

She nodded.

Instead of leading her out the main doors, he went up a side staircase. Vhalla slipped on one of the steps, and he caught her as they both burst into laughter. She leaned against the wall, trying to get her giggles under control.

"Vhalla, you're too smart to be this stupid when you're drunk," Daniel wheezed between laughs. Something about the giddiness was infectious, and Vhalla slid against the wall. He caught her arm, pulling her to him. "Come on, we've barely taken ten steps."

Daniel helped her upward, and the stairs led them onto the roof. They weren't the only ones with this idea as a few others milled about enjoying the night air. Vhalla walked out to an empty corner of the roof and gasped faintly.

"It's beautiful," she whispered in misty awe. The Crossroads was lit up across the horizon. The rectangular windows of the flat-roofed square buildings glittered across the black desert. In some windows, bright curtains of reds and maroons tinted the light; in others, stained glass projected colors onto the roads and nearby buildings.

"It's your first time, right?" Daniel sat onto the small ledge that bordered the edge of the roof. Vhalla sat also, swinging her legs over the side. "Vhalla, careful." He grabbed her upper arm.

"Silly," she laughed, swaying and placing her hand on the stony clay to lean close to him. "I can't be hurt falling— well I can't *die*." He tilted his head curiously. "Fire can't hurt Firebearers, water can't hurt Waterrunners, earth can't hurt Groundbreakers, I guess?" Vhalla found herself giggling again, she had no idea. "But wind can't kill me; I've fallen from higher places and lived." She began to ramble, turning away from him.

"It's how I had my Awakening, actually. An Awakening is when a sorcerer first has their powers really shown in full to them. Before then they just Manifest in some ways here or there without control. This is the second time a man took me to a roof. But, the last time Aldrik decided to push me off." She made a pushing motion with her hands and started laughing. "By the Mother, I was cross with him. I was a mess too. He gave me a pretty good apology after though. Aldrik's wonderfully complex, had a reason for most of it, even if it's still pretty awful knowing the reason. I wish more people could've seen his face when he apologized—he looked like a little kid!" Vhalla roared with laughter. Hadn't she been upset with him a few hours ago? Slowly, her giggles faded as she caught a glimpse of Daniel's face. "What?"

"Vhalla—" he murmured, bringing his heavy flagon to his lips, "—you've drunk too much." He smiled tiredly and reached over. Daniel placed his palm on her head and stroked her hair once. "No more of that, before you say something you'll really regret in the morning."

She found she was somehow still holding the mug of water,

and she drank deeply. Vhalla found herself swaying slightly in the breeze, or perhaps it was the feeling of ale in her head. She leaned to the side and her temple found his shoulder. They sat silently, he looked back toward the roof, and she looked out over the city.

"He's lucky," Daniel whispered.

"He doesn't want me," she said for the first time aloud. Daniel's silence was an invitation for her to continue. "I think I'm a burden, or a tool, or an amusement. Nothing more."

"I don't think so," Daniel murmured. "I've seen him around you—we all have."

Vhalla wondered if she imagined the swordsman leaning toward her a fraction.

She took a deep breath and grabbed for his flagon, the water forgotten a moment. Daniel relinquished it. "He wants me for his father, for their war, that's all."

"Then he's more of a fool and an ass than people give him credit for." Daniel's fingers brushed hers as she passed the flagon back to him.

"Do you have someone?" Vhalla already was certain she knew the answer was not going to be affirmative. If she was honest, she'd already begun to see the way her fellow Easterner looked at her when he thought she wasn't paying attention.

"I did." He took a long drink. "I returned from my last tour and found she'd decided that 'when the war is over' was too long to wait."

"I'm sorry," Vhalla sighed, accepting his flagon back.

"I'm getting over it." He shrugged. He wasn't convincing in the slightest.

"You know what will help?" She swung her legs back around and stood with a stumble and a laugh. "More alcohol, more dancing." She held out her hands for him and he chuckled, resigning himself to her.

They both had something to run from, Vhalla realized, or rather *someone.* He ran from the shroud of this other woman, and she ran from the painful possibilities that surrounded her and Aldrik. Vhalla took the stairs with resolve, his hand wrapped in hers as she led him back below. Tonight they would run together.

The first stop was the bar. Just because she realized she was running didn't make her judgment any more sound. Her hand was in the air and she ordered two shot glasses of a liquid that burnt all the way down.

Daniel coughed. "How are you drinking this?" He slammed the glass back down on the bar.

"You're drinking it too," she coughed. Vhalla felt the alcohol hit her system and she swayed, laughing again. "Come on."

Daniel paid the bartender and they were on the dance floor anew. He took her hands and spun her three times. Vhalla's insides bubbled, and she was laughing again. Her hips swayed and her hands clapped to the music as they stepped and twisted their hips. She kicked to his left and he to her right, before changing directions.

They came back together and one hand was wrapped in his, the other on his shoulder and his on hers. Vhalla found herself beaming from ear to ear. They were both awful dancers. But she was completely intoxicated on the alcohol, on the crowd, on the heat, on Daniel's sweet smiles, on his gentle admiration, and on his hands.

Finally her feet felt as though they were on the verge of falling off, and her joints screamed in protest of further movement. Vhalla fell out of step by placing her hands on his shoulders, leaning on him for support. She felt Daniel's palms fall on her hips.

"I'm *so* tired," she shouted in his ear over the music and noise of the people.

"Thank the Mother, me too." He laughed and led her off the dance floor. They walked over to the main entrance and hovered by the door.

"Where is everyone else?" The band never stopped playing so the floor never stopped moving. They both tried to locate just one of the people they came with.

"Who knows? They know their way back." Daniel yawned, he turned and stumbled into the street. It was his turn to almost collapse, and Vhalla ran up beside him, throwing her arms around his waist. He grabbed her for support and they almost fell together.

"You-you're drunk." She punched his gut.

"Ungh," he grunted. "Don't do that or I'll be sick on your shoes."

"You wou-oudnt," she laughed and slurred her words, her arm situating around his waist and his around her shoulders.

"Now who's drunk?" He put his thumb on one side of her mouth and index finger on the other, pinching her lips together to make a talking motion.

Vhalla laughed and slapped his hand away. "Don't make fun of me," she pouted.

"Now there's a face that could break the strongest of men." He grinned. Vhalla noticed one side of his mouth went up more than the other. It didn't have the same curl as Aldrik's but there was something similar and charming in it.

They stumbled through the streets teasing each other and grabbing at walls and railings for support. In all it was rather a miracle that they didn't end up horribly lost. On the way they passed a public fountain, and Daniel insisted she drink liberally.

"I can't drink anymore." She lay out on the dusty ground, her face wet.

"Get up off the ground," he laughed.

"No, it's nice here." She grinned, which was interrupted with a yawn. The fuzziness in her head was beginning to change to exhaustion.

He extended a hand to her. "It's not far now, Vhalla. Bed is better than the ground. Plus, I think there are a few people, whom I'm rather fearful of answering to, that would be cross if I let you sleep on the road."

She found her feet again, and they stumbled into the inn not long after. The main lobby was quiet, and he helped her upstairs. Vhalla dissolved into a fit of giggles, collapsing against the wall.

"You're so loud," he scolded between uncontrollable laughter.

"No, you are!" She covered her mouth with a hand, her sides aching from bruises and amusement.

Daniel smiled down at her charmingly. His hair hung around his face. He was plain looking, normal for an Easterner. But for Vhalla he was handsome with nostalgia, and his voice, worn from too many years of calling across battlefields and training grounds, was beginning to sound smooth. "Come on, to bed with you."

"Thank you, Daniel," Vhalla whispered, pausing in front of her door.

"For what?" he asked.

Even drunk, she wasn't naive. This would be the moment most other men would ask to come into her room. Vhalla leaned against the door with a sincere smile. The glitter of intoxication would fade with the dawn. But the sweet wash of his presence already promised to linger. "I haven't had that much fun in a long time."

"Me neither." Daniel took a few more steps backwards. "If you need anything, I'm upstairs, first to the right on the landing."

"Thank you." She yawned.

"All right, to sleep, you beautiful Windwalker." He gave her a lazy smirk and Vhalla reciprocated before slipping into the dark room.

She didn't even find it in her to change. Vhalla headed straight for the bed, collapsing on top of another comatose body. She nearly jumped out of her skin.

"Welcome back, Vhalla," Larel mumbled groggily.

"What are you doing here?" Vhalla relaxed, wiggling under the blankets.

"I wanted to make sure you made it back," the Westerner yawned. "How was the rest of your night?"

"Fun." Vhalla snuggled up to the familiar warmth of Larel.

"Fritz?" Larel closed her eyes.

"Don't know," Vhalla said honestly, and wondered if she should feel guilty.

"He's likely still trying to pick up boys," Larel laughed tiredly. Her words slurred slightly—Vhalla hadn't been the only one drinking. "Daniel?"

"Yes, he walked me back." Vhalla rubbed her face on the pillow.

"He didn't do anything untoward, did he?" Larel cracked her eyes open to study Vhalla.

Vhalla laughed. "No, he's wonderful actually," she admitted treacherously. "I should be with someone like him . . ." When Vhalla thought about it, he'd be a sensible choice for her. Only just above her station, Eastern like she was, thoughtful, kind, handsome. She felt strange just musing over the growing list of reasons why Daniel was a good match.

"Aldrik?" With the name alone Vhalla's rationalization over Daniel and her halted.

"I love him," she sighed. She loved him so much her heart ached at the thought. One night and too much alcohol couldn't change what had been growing and building for months, even if it may be for the better. Vhalla picked at the blanket. "What did you feel for Aldrik?"

"What did I feel?" Larel shifted onto her back. "I felt like he was one of the only people who I really had in the world, who really cared for me. I suppose that's why I called it love."

"How do you mistake love?" Vhalla asked. *Maybe she was mistaken also?*

"There are many kinds of love," Larel said.

"Are there?"

"Do you love Aldrik as you love your father?" A grin was in Larel's voice.

"Family is different!" Vhalla pushed the other woman's shoulder.

"I love you," Larel said softly, stilling Vhalla. The Western woman leaned close, placing a gentle kiss on Vhalla's forehead. "I don't love you as a lover. But I love you wholly and completely nonetheless." Vhalla suddenly felt like crying. "And I love Aldrik—but as my friend; I didn't and don't want him between the sheets. When I kissed him, it was strange, awkward; there was nothing to it other than a kiss."

"I see," Vhalla barely said over another yawn. She wondered if she kissed Aldrik what she'd feel.

"Let's go to sleep, Vhalla. It's late." Larel shifted closer, before settling.

Vhalla closed her eyes. She imagined Larel's slow and steady breathing to be Aldrik's. She imagined it was his warmth radiating close by. Vhalla sighed softly. There was an ache that made her legs shift under the covers. If it was the alcohol or the exhaustion that brought her to admitting it, she knew without doubt, she wanted the crown prince as a woman—as a lover— would.

CHAPTER 16

THROUGH THE OTHERWISE dark room a slit of light streamed between the curtains, causing Vhalla to blink blearily and her head to pound.

"I feel sick," she groaned softly.

"You drank too much," Larel mumbled.

"You two, *silence*," an agonized whisper ordered.

Both women sat up at the sound of the male voice.

Vhalla peered over the edge of the bed to see a disheveled Fritz collapsed on the floor. "When did you get here?" She paused. "*Why* are you here?"

"Larel wasn't in our room, and I was worried. Then I got sleepy," Fritz groaned, rolling away from the light. "No more talking."

Just when Vhalla was going to give into the idea of sleeping the day away, there was a knock.

"Damn that person to the Mother's fiery justice," Fritz spat spitefully.

"Vhalla?" It was Daniel.

Vhalla pulled herself to her feet and tugged at her rumpled, alcohol-smelling clothing. Larel and Fritz had already collapsed again when she opened the door. Daniel seemed to be in a better state, but not by a large margin. His hair was wet, and Vhalla guessed a bath would likely help her also.

He chuckled when he saw her. "Still sleeping?" he remarked rather obviously.

"No, practicing an ancient Tower ritual," she retorted with a tired grin, leaning against the doorway. Vhalla scanned the tray he held in his hands. "You come bearing gifts?"

"A little something. May I?" Daniel held up his offering of food, water, and some vials.

She nodded and stepped aside for her fellow Easterner to slip into the dark room. Larel and Fritz stared at him red-eyed and squinting but didn't question.

"I thought you two might be here." He shook his head in amusement. "I brought water for each of you and some potion that'll help with your heads. I managed to find some before they were all gone."

"And *man'nik*." Larel was on her feet, headed for the tray. She grabbed a steaming bun, biting into it ravenously.

"That." Daniel didn't even try to pronounce the name of the Western food. He glanced at Vhalla's confused face. "It's filled with meat."

"Eat one, Vhalla." Larel shoved one into her hands, grabbing for the water.

"Thank you, Daniel," Vhalla said sincerely, downing the potion and chasing the taste with water.

"It was my suggestion to go out last night." He grinned as Fritz dragged his feet over. "And I could tell none of you were really used to that type of affair."

"And you are?" Fritz took his share of Daniel's gifts.

"Not really." Daniel chuckled. "We're going out for a quieter night tonight, if you'd all like to join."

"No alcohol," Larel mumbled.

"No alcohol," he confirmed. "I'll be back around dusk. We're all meeting in the lobby downstairs." Daniel started for the door.

"Where are you going now?" Vhalla asked.

Daniel paused, his gaze questioning. "I thought I'd go to the main market today."

"Can I come with you?" She wasn't sure what overtook her in that moment.

"I don't mind if you come along." Daniel flashed her a toothy smile, and Vhalla found herself unable to stop herself from smiling back.

"I need to change . . ." Vhalla pinched her rumpled clothes, catching a whiff of herself. She felt as gross as she smelled from dancing last night. "And bathe."

"I'll wait downstairs," he said, opening the door. "Take your time."

"Daniel, huh?" Fritz gave an appraising hum.

"What?" Vhalla asked, defensive.

"Nothing, just a shame he doesn't seem interested in boys. The march is long," Fritz sniggered.

"Oh quiet." Larel shook her head at Fritz. "You have someone."

"You do?" Vhalla blinked. The Southerner seemed so intent on finding men all night.

"Not really . . ." Fritz was more uncomfortable than Vhalla had ever seen him.

"Grahm, it's Grahm." Larel rolled her eyes.

"Grahm?" Vhalla remembered the Eastern man Fritz was rarely seen without in the Tower. How they'd sit, thighs touching, shoulders brushing. "You and Grahm?"

"It's nothing official, I don't know . . ." The scarlet on Fritz's cheeks told Vhalla everything she needed to know. Whatever was "not official" about them wouldn't be that way for long when Fritz returned.

"If you're going to the market, you'll need these." Larel tapped three golden coins on the dresser.

"Where did those come from?" Vhalla had never seen so much money at once in her life.

"Pay," Fritz yawned, making for the door.

"Pay? For what?" Vhalla was confused.

"Soldiers get paid." Larel smiled.

"But I'm not a soldier." Vhalla fidgeted with her fingers. "I'm owned by the crown."

"I think saving the army deserves three gold coins." Larel patted her shoulder and ushered Vhalla off to the bathroom.

It was a shared bathroom for the floor but it was thankfully empty. The tub was sized for one and Vhalla took her time. Someone, she suspected Larel, had bathed her when she was unconscious but it didn't compare to how clean she felt when she could be thorough.

When Vhalla returned to the room, Larel was still waiting persistently to check her injuries. Vhalla doubted she could dance the night away if her wounds were still significant, but she indulged Larel anyway. Larel saw her dressed and then used magic in a way Vhalla had never conceived.

She ran her palms through Vhalla's hair and the heat instantly set the water to steam. Larel explained how it took many tries to get the right balance of tension and heat, but it was a useful trick when mastered. As Vhalla looked at her hair in the mirror, suddenly smooth and straight, she easily agreed.

Daniel was sitting, charcoal moving without pause over the pages of a worn-looking leather book, when she arrived downstairs. He had a canvas bag slung across his chest, a bag into which the book quickly disappeared upon his noticing her. Vhalla adjusted her pack on her shoulders, empty save for a golden coin.

"Sorry to make you wait," she said apologetically.

"Not a problem." Daniel stood with a shake of his head. "Ready?"

She nodded.

The alleyways of the Crossroads were completely different in daylight. Most of the stores that had been shut by dusk were now open and alive. Tables were set out with all manner of jewelry, food, baubles, and trinkets. Vhalla found herself slowing down by every other one to inspect something she'd never seen.

"We're never going to make it to the main market like this." Daniel chuckled.

"Sorry!" she said, skipping to catch up with him. "It's just all so, *so* different."

Vhalla made it a point to keep step with Daniel and not lag behind. Eventually his roundabout way led them to a wide road—the East-West Way. Vhalla gasped at the hive of people that bustled within the greatest market in the world. Everything was busy, everything was colorful, everything was alive, and everything seemed to have a price.

People pressed in against each other and pushed purposefully to get to wherever it was they were off to next. Some carried large baskets on their heads, others held platters, and some had cages with wild beasts that Vhalla had never before seen. A man pushed between them and Vhalla glanced back for Daniel, but the crowd had enveloped him.

She scanned her left and right, trying to find where he may have gone. Vhalla walked in his general direction. "Daniel?" A few passersby looked at her strangely but kept going. "Daniel!" she tried a little louder.

"Vhalla!" A hand shot up from the edge of the crowd. "Over here." Vhalla had to jump to see where he was, and she pushed through the mass to get to him. He chuckled. "Sorry about that."

"Not your fault." She shook her head.

"Let's look in here." He held back a heavy curtain to a dimly lit shop.

Vhalla's eyes adjusted slowly to the lighting. A dense haze hovered in the air that held the smell of spices and wood. Glass cases lined the walls and a few stood freely in the middle of the room. Vhalla ran her hand over them, looking at the treasures within.

"*Irashi*, welcome." A young woman wearing a robe revealing her generous cleavage—too much revealed, in Vhalla's opinion—sauntered over to them. She had long, straight black hair. Half was down flowing over her shoulders and back. The other half was braided like a spider's web on top.

"Welcome to the finest Curiosity Shop in all the land." She leaned against one of the cases, the tan skin of her leg slipping out through a slit in her bright ruby robe—a stunning contrast. "And what can I help you with today?" The woman smiled thinly.

"I think we're just looking." Vhalla took a step closer to Daniel and away from the woman. He seemed to be unbothered, but something about this woman put Vhalla's hairs on edge.

"No one is 'just looking.' All desire." The woman folded her arms under her breasts. "Tell me, what is yours?"

"Sorry to disappoint." Vhalla dodged her question and looked at Daniel. "Let's go, I'm hungry." She grabbed his arm and turned to leave.

"There is not one curiosity you have, Vhalla Yarl?" Vhalla stopped short. "I know your winds will not tell you what the flames will tell me."

Daniel took a step forward; he put his body half in front of Vhalla's, an arm stretched across her protectively.

"How do you know my name?" Vhalla whispered in shock.

"I can know many, and tell more, if you wish it." The woman flipped some hair over her shoulders. "The fire burns away all lies."

"You're a sorcerer," Vhalla stated; it was as though she could smell the magic radiating off the woman.

"I am a Firebearer," the woman affirmed with a nod.

"What is your name?" Vhalla pushed Daniel's arm down, taking a step forward.

"I've had many names, I could give you one, or I could let you chose a name for yourself. Then it will be something we alone can share." The woman continued to lounge against one of the cases. "Tell me the name you would like me to call you. Invented or otherwise." Instinct told Vhalla to make as few choices as possible when interacting with this woman.

"Vi," the Westerner said simply. "Would you like me to read your curiosities?"

"Read our curiosities?" Daniel asked.

"I am a Firebearer, I am one with the flames, and with my eyes I can see into the future. You come with curiosities, *questions*, in your heart and I will give you answers," the woman proclaimed.

Vhalla was skeptical, but the woman *had* known her name. "I'll do it." She felt overcome with bravery.

The woman gave her a knowing smile. "You must pick four things: three to burn, one to hold." The Firebearer motioned around the room at the cases, and Vhalla understood. These things weren't for sale; this was a fortune teller and these were tools for her trade. Vhalla began to stroll about the space, Daniel hovering over her shoulder.

"Are you sure this is a good idea?" he whispered directly into her ear so the woman would not hear. His proximity was warm, even compared to the heat of the day.

"It'll be fine. Why not live a little? I am here, and somehow she knew my name."

Vhalla scanned the strange objects; there was an impossible amount of knickknacks at random order in the cases. A jar of quills caught her eye. Vhalla reached over, thumbing around. Selecting a gray silver plume Vhalla brought it to the counter the woman rested on.

Then Vhalla was wandering again. A bunch of wheat—*home*—and rose petals, a different feeling of home, collected on the counter. The last thing—something to hold—was the hardest to find. She spent far too long going from case to case looking at this or that.

In the end, it was a fine silver chain that was draped out of a halfway closed jewelry box that caught her eye. Vhalla slid open the glass of the case and pulled lightly on the chain. It was a simple, silver pocket watch that was designed to be worn around the neck. Vhalla stared at it closely. The links were oddly familiar. It reminded her of Aldrik's, she realized. "This . . . this is what I will hold." Vhalla walked back over to the woman.

"An interesting spread." The Firebearer sounded amused. "Come." Vi carried the burning goods into an even smokier backroom. Their shoes were removed as though it was a sacred place. Tapestries and rugs covered the floor and walls, making it feel very small and intimate. They each took a place on either side of a smoldering fire pit.

"Are you certain you wish an observer?" she asked, looking at Daniel. "I will read the futures as I see them."

"I suppose . . ." Vhalla looked up uncertainly at Daniel. "If you don't mind?"

"I'll wait right out here." Daniel slipped back out of the heavy curtain, and Vhalla heard his footsteps fade away.

The woman knelt over the fire pit and reached into the smoldering coals. She lifted them up and dropped them, their orange-hot glow bright in the dim light. Flames licked around her fingers and soon her arms up to her elbows were covered in soot. The woman reached across and held out her thumb, marking Vhalla's face.

"Vhalla Yarl, blessed bird of the East. The one who can soar without wings. The first chick to fly the cage. The first to return to our land."

The woman leaned back. Taking the quill, she threw it into the fire pit. Flames roared white. Vi grabbed the wheat, adding it to the fire. The color changed to orange. Finally the rose petals were sacrificed and the fire changed a deep unnatural crimson, almost black.

Vhalla held her breath as the woman eased her face into the flame. Face-down she opened her eyes to the fire, and Vhalla let out an uneasy sigh as the Firebearer was completely unaffected by its heat. Slowly the flames began to die down, leaving a light-purple ash at the bottom of the pit.

"The present burns away, leaving the future to rise from its ashes." Vi leaned over and took a large handful of the ash and threw it into the air over them. The fine powder began to slowly swirl and trickle down, lighter than snow, and hovered before her, making unknown shapes before finally settling to the floor. Vi's eyes burned a bright red color.

"You will march to victory, and it will be won upon your silver wings. But the winds of change you will set free will also shatter that tender hope upon which you fly. *You will lose your dark sentry*," the woman foretold.

Vhalla clutched the plain pocket watch, her heart beginning to race.

"Two paths will lie before you: night and day. Go west by night. Fade into the comforting obscurity of a shroud of darkness. You will find a familiar happiness there, if you can ignore yearnings for the sun." Vi paused, looking at the glimmering ash about the room. "The other road will burn away your falsehoods by the light of dawn. You will own your wants for all to see. But take caution, for the fire that will expose you will give birth to an even greater power that will consume the land itself."

A silence fell over the room as the last of the ash fell to the floor. Vhalla breathed shallowly. Each of the woman's words seemed to have been carefully and perfectly chosen for an exact meaning. But what that meaning was Vhalla still considered. Vi's eyes slowly faded to black again.

"And now, for payment." The woman settled into a more comfortable position.

"Ah, right." Vhalla put down her sack and reached for her gold.

"I do not want coin." Vi stopped her.

Vhalla paused, an unsettling feeling worming its way into the back of her skull. "What, do you want then?"

"That watch." The Westerner pointed to the one which Vhalla was holding.

"This one?" Vhalla held it up; it was the woman's to begin with. Vi nodded. "All right, of course."

Vhalla passed it over. She had never expected to keep it, but something strange tingled across her fingers as Vhalla gave it up. It was physically difficult to see it in the other woman's hands.

"Our current business has concluded."

They both stood, and Vi held open the back curtain while Vhalla slipped into her shoes.

"Heed my words, Vhalla Yarl."

Vhalla could only nod at the cryptic message and walked out into the shop proper. She rubbed the soot off her face, trying to figure out how much the woman's fortune telling bothered her. Vhalla nodded to Daniel and they left silently, back out into the chaos of the market. Somehow, she felt the fiery glow of the woman's stare halfway down the street.

Vhalla linked her arm with Daniel's to avoid getting separated from him again. He was also steady and, in truth, she felt a little shaken. Vhalla flexed, gripping him tighter.

"How did it go?" he asked as lightly as possible.

"It was an experience." Vhalla attempted a chuckle. She could tell he didn't buy the brave front, but he didn't follow up with any questions on what type of experience it was.

Daniel was in good form the rest of the day as he showed

her the market. He let her walk as close as she liked to him and neither pushed her away nor pulled her closer. Normally they were arm–in-arm for practicality, but if she was completely honest, she was enjoying the position of being physically close to someone who wasn't confusing or frustrating.

They stopped at a food stand and purchased balls of rice that had vegetables inside. Vhalla laughed as she fed him a bite of her flavor and half dropped out onto his lap. For dessert, they tried a square sweet had a strange stiff, jelly-like texture. Vhalla bought a small box to bring back to Larel and Fritz.

After the morning's affair finally faded, the day gave way to an all-around positive experience in the market. Vhalla purchased a small bottle of perfume and a potpourri ball for her bag from a scents shop, thinking they may come in handy during the rest of their march in the desert.

They passed a candy shop and found the lemon peels that Aldrik had mentioned. Vhalla picked up two bags, one for her and one for him. He had brought them up, and he had liked the lemon cake. Daniel purchased a new dagger that could be worn on the leg and short swords that he insisted were worlds better than his own. When Vhalla told him she had no weapons, he was aghast and that hunt absorbed the rest of their afternoon.

She finally decided on a thin, almost needle-like dagger that was just a little less than the length of her forearm. It came with a holster to wear on the arm, the hilt right near the wrist. Daniel pointed out that she'd lose a lot of stability and strength choosing such a small option. But as Vhalla clipped it onto the underside of her forearm and rolled her sleeve down over it, she instantly liked her choice. With a normal shirt, it was perfectly concealed. The hilt was just the right length to not impede her movement. Yet in a quick motion she had it drawn.

In all, the day cost her almost all the money she had brought.

But they were only in the Crossroads for a few more days and most things seemed to have been taken care of for her. Even outside the market her arm still lingered around Daniel's. The night chill was setting in and he was familiar and warm. Vhalla smiled, fussing with the dagger strapped to her left arm.

"It doesn't work as a concealed weapon if you're showing people it's there," Daniel scolded with a grin.

"You're right, I suppose," she agreed with a laugh. He hadn't touched the new dagger strapped to his calf for hours.

They strolled through the market and back to the central square, where the East-West Way met the Great Imperial Way. Firebearers walked about lighting the lamps, and Vhalla found it amazing to see a society that had sorcerers so integrated in helpful ways. She smiled, eyes following one in particular for no reason. He moved to a building with large circular stained glass. Vhalla paused shifting her bag on her shoulder.

It was a bad idea. She was having another moment where she needed to admit it, and stop herself. Vhalla took a breath. "I—" She paused, glancing between Daniel and the building. "I need to make a quick stop. The inn is right over there. You can go ahead."

"No, I'm not letting you walk alone in the Crossroads at night," he said definitively. "It can be dangerous."

"Very well," she sighed softly. "Then wait out here for me?"

"That, I can do." There was apprehension locked in his eyes, but Daniel kept it away from his tongue and spared her comment.

Vhalla took a breath and summoned her courage, walking to the front doors. She wasn't sure if she wanted to see Aldrik again. *Wasn't she mad at him?* But at the root of all her conflicting feelings was the need to see him, to say what needed to be said: the truth.

Soft music, a Southern sound, played from one of the rooms off the main lobby. Vhalla looked uncertainly at the shut doors and opulent parlors. A man cleared his throat from behind the front desk.

"I have a delivery for the Crown Prince," Vhalla announced.

The older man folded his bony fingers and regarded her skeptically. "What could you possibly have?"

"I'm the Windwalker," she declared, attempting to use credentials to dodge the question.

"That is most excellent, and what is so important that he would not leave word?"

Deflated that her approach hadn't worked, she lost her resolve and mumbled, "He . . . We have work to do . . . for the Emperor."

"I'm sure . . ." The man didn't believe her in the slightest. "Unfortunately the prince has explicitly asked not to be disturbed. Do take care."

Vhalla sighed softly, resigned.

"Vhalla?" Prince Baldair stopped in a hallway joining the lobby with other rooms, walking over to her. "What're you doing here?"

"My prince, I was just leaving." Vhalla keenly remembered the last time she and Prince Baldair had spoken.

"She was asking to see the crown prince," the treacherous clerk informed.

"Vhalla." The golden prince frowned, glancing at the man and thinking better of continuing. "I'll take her there myself."

"You will?" Vhalla and the desk man said in unison.

"He's shut himself up; I've not seen him once. Company is a good thing, no?" Baldair placed his hand on the small of her back and practically pushed her up a wide staircase.

"You're really taking me to see him?" Vhalla asked as they reached the second floor landing.

"Of course not, but I am going to ask you what you think you're doing here." In private, the prince dropped all decorum.

"It's nothing important," Vhalla muttered. She was already second guessing her mission.

"I thought I told you to stay away." Baldair frowned.

"It's not your business." Vhalla pulled the bag of candy from her pack. "And I also wanted to give him these."

"Lemon peels?" Prince Baldair recognized the sweet shop's marking. "Vhalla . . ." he sighed. "I don't know what kind of relationship you think you can have with my brother—"

"I don't want one," she said defensively. The words crossed her lips before Vhalla could think about them, fueled by spite.

"No, you do. He has you under his spell," the golden haired prince insisted.

"What are you talking about?" Vhalla took a step away.

"Why else would anyone want my brother?"

He caught her wrist as she tried to leave. "Let me go."

"I'm trying to help you." Somehow, Prince Baldair managed to sound sincere.

"Let me go!" Vhalla tugged against his firm grip.

"What is all this commotion?" a voice called from the end of the hall. Vhalla's blood turned to ice in her veins. Elecia, in a loose sleeping tunic and nothing else, stood barefoot and groggy eyed. She yawned as she came closer. "*Vhalla?* What are *you* doing here?"

"Nothing!" Vhalla said, trying to make a hasty retreat. "I'm trying to leave right now." She clutched the lemon peels to her chest and tried to turn, but Prince Baldair still held her wrist.

"You're still in there? At this hour?" Prince Baldair's surprise at the sight of Elecia caused him to ignore Vhalla's tugs against his grip.

"Baldair, quit being an ass-face, take the girl, and go," Elecia snapped. She seemed exhausted and worn thin. Somehow even her hair seemed less fluffy than normal.

"Just what have you two been doing all this time?" Prince Baldair inquired.

"Can your curiosity be satiated solo?" Vhalla asked weakly, still attempting to leave.

"Brother, by the Mother, I swear . . ." A low voice, rough sounding, as though it hurt to speak—yet still very clearly annoyed—came from the back of the hall. Elecia turned and sprinted back to Aldrik.

"You need to go back to bed." The other woman stood in front of him, a dark-skinned palm contrasting with the pale skin of his bare chest.

Vhalla's eyes widened as she took them in. Elecia barely dressed, tired, her hair a mess. Aldrik looked as close to sleep as she'd ever seen him—and half-dressed. His pale, well-sculpted chest brought a hot flush to her cheeks. Aldrik didn't just tolerate the contact; he didn't seem to mind Elecia's proximity, her touch. He moved his hand to place it on the other woman's shoulder.

The bag of lemon peels slipped from Vhalla's hand and dropped to the floor.

The noise of the bag dropping and the candy scattering silenced all parties involved. Aldrik's eyes were the last to find Vhalla but they met hers with a mix of surprise and confusion. Vhalla took a quivering breath.

There was nothing to say. The silence stretched another painful minute. Just before it was about to break she turned on her heels, wrenched her hand from Prince Baldair's slack grip, and sprinted.

Vhalla ran down the stairs, out the doors, and into the square. She tilted her head back and took a deep breath. The cool air hitting her lungs made her choke, and Vhalla doubled over. The sobs had already started. She pressed her eyes closed and felt her whole body trembling.

A pair of hands tentatively placed themselves on her shoulders, hovering a moment before making contact.

"Vhalla," Daniel whispered.

She spun. Her cheeks soaked with her barely-silenced crying. "I told you, I am the queen of bad ideas." Vhalla tried a smile that was quickly consumed by the tears.

Daniel pulled her to him and wrapped his arms gently around her shoulders. He whispered soothing words into the crown of her head and held her. Vhalla pressed her face into his chest, clutching his shirt. She felt her knees give out.

Daniel supported her. He held her, saying nothing, asking nothing, as she sobbed. Vhalla didn't care who saw her. Behind her eyes was the singular image of Aldrik and another woman. A woman whom she knew had been in the palace for some time, of some noble birth if every suspicion was correct. They were both adults, of the right age, and of the right breeding. They were together, interrupted from *something*, in the night. She thought of his bare chest and it stirred something within Vhalla, which only made her weep more.

Vhalla clutched Daniel as though his arms were the last thing holding her sanity together.

CHAPTER 17

THE SUN WAS *setting over the rooftops of the Crossroads.
Vhalla raised her hands to his face. Aldrik leaned into
her, took them in his, and kissed her palms lightly. She
whispered to him and he whispered back, the words which
she had been longing to hear. She shifted closer to him, his lips
parted.*

*Then Vhalla was only watching, Elecia's beautifully long fingers
were across the pale of his face. They leaned closer, and Vhalla let
out a cry.*

She gasped in the night air, waking with a start. Vhalla looked
around frantically, remembering where she was. Daniel was
fast asleep in the chair Larel had previously occupied. The
Westerner and Fritz were still out eating dinner, oblivious to
Vhalla's shattering world, and Daniel had refused to leave her
alone. Vhalla collapsed back onto her pillow, forcing her eyes
closed.

*The next time, her hands were his. The fingertips ran over a
shadowed face in the dark. She couldn't make out the features
but Vhalla knew they were not her own. Were they Elecia's? Her
mind wandered while trapped in the prison of the dream. Her*

heart beat fast and she felt blood shifting its attention. There was a carnal desire it wanted to attend to.

Vhalla rolled over and opened her eyes, staring blankly at the wall. She whimpered softly and pulled the blankets over her head.

She ran through streets of fire and death. The bodies were already mutilated, their battered limbs and shattered skulls littering the ground. Vhalla sprinted through the streets, through the shadow people. Tonight, tonight she would be fast enough, her feet told her, and she allowed the wind to pick up beneath her.

Vhalla came to a skidding halt before the demolished building and she tore at the debris. Each rock that moved made her heart beat a little faster. Eventually she saw a face beneath the rubble. Vhalla paused; he wasn't supposed to be there. She tore away the remaining remnants and took Aldrik's body into her arms, weeping.

She awoke for a third time, and then a fourth and a fifth. Her mind was too heavily armed with the stuff of nightmares. Daniel was gone, and she heard talking muffled through the door. Vhalla instantly recognized one voice as Larel's and waited for the other woman to slip silently into the room.

"Larel," she whispered weakly, feeling the bed shift to accommodate the new person.

"What happened?" Larel ran her hands through Vhalla's hair lovingly.

"Aldrik—" Vhalla choked on his name. "He and Elecia . . . they . . ."

"They what?" Larel coaxed gently.

Vhalla recounted the events from earlier in the evening, and Larel listened dutifully. She said nothing, good or bad, absorbing the whole story. Vhalla broke down again when she retold the moment of seeing Elecia and Aldrik together.

"I know she's noble. The way she acts around him, the way she calls him by his name . . . There's something there, Larel. I just—I didn't want to see it." Vhalla sniffled loudly.

"She is," Larel said softly.

"She is what?" Vhalla rubbed her eyes.

"She's noble," Larel confirmed.

"What?" Vhalla stilled. "How can you be certain?"

Larel sighed and averted her eyes. Whatever she was about to say Vhalla knew she wouldn't like. "She didn't start coming around until he was older. During the few years we were very distant from each other. He spent a lot of time with her, when she was around. I didn't remember until I heard the reception for her here in the Crossroads. She's a Ci'Dan, a noble family from the West with ties to the crown. I never really studied history—that's Fritz's area—but I always assumed she was a potential bride, given his age when she appeared."

"You knew." Betrayal was a hot poison. "*You knew and you didn't tell me?*"

"Vhalla, listen," Larel demanded, pinning her to the bed with an arm. "*Listen.*"

Vhalla stopped fighting, but that didn't stop the anger pulsing through her veins. The world was out to lie and cheat her; maybe Prince Baldair was right.

"I didn't tell you because I didn't believe—I still don't believe—that you have anything to worry about."

"How can you say that? She's a noble woman, she's known him for years—*I saw them together!*"

"Hush." Larel tried to calm Vhalla's hysterics. "When you are together, Aldrik looks for you, only for you."

"He spent a lot of time with her."

"He did," Larel conceded. "But he never looked at her the way he looks at you. He never reached for her the way he reaches for you. Vhalla, Aldrik cares for you deeply, I know he does."

"You don't know anything," Vhalla mumbled.

Larel just sighed and rubbed Vhalla's back as the younger woman cried softly.

Vhalla was shocked later when a messenger brought her an Imperial summons. It was a tri-folded card sealed with the blazing sun of the Empire in black wax.

"Are you going to open it?" Larel asked after Vhalla's tenth lap of the room.

"I will," she said with false confidence.

"Today?" Larel had the audacity to tease her.

Vhalla shot the other woman a glare, and Larel was only moderately apologetic. The Westerner hadn't changed her tune that Aldrik had no interest in Elecia.

"I will," Vhalla repeated, placing her finger under the seal. She took a breath and unfolded the note before her hands dropped it from shaking so much. "*Your presence is requested,*" she read aloud. "*Prince Aldrik C. Solaris.*"

"That's it?" Even Larel seemed surprised.

"It's better this way." Vhalla threw the note onto her pack, rummaging through the clothes on the floor that had never made it into drawers. "*It is.* I'll go and tell him I know everything."

"Vhalla," Larel sighed.

"We can stop this sham, and I'll just do what I need to for my freedom," Vhalla vowed, tugging on a clean shirt and leggings.

They walked down the stairs in silence, Larel seeing her out of the inn and all the way to the fancy hotel where the Imperial family was staying. Vhalla spent the walk attempting to shield her heart as much as possible. She imagined each rib a barbed wall that nothing could enter into or get out of. She would do whatever Aldrik and the Emperor needed, and then she would go. She didn't even want to bring up what she'd seen. It wasn't her business after all; she had trespassed on his privacy.

By the time Vhalla arrived at the glittering building on

the main square, she had scripted and repeated so many conversations in her head that she felt prepared for every possible outcome. No matter what, she would keep it together and leave as quickly as possible. Yet none of this stopped her heart from threatening to burst out of its thorny cage as she pushed open the door, leaving Larel behind.

"How may I assist?" the woman behind the desk asked stiffly.

"I've an appointment with the crown prince." Vhalla didn't allow herself to say his name. "Vhalla Yarl, the Windwalker."

The woman pulled out the same ledger as the man from the night before and ran her finger down the pages. "Ah yes. Go ahead—second floor, right wing," the woman instructed needlessly. Vhalla had already started up the stairs.

Each step coincided with the pounding in her ears. Every scrap of common sense screamed for her to leave a message that she was indisposed. But she knew she could only run so long. In four more days they would be riding together, with Elecia too.

Vhalla paused and took a deep breath, focusing only on the sound of the air moving. *She could do this.*

Arriving at the landing, she stilled. Vhalla shook away the image of Elecia and Aldrik standing in the night and proceeded to the door. With the last of her resolve, she gave a few short knocks.

It was a tense minute as she waited; she was fully prepared to make a hasty retreat and explain she thought he was out. The door handle turned. Aldrik stood against the colored light of large stained glass circles that dominated the wall opposite the door. He wore a black leather jacket that went to his knees with a single line of gold buttons opened at the collared white cotton shirt underneath. Well-fitted trousers fell straight to *bare feet*, Vhalla noted curiously. His hair was fixed again, and just the sight of him was painful because it now contrasted so sharply from the disheveled man who had been woken from sleep, likely from lying in the arms of his lover.

"Hello, Vhalla." He seemed as happy to see her as she was him.

"My prince," Vhalla glanced away, unable to keep eye contact any longer.

"Come in." He took a step back and turned.

Vhalla let herself into the room, closing the door softly behind her.

It was an astounding space. High ceilings with mosaics of classic stories along with some characters Vhalla had never before seen. There was a large sitting area with two lounging chaises that faced a large couch, a table between them. A stocked bar dominated the wall to the left of the door—Vhalla instantly wished for something strong—and a large standing table with all manner of papers and uncorked bottles was to the right. To her left was a wall with open sliding doors that revealed an additional room with a large bed covered in blankets and pillows. Perhaps the most astounding feature was a window, which was one she had seen from the square. It was big enough that pillows were piled up on the windowsill, and it looked like it could easily seat four.

Vhalla took another tentative step, instantly uncomfortable being in his space. She couldn't help but look at the bed, wondering if Elecia had shared it with him the night before. Aldrik had crossed to the table and was shuffling the papers.

"You are quiet." He glanced at her from the corners of his eyes.

"I'm sorry," she replied, unsure of what else to say.

"Sit," he ordered curtly.

Vhalla waded through the tension between them, nearly drowning before she managed to sit on one of the chaises.

Aldrik found the paper he was looking for, placing it on the lower table before the couch as he sat opposite her. They stared at each other, waiting for someone to say the first word. Vhalla swallowed.

"This is for the demonstration? For your father?" *Work*, she had to stick to work.

"What else would it be for?" he mumbled, the words like needles.

"Of course," Vhalla replied weakly.

"My father will want us to play a game of scavenger hunt." Aldrik looked at the paper as though it was the most fascinating thing in the world. "Based off what I told him you are able to do at present, first he will have you Project to a person who will tell you a location and an item. You will return to me and direct me to something—unknown to me at the start of the demonstration—based on the instructions."

"It seems simple enough." She nodded.

"Does it?" Aldrik arched an eyebrow at her.

Vhalla shifted under his skepticism. "We've been doing things like this for weeks."

"What exactly have we been doing, Vhalla?" Aldrik's voice was void of any familiar warmth.

She didn't know how to answer. He wasn't asking about the Projection, he was asking about the dance they'd been doing around something both of them had been too terrified to name. Now, it felt like he was accusing her.

"Never mind." Aldrik stood. "Do not answer that. I already know."

"What?" She was on her feet also. "What do you think you know?"

"You think I would not find out?" He glared at her.

"Find out what?" Vhalla's voice had a shrill edge from the tension his eyes evoked in her.

"You are not the first one who has used me to get to him."
Aldrik looked away in disgust.

"What are you talking about?"

"You and Baldair."

Vhalla's mouth dropped open in shock. "What?"

"I caught you both together last night, your hand in his."
Aldrik drew his height, his body language was imposing.

"My hand in his?" Vhalla balked. "You mean him grabbing my
wrist? Him holding me in place so that I'd be forced to witness
you and Elecia?" she accused, pointing at the crown prince.

"Elecia?" Aldrik seemed to forget the other woman was even
with him the night before.

"Were you even going to tell me?" Vhalla's lower lip quivered,
and she swore she would not lose it, she wouldn't cry in front
of him.

"What does Elecia have to do with this?" Confusion eased
his shoulders.

"No." Vhalla shook her head. "No more, I can't. I'm done."
She turned, starting for the door.

"Vhalla!" he snapped. "You asked me for no secrets, for the
truth, and you're turning your back on me?" Aldrik chuckled
darkly. "The irony of *that*."

"The truth?" She stopped, only ten paces from the door. She
should just leave. But something made her turn. She stared at
him in hopelessness. It would all be better if he'd just admit it.
"The truth is . . . the truth is . . ." Something in her snapped.
"The truth is that every time I close my eyes all I see is you and
her!" Vhalla's voice broke halfway through and she threw her
arms up in defeat. The tears burned at the corners of her eyes
and she sniffed, keeping them at bay.

"Why?" Aldrik took a step toward her.

"Because—you know why!" *Was he really going to make her
say it?*

"Why would you care about Elecia if you desire my brother?" His voice was losing its edge, his probing becoming more exploratory over jabbing.

"Aldrik," Vhalla covered her eyes with her palm. "You are a fool." She gave him a defeated laugh. "I don't want your brother, my dear Prince Aldrik C. Solaris. Not every creature with breasts thinks Prince Baldair is a god among men."

"Then why, why do you care?" He took another step closer. Vhalla opened her mouth and shut it, turning for the door.

"Tell me, why does Elecia matter?" Aldrik grabbed her elbow, stopping her from fleeing from the room.

"What does she matter?" Vhalla wasn't sure if she had ever met a man who could be so astonishingly smart about seemingly everything and yet so daft about the person whom he was supposed to be more connected with than anyone in the world. She twisted to face him, tearing her arm from his grasp. "She matters the same as titles do. The same as my birth and yours does. The same way it matters why your brother insists on tormenting me with awful stories about you."

"Stop avoiding my question!" he demanded.

"I am not!" The last of her resolve shattered and her control slipped away. Tears were going to fall at any moment, and if the two of them were going to break they may as well shatter. "*I love you, Aldrik!*"

Her voice echoed on the shockwaves that shook them both. Vhalla's palm clamped over her mouth. She hadn't meant to say it, and Vhalla stared at him wide eyed. She watched his face closely. She witnessed the words settle in on him, the shock that started in his eyes, raised his eyebrows, and dropped his mouth open.

Vhalla's heart raced, and she felt a soft whimper rise in her throat. She wanted him to say something, *anything*. If he would pass judgment she could leave and finally move on from all he was. She could leave his ink black hair and dark eyes behind. She could let his voice fade away from her dreams and let his form no longer haunt her in the daylight.

Aldrik's mouth closed. He swallowed hard.

Vhalla couldn't tolerate the silence any longer, and she grabbed for the door handle as though it was her only lifeline. She would walk away now, and let it all stay broken.

The prince had other plans, and he grabbed for her.

"Aldrik wh—" She half turned, and he spun her the rest of the way.

His hands released her arms and cupped her cheeks in a single fluid motion. Vhalla had only a half a second to register his face closing in on hers. She inhaled sharply at the shock of feeling his lips on her own. His scent, his breathing, the warmth of his palms, the feeling of his mouth, all assaulted her senses and Vhalla closed her eyes, leaning into the kiss.

CHAPTER 18

VHALLA SIGHED SOFTLY, her mouth still gloriously occupied with his. Something audibly clicked back into place, and suddenly her head silenced the noise of the past few months. His palms were hot on her cheeks, and they stayed the tears that had so insistently found their way out seconds before. She felt him pull away slightly, but Vhalla pressed forward, stealing one more moment of his lips. Her eyes opened and met his. Despite being the initiator of the kiss, he looked as bewildered as she.

Still holding her face, Aldrik sighed softly and leaned forward to press his forehead against hers, their noses barely touching. "Say it again . . ."

Vhalla closed her eyes. "I love you, Aldrik." Saying it out loud, to him, sent sparks up her chest.

He pulled her face back to his, claiming her mouth again fiercely. Vhalla's hands found their own life, meeting his fervor. They pressed against his chest, her palms running up to his shoulders. Vhalla buried her fingers in his hair at the nape of his neck, itching to unravel his pristine visage. Her nails ran against his scalp, and his hands dropped from her face to her waist.

Aldrik pulled her closer and her arms bent. She felt her hips meet his, and her chest brush against the warm length of his body. Vhalla shivered—and he held her tighter. She broke the kiss for a moment, taking a shaky breath. Just as she opened her eyes, his mouth was on hers again and he annihilated her every thought with just his taste and touch.

The time that passed between them wasn't nearly enough before she felt his neck push against her fingers and his lips pull away from hers. Vhalla resigned as gracefully as possible, barely restraining herself from clutching him and holding his mouth to hers forever.

Aldrik stared down in bewildered adoration; she'd never seen a flush to his cheeks before, but now it was a soft rosy color that looked almost healthy on the natural pallor of his skin. His lips parted and he breathed heavily. A hand shifted from her waist back to her face, and he stroked her cheek with his fingertips.

"Aldrik," she whispered, her lips aflame. She still felt inebriated on his nearness; however, without the immediate distraction of his mouth, confusion began to slip back into her brain. "What about Elecia?" she whispered—just the name made the happy bubbles in her stomach settle.

"Come," Aldrik said, taking her hands in his as he led her back to the couch. This time she sat next to him. "Who do you think Elecia is?"

"I don't know." Vhalla didn't want to play guessing games, and her theories on Elecia ran as long as the Great Imperial Way. Thankfully, Aldrik didn't drag her along.

"Elecia is my cousin."

"What?" Vhalla asked on a quick inhale of air.

A knowing grin curled up the corners of his mouth at her obvious shock. "My mother, as I'm sure you know, was a Western princess. When the West was overthrown, her father was removed from his throne as king. But in an effort for a peaceful transition, his eldest son—my Uncle Ophain—was appointed as the Lord of the West. My uncle had a son who later married a Northern woman and had a daughter."

"Elecia?" Vhalla whispered, wide-eyed, mentally following along. It explained everything about the woman. Her appearance, her demeanor, her protectiveness of Aldrik, Vhalla understood it all.

Aldrik nodded. "She was born when I was seven. We made a trip back to the West not long after but she was only a toddler. I didn't know her well until we were adults," he continued.

There was a ringing in Vhalla's ears and relief tingled across her skin. *Elecia wasn't a lover.* She wasn't his betrothed. She was his family.

"I thought you already knew."

"How would I have known?" Vhalla asked, a touch exasperated. She read a lot of books but it wasn't as though she specifically studied lineages and would just happen to recall that bit of information.

"We have the same name," Aldrik said, matter-of-factly.

"What?" Vhalla regarded him as though he was crazy.

"Ci'Dan, my mother's family name."

The mysterious "C" finally had an explanation.

"Aldrik *Ci'Dan* Solaris," Vhalla whispered. "Then, what was she doing in your room—at night?" Vhalla refrained from commenting on their extremely casual state of dress.

"Ah, that." Aldrik glanced away. "I didn't say anything before because I was worried it wouldn't work."

"What?" Vhalla asked, wondering what other obvious thing she could have missed.

"Elecia is a Groundbreaker. She's talented in a great many things, but healing is something she has a natural gift for. She reads bodies like books." Aldrik smiled and stood. "Vhalla, look at me." She pursed her lips together, seeing nothing. "With magic sight."

Vhalla shifted her vision and saw a sight unlike any she'd seen before. His body was swathed in a golden-white flame, so brilliant that his skin glowed faintly. She'd never seen him so bright. It was then she realized the reason. The dark spot at his side was gone.

Vhalla was on her feet, reaching out and placing her hand on his hip. She shifted back her vision and looked up at his face. Aldrik continued to smile through Vhalla's surprise.

"Y-you're cured?" she asked tentatively.

"I am," he beamed. "It was a process, though; it took almost two days of her work and mine. She was here around the clock."

Vhalla breathed slowly. She had never seen the prince smile so much. Laughter bubbled up from her stomach and escaped with a joyous melody. As long as she had known him he had been suffering from this wound. It was literally a dark spot on him for months. Now he was free.

"I wish I could've helped," she said softly.

"I didn't want to tax you," he replied, timidly running his fingers over her cheek. They left a flush in their wake. "Especially not after the sandstorm."

"Next time, at least tell me," she said sternly.

"I promise," Aldrik vowed.

"I thought . . ." Vhalla shook her head with a small laugh. "I thought you were with her," she confessed, looking away.

"I thought everything was obvious to you," he said softly, astounded at her confusion. "Not just about Elecia, but—" Aldrik ran a hand across his hair, noticing the mess she'd made in the back earlier with a small smile, "—with everything. I was certain that, with how I acted toward only you, you knew."

Vhalla blushed and stared at her toes. Larel had tried to tell her. It would be false if Vhalla said she hadn't hoped. But of course she had never thought it was true. There was always a more likely, convenient explanation. Something else crossed her mind and her eyes snapped back to his.

"If you're cured, then the Bond . . . is it?" She felt a small panic rising in her.

Aldrik chuckled. "It is still there. My sincere apologies, Vhalla Yarl, but to the best knowledge of the academic community of sorcerers, we are Bound for life."

"Forgive me for not being torn up over that." She smiled from ear to ear.

He chuckled and squeezed her hand lightly.

Vhalla sat back onto the couch with a relieved sigh. The past half hour hit her all at once, and she suddenly felt exhausted. Aldrik returned to his place next to her, placing his arm behind her, his side flush against hers, and she leaned into him instinctively. Her head rested on his shoulder, and she was pleased to find he made no motion away.

"Vhalla," he whispered softly.

"Aldrik?" she replied, her eyes dipping closed as she allowed herself to enjoy his warmth.

"Did you mean what you said? Or was it just a moment?"

Vhalla sat up straighter to study his face. "What?"

"Earlier." Aldrik glanced away. "You told me that, your feelings . . ."

Vhalla paused, hesitant. *Was he giving her the choice?* Was he asking her to decide? He seemed unable to meet her gaze and looked across the room at nothing in particular. Vhalla took a shaky breath. Reaching out, she put her fingertips under his chin and guided his eyes back to hers.

"Aldrik, it was *not* an impulse," Vhalla spoke slowly and deliberately. "It was not even the first time I had said it aloud." She smiled softly at his surprise.

"When?" His lips barely moved.

"When did I admit it? Only after the sandstorm. When

did it happen? Long before that." She shrugged slightly; it was hopeless to attempt denial. Vhalla returned her hand to his, looking at their intertwined fingers. The sight of that alone filled her with joy.

"I tried," he sighed, the sorrow in his voice contrasting starkly the tone of their conversations prior. "I didn't expect it, then I didn't want it to happen. I tried to explain it to you the day of the verdict. Being involved with me at all is dangerous."

"I don't care." It came out of her mouth before she had time to filter it. But as he shook his head at her she found she didn't regret it.

Aldrik chuckled softly and stood. "You're a rather impossible woman."

"Pot meet kettle." Vhalla gave him a snarky grin.

She was rewarded with the rich sound of his laughter as Aldrik helped her to her feet. "I must do some work," he explained his apologetic look.

"On what?" Vhalla stalled him, not ready to be dismissed.

"Strategy, planning for the troop addition, acquiring any extra rations we may need," Aldrik listed.

"Could I help?" Vhalla was glad that she hadn't thought the words through first, otherwise she may not have said them. Offering to help the crown prince with matters of state was too bold, too far beyond her station. *Then again, so was kissing him.* Vhalla shifted her weight from one foot to the other, weighing his surprised stare.

"Actually," Aldrik thought aloud, "you could."

Aldrik led her over to the table eagerly. He scattered the papers and began to give her an overview. Vhalla was surprised to find how good it felt to use her mind again. For months she'd been out of her element, away from books and knowledge. It was like stretching a muscle that'd been languishing for far too long.

He twirled a gold-tipped raven's feather quill between his fingers as he spoke, and Vhalla chewed thoughtfully on the end of a spare she'd made her own. One positive, she discovered, about her intellect was that she could focus on what he was saying and his dexterous fingers at the same time. Vhalla missed nothing, his knowledge or how nimble his long hands actually were.

"How many stone's worth of smoked meat is being provided by the West?" Aldrik asked from the other end of the table.

"Two-thousand," Vhalla replied, quickly marking the numbers on a new list as he'd showed her.

"That's not enough," he mumbled. "We'll need to ask the Western lords for more."

Vhalla stopped her quill, looking across at the dark-haired prince who was deep in thought. She could almost hear the words echoing through his mind. "I know how you could get more."

"What?" Aldrik looked up, startled.

She took a deep breath, hoping she'd arranged her thoughts well enough. "The West survives off shrub game and fishing from the coast as well as imports from the East and South." She recalled reading. "You can't ask for any more from the lords and ladies this far into the Waste. They're likely already worried about making it through the off-seasons of trading."

"So then what do you propose?" Aldrik rested his fingertips on the table, assessing her as a prince.

Vhalla faltered, but only briefly. She knew what she'd read and lived. "Every year in Paca, Cyven, there's a Festival of the Sun with prize hogs. They're slaughtered shortly after and smoked in the winter to be sold at the Crossroads. It's part of a sort of meat migration that supports the West."

Aldrik's eyes glittered, suddenly following along.

"The Empire buys eighty percent or so, of this influx in the market and you'd likely have your difference for the war. But, to make sure the Western lords and ladies don't worry about their storehouses, you should send the farmers back to the East with orders to return with extra grain and subsidize the cost of the farmer's travel," Vhalla finished.

"Yes," Aldrik breathed, a wide smile arcing across his lips. "The double round of trading should also help the economies of both East and West."

He was furiously scribbling, folding three quick letters, and sealing them with some heated wax. Vhalla watched his golden seal move in shock. *Had she just done that?*

"I should get these off immediately." Aldrik started for the door, pausing briefly to stare at her in what Vhalla dared to say was awe. "When I return, I'd like to run a few more thoughts by you."

"Of course, my prince." Her own smile broke through her daze.

Aldrik returned in record time and their previously quiet work was suddenly very chatty. Vhalla learned quickly that the prince wanted her to challenge him. It went against everything she'd ever been taught to oppose the prince's word, but Aldrik thrived off it. He held nothing back, and Vhalla had to draw from every book she'd ever read on the geography, history, economies, and people of the Empire to keep up.

It was exhilarating, and exhausting.

Vhalla put her hands on the small of her back and stretched. The sun had begun to hang low, turning the room into a kaleidoscope of rich colors cast by the stained glass window. "Do you ever stop working?"

He grinned at her. Aldrik couldn't hide his enjoyment all afternoon and neither could Vhalla. "An Empire doesn't run itself." He tapped his quill on the table twice. "And, I'm three times as productive with you around, so I must take full advantage of that. I had no idea I was with such a natural stateswoman."

Vhalla blushed.

"Are you hungry?" He stared at the stained glass a moment before pulling his watch from his pocket. Time had crept up on him as well.

"A little."

"What would you like? I will get you anything you desire." Aldrik grabbed the coat he'd discarded on the floor at some point in the afternoon and shrugged himself into it.

"Anything?" she asked.

"I *am* the crown prince," he smirked.

"Such an abuse of power," she scolded teasingly.

Aldrik straightened, finishing the buttons at his neck. "The things we do for love." He shrugged, running his hands over his hair.

Vhalla's eyes widened. She stared at him as he turned back to face her, struggling with the meaning of those words. "Aldrik," she whispered.

He paused, his hands dropping to his sides. "Food?"

"Surprise me." Food had become the farthest thing from her mind.

He nodded and strode briskly out of the room.

Vhalla stared at the door dumbly before turning to one of the candles on the table. She watched the flame, losing herself to her thoughts. It seemed to radiate his essence, echoing Aldrik's words in every flicker. Vhalla reached out a hand, running it over the top of the fire absentmindedly.

Aldrik returned faster than expected. "It will be up—" His words faltered. "What are you doing?"

"Oh, something that children dare each other to do. Well, children who aren't Firebearers." Vhalla laughed, quickly stopping when Aldrik's intent expression hadn't changed. "It doesn't hurt," she explained, thinking he may have no idea what non-Firebearers could manage when it came to fire.

"Are you certain?" His eyes flicked to her hand.

Vhalla returned her attention to the appendage in question and stared in shock. Her fingers had been directly atop the flame the whole conversation, frozen from the moment he'd caught her. She stared dumbly, watching the fire flicker over her skin as nothing more than heat.

"What . . ." she whispered in confusion, pulling her hand from the candle. Vhalla stared at her fingers; they weren't even red. Aldrik crossed the room, inspecting as well. "Why am I not burned?"

"Likely the Bond," he whispered, suddenly fishing for a blank piece of parchment to scribble across. "You have some of my magic in you, and I have some of yours in me, maybe more than *some* with the Joining. I cannot burn myself with my own flames so it stands to reason that such protection could extend to you."

"My wind has never affected you like it does others." He considered her thoughtfully and Vhalla used his paused expression as an invitation to continue. "The twister on the Night of Fire and Wind."

It surprised her the ease to which the infamous event could roll off her tongue. It still left a lingering sour taste in Vhalla's mouth, the reminder of something foul. But it no longer repulsed her.

"Let's test it?" she suggested. "Your fire is easier than my wind."

Aldrik held out a fist, opening it for a dim spark, mostly red with a hint of orange. She knew he could make the flame surround her hand just as easily but instead it remained in his palm. He looked to her uncertainly and Vhalla realized he was waiting for her.

She wanted to laugh. Wasn't that how it always was between them? He held out knowledge, power, desire, in his palm just before her. But he never took the step forward, he never forced it upon her. Their whole relationship he stood waiting. Every time, she met him.

Vhalla sunk her fingers bravely into the inviting warmth. It wasn't quite like the wind, but something tingled on the edge of her senses that she could only describe as the essence of fire. She smiled in awe.

Aldrik's hand closed suddenly around hers. Tongues of flame slithered between their fingers, eagerly tickling up her arm and singing her tunic. At such close proximity they cast a breathtaking array of reds, oranges, and yellows over the angular visage of the crown prince. He raised his other palm to her cheek, fire glittering under his thumb as he ran it over her flesh.

Vhalla's eyes fluttered closed, his magic rubbing against hers like a whispering invitation. It was a foreign and savory sensation that quickly enthralled and commanded her. She obliged his light tugs on her chin, guiding her forward and upward. Aldrik's lips ghosted across hers and Vhalla inhaled sharply, breathing fire imbued with his raw essence.

A knock on the door startled the two apart. The flames vanished quickly. "Don't worry," he whispered. "I am always a private person so that no one questions when I have a reason to be." The prince wore a conspiratorial grin. "Leave it," he called through the door.

Vhalla ran her fingers over her lips. Food was the last thing on her mind. She'd found a different sort of sustenance.

Aldrik pushed in a rolling tray with a veritable feast, quickly motioning to it when he caught her hungry look. Vhalla witnessed the instant flush on his cheeks, his shorter breaths. She knew if she were to put a palm on his chest his heart would be racing, racing at the same speed as hers.

"We're going to waste so much food." With a light laugh, she eased away from the heated moment.

They ended up pushing together the two chaises, making a platform upon which they dined. Aldrik sat in one corner of the half square the backs made when put together and Vhalla occupied the other. He told her the different foods that surrounded them with expert precision, offering insights onto their origins or the best way to enjoy them. They spoke about dining etiquette and differences in cultures.

"Do you like the West or the South more?" she asked between bites.

"For what? Food?" He spooned a bit of rice.

"Everything," she specified.

"That is a hard choice. Sorcerers are undoubtedly treated better in the West; I'm generally more loved here as a result. But I grew up in the South; my ties here are only through visiting. The palace is my home." Aldrik turned the question to her. "And you? East or South?"

Vhalla chewed on her food a moment to give herself time to think. "It's not too difficult really . . . I come from very little in the East." Vhalla looked down at the food; she hated the reminders of who she really was at times like this. They shattered her fantasies. "The palace is home for me also in most ways."

"What is your childhood home like?" Aldrik stretched to reach a platter.

The idea of home held a bittersweet sort of beauty. "My home, it's a small place. It's stone, a roof that was badly in need of replacement the last time I was there. We've a wooden barn to keep a horse for plow."

"I would like to see it," he said casually. Vhalla couldn't stop herself from laughing, and he frowned at her. "I would."

"The crown prince? In Leoul? In my home?" Vhalla's laughter

rang out again. "My father may disown me for letting someone like you inside."

The rest of the conversation was relaxed and easy between them. They spoke, lounged with food about them on the chaises and table, and talked well into the evening about everything and nothing. When it was clear they'd both had their fill, he got up to clean the plates and Vhalla helped. Old habits died hard; it felt strange to see the prince of the realm cleaning his own food when she was there. He insisted he could do it himself—she insisted she would help him.

She hovered as Aldrik returned from placing the cart in the hall for the wait staff to take care of. The outside of the stained glass was dark and Vhalla knew it was late.

"I should go," she whispered.

Aldrik stared at her silently for a long moment, taking both hands in his. "Stay."

"Aldrik?" Vhalla questioned.

"Stay here," he affirmed. Vhalla bit her lip, unsure of what he was really asking. "I have more than enough space. Elecia said the chaises are comfortable."

"Why?"

"Because I want you near me. I don't want you to leave." His directness pierced her and she felt her heart begin to pick up the same speed as earlier.

"I shouldn't." Her words were weak and faint. *Was he asking what she thought he was?*

"You're right." He nodded, his voice was soft and deep. "Will you?"

Vhalla tried to find grounds to object. Fritz and Larel surely wouldn't care, and there were few other people who would notice her absence. He hadn't explicitly spoken of her sharing his bed, but would it happen? Vhalla swallowed hard. If it did, *was she ready for it?* If she wasn't, she knew Aldrik wouldn't force it upon her. All of Vhalla's reason objected that it was a poor decision.

But she was too overwhelmed by his proximity.

"I will. I'll stay," she whispered.

He laughed softly with a shake of his head. "It's the first time."

"What is?"

"That I've asked a woman to stay with me while being completely uncertain about how she will respond." Aldrik looked at her in relief. It was an odd thing to say, but Prince Baldair's words came back to Vhalla. His stories of the hunt, of his brother knowing exactly what would happen, exactly what even she would do. Yet, it seemed like the infamous silver-tongued prince hadn't calculated what was happening between them. Her own relief spread over her.

"How many times have you asked a woman to stay with you?" she teased gently.

"Well," Aldrik seemed to be at a loss for words. "Before this? Not many who mattered even slightly."

Vhalla felt a flush rise across her whole body. She took a half step closer, closing the gap between them. Aldrik tilted his cheek into her bold fingertips as they made feather-light trails over his pronounced cheekbone. Vhalla outlined his brow, down over the bump in his nose, the edge of his jaw, she wanted to remember every detail exactly. Her thumb brushed the corner of his lips and she felt herself move without thinking.

Aldrik tilted his head to meet her halfway, ensnaring her in a slow and purposeful kiss. Every shift, every brief opening of his mouth, made her ache for more. Aldrik's fingers buried themselves in her hair. She was pulled against him, sighing in soft release as she felt his magic slip over her skin once more.

The prince pulled away suddenly.

Vhalla swallowed, blinking. "Aldrik . . ." Her voice was strange even to her own ears, desire changing it.

"I love you, Vhalla," Aldrik forced himself to say.

Vhalla pulled her head back in shock, her eyes wide. Her heart pounded and she repeated his words in her mind. "*What?*" Somehow she'd pushed from her consciousness the notion of him having the same feelings for her as she had for him.

"I love you," he repeated, a determined fire lighting his eyes. "It is one of the worst things I could ever do," Aldrik confessed. "I swear to the Mother, I have tried not to damn you with it. But you're a rather persistent, beautiful presence in my life. And, for once, the silver-tongued prince is tired of pretending."

CHAPTER 19

VHALLA SHIFTED A pile of blankets about her. Her head was hazy with sleep as she rolled over. Long fingers ran through her hair, snagging lightly on tangles. She nestled into the pillow, not opening her eyes. Vhalla reached out for Aldrik under the covers, finding him but unable to touch. Her eyes cracked open.

"Good morning." Aldrik sat next to her on top of the blankets. He leaned against pillows and the headboard. His far knee was bent, a board with papers on top of it. Vhalla noted the fingers of his right hand were already stained with ink; he must have been at it for a while.

"Good morning, my prince." She smiled up at him. Vhalla remembered curling up with him on the chaises for a thousand kisses the night before, but she couldn't seem to recall how they'd made it to the bed. However, it was a mountain of fluff that she could sink into; her clothes were still in place; and she didn't recall taking anything that would have made her lose her head, so she wasn't particularly worried about anything untoward.

Vhalla propped herself up on her elbows, rubbing her eyes. The curtains in the side room had been pulled back a tad and the beam of sunlight cutting through the air told her that it was sometime past dawn. "What time is it?"

Aldrik shifted. He only wore a cotton shirt—black this time—and black pants. Vhalla mused over how she had never seen him in anything less than long sleeves and long pants, save for the night with Elecia. He pulled a familiar silver watch from his pocket.

"Just after eight-thirty." He clicked the watch closed and stashed it away.

"Just after eight-thirty and you're up and working. *And* you've bathed." She noted his hair was fixed. "Do you sleep?" The pillow muffled the end of her words as she fell back into it.

"Normally, not very much." His quill scratched against the parchment.

"Normally?" she repeated, twisting her face to look at him from under the blankets.

"I slept well last night."

"How did we make it to the bed?" she couldn't help but ask.

"I brought you in when I noticed you'd passed out. I suppose my story on the Kingdom of Mhashan was *that* boring." Aldrik glanced at her from the corners of his eyes.

Vhalla laughed guiltily.

"Elecia was right though," he continued. "I couldn't find one complaint with the chaises."

Vhalla chewed that over for a second. "Wait," she paused, "*you* slept on the couches?" Vhalla rolled onto her side to look up at him.

"Of course." His brow furrowed slightly. "Did you think I would creep into your bed as you slept and spend the night lying with you without your permission?"

Vhalla stared at him. She had assumed falling asleep in his arms after kissing half the night away to be permission enough, but the chivalry in the statement was noted. However, any tenderness over the sentiment was quickly lost to laughter.

"What?" he asked, staring at her queerly.

"I kicked the crown prince out of his bed." She rolled onto her back with laughter. "Oh, that is a story I wish I could share with someone."

Aldrik grabbed the blankets and threw them over her face. "You're annoying in the morning," he said with a hint of amusement.

It sent Vhalla into a fit of giggles. "Oh I am sorry, mighty Aldrik." She sat up, throwing the covers off her. "Am I a disturbance to your routine?" Vhalla put her hands on the bed between them and leaned over.

"Very much so," he smirked.

"Fine, then I shall leave promptly." Vhalla swung her feet off the bed.

She heard the rustle of his papers as he reached and grabbed her shoulders, pulling her onto his lap. He leaned over, and his lips were on hers. Vhalla sighed softly, she could get used to waking in this manner.

"I haven't cleaned my mouth yet." She quickly covered it with her hand as he pulled away.

"I know. It's foul too. Washroom is there." He grinned and pointed at an adjacent door.

Vhalla glared at him as she stood. She never knew a man who could be such an ass while still being so handsome. The moment the bathroom door closed, Vhalla suppressed another fit of giggles.

It was absolutely insane what was happening. It was absolutely insane how happy she was. Vhalla hummed as she ran her hand across the counter. It was a dark black marble, and the spigot was cast in gold. The tub was large enough for four people to sit comfortably, like a small pool carved from stone. There was an adjacent closet filled with more clothing than she knew he carried with him on the journey. The whole room was as opulent as the building itself, and Vhalla couldn't believe that she had a place here.

There were a few bottles on the counter. She noticed one or two mostly empty clerical elixirs among them. Vhalla mused over which one he used for his hair, smelling a few that had the fresh scent of eucalyptus, as she located the one to cleanse her mouth with. Vhalla washed her face and ran her wet hands through her hair. It stayed back slightly from the dampness and she laughed.

"Look, I'm you." Vhalla opened the door.

He glanced at her and then returned to his papers. "It looks awful," he murmured.

"Now, now, don't be mean to yourself," she laughed lightly, sitting across from him on the end of the bed. "I think it's striking on you." Vhalla ran her fingers through her hair, teasing it back into its normal mess. Aldrik looked over his papers at her and said nothing, though she could have sworn there were the makings of a smile on his face.

"So what will you be doing today?" he asked.

"I'm not sure. I suppose I'll go back and . . . see what everyone else is up to." Vhalla shrugged.

"Will you return tonight?" Aldrik paused, searching for her reaction.

"Tonight?" She hadn't thought of it.

"Yes, my parrot." He grinned at her scowl. "Tonight, will you come back?" Aldrik placed his papers carefully on the pillows she previously occupied. He returned his quill to the inkpot on the bedside table.

"Do you wish it?" Vhalla wanted to hear him say it directly.

"I do." Aldrik nodded.

"Then I will."

"Do you wish it?" he returned the question.

"Of course I do." Aldrik seemed relieved by her response. "Being near you is—"

There was a pounding on the door; they both looked out to the other room. Vhalla turned back to him, a deep scowl written across Aldrik's features.

"Brother?" a voice boomed from the hallway. "Are you awake?"

"Stay here," he said softly to her.

Vhalla nodded silently.

Aldrik swung his feet off the bed and stood. He started for the door and paused briefly. Wrapping his hand around the back of her head, Aldrik leaned down and kissed her forehead lightly. She beamed up at him and he gave her a tired smile.

He closed the sliding paper-screen doors behind him as he left the room. Vhalla fell back on the bed with a contented sigh. She would be happy to never leave the Crossroads. The war could just go on as it was, and the Emperor could return back to the South to rule. She would be happy if she and Aldrik could hide away here forever.

Vhalla held her breath as she heard the door open.

"Good morning, brother." She could hear Prince Baldair entering the room as he spoke, even though Vhalla was fairly certain that he hadn't been given permission to by his older brother.

"Baldair," Aldrik said curtly. Even she had a hard time imagining that voice belonging to the man who laid kisses upon her moments before. "To what do I owe this . . . *pleasure?*"

"I'm not interrupting anything, am I?" the younger brother inquired.

"Clearly not," Aldrik sighed. "Is that all you came for?"

"Ah no, scouts have arrived. The Western forces will be joining us within an hour, two at most." Vhalla heard Prince Baldair's voice drawing closer.

"Oh? Excellent, I shall need to prepare for their arrival then." Aldrik's voice was also louder.

Vhalla sat. *Should she hide?*

Aldrik's shadow appeared on the other side of the carved doors, blocking his brother's path. "If you'll excuse me."

"Good morning, Vhalla," Prince Baldair called.

Her stomach turned to stone. *One night*, she had indulged herself for one night and the world couldn't even give her that.

"You look rather foolish shouting at empty rooms," Aldrik drawled.

She wondered how he kept his composure so well.

"You look rather foolish, brother, for being caught with something so simple," Prince Baldair retorted. "You picked this place for their security, for their record keeping." His laughter rang out and Vhalla winced, wondering how she ever thought it to be a charming sound. "It's amazing for you to make a mistake so simple."

"And what, pray tell, is that mistake?" Aldrik growled.

Vhalla's heart raced. She didn't have to see him to know his jaw was clenched tight; he might even have a hand in a fist, he was telling his brother exactly what he wanted to hear without using a single word.

"A one Miss Vhalla Yarl was recorded in last night, but was never recorded out," Prince Baldair proclaimed, almost victoriously. Vhalla wanted to panic, but the first emotion was a strange curiosity—Prince Baldair was checking on his brother. That wasn't information he could have accidently happened across. "Really, brother, it isn't like you; it's sloppy."

"It sounds like all that is sloppy is their record keeping," Aldrik attempted.

She wondered if it sounded more convincing to a person who wasn't her.

"What do you both think you're doing?" Prince Baldair retorted. He was clearly not buying what Aldrik was selling.

"Nothing that you need to concern yourself with," Aldrik snarled.

Vhalla cringed, realizing what was coming.

"Oh? No more denials?" Aldrik's brother had caught him in his own words. "Do not let yourself be played by him, Vhalla." She bit her lip to keep from calling out and putting the younger prince in his place.

"Enough of this. *Out, Baldair.*" Aldrik's patience was almost gone.

"Fine, Aldrik, if you wish to be that way." She heard the click of Prince Baldair's boots fading away. "But you should doctor the book before Father has a chance to see."

"Thank you," Aldrik said begrudgingly.

Vhalla blinked. He was thanking his brother, after all that? She couldn't fathom a reason.

"I'll see you within an hour." The door closing signaled the younger prince's departure.

Aldrik pulled back the sliding doors, and Vhalla stared at him hopelessly. He picked up on her emotion and crossed quickly to sit next to her, taking her hands in his.

"It's okay." He raised her knuckles to his lips. "It's all right."

"But . . ." she protested weakly.

"I'll change the book. It will be no trouble." Aldrik cupped her cheek.

"Your brother?" she asked.

"Ignore him," Aldrik sighed.

"Why is he like this?" Vhalla asked, allowing her prince's touch to calm her.

"It's a long story between us. But for now, I must go change that book before it has a chance to be brought to my father's attention."

Judging from the way Aldrik spoke, it was a long story she would not be hearing. "What would happen if your father saw it?" Vhalla knew Prince Baldair entertained women all the time. While she hardly wanted to be thought as that type of woman, especially to Aldrik, it seemed rather unfair one brother could get away with having women in his room and the other could not.

"Don't worry yourself with it," he sighed.

"What would happen?" she pressed. "Aldrik, stop shutting me out. Even if you think it's for my own good."

He averted his eyes. "I need to prepare for the troop arrival."

"*What would happen?*" she snapped. He looked back at her, startled. Vhalla took a deep breath, calming herself. "Just tell me."

"After I gave my testimony at your trial, my father spoke with me." The prince's voice was faint and his eyes never found hers. "He asked if you were going to be a problem."

"A problem?" she whispered. Something about his tone unnerved her more than the entire exchange with Prince Baldair.

"A . . . *distraction* from my obligations." He finally turned back to her. "I'm sorry."

"For what?" Vhalla was confused.

The prince just sighed and rested his forehead in his palm. "I told my father that I saw you for what you were. A tool that we needed and nothing more. That I had you in my palms, and you would do as I told you. That it—*we*—were nothing more than a means to that end." Her chest tightened at the weakness in his voice. "Vhalla, I don't—"

"I know." She cut him off. It hurt to hear he said it, but she knew he only did what he felt was best. Or at least, she hoped. He looked at her skeptically and she squeezed his hand lightly.

"My father told me that he hoped I was correct because too much rested on my shoulders for the Empire to exhaust or invest much on a common girl, no matter how magically special." Aldrik rolled his eyes at the paraphrased statements.

"Your brother was there, wasn't he?" Vhalla realized.

Aldrik gave her a small nod.

If not for your sake, then his, Prince Baldair's words repeated in her mind. *He's using you, Vhalla.* It made her pause. Baldair would've seen all of Aldrik's interactions with her in a very different light than she did—as the object of the crown prince's affections.

"What will your father do? If he . . ."

"If he found out you stayed the night with me?" Aldrik asked. "Or that I've fallen in love with that special common girl?" He smiled sadly at her.

"Both?" Vhalla reminded her insides that now was not the time to be fluttering.

"The former, I may be able to talk my way out of." Aldrik pinched the bridge of his nose. "The later, I'm not sure."

Vhalla took it for the truth, though something in the distance of his eyes made her suspect that he had a guess. She let it drop; perhaps some things were better left unsaid. "Thank you."

"For what?"

"For telling me honestly." It wasn't lost on Vhalla how hard it likely was for him.

Aldrik laughed and shook his head. Vhalla pulled him closer to her and he obliged, leaning forward. Their lips met briefly, but that was all it took to reassure her about almost everything she thought she knew in the world.

"You need to get ready and edit that book."

Vhalla stood, and he grabbed her wrist. "Will you come again tonight still?"

She blinked at his question. After all he just told her?

"I don't know if that's really—" she started, knowing full well now that it wasn't just a bad idea, but a potentially dangerous one.

"There's a secret entrance," he said quickly.

Vhalla stared incredulously at him. "If there was a secret entrance, how come I didn't use that to begin with?"

"Because I had a reason to see you." A sly lopsided grin tugged at his lips. "Because I wasn't expecting you to stay the night."

Vhalla blushed and averted her eyes from his handsome face. "It's still a poor choice," she whispered.

"It always will be." Aldrik stood. Her breath quickened by his proximity alone. He hooked his fingers under her chin and pulled her face upward gently. "If you want to make the widely accepted *appropriate* decision, then leave now, have mercy and end this before you entice me further. Because I promise, this will never be easy—for either of us—and I refuse to love you halfway."

Once again, she felt the choice given to her. The problems were nothing she hadn't told herself before. The challenges nothing she didn't already realize. Yet, hearing him say it made it all the more terrifying. He seemed frightened as well, and if it frightened him, she had every right to be scared. But he also acknowledged it, telling her that he would fight if she would. There were a thousand things she wanted to reply with.

"What time?" were the only words that left her mouth.

"Six?" Aldrik's face found its smile again, and Vhalla felt warm knowing she contributed to it.

"That's fine."

Aldrik nodded and led her out into the main room and behind the bar that occupied the space to the left of the doorway. Walking over to a shelf, Aldrik pulled a bottle and Vhalla was surprised to see it attached to a hidden metal lever. There was a click from somewhere in the wall, and he tugged open the shelves to reveal a passage. As they descended the short distance, a mote of light appeared over his shoulder.

"How did you know this was here?" she asked.

"I don't enjoy feeling like I could be trapped somewhere. We stayed at this hotel at the start of the war, and I've insisted on it ever since after the owner showed this to me," Aldrik explained as they reached the ground floor. "Six," he affirmed.

She nodded.

"Be sharp, I'm the only one who can open this door."

"I'll be here, I promise."

He pressed his lips to her forehead. "Take care, lest I have to burn the Crossroads to the ground in a rage."

Vhalla laughed softly, very well realizing that it may not entirely be a jest. She grinned up at him playfully. "Take care yourself, lest I have to blow the Crossroads away in a rage." She was rewarded for her cheekiness with his laugher and another firm kiss.

Aldrik placed his palm on the door and pushed. Vhalla realized the truth of what he said earlier as the metal where a lock or knob should be began to melt around his hand. The molten metal parted and the door swung open. Vhalla stepped into the light beyond. She said nothing and he gave her a nod, closing the door that looked like the stone of the outside wall.

Vhalla waited a moment, her head reeling from all that had happened. Taking a breath, she turned and started the walk through the alleyways around the building and back to the main square. Somewhere along the way she found herself unable to contain giddy laughter.

Her hotel's lobby was quiet, and Vhalla was thankful she could sneak up the stairs and into her room. Vhalla turned around the door, leaning against it with a blissful sigh. If this was a dream, she never wanted to wake.

"Fritz, get up; she's back." Larel stirred.

"What are you two doing here?" Vhalla blinked at the two people occupying her bed.

"Fritz, *up*." Larel shoved at the man sleeping next to her.

"Larel, nooo . . ." Fritz pulled the covers over his head.

"*She's back,*" Larel hissed.

Fritz was suddenly also sitting at attention.

"Good morning, Fritz, Larel," Vhalla greeted them like a girl caught out late by her parents.

Fritz was across the room in a moment, his hands on her shoulders. "Don't you 'good morning' me." He peered at her. "You were out all night! We were worried!"

Well, that explained why they had decided to occupy her room. "I'm sorry," she said honestly.

"We couldn't even ask someone because, well, we didn't know if . . ." Fritz glanced back to Larel.

"If you stayed with him," Larel finished.

Fritz gaped at the Western woman but then turned back to Vhalla with a nod. "*So?*" Fritz asked.

Even Larel examined her quizzically.

Vhalla sighed. It wasn't that she had never planned on telling them, or that she hadn't expected them to find out, but it felt like half the world had discovered her secret within the first few hours of it happening. "Yes, I did."

Fritz squeaked. He seemed to vibrate with excitement. "Tell—us—*everything.*" He punctuated his words, making each a demand.

"She doesn't have to tell us *anything,*" Larel scolded. He whimpered at the other woman.

"I'm sorry for making you worry, foremost," Vhalla apologized. "It kind of just, happened . . . obviously." Fritz's excitement put the giddy feeling back in her chest. "There's not much to tell, though. We didn't . . ." Vhalla blushed, realizing what people would likely think. "We didn't even share a bed." It was a half-truth, they didn't share a bed for the whole night but she had fallen asleep in his arms and woke up with him next to her.

"Elecia?" Fritz asked.

Vhalla shook her head. "Elecia *Ci'Dan* is his half-Northern, half-Western, cousin. Aldrik *Ci'Dan* Solaris," Vhalla explained. If her face had looked anything like theirs at the revelation of that fact then it was no wonder Aldrik had gained amusement from it.

"Of course," Larel groaned and put her face into her hands. "We're so dumb."

"So then, if you didn't share his bed . . . what did you do?" Fritz seemed genuinely confused.

"He worked, some magic," Vhalla outlined vaguely.

"You're adorable," Larel said knowingly, earning a look from her and Fritz. "You're going back tonight, aren't you?"

"How did you . . .?" Vhalla wondered if the woman was psychic.

"You are?" Fritz asked, dumbstruck. Vhalla could only blush. "By the Mother, this is the most insane thing I've ever heard of! Prince Aldrik? The Fire Lord? The black prince? He whose temper is short and his wrath is long?"

"And your point is?" Vhalla peered at him.

"He's acting like a normal man!" Fritz laughed.

Even Larel found a conspiratorial smile. Vhalla hid her face, embarrassed.

Vhalla avoided filling them in on many more details. She'd already inadvertently revealed more than she intended, and she wanted some things kept private. They spared her further inquiry and kept Vhalla company as she filled her pack with a few things for the night.

Hours later, and Vhalla was slipping back into a side alley off a cart path. She glanced about—not a soul was nearby. Vhalla's heart beat nervously as she prayed that she arrived early enough and hadn't missed him.

The passage entry swung open and Aldrik wore an excited

grin. Vhalla slipped inside and he closed the door, welding it shut. Vhalla placed her hands on his hips and leaned up. He obliged, tilting his head down. Kissing him enflamed a hunger that had been growing throughout the day. Now that she had him, all she wanted was him. Her need was insatiable. The crown prince sighed softly into her mouth, a deep noise rumbling the back of his throat that she hungrily consumed. Vhalla moved her hands to his neck and he eagerly scooped her up. Vhalla tried to use the passion-heat between them to fuse their bodies from hips to chest. Aldrik clutched her tighter, his fingertips pressing against her woolen tunic as if to bore holes in pursuit of her skin. Vhalla's lips parted slightly, but he pulled away quickly with a shake of his head.

"We can't." His voice was deliciously thick, making her want to be all the closer to him. "Not right now. I have someone I want you to meet."

Vhalla's curiosity hid the resentment for having to stop what they had started. Aldrik intertwined his fingers with hers as they walked up the stairs.

"I want you to know," he said softly, "I trust him *completely*, so don't fret. I would've told you earlier, but his presence was a surprise for me also." He didn't give her a chance to ask who he was talking about as Aldrik pushed open the portal to his room.

Vhalla stepped in first, tentatively. She set her bag next to the hidden door as Aldrik settled it back into place. Vhalla scanned the room, her gaze falling on a man sitting on the couch in its center. There were papers and ledgers spread out on the table, and Vhalla could instantly tell the chaise Aldrik had occupied by the gold-tipped quill and ink that sat out without an owner.

The man stood, and Vhalla brought her hands together, pulling at her fingers. He was as tall as, or maybe even a little taller than, Aldrik. His black hair was cut very short and it seemed to spike up slightly in odd directions. He had a closely trimmed dark beard that ran along his jawline and up his chin to his lower lip. None of this was what startled her though. His eyes were like looking into a mirror image of a very familiar set that she was particularly fond of.

Aldrik walked behind her, placing a palm on the small of her back to help her find her feet again. The man studied her with a guarded gaze as she rounded the bar and crossed the room over to the sitting area. Aldrik held out a hand in the man's direction.

"Vhalla, meet Ophain Ci'Dan, my mother's brother and Lord of the West."

She glanced between the men; Aldrik had a relaxed smile, the other man continued to assess her with interest.

"Vhalla Yarl," the lord said slowly, his voice was among the deepest she'd ever heard. "I have been looking forward to meeting you."

CHAPTER 20

VHALLA SOUGHT REAFFIRMATION, and Aldrik gave her a small nod. The Western man extended an open hand to her, and Vhalla tried to smile politely as she took it. The lord's skin was just as warm as her prince's, and she wondered if he was a glimpse into Aldrik's future. He was beginning to grey by his ears, but it gave him a handsome and stately appearance. His shoulders were broader and seemed to carry more muscle.

"My lord, it is an honor to meet you." Vhalla told herself not to be nervous.

The man nodded and sat upon the couch across from her in an open stance, his arms splayed across the back. Aldrik returned to the chaise he had previously occupied. Vhalla sat on the remaining chaise and folded her hands in her lap, attempting to sit nicely and not fidget.

"I cannot recall any other time when one of the first words out of my nephew's mouth has been a lady's name. Combined with hearing that same name on the Emperor's and the other prince's lips, well, needless to say, I had no choice but to meet this woman."

Vhalla wasn't sure what to feel, knowing she was the subject of so much chatter.

"Then again, had none of this been true, I would have insisted upon meeting you anyways." Lord Ophain placed his elbows on his knees, folding his hands between them and leaning forward. "After all, you are the first Windwalker in the West in over a hundred years who was not brought in wearing chains."

"Well, I don't know if I am free from chains." Vhalla could not stop the dry remark from escaping.

"Why so?" he asked. Even Aldrik was curious.

Vhalla focused on the prince as she spoke, praying he did not twist her words. "I am the property of the crown. My chains are invisible, but just as heavy."

Pain flashed through Aldrik's eyes briefly, but there was no hostility at the truth she bore.

"You did tell me she had a bit of fire in her." Lord Ophain chuckled at Aldrik before returning his attention back on her. "I know of the accusations against you. And I know of the magic you wield. But what I wish to know most is about the woman behind it all."

Vhalla noted that he used the word "accusations" instead of "crimes."

"Well, I was born in an Eastern town called Leoul. It's west and a little south of Cyven's capital, Hastan. About three day's travel from the Western border?" Vhalla had never travelled it herself, but she had heard about the journey from farmers. "When I was eleven, I was brought to the capital by my father and ended up working in the palace as a library apprentice."

"Which explains how you could come into contact with a prince," the lord mused.

Vhalla nodded, curling and uncurling her fingers. "Yes, my lord, though it was all rather strange and lucky."

"There is no such thing as luck, Vhalla." She prompted him to continue with an inquisitive stare. "The Mother has given us a line to follow until the end of our days. It is filled with meetings and partings, none of which are chance." He paused before adding, "At least, this is what I choose to believe."

Vhalla paused, trying to decide how much of that curious statement she considered to be true. "I see, my lord." She was unsure of what else to say.

"You are skeptical," he stated with a grin.

"There are a great many things I do not understand; it would be presumptuous to rule out any superficially," Vhalla retorted, both a truth and a polite response.

"I am sure you are made all the wiser for such an attitude. I can offer you proof, however; should you take it." She tilted her head, listening intently. "I believe were such things not a fact, then some Firebearers could not use these lines to peer along into a person's future."

"Firebearers *can?*" Vhalla interjected eagerly.

"Some," Lord Ophain nodded.

"Very few," Aldrik scoffed. "Most are curiosity shop charlatans with smoke-and-mirror parlor tricks."

Vhalla decided then to keep the incident with the Firebearer named Vi to herself.

"Fine. Since my nephew seems keen on dismissing that theory." The lord looked between them knowingly. "The ties that Bond two people together are made of the same red lines of fate."

Vhalla's eyes grew wide. Lord Ophain allowed himself a satisfied smile. Her heart began to race and she glanced over at Aldrik. Her prince chuckled softly and shook his head.

"Don't worry, Vhalla. I trust him," Aldrik reaffirmed.

She stared in shock at the prince and then back at Lord Ophain. It spoke volumes of the relationship these two shared if Aldrik trusted him with the knowledge of their Bond. Vhalla began to immediately warm up to the Lord of the West.

"To not even be Awoken and form a Bond." Lord Ophain ran

a hand across his chin. "You are a curious creature indeed. I am truly excited for your demonstration tomorrow."

"It's tomorrow?" Vhalla asked the room.

"Father told me earlier." Aldrik nodded.

"Have you thought of introducing her to crystals for all this?" Lord Ophain asked Aldrik.

"No, and do not breathe a word of it to my father," the prince threatened. "As far as he is concerned, she cannot handle them without risk of taint, just like any other sorcerer."

"And how did you get him to believe that?" The Lord of the West seemed impressed.

"I told him I tried." Aldrik shrugged. "I have been providing him carefully doctored notes based on my own to paint the picture I want him to know."

"Clever," Lord Ophain praised.

Vhalla ignored the guilt she felt for ever suspecting that Aldrik would share the intimacies of their Bond without care. "But, I *can* handle them . . ." Vhalla thought back to the stones Minister Victor used on her after she was first Awoken. They had worked so effortlessly with her magic it was as though they'd been made especially for her.

Lord Ophain grinned broadly at Aldrik, clearly excited by her admission. The prince pinched the bridge of his nose and sighed. "Vhalla, don't repeat that out of this room."

"Why?" she asked.

"Do you know how the War of the Crystal Caverns was started?" Lord Ophain asked her.

"Well, my father was a soldier during the war . . ." Vhalla thought back to what he and her mother had told her. Aldrik was suddenly fascinated with a corner of the room, avoiding the conversation as though it weren't happening. "He said that it was because of the chaos locked in the crystals escaping and disrupting the Mother's day and order. That we were fighting the darkness. I read that it also had something to do with sorcerers meddling with forces they shouldn't."

"But *why* were they meddling with those forces? What prompted them to be there?"

Vhalla didn't have an answer for the lord's question.

"Uncle, enough of this!" Aldrik was on his feet, his hands clenched into fists. Vhalla could feel the power radiating off him.

"Aldrik, relax. I know when a story is not mine to tell." The man's voice was stern, yet it had a gentle touch to it. Aldrik stood rigidly for another moment before his hands fell limply to his sides. His eyes were tired and distant as he huffed over to the bar.

"The Crystal Caverns have long been a mysterious enigma," Lord Ophain continued, ignoring his temperamental nephew. "Some claim it to be the gate to the dark realm that the Father built to keep our world separate. Others theorize it's solidification of raw magic from when the Gods created life. No matter what you choose to believe, there is something about the properties of the stones that can be found there which can alter a sorcerer's natural abilities." The lord took a sip from his drink. "The war was started because people had returned to the Caverns in another failed attempt to claim its powers for their own selfish greed—powers that have the potential to warp even the strongest of sorcerers, faster even than a Commons because of a sorcerer's magic Channels."

"What does this have to do with me?" It was interesting history, but she didn't know why it was relevant.

"Why did the West want Windwalkers?" Lord Ophain returned her question with a question. She was beginning to see where Aldrik got his teaching style from.

"For their magic," Vhalla said uncertainly. She'd only read one book.

"To access the caverns." The lord leaned forward with grave seriousness.

Aldrik nursed a drink from behind the bar, still ignoring them.

"Why . . ." Her voice had dropped to a whisper.

"Because Windwalkers are the only ones, of all sorcerers or Commons, who cannot be tainted by the crystals." Lord Ophain finally gave her the answer that she hadn't wanted to see on her own.

"So then—" Vhalla looked to Aldrik and stole his attention. "You don't want your father to know because you don't want him to have this power."

"If *he* can have it or not is irrelevant." Aldrik topped off his glass before returning to his seat. "I don't want you used by *anyone.*"

Vhalla's heart couldn't even skip beats at his words, her mind was too heavy. She had a power that could give access to an even greater, ancient magic that had the ability to warp the hearts, minds, and bodies of men. Vhalla gripped her hands tightly. Minister Victor had asked her to bring him a crystal weapon. She now knew why, and why it had to be her.

"But enough on history and dark 'what ifs.' " Lord Ophain attempted to disperse the cloud that now hung over the room. "May I have a demonstration of your abilities, specifically this Projection I have heard of, in advance of tomorrow?"

Vhalla obliged him and was better for it. The wonder and excitement Lord Ophain had toward her magic helped Vhalla overcome the worries and fears of the Crystal Caverns. The war was over and people had learned their lessons when it came to crystals. While Vhalla agreed with Aldrik's decision to keep secret the fact that they did not affect her negatively, she also decided not to worry about it.

They talked over dinner and into the evening. Vhalla began

to contribute more yawns than words to the conversation, and Aldrik finally noticed their dozing companion. "You should rest."

"Oh, no, I'm fine." It would have been more convincing if she hadn't punctuated the statement with a yawn.

"You need your energy for tomorrow." The prince stood, offering her a hand. "Get some sleep."

Vhalla realized with the way he turned his body that he was about to lead her into the bedroom. "I could go back to the inn," she said quickly.

"No, I want you here with me." He paused. "If you still wish it also."

Vhalla smiled softly at his addition; in a way, it was adorable to watch a born and bred royal attempt to be less princely. "Of course I wish it." She squeezed his hand lightly. "I'll sleep out here tonight," she offered.

"No." Aldrik shook his head. "I will be burning the midnight oil with my uncle. I have not seen him in too long. Take the bed, it will be much quieter."

Vhalla nodded, and Aldrik relinquished his hold on her, satisfied that she was not about to leave. Vhalla turned toward Lord Ophain as the prince went to retrieve her pack from behind the bar. The Lord of the West had a knowing smile.

"Lord Ophain, it has been a delight to meet you," she said earnestly.

"I can only say the same, Vhalla. A *friend*—of Aldrik's is a friend of the West. I will see you tomorrow."

Vhalla noticed his smirk and couldn't stop herself from blushing. All too eager to hide her embarrassment, she grabbed her pack from Aldrik, bid them both goodnight, and slipped behind the wooden sliding doors into the dim bedroom beyond. A flame flickered by the bedside and in the bathroom, hovering above a metal dish that had been set out. Vhalla made a note to someday ask Aldrik how Firebearers left their flames, but for the time being she was grateful for the light.

Knowing Aldrik was going to take his time, Vhalla decided to take hers, enjoying the luxury of his bath. The water came out piping hot and she let it seep into her bones. The heat relaxed her and staved off the tension in her muscles from turning into fear and worry at the unknown of what the Emperor's impending demonstration would bring.

She was wrinkled in her fingers and toes when she emerged. Drying and dressing in basic sleeping clothes, Vhalla dragged her feet back into the bedroom. Dim lights still flickered beyond the sliding doors that did almost nothing to block the deep resonance of Aldrik's words.

"Would you like another one?" he asked, likely from behind the bar with the way his voice carried.

"No, we have a long day tomorrow. You should stop too," his uncle warned.

"Just a nightcap," Aldrik assured.

"You were past a nightcap two drinks ago." There was a tone of scolding in Lord Ophain's voice that made Vhalla grin slightly.

"Don't fault me for this." She heard Aldrik crossing the room, the sound of the furniture scraping as he sat heavily.

"You know I do. And I will especially if you are in an alcohol haze and can't perform as you need to tomorrow," the lord said sternly. "I do not think you want to be the cause of her demonstration going poorly."

"I would *never* do anything that could jeopardize her," Aldrik said sharply.

Vhalla took a step closer to the doors, her heart racing. She knew she shouldn't be listening, that it was an invasion of his privacy. But she couldn't stop her feet from carrying her up to the papered and carved screens.

"It sounds as though you already have." Lord Ophain's words were strong, but his tone was not.

"Don't you dare tell me—"

"What?" the older man cut off the prince. "That you have clearly broadcasted your relationship with the woman to your men, your leaders, your *father* of all people?"

Aldrik was silent.

"He mentioned the trial in a correspondence. He asked me to come and speak sense into you."

"And here I thought you were paying your dear nephew a friendly visit." Aldrik punctuated his words by bringing his glass down upon the table a little too hard.

"Your father summoned me to reject this. But, you summon me seeking my advice and my approval. Why else would you bring her before me as you have?" Lord Ophain had a point.

"Well," Aldrik asked finally, "what *is* your advice?"

"Make her a ward of the West." Vhalla inhaled sharply at Lord Ophain's words. "Send her back to Norin with me to study at the Academy of Arcane Arts. Put her out of your father's reach, and yours."

"That would be the smart thing, wouldn't it?" Aldrik sighed.

Vhalla gripped her fingers so tightly she thought one may break. She should be happy. Being sent to Norin to study at one of the oldest academies in the world, nevertheless an academy for sorcery, should sound like a dream compared to marching to war.

But it would not be by his side.

"You're not going to do it, though." Lord Ophain heard something in Aldrik's words that Vhalla hadn't. The clanking of ice in glasses filled the silence. "What is this woman to you?"

"*Vhalla*, I need her in so many ways, Mother help me," Aldrik groaned. "I need her as my redemption, I need her kindness, I need her forgiveness, I need her smiles, I need her humanity, I need her ignorance, I need her innocence, and, yes . . . Mother Sun, *yes*, I need her as a man."

Her breathing was short as she leaned closer to the door. Vhalla's heart threatened to beat over Aldrik's soft words.

"You love her."

It was not a question, but Aldrik answered it anyway. "More than I ever thought possible."

"Aldrik," the lord said thoughtfully. "You have yourself in quite a spot, don't you?"

"I don't know what to do." His voice sounded weak compared to its normal fullness.

"You know your place in life, your duty to your people." Vhalla didn't like where Lord Ophain was headed with his logic. "Someday you will be Emperor and no one will be able to question your decisions. No one *will* question them if they feel that your law comes from a place of honor, sensibility, and compassion. The crown is a heavy burden and you will have to make choices between your wants and your Empire."

"I know all this, Uncle." Aldrik's voice was muffled a moment as he buried his face in his hands. "But I can't."

Vhalla released a breath she hadn't realized she was holding.

"I know," said Lord Ophain. "You remind me so much of your father."

"What?" Aldrik's anger was quick at the comment.

"Calm down." The lord laughed. "You never saw them together, but he was over the sun for your mother. Of course, she was still a princess, but the logical choice would have been one of your older aunts. He should not be so hard on you because it is not as though he has been exempt from chasing a stolen heart."

Vhalla blinked, she'd never heard anything of Aldrik's mother. She should leave now; this was certainly a private moment.

The lord sighed. "She was too young, younger than you now . . ."

"Enough," Aldrik said softly. There was a long pause. "We have quite the day ahead of us." It sounded like Ophain stood. "And you have a beautiful woman in your bed," he added with a chuckle.

Vhalla fought a blush.

"There she will stay without me," Aldrik sounded resolute.

Vhalla fought unladylike disappointment.

"You and your nobilities. You are a prince, Aldrik, people expect you to enjoy yourself when no one is watching." The lord's voice diminished as he headed for the door. "It is a true shame that the seat of power was not kept in the West. Our people would be all too eager to accept a woman like her as their princess."

Vhalla tried to absorb what the man was implying, *what he was outright saying.*

"One step at a time . . ." Aldrik's voice faded as she padded over to the bed.

Vhalla settled the covers around her. Her blood felt on fire with shame for listening in on a conversation that wasn't meant for her ears. But that was not the only thing burning her. She wanted to touch him, to kiss him, to let him know that she felt much the same and more and that she was never going to let the world rip him from her needy grasp.

The sound of wood on wood filled the silence as the door was slid open and Vhalla sat.

"You're awake." His cheeks were lightly flushed and his lips parted.

"I am." All eloquence left Vhalla when she looked at him.

"I . . ." He glanced between her and the sitting area in the main room.

Vhalla saw the debate on his face and put an end to it. "Stay with me."

"I shouldn't." His focus was now solely on her and it sent sparks up her chest.

"You shouldn't? Just like you shouldn't have me in your bed right now, or kiss me, or love me? I'm not, I'm not asking for—" Vhalla gripped the covers and blushed, forcing herself to act a woman, "—for you to make love to me tonight. But I want you near me."

Aldrik sighed heavily, and Vhalla prepared herself to see him leave for the other room. But he crossed to the bed, crawling over the sheets on his hands and knees to her. Vhalla felt deliciously ensnared, pinned to the pillows before a predatory beast.

The lights extinguished magically as he kissed her, his weight assaulting her senses. Vhalla snuck a hand around his neck, holding his face to hers. He tasted of sweet liquor and every delicious dark dream she'd ever had. She wanted to lose herself to him, to give him everything she had. When he pulled away countless kisses later it didn't feel even close to enough.

"Aldrik," she sighed breathlessly.

"No, I won't. You said not tonight." The prince read her mind.

"But—"

"No," Aldrik repeated. He scooped her up into his arms and twisted onto his back, pulling her half onto him. "I also don't want you to think that I take women to bed lightly."

"You don't need to worry. I know." Vhalla caressed up his stomach, feeling the groves of muscle carved by years of duty through the thin fabric of his shirt. "I don't care how many it has been, or why. I just want to be here now."

"How many do you think it has been?" He actually sounded amused.

"I told you, I don't care." Her movements stilled.

"*Ah-ah*, Vhalla, I practically invented dodging questions. You've much to learn yet." He tucked some hair behind her ear.

"I don't know," Vhalla resigned. She didn't want to offend him with her guess being wildly off. He was six years older than she was, and judging by his brother's comments he had been significantly more active from a younger age. "Eight?" She took a stab at a number, thinking it would be too low as it was less than one a year since his coming of age ceremony at fifteen.

His laughter rang out through the darkness. "Three."

"Three?" she repeated. It was more than her grand total of one, but it was far fewer than she had expected.

"Is that a pleased repeat, my parrot?" He pressed his lips to her forehead.

"I suppose so." She shifted slightly closer to him. "More than me."

"I'd assume so."

"What does that mean?" Vhalla huffed in mock offense.

"I used your lack of experience to throw you off balance right off, remember?" He ran his hand down her arm to intertwine his fingers with hers.

"Two isn't *that* big of a difference," Vhalla muttered, unsure how it had become a contest.

"Two." The simple math took Aldrik far too long. "You mean, you have . . ."

It was Vhalla's turn to laugh. "The East doesn't really have your Southern notions of a woman's virgin blood. Yes, one man."

"And here I thought I was corrupting you." Vhalla heard the grin in his voice, and she moved her hand to his cheek, feeling how his mouth curled.

"I'm fairly certain you are," Vhalla teased lightly.

"You're right," he teased back. "I am out to dine upon your still beating heart."

"If that's all you wanted, you should know I gave it to you a while ago." Vhalla was confused when she felt the grin slip from his face. "What?"

"How have you not seen it yet that I am not worthy of you?" He grasped her hand, pressing his lips against her fingertips.

"How have you not seen it that you are and more?" Vhalla retorted.

He gave a huff of amusement and squeezed her hand tightly. "I love you, Vhalla Yarl."

"How fortunate for me." She yawned. "For I love you as well, my crown prince."

His breath ruffled her hair slightly as Vhalla pressed closer to the prince, and he filled her senses as she drifted to sleep.

CHAPTER 21

S HE STARED AT the face of a man who was painfully, horribly familiar, and yet was completely different. Egmun wore his hair cropped short to his head, though the wrinkles at the corners of his eyes were smoother, the lines around his mouth lighter, and he wore a hint of stubble across his chin. The sight of the younger senator sent Vhalla into a rage-filled dread, the emotion conflicted with what her dream-self was feeling, a sense of calm trust.

Vhalla fought against the vision, struggling to escape, to push Egmun away. She pulled and pried and twisted mentally until something fractured at her raw panic. She stood outside of the body she previously occupied, what should be her body in any other dream.

Aldrik looked like he could be no older than fifteen. His hair was longer, down to his shoulders and tied back at the neck. Messy bangs framed his face, and Vhalla looked on with a strange mixture of love and fear for the wide-eyed boy alone in this dark place with a man she hated more than anyone or anything else.

The room was filled with a haze that mingled ominously with the darkness, making only certain details easily distinguishable. There was a single flame flickering in the cavernous space, and *wherever it was, neither the ceiling nor walls were visible by the light. The floor was stone, inlaid with what seemed to be shards of shimmering glass. She tried to get a closer look but a fog covered them every time she tried to focus. There were old looking markings carved beneath their feet, spiraling toward the center where a man was kneeling, bound and blindfolded. He shivered and shook. The fabric covering his eyes was wet with tears.*

"Prince Aldrik." *Egmun took a step forward. He wore a formal black coat and dark trousers; there was no sign of his Senatorial chain.* "Someday, you will be Emperor. Do you know what that means?"

"I-I do."

Vhalla turned to the stuttering child.

"So you know that justice will fall to you." *Egmun took another step forward, and Vhalla's heart began to race, feeling hopelessly trapped. She didn't want to be here, she didn't want to see this.* "It was your mother's last request for your father to spare you these duties as long as possible."

"My mother's?" *Vhalla saw a sad flash of hope in the boy's eyes at the mention of the mother he never knew.*

"But you will soon be a man, won't you?" *Egmun asked softly.*

"I will." *The boy prince took a deep breath, as if to grow into all his height in one moment.*

"It is rather unfair, no? For your father to be treating you like a child?" *Vhalla watched the man grin, and she knew this Aldrik had not yet perfected his powers of perception and manipulation. If she could see Egmun for what he was in that moment, she had no doubt the adult Aldrik would as well.* "Are you prepared to be the crown prince this realm needs?"

"I am," *Aldrik repeated through obvious doubt. Even though the space was cold, sweat dotted his brow.*

"Then, my prince, for justice, for the strength of Solaris, for the future of your Empire, slay this man." *Egmun dropped dramatically to a knee. He pulled at the rope which attached a short sword to his belt and held out the blade expectantly.*

Vhalla wasn't sure if it was her heart that was racing or if it was the young Aldrik's.

"But . . ."

"This man has stolen from your family; it is a treasonous crime. He is not an innocent," *Egmun assured.*

"Should my father not—"

"I thought you were a man and a prince. I did not take you as someone who shied from justice or power, Prince Aldrik." *Egmun seemed to stretch his arms to hold out the sword further.* "Why are you here?"

"For my father, to conquer the North," *Aldrik said uncertainly. The war on the North had only started four years ago. Aldrik should be twenty, not a child.*

"With this, all will bend to you." *Egmun smiled encouragingly, and Vhalla was reminded of a serpent. Aldrik took the sword hesitantly.*

No, *she whispered mentally. She was, of course, helpless and unheard. Aldrik turned to the kneeling man.*

"M-my prince, m-mercy please. T-take my hand for m-my theft. Spare m-me." *Vhalla heard the rough voice of the man through his tears. Aldrik looked back to Egmun.*

"Minister . . ." *he said weakly.*

"The guilty will say anything to you, my prince, to save their skin. This, too, is a lesson." *Egmun returned to his feet, he seemed to be holding his breath.*

Aldrik unsheathed the sword, passing the scabbard back into Egmun's eager palms. The blade shimmered as though it gave off its own light.

Egmun, stop. *Vhalla shouted.*

"M-mercy," *the man begged. Aldrik stared at Egmun hopelessly.*

"Kill him, Aldrik."

Vhalla gaped in shock at the sudden harshness in Egmun's tone. His patience had finally run thin. Aldrik didn't seem to notice. She only had a moment to contemplate what, exactly, had the senator so eager before Vhalla saw the boy set his jaw in grim determination.

No. *She felt Aldrik's terror, his uncertainty, his youthful hopefulness, the ever encroaching end of his innocence, and she felt herself at the point of weeping.*

Aldrik raised the blade. It hovered, just a moment above his head. The young prince stared at the helpless man before him, the life she knew was about to be cut short. Vhalla saw the flash of the firelight on the surface of the sword as he brought it down clumsily onto the man's head.

No, *she repeated as she saw the man shudder violently at Aldrik's weak and clumsy swing. Aldrik raised the sword again.*

No! *Vhalla cried as he brought down the sword again, blood splattering across his perfect, youthful face. Aldrik raised the sword again.*

"No!" Vhalla shouted, lunging forward at a figure that disappeared with the opening of her eyes.

An arm wrapped itself across her shoulders, holding her tightly to a man's chest. A hand clamped over her mouth firmly. Her mind was in a daze and she cried out again, muffled by the fingers covering her lips. She twisted and kicked to free herself from the person's clutches, instantly thinking of Egmun, her cheeks wet with tears.

"*Vhalla.*" A voice that was made of midnight itself soothed from behind her. It broke through the chaos in her head. "Vhalla, stop. It's all right. It's me."

She gave a small whimper of relief and took a breath through her nose. Then another, until Aldrik finally removed his hand from her mouth, assured she would not alert the whole world to her presence in his bed. In her sleep she had rolled onto her side and Aldrik had curled behind her. Vhalla rolled to face him.

"Aldrik," she said weakly. Vhalla scanned his face. After seeing his younger self, he suddenly appeared every year of his age and too many more. She choked down a small cry of relief to see his cheeks free of blood. "Aldrik," Vhalla whimpered before using his chest as a shield from the world.

The prince's arms closed around her, and he kissed the top of her head. "I'm here. You're safe. It was just a dream. It isn't real," he reassured, running a hand up and down her back.

"It is." Vhalla choked out in-between shaky breaths and the remnants of tears. She couldn't deny it any more. The earlier dreams had been too mingled with his consciousness to know for certain, but now she was sure.

"Vhalla, I know of a great many powers in this world . . ." He pulled back and ran a thumb over her wet cheeks. "I know of powers to see the future in flame and ash. I know of powers to listen to echoes of the past in waves. I know of powers that can heal almost any illness. I know of powers to walk outside of one's own body." Aldrik smiled gently at her. "But I know of no power of dreams."

"It-*it was real.*"

"Hush, you're not making sense. Take a breath and go back to sleep. It is barely dawn, and my father didn't speak of having your demonstration until noon." He kissed her forehead lightly, and Vhalla's guilt made her pull away from him to sit up.

"You don't understand. It was real. My dreams, they're not—" A shiver ran down her arms. "They're not always dreams."

"Come, you're cold," Aldrik sighed. "What is it you think they are?" He yawned, blinking sleep away and propping his head up with his elbow.

She relented, lying back down into the covers but avoiding

his embrace. "They're," Vhalla sighed and closed her eyes, bracing herself. "They're your memories."

"What?" Aldrik studied her.

"My dreams, at least sometimes, are your memories. I don't know how, or why, or when they will happen, but they do." She gulped at his silence.

"Why do you think that?" he asked, turning serious.

"Because there's no reason why I should dream anything like what I see," she whispered.

"Dreams are strange, Vhalla. Who knows why we dream what we do." Aldrik laid back down.

"No," she snapped; he wasn't taking her as seriously as she had wanted. She recalled a prior vivid dream. "The man who stabbed you was your brother's guard, he was a Westerner, and his son was in the town that you attacked."

Aldrik's eyes grew wide. "Did Baldair tell you that?"

"No!" Vhalla fought to keep her head from turning into an emotional mess. "Aldrik, they are my dreams! You were at a garden in the West with the sculpture of a woman on an obelisk with a gold and ruby sun. There was a man there who told you—of all people—to stop fidgeting."

"My mother's grave." Aldrik's lips barely moved. His eyes were suddenly burning with a dark intensity, and he grabbed her shoulder. "What else?" he demanded. "*What else have you seen?*" His fingers dug into her skin.

She struggled to remember anything else but her most recent dream. "You in the dark, with another woman . . ."

"Mother . . ." He hung his head in shame.

"With, when-when Egmun made you . . ." Vhalla struggled to find words, still reeling.

"When he what?" Aldrik's teeth were clenched. "*When he what?*"

For the first time, Vhalla felt a small twinge of fear at his quivering hands. "When-when he made you kill that man," Vhalla whispered, her lips barely moving.

Aldrik stared at her. "Is that all? What do you know? Tell me, Vhalla, and do not lie to me." His voice was rough and void of compassion.

"I have never lied to you!"

"Of course not, just rummaged through my head," he raged.

"How dare you!" Vhalla jerked out of his grasp, offended by his presumptions. "I only just realized it. I was only now, this morning, able to separate myself enough from you in the memories to realize." She saw the recognition of those facts calm his anger some.

"Was that all you saw?" he repeated more calmly.

"Of that dream? Yes," she sighed. "I don't even know where it happened. It was all dark."

The prince sat and brought his forehead to his palm with a heavy sigh.

"Aldrik," she whispered. "There's another . . ."

"Gods, what?" he sighed. "*Vhalla*," he urged softly.

Vhalla bit her lip. She wasn't sure how to form the words. Something about all that had been said, her recent dream, his low opinion of himself, placed this singular memory in the forefront of her mind. Vhalla sat and took his hand gently in hers, bringing it to her lips first in reassurance. He looked at her, a mix of pain, shame, and anger furrowing his brow. She sighed and turned his hand over, so the inside of his wrist faced upward. With her free hand she placed an index finger just below his palm running it up his forearm. Her fingertip caught on his sleeve and pushed it upward, revealing the ghost of a scar which she knew would be there. It was so faint that on the pale of his skin it was nearly invisible, but she knew to look for it. Vhalla brought her gaze up to his slowly.

Aldrik's face drained of all the other emotions except horror as his lips parted. Vhalla held her breath, letting the shock hit him in silence. He wrenched his hand from her fingers, as though she had actually cut along his forearm. Vhalla could only look at him sadly before his eyes bore into her long enough that she was forced to avert her attention.

They sat facing each other on the bed as the silence dragged on into eternity. His breathing was rough, and he clutched the arm she had touched as though he was in pain. Vhalla couldn't bring herself to look at him as she awaited the verdict.

"I never meant to violate you so," she said weakly. Intentional or not, it remained that she had forced herself upon his most private of spaces, pilfering things that were not freely given.

Aldrik said nothing; he continued to attempt to get his breathing under control as his eyes fixed on her. Vhalla felt power radiating off of him; he was angry, he was hurt, and it made her feel all the more awful.

"I never wanted to." She tried to explain, "I would've never done so—"

"Of course not," he spat. "Who would ever want to see the twisted broken histories that lurk in my head? Only one person in this world should deserve to endure it." That brought her eyes back to him.

"Aldrik, don't say that," she whispered softly, breaking under the anger in his gaze that she saw wasn't really directed at her.

"Oh?" He laughed dryly. "How can you think so? You know what's there now. What's worse, you've lived it. Tell me, Vhalla, what's it like to find out your prince is a coward? Is weak? Is scared? Is wicked? Is—"

"*Human*," she said firmly, cutting him off. Aldrik paused. "Aldrik, I don't know why . . ." She took his hand in hers again, looking down at his arm.

"I won't tell you," he said sharply. Vhalla shifted, startled, she had hardly been about to ask. "Damn it." He stood, pacing the room. "Even if I don't tell you, every time you sleep it's a roulette to see if you'll find out." He spouted a series of foul words.

Vhalla grabbed the blanket tightly; she'd never heard him use such vulgarity. "I wouldn't say anything to—"

"Not even my brother knows, Vhalla." He turned back. "Not even Larel knows, and she's the closest person I've ever had to calling a true friend. I tried to tell her once and that just went over awfully." He sighed and rubbed his eyes with his palms.

Vhalla had come to think of Aldrik as one of the strongest people she knew. Seeing him so close to his breaking point pulled her to her feet.

"End the Joining."

He grimaced, shook his head, and pinched the bridge of his nose.

"It only started after the Joining." She pleaded, "Aldrik, please, I don't want to hurt you. I want you to close what was opened."

"And I want you to survive this war!" he nearly shouted.

Vhalla blinked as his words stung the corners of her eyes. *Still*, he still was mindful of her wellbeing. Even when he was in so much pain, even when she had pilfered intimate knowledge of him, he refused relief for her sake.

"Mother Sun, woman," Aldrik groaned. He crossed the room and stood before her, releasing his tension with a sigh. Slowly, gently, Aldrik wiped her cheeks. "Why are you crying?"

Vhalla hiccupped. "Because you may be the most amazing person I have ever met."

"I am not. If it had been anyone other than you, I likely would have killed them on the spot and burned their body until there was nothing left but dust," Aldrik swore darkly.

She knew it shouldn't, but just hearing it put that way brought a small smile to her mouth.

Aldrik sighed. "I don't know if I'll ever be inclined to talk about these things."

Elise Kova

"That's fine."

"Tell me, from now on, no matter what they are. Whatever you see, I *need* to know," he said gravely.

"I promise." She nodded, apprehensive of what was locked away in his memories that gave him such fear.

Aldrik sighed and stepped away. "Vhalla, I need some time." He rubbed his eyes tiredly. "I understand you didn't choose this." He swallowed hard. "I-I am not angry at *you* for it. I am not blaming you. But, this . . . *this*, letting someone in is already so far beyond what I am accustomed to."

"I didn't realize." Vhalla rubbed her eyes, hanging her head.

Aldrik tapped her chin, summoning her attention. "Good. It's been better than good." He shook his head. "I can't even . . . form sentences. This, you and I, my being pushed beyond the personal hell I built for myself, has been good. I've felt more like a man in the past months-weeks, in the past days being with you, than I have in years. As though I can enjoy things without—guilt. Good isn't even the right word to say for it. You've let me be the person I always wished I could be and, I . . ."

"I understand." Vhalla spared him further struggle. "I'll wait, take your time."

"I just need to really understand what it's like to have someone whom-whom I trust." Aldrik avoided her gaze, scowling at himself. "Someone who knows my dark truths and who isn't seeking something from me or is trying to use something against me."

Vhalla nodded, taking a breath for courage. She pressed her palms against her eyes briefly to hold in more tears of hurt and frustration. Intentional or not, she had hurt him and that ground her heart into pieces. And now she had to leave him at his request; even if he needed time, it didn't sit well with her.

Aldrik's form was hunched and his eyes were somber as he led her down the passageway. There was a sorrowful resignation between them at the suppression of something that had just begun to blossom. It may be stinted, but Vhalla vowed she wouldn't let the flame that burned between them be extinguished.

As if reading her mind, Aldrik turned. "Thank you."

"For what?" She blinked at him.

"For not fleeing my side after you . . . had to experience all that." Aldrik rubbed his forearm.

Vhalla wondered if he even realized he was doing it. "I may not understand it all," she whispered, braving a step closer to him. "But who you were made you who you are now. I wish you'd never had to suffer. But I'll take the past gladly so I can share the present."

She saw the beginnings of a smile that he quickly abandoned. Aldrik pulled her in for a tight embrace, and she heard his breath quiver. Before he could lose his composure, he turned and pushed open the secret door.

"Return at noon. My father will be expecting you then." His voice was distant.

"I will see you then," Vhalla said hopefully.

But the door had already closed.

Larel and Fritz were playing a game of Carcivi when Vhalla mindlessly stumbled into the downstairs of their inn. She gave them one glance, nothing more than acknowledging they were there, before dragging her feet toward the stairs. A chair scraped against the ground.

"We'll finish later," Vhalla heard Larel saying. The woman was quick on Vhalla's heels.

"Larel," Vhalla whispered weakly.

"What is it? What's wrong?" Larel rested her hands lightly on Vhalla's quivering shoulders.

"I hurt him, Larel . . ." Weakness burst forth from her, and Vhalla relied on the other woman's support once more to put her back together in time to face the Emperor.

CHAPTER 22

VHALLA OPENED HER eyes to the stunned faces of royals, lords, and ladies. The only person in the room who wasn't impressed was Aldrik. Despite her demonstration being better than even she expected, the prince maintained his withdrawn and ambivalent look. She knew he couldn't show her favor in front of the nobles, especially after hearing Lord Ophain speak on how careless he'd been with the affections he'd already displayed, but there was a larger wall there than just acting. Be it the Joining, the Bond, time spent together, or a combination of it all, he was poor at hiding his feelings from her, and Vhalla could see the hurt and fear in the depths of his eyes every time he looked her way.

Everyone gave her space as she pushed herself off the plush furniture. No one said anything. The majors who had been assembled, the highest of the Emperor's command, looked between her and their leader, reserving all judgment until they had heard his assessment.

The most powerful man in the world leaned forward, his eyes glittering. "Well, Miss Yarl, that was certainly impressive."

"Thank you, my lord." Vhalla lowered her eyes in respect.

"This demonstration is replicable an infinite amount of times?" The Emperor turned to his eldest son.

"As long as her magic Channel is not blocked in some way, like depletion or Eradication," Aldrik affirmed with a nod.

The Emperor stroked his beard and turned to the nobles assembled. "My son has already formulated some plans on how we will be able to use this power effectively in the North. However, I would like each of you to put together your own strategy before we reach the Northern border."

They spoke as though she wasn't there. Vhalla shifted in her seat, folding and unfolding her hands in her lap. She was a tool to these people, designed to be used in whatever way they saw fit.

A pair of eyes caught her attention. The only person focused on her was the younger prince. She met Prince Baldair's gaze and was surprised to see sympathy there. Vhalla averted her eyes. She didn't want his pity.

"Very well, this is sufficient for today. You are dismissed, Miss Yarl." The Emperor waved a hand in her direction.

"Thank you, my lords and ladies." Vhalla stood, keeping her eyes downcast.

"*Ah*, one more thing," Lord Ophain interjected.

Vhalla searched him with a questioning stare. *What was he doing?*

"This is the first Windwalker in the West in decades."

The other nobility were confused; even Aldrik didn't seem to understand why his uncle was approaching her.

"Vhalla Yarl," Lord Ophain began, looking down at her. "I cannot correct the mistakes of my forefathers. I cannot expunge the blood of Windwalkers from the stones of my castle. What the Knights of Jadar did to your brethren can never be remedied."

Vhalla shifted her weight from one foot to the other. Speaking of the genocide of her people after learning more about the reasons behind it put an uncomfortable feeling in her gut that tingled down to her toes. It wasn't something she even wanted mentioned.

"But what I *can* do is be a catalyst for a future of hope, peace, and prosperity between sorcerers of all types and Commons. To show that the value I see in you is far greater than your magic."

She wondered if he was sincere. But the second Lord Ophain's eyes darted over to the Emperor's, she had no doubt. This was a statement, one which Vhalla wasn't sure she was prepared to be involved in or even fully understood the implications of.

"Therefore, it is my honor to bestow upon you a Crimson Proclamation."

Murmurs clouded the air the moment the words left the Western Lord's lips. Vhalla shifted uncertainly. Even Aldrik wore a look of dumb shock on his face. Some nobles were confused, but the other Westerners seemed quick to fill in the blanks.

Lord Ophain focused only on Vhalla as he produced a crimson ribbon from his inner coat pocket. It was just over half the length of her forearm and as wide as three fingers. He handed it to her, and Vhalla instantly ran her fingers over the silk. Upon it were Western symbols in silver thread, on the bottom was an ink seal bearing the flaming phoenix of the West.

Vhalla looked back up to him quizzically.

"In truth, this is a hollow title." Lord Ophain did not make her ask outright. With a nod in the Emperor's direction, he continued, "Only the Emperor may elevate lords and ladies to the court of nobility. But the West maintains its traditions and honors the old ways. Any who are able to read those words will know that the Lady Vhalla Yarl is considered a Duchess of the West by Order of Lord Ophain Ci'Dan."

Vhalla stared in awe. Hollow title or no, it was more esteem than she had ever contemplated in her life. She made the mistake of looking to the Emperor and resisted the urge to push the fabric back in Lord Ophain's palms. Emperor Solaris's eyes were steely. She gripped the ribbon tighter. It meant nothing, it was a symbol of good faith, of righting wrongs of the past. It posed no threat of change to her current status. *Surely the Emperor knew that?*

"You honor me, my lord," Vhalla mumbled, lowering her eyes.

"If you are quite finished, Lord Ophain," the Emperor said coldly, "Miss Yarl has other places to be."

Vhalla didn't, but she was eager to be out of the suddenly oppressive room. She gave one last bow and noticed that suddenly the Western nobility gave her small nods of their heads. All, save for one; a mustached major, whom Vhalla had never so much had laid eyes on before the demonstration, regarded her with thinly veiled contempt.

It was impossible to leave the room fast enough, retreating back to her inn.

Larel and Fritz were waiting for her when she returned. They lounged in a sitting area to the left of the lobby's entrance. Daniel and Craig occupied the Carcivi board to the right. All of them looked up in interest the moment she entered.

"How'd it go?" Fritz was the first to ask.

"Well," Vhalla held up the ribbon in white-knuckled grip. "I got a Crimson Proclamation."

"A what?" Larel asked.

Daniel and Craig seemed equally lost.

"A Crimson Proclamation?" Fritz was on his feet, rushing over to her. "I didn't think the West gave these anymore."

"What is it?" Larel asked, crossing over to Vhalla and Fritz.

"Crimson Proclamations were how the old kings of the West built their court. They raised people to noble status with them," Fritz explained.

"So, are you a noble now?" Daniel went to get a look himself.

"Not really," Vhalla remembered what Lord Ophain said.

"The Emperor abolished the Western Court," Fritz continued. "When Mhashan was absorbed into the Empire and became just 'the West,' the Emperor didn't want an uprising from the people who were old nobility. So he formed the Imperial Court as a way to appease them, giving the old nobility new Southern titles and elevating his own lords and ladies to sit among them."

"He took control of their power then?" Craig rubbed his chin.

Fritz nodded. "And, in effect, absorbed the wealth of the oldest families in the West. But why did you get one?"

"Lord Ophain said it was a gesture of good faith, for the Burning Times," Vhalla summarized.

Comprehension sunk into Fritz's face.

"The Burning Times?" Daniel asked.

That launched Fritz into a whole new history lesson. One that, given Daniel's interest in Windwalkers, took significantly longer. Vhalla listened quietly, still digesting the afternoon.

The Emperor seemed pleased with her demonstration . . . *but his eyes.* She suppressed a shiver. His eyes were void of all emotion each time they fell upon her. The more interactions she had with Emperor Solaris, the less doubt Vhalla had that her place beneath him would never change.

"So, they just, killed them all?" Craig leaned back in his chair in shock.

"Yep." Fritz nodded. "And Vhal's the first one since."

She met her friend's proud smile with a tired curl of her lips.

"However . . . horrible that is, we can't change it now, and I think we should celebrate Vhalla's proclamation." Daniel leaned forward in his chair.

"I don't know if I can handle another night of celebration," Larel said uneasily.

"Something quieter. There's a delicious Western restaurant not far from here." Daniel stood. "I'd love to treat the Windwalker and her friends."

Daniel extended a hand to her, and Vhalla stared at it. She wished she could feel his joy. She wanted the excitement that had been evoked in her the first night in the Crossroads, excitement in spite of the sea of power plays and manipulation that she found herself adrift in. Vhalla took Daniel's hand, allowing him to pull her to her feet. Sitting and brooding wouldn't help her find that joy again, and Daniel had been a catalyst for it before—maybe he would be able to summon it again.

The Crossroads did not disappoint. The night was warm, interrupted by a cool breeze drifting through the dusty streets and alleys. Colors were splashed upon every building in the forms of bright murals, tapestries, and awnings. Music and laughter could be heard all around, in harmony with gambling parlors and pleasure halls—*it was a good place to forget who you were*, Vhalla decided.

The restaurant was nicer than Vhalla expected, and she was instantly overwhelmed by the menu and table setting. Fritz seemed equally lost and Larel surprisingly comfortable. Vhalla could only suspect that growing up the friend of the Crown Prince gave the Western woman insights into etiquette she wouldn't have otherwise.

Vhalla leaned back in her chair, nursing her drink between plates. She was on the edge of a haze that seemed very inviting and, while she did not want to induce morning-after headaches, she did want to take the edge off the day. Daniel leaned back as well, allowing the table conversation to continue before them.

"What do you think of Western food?" he asked soft enough to be heard only by her.

Vhalla was startled out of her thoughts. "What? Oh, it's delicious."

"I think so too," he agreed. "I didn't know what to expect the first time I tried it."

"When was that?" she asked.

"My first campaign." He sipped his glass thoughtfully. "It was my first time into the West. My family never travelled much."

"How did you end up in the palace?"

"I enlisted." Daniel shrugged and added, "I thought it'd be a chance at a better life."

"Hasn't it been?" She heard the edge of disappointment in his voice.

"On paper, I suppose. I am a lord now, after all." He had the look of someone who was seeing shadows of the past rather than the glittering splendor that surrounded him in the present. "But at night I wonder, if I had never left the East if I would still have her."

His tone made Vhalla's chest ache. "Don't think that way." Vhalla shifted in her chair to get a better look at her fellow Easterner. Daniel regarded her thoughtfully, his complete attention a heavy load. Vhalla swallowed, hoping she could find the right thing to say to support her friend. "I-I almost Eradicated my magic."

"Eradicated?"

"Got rid of." Daniel gaped at her in shock, as though the notion was incomprehensible to him. "I was scared when I found out I was a sorcerer. And then, the Night of Fire and Wind, I thought—I thought everything was the fault of my magic." Food was placed in front of them but neither made a motion toward it. "My friend died because of it."

"Vhalla . . ." he said with a sympathetic tone.

She shook her head, dismissing his sympathy. "I can't go back, and neither can you. We both have to move forward and find what beauty we can in the world as it is."

Daniel stared at her in awe. His gaze brought a heat onto her cheeks, and Vhalla quickly placed her glass on the table, digging into the plate before her. She felt the weight of a second stare on her shoulders, and Vhalla looked up, surprised to find Larel's waiting eyes. The Western woman smiled gently at Vhalla.

When they were done with dinner and had returned to their hotel, Larel followed Vhalla to her room following bathing. Vhalla sat on the bed, the other woman behind her, combing through her wet hair with magic fingers. "Did you mean what you said at dinner?"

"To Daniel?" The question was pointless, Vhalla knew what Larel was talking about.

Larel hummed softly behind her in confirmation as she continued to dry Vhalla's hair.

"I did." Vhalla nodded.

"I'm glad." Larel pulled Vhalla in for a tight hug. "I've been worried for you."

"You have?" It was a dumb question and Vhalla knew it. This was the woman who had held her through shivers and shakes. Larel had been the one who pieced her back together after the Night of Fire and Wind. She knew every jagged piece that was still cutting into Vhalla's heart.

"You're not someone to live in darkness or sorrow." Larel reclined on the bed, inviting Vhalla to do the same. "You're a light that can shine brighter than even the sun."

"That sounds treasonous," Vhalla teased.

"I mean it all the same." Larel leaned forward and pressed her forehead against Vhalla's a brief moment. "You have something in you, Vhalla, something most never have or lose quickly. I cannot wait to see when you realize it yourself."

"I'm nothing . . . I'm not even myself, I'm property of the crown." The more she said it, the deeper it sunk into her. She needed to accept this truth to make it through the war.

As if sensing that fact, Larel didn't outright object. "You are, *for now.* But soon you'll be back in the capital studying and doing great things."

"But I can't—"

"Oh, stop arguing." Larel laughed lightly, running her fingers through Vhalla's hair lovingly. "You'll see it eventually."

Vhalla closed her eyes. "What if I don't?"

"You will."

"Will you still be there to help me? Even if I don't?" Vhalla asked softly, feeling like a child who still needed her security blanket to face the monsters that lurked in the night.

"You know I will be," Larel promised.

"Thank you," Vhalla whispered. "Good night, Larel."

"Good night, Vhalla." Her friend replied, holding tightly to Vhalla's hand as she drifted into sleep.

The door eased open quietly and the soft sigh of the hinges lingered on Vhalla's ears. Fritz had stayed out with Craig and Daniel after the restaurant. Vhalla wondered how drunk he was to come crawling into her room again. She rolled over, pressing her face into the pillow.

The footsteps barely made a sound. Her ears picked up the movement of air more than the noise upon the floor. There was something amiss, but her sleep-filled mind couldn't quickly place what it was. Something about the footsteps . . .

Footsteps. Two sets of footsteps.

Vhalla yawned, bringing a palm to her eyes. She expected to see Craig and Daniel, or some combination of them with Fritz. But when Vhalla blinked the sleep from her eyes, the figure standing at her bedside was a nightmare come to life.

She recognized the Northerner staring down at her. Vhalla remembered a night of fire, a night of running through burning streets with a prince on her heels. She remembered being attacked but cautioning the prince that despite there being four assailants, *two were still missing.*

Moonlight glinted wickedly off the wavy blade the Northerner raised. Vhalla stared in frozen shock.

Another sword cut through the air, and Vhalla turned instinctually toward the sound. The first blade sliced deeply on her back, narrowly missing impaling her due to her sudden and unpredicted movement. The pain of the weapon digging into her flesh didn't even register as Vhalla's mind tried to process what was occurring.

She stared at the blade of another swordsman, plunged straight through Larel's stomach. Blood, inky black in the darkness, poured out from the wound. Larel's dark eyes were jolted open in shock. A strangled gurgling noise accompanied the loll in her friend's eyes as they drifted to Vhalla, blood bubbling through her gaping mouth.

Vhalla screamed.

CHAPTER 23

THE NOISE VHALLA released sounded more animal than human. It was a high-pitched shriek, wordless but perfectly expressing the agony that rushed through her veins on the back of adrenaline. The sword was pulled from Larel's stomach and the assassin twisted it through the air quickly, preparing for a second attack. The woman behind Vhalla was doing the same.

A singular instinct overtook Vhalla: the instinct to survive. She launched herself at the male assailant before her, scrambling across the bed and over the body of her friend. The swordswoman's blade narrowly missed for a second time, slicing Vhalla deep across the calf as she was mid-lunge.

Vhalla tumbled with the swordsman, biting and scratching like a rabid beast. A heartbeat overwhelmed her senses, and Vhalla allowed Aldrik's knowledge of combat to take over. She wanted to know every horrible way he could ever conceive to reap pain and torture upon these vile creatures.

She moved a hand, quickly disarming the man. He was well-trained and swung with his opposite hand, sending Vhalla off him with a jab to her face. She rolled, recovering quickly despite the searing pain in her calf.

The woman was upon her, and Vhalla barely had time to

wave her hand through the air and deflect the blade mid-swing. That movement allowed the man to recover his weapon, and Vhalla was forced to duck to miss another attack. She was outmaneuvered and outnumbered in the small room.

Vhalla made a dash for the door, having to push it open from her knees to avoid the blade that sunk into the wood where her head had been moments before. Vhalla scrambled into the hall, other guests of the inn opening their doors in confusion as the Windwalker sprinted down the narrow stair. Adrenaline was the only thing keeping her upright.

The female assailant let out a cry of frustration, quick on Vhalla's heels. "Die, *Wind Demon!*"

Vhalla half-turned to dodge a dagger thrown at her, tripping down the last of the stairs. The night owls roosting in the lobby were quickly pressed against the outer walls as the Northern assassin and Windwalker rolled head over heels. Some were soldiers who quickly reached for weapons that weren't there. One lunged bare-handed only to be cut down by the Northern man.

She had no time to consider the demise of the nameless Southerner. Her calf burned with what Vhalla suspected was more than pain. Her movements were becoming sluggish and delayed, despite Aldrik's instincts remaining sharp with every pulse of her heart. She bumped into a chair and lost her balance. The swordsman raised his sword as the woman recovered from a gust of air Vhalla had sent her way.

A woman plowed into his side, knocking the Northerner off-balance and sending his blade in a wide arc. Vhalla met the unfamiliar pair of eyes. "Run!" That was the last word the brave woman said as the Northerner plunged the curved blade through her throat.

Vhalla didn't know what running would do, but she did so anyways, barreling through the doors of the inn and into the square. The army was unarmed and off-guard. The soldiers were fat and lazy from the days of peace and relaxation that the Crossroads had afforded. It was so far from the North that they'd all so wrongly assumed they were safe. Even if they had been armed, half of the Crossroads was drunk by this time of night anyways.

But there was one ally ready to greet her. Vhalla felt the wind and quickly turned it on the man racing out to her. It sent the Northerner tumbling head over heels, his head cracking hard against the wall of the inn.

She had expected that to kill him, knock him out, *daze him at least*, but the man seemed to be made of metal or stone as he just blinked and rose again to his feet. She took a step back, sending another gust of wind at him, but it was equally ineffective. She had killed these people before—*why couldn't she kill them now?*

A bloodthirsty cry summoned Vhalla's attention as the Northern woman was nearly upon her. Vhalla swung out her hand, preparing to deflect the attack. The numbness that had been seeping from her calf had spread into her fingers and the wind didn't heed her call.

"The eyes!" a voice cried from behind her.

A dagger crafted of blue ice shattered on the assassin's face, narrowly missing her cheek. The distraction gave Vhalla enough time to roll out of the way of her blade. Vhalla turned, breathless, toward the source of the voice.

Fritz pulled back his hand, another ice dagger appearing in his fingers. He threw and missed again, leaving Vhalla to roll helplessly between sword swings.

Daniel charged as the woman lunged a third time. He had a breathtaking command over his body as each tight step narrowly preempted the assassin's motions. Vhalla recognized the dagger he wielded as one he'd purchased when they'd gone shopping. *The soldier had been wearing it under his pants leg since.*

The Easterner demonstrated how he earned a golden bracer by not even blinking as he sunk the dagger to its hilt into the Northerner's eye. The woman shuddered but didn't make a sound as her body limply fell to the ground, sliding off Daniel's blade. Vhalla stared at the lifeless body but found no sympathy. Instead she turned her rage to the remaining target.

The other assassin, seeing himself outnumbered against the army that quickly gathered with weapons in hand, turned to run.

Vhalla tried to jump to her feet, throwing out a hand uselessly. Whatever poison that they had laced the blade with sent shivers up her spine that blocked her Channel. However, as if summoned from her fingers, an inferno sprang up, sending the Northerner tumbling backwards as he tried to avoid running into the flames.

She twisted on the ground, looking for the origin of the fire. The crowd scattered like rats, fearing the blinding light of the fire that burned from Aldrik's fists to his elbows, searing off the rumpled shirt he wore. His dark eyes were alight with flame and pure malice. Vhalla did not recognize the man before her as the man she had held and kissed a day prior.

This was the Fire Lord.

Aldrik's focus was past her, toying with the Northerner as he sent the assassin scurrying to avoid one blindingly powerful magic flame after the next. Baldair was quick to follow behind his brother, freezing in his step as he took in the carnage before him. Vhalla pushed against the ground, trying to keep herself even partly upright. She was safe now and the heartbeat was beginning to fade. Behind it lurked an agony that threatened to tear her apart.

Aldrik had finally made it to her, and she saw his shoulders quiver with rage as he looked down upon her mangled and bruised body. "Lord Taffl, Baldair," Aldrik spoke to Daniel and his brother but his eyes never left her. "Apprehend that man and bring him here—*alive.*"

The prince knelt at her side. "Vhalla," he whispered.

"Aldrik," she choked out, emotions overwhelming her. Vhalla's face twisted in agony. "Aldrik, she's-she's-I, it's my fault, *it's my fault.*"

"Vhal . . ." Fritz had been the only one of the steadily growing onlookers to approach the two. He sunk to his knees as well.

Vhalla hung her head between her shoulders and wailed in mourning.

"Mother, no . . ." Fritz gasped. Vhalla expected him to be staring in horror at her. But he looked beyond.

She followed the Southerner's gaze over her shoulder, past where Baldair and Daniel were dragging the overpowered assassin toward Aldrik. Her eyes followed the bloody trail she'd left to the inn that was now in need of repair from where she'd slammed a stone-skinned Northerner into its side. Vhalla's eyes fell on a small row of bodies that was being lined up before the doorway. There was the man who'd been cut almost in half through the abdomen, the woman with the wound to her neck, another two Vhalla didn't even remember falling in the scuffle, and then a Western woman.

Vhalla scrambled to her feet, Aldrik and Fritz in too much of a daze to stop her. Limping the pain away, she broke into a clumsy run. Daniel tried to grab her as she passed but his hands were too busy keeping the Northerner under control.

She pushed away the man who was situating Larel's body in the line of the fallen, collapsing at her friend's side. "No no no no no Larel." Vhalla pressed her palms against the woman's mortal wound, as if she could somehow heal it now. "You can't, you can't do this to me!"

Her throat was raw from screaming, but Vhalla's ears could barely make out any sound. She leaned forward, pressing her face into Larel's still warm shoulder, gripping onto the shade of her friend. It was too much. She rocked back and forth with every sob. *It was too much.*

"Vhal," Fritz placed his palms on her shoulders. Vhalla didn't move. "You-you need to get tended to."

"Don't touch me!" she shrieked, twisting out of his grasp, pressing herself closer to Larel.

"Vhal." He grabbed her.

"I said, don't touch me!" Vhalla twisted, swinging at him. She didn't have the strength for an even halfway decent attack, but Fritz still took it upon his tear stained cheek. Quiet sobs heaved his shoulders.

Vhalla stared up at him at an utter loss.

"Bring the Windwalker." The Emperor's voice cut through the rising commotion of the square. His icy blue eyes found hers.

Vhalla gripped Larel's arm tighter. "No," she whispered.

"Vhal, you need to go," Fritz pleaded, kneeling quickly to block the Emperor's view of her disobedience.

"No," she pleaded with Fritz, shaking her head. "I can't, I can't leave Larel like this. She needs me."

"She's dead, Vhalla." Fritz's harsh words were a knife that cut through the last scraps of hope in Vhalla's heart. "And you might be dead too if you don't heed the Emperor's call."

Fritz pulled her upright and herded her toward their ruler.

"It's my fault . . . It's my fault . . ." Vhalla whispered, repeating the mantra over and over in her head.

"What happened here?" the Emperor demanded as she arrived.

All eyes were on her. Vhalla swallowed and turned to the Northerner. "He was a juggler, at the festival."

"Speak clearly, girl!" the Emperor took a step forward.

Aldrik stepped forward as well, wedging himself protectively between his father and Vhalla.

"The people who attacked on the Night of Fire and Wind, they were the jugglers from the festivals, the ones who came to the capital. There were two missing in that attack." Vhalla's voice echoed emptily in her ears.

"And our attack was a success! We had no idea Emperor Solaris was growing Wind Demons," the man spat. His accent was thick and heavy and it would have been difficult to understand if its inflection hadn't already been seared on Vhalla's ears from that fateful night long ago.

"You speak forcefully for a man who is about to die," the Emperor said quietly.

"A warrior doesn't fear death," the man replied haughtily.

"How about dying with the shame of failing to kill the one who slayed your comrades?" The Emperor gave a tilt of his head toward Vhalla.

That set the man off, and he was suddenly raging against Craig, Daniel, and Baldair, who all struggled to keep him on his knees.

"Let him go," the Emperor commanded.

"Father—" Baldair began in shock.

"I said, release him!" Emperor Solaris was not to be trifled with, and they released the Northerner.

The assassin sprang forward like a sprinter from the blocks. But he did not lunge for the most powerful man in all the realms, the man who had killed his people and invaded his homeland. The Northerner lunged for Vhalla.

She didn't even flinch when the flames erupted right before her. They singed her tattered sleeping clothes and licked by her face. But they did not burn her.

The man seemed to resist the heat as well, but only for a brief moment until he was magically overpowered and set to writhing and rolling on the ground. His flesh bubbling and singed.

The Northerner began to rasp, pulling himself into a seated

position. "Tiberum Solaris, the mighty Emperor, *chosen of the sun*, hiding behind his son and a child."

"I am not a child," Vhalla threatened. Her whisper was heard by all and even the Emperor stilled his tongue.

"You think you will lead them to victory?" the man sneered up at her, his face a mess of mutilated flesh. "We sent birds, we reported, we have *friends* here in the West who hold no more love for you. Every sentry; every soldier; every man, woman, and child will aim their arrows, their blades, their stones, their axes, their fists, their picks, and their poisons at you. You cannot comprehend our power, and you will die."

"Daniel, give me your dagger," Vhalla demanded softly.

"Vhalla—"

"Give it to me!" She pried her eyes away from the Northerner, the pain manifesting as hot rage.

Daniel looked hopelessly to Baldair, who turned to the Emperor. The royal considered it only briefly, before nodding at the Golden Guard. Daniel flipped the weapon, carefully grabbing the blade to hold out the hilt to her.

The metal of the hilt felt like her magic did the first time she'd opened her Channel. It was a rush of power. But this was darker, of a more twisted and primal nature. Vhalla limped forward toward the disabled man, her calf beginning to protest her weight. Her clothes were soaked in blood, her own and otherwise, and her shoulders were heavy with guilt.

The Northerner squinted up at her with hatred and rage. For the briefest of moments, Vhalla wondered if he had loved those she'd killed on the Night of Fire and Wind the same way she had loved Larel. If she simply stared into a mirror of herself, she just happened to be on the lucky side of the reflection.

The man snarled and lunged. Vhalla moved to meet him. She did not need the Joining; she would do this alone. Vhalla remembered what Daniel had said as she felt the resistance of the blade sink straight through the man's eye, embedding itself into his skull.

There was no sound but the wind as Vhalla remained frozen in time, staring at the remaining wide-eye and lifeless face of the man she had killed. This was not a blind rage, it wasn't a burst of power, and it was not a memory her mind would later block. It was the deliberate end to a life, and it had been horribly simple.

Vhalla suddenly felt sick, and she swayed as her whole body trembled. She felt empty and yet so full with agony that she was certain she was going to split apart at the seams and die.

Her calf gave out with the waning resolve, and Vhalla staggered, falling.

Daniel moved to catch her, but Aldrik was faster. The prince caught and twisted her. Vhalla found herself weightless as Aldrik hoisted her into the air, holding her to his chest. She grimaced as he shifted his arm around the severed flesh of her back, finding a way to hold her with the least amount of pain possible.

When the prince turned, Vhalla could see the face of the Emperor. It was deathly still and the malice in his eyes at the sight of her in Aldrik's arms was palpable, but the prince said nothing. He looked past his father and started for the hotel in which he'd been staying. Vhalla felt every wide eye and saw each gaping mouth as the people parted to make way for the crown prince and Windwalker.

"Aldrik," she breathed, trying to be quiet enough that only he would hear. "Aldrik, you-I-they . . ."

"Let them say something," Aldrik ground out through a clenched jaw. "Let one person say something and give me a reason to burn it all."

Vhalla felt the heat in his palms, the raw strength he wielded that promised to make good on his threats, and she closed her eyes. Vhalla leaned against the shoulder of the crown prince as he carried her into the temporary home of the Imperial family. She pressed her face against him and allowed his strength to shield her weakness as her shoulders began to shake and tears fell once more.

CHAPTER 24

A
LDRIK LAID HER down gently on a chaise, a boneless
shell of grief and tears. Vhalla curled on her side, almost
choking as she sobbed. Aldrik sat next to her, his fingers
lightly caressing her hair.

Whatever peace he could offer her was quickly ruined by the
door slamming open.

"You have lost your mind!" Lord Ophain took giant steps
toward his nephew.

"Leave us, Uncle." Aldrik didn't pull his eyes away from her,
his fingers losing themselves in her hair.

"I thought you wanted to protect her—"

"And she is clearly nowhere safer than at my side." There was
a foreboding calm to Aldrik's words.

"No, what you did just now was put an even bigger target on
her back by showing everyone that *she's* the chink in the crown
prince's armor!" Lord Ophain pleaded, "Aldrik, you need to
move her to a clerical room and cover for your actions. That
you acted as you did only because we need her for the war. You
want her to think that—"

Fire erupted next to them as the opposite chaise burst into
flame. The sudden brightness and flames at Aldrik's back made
Vhalla stir.

"Uncle, I swear to the Mother, if you or anyone else tries to take her from me—"

"That's enough, Aldrik." Vhalla rested her hand over one of his clenched fists. The flames instantly extinguished. She slumped against him, his arm quickly wrapping around her shoulders. Vhalla didn't know which one of them was shaking. "He's trying to help. Should I—"

Aldrik tightened his arm, half-pulling her onto his lap. He held her against him as if he was desperately trying to piece back the broken thing she was with his quivering caresses. One arm clutched at her waist, and he drew a shaky breath. "No, I will not." He scowled at the Lord of the West as he spoke to her. "I will not let you go."

"You'll need to let her go if you don't want her to die from infection." Prince Baldair stood in the doorway. "I'll see to her here." He crossed over, placing one of the largest cleric's boxes Vhalla had ever seen on the ground by the chaise.

The two brothers regarded each other, and Vhalla began to think Aldrik was going to make good on his promise. But his arms finally relaxed, and he eased her back into a reclining position. Aldrik quickly resituated himself so that her head could rest on his thigh.

The younger prince pulled at the hem of her shirt, slicing through the tatters in the back all the way to her collar. Vhalla didn't have the energy to worry about her modesty. She didn't have the energy to do anything other than cry and let Aldrik wipe away the tears.

"Father is assembling the majors," Baldair said finally. "You need to go."

"I'm not leaving her," Aldrik repeated.

"She needs to rest," Prince Baldair retorted.

"You should go, Aldrik." Lord Ophain was much more collected. "If you want to protect her then you *must go*. You are the only one who can represent her interests at that table, *both* of your interests."

Aldrik's hands stopped moving. His pain palpably washed over her and numbed Baldair's probing in the gash on her back. Vhalla clutched the crown prince's thigh with white knuckles. Her fingers would leave bruises in their wake.

He was going to leave her. She knew he had to but that made it no easier. The world was taking him from her too. Vhalla couldn't handle it.

"Baldair," Aldrik choked on the *a* but quickly recovered.

Larel had been his friend too, his only friend in many ways. Vhalla had taken her from him as well. *It was all her fault.* Vhalla pressed her eyes closed, her whole body shaking.

"You don't let her out of your sight. You protect her with everything you have. You see her healed and well. Do this for me and I will never ask a single thing of you again," Aldrik's voice was raw as it forced through tears he wasn't letting fall.

Prince Baldair's ministrations paused as the two princes shared a look of understanding that had not been there in some time. "You have my word, brother. On my honor."

Aldrik began to pull away from her. Vhalla gripped his hands with both of hers, willing him to stay. "D-don't, Aldrik. Please, don't leave me yet. I know you have to but not, not yet."

Her eyes nearly broke him.

"Aldrik, *please*," she pleaded, tears streaming down her cheeks.

He eased her back down onto the chaise, standing at its side. Aldrik leaned forward, smoothing her hair away from her face one more time and pressed his lips to her temple. Vhalla sobbed.

"I will return as soon as I can."

"Promise me." She gripped for his fingers again. "*Promise,* and I'll believe it."

"*I promise,* and I will never break a promise to you, my

Vhalla." He took his hand from hers and straightened. Vhalla watched as the stony façade of the crown prince slipped back into place. He wore the distance of nobility, the ferocity of the Fire Lord, and the armor of his title. He was a warrior ready to do battle.

Vhalla balled her hands into fists and buried her eyes in the pads of her palms, letting out a wail the moment the door closed behind Aldrik and his uncle. "It's my fault, it's my fault."

"It is not." She hadn't been speaking to the younger prince, but he responded.

"What do you know?" Vhalla spat bitterly. "You know nothing about your brother, nothing about me. You've never even tried to know. You were too busy with your misplaced warnings. So just be quiet for once."

The prince obliged her for a time as he placed gauze over the wound, coating it in a sticky substance that turned icy as it hardened. He pressed on her shoulder lightly and Vhalla understood that he needed her on her stomach to access the wound on her calf. The prince began stitching the deep wound without even warning her first.

"That one had poison in it," she mumbled.

"What?" His fingers stopped. "Are you sure?"

"It was affecting my magic." Vhalla nodded, her tears subsiding into numbness.

"I'll need to get someone else to see to that." The prince fumbled among the vials of elixirs, salves, and antidotes. "I have no idea which is which for poisons."

"Aldrik will know." Vhalla was certain. Prince Baldair returned to his stitching and packing the wound with a thick salve. When he was finished, he came around the chaise to kneel before her face. The prince dipped his first two fingers into the tin and began to massage the ointment over Vhalla's black eye.

"Thank you, my prince," she begrudgingly offered.

"Baldair," he corrected.

"Baldair?" The name sounded surprisingly easy on her tongue.

"You call Aldrik by his name; it's weird to have you continue to call me by my title." Baldair packed up his case and stood. "I'll fetch Elecia; she'll see about an antidote."

"I said *Aldrik* would know." Vhalla had no interest in seeing the Western woman.

"And Aldrik will not return for many hours," Baldair replied firmly. His tone softened when he saw her deflate. "Elecia will help you."

Vhalla nodded and began mentally withdrawing herself to endure the assault Elecia was likely to heap upon her. It had been days since they spoke, and in such time Vhalla had become the secret lover of the crown prince, Elecia's cousin. Vhalla closed her eyes and attempted to think about nothing.

When the door opened again Vhalla didn't even turn. She held herself tightly, trying to fight away the shivers. *Her fault, her fault, it was all her fault.*

"Vhalla." Elecia touched her shoulder gently, and Vhalla spooked, nearly jumping out of her skin at the contact. "Let me see you."

Elecia's manner left no room for objection, and the Westerner's hands were suddenly wrapped carefully around Vhalla's neck. She moved her fingers up Vhalla's cheek, the other hand ghosting over her shoulders, down the middle of her chest and on her thigh.

Vhalla pressed her eyes closed.

"It's the same nonsense they used on Aldrik," Elecia sighed. "But much weaker. Shouldn't be a problem."

It was weaker than what Aldrik had endured? He had more and could still use his magic, where hers had already faltered. Vhalla had a whole new appreciation of the crown prince's strength.

"Where is Aldrik?" she couldn't stop herself from asking.

Elecia sighed, rummaging through the small bag she'd brought.

"Figuring out how to keep you safe." Elecia sat down next to her, inspecting Baldair's work and making her own additions. "You and him . . ."

"I love him." Vhalla shook again, the words bringing a fresh batch of tears to her eyes. "I love him, but I am only death. I am death to everyone I love. Someday I will be the death of him."

Elecia grabbed her face roughly, turning Vhalla to face her. The woman's emerald eyes burned red at the edges from exhaustion or tears. "You will not be. I will not let you be."

"But—" she whined.

"If you are going to be with him, then you will find the strength to wear that mantle. You don't get it both ways, Vhalla Yarl," Elecia said fiercely. "He's risking everything for you tonight, so you better be ready to do the same. Because if you hurt him, I swear I will kill you."

Vhalla made a choked noise when her lips failed to form words. Elecia put her hand on Vhalla's back with a frustrated sigh, creating a tingle as her magic activated the salve she had applied. She repeated the process on Vhalla's calf and forced two more vials down Vhalla's throat before thrusting the third into her hands.

"Deep Sleep?" Vhalla instantly recognized the smell from what Baldair had given her months ago during her trial.

"You can't heal if you don't sleep. Get the rest while you can." Elecia stood.

"Wait, don't leave me." Elecia was the last person Vhalla ever expected to cling to. But grief wasn't logical.

"I can't do anything more for you." Elecia frowned down at the Eastern woman, but didn't pull her hand away.

"Don't leave me alone, please." Vhalla bowed her head again.

Larel, she wanted Larel. She wanted to feel safe and warm and unconditionally loved. *She wanted Larel.*

"Lie down," Elecia sighed and sat. The woman didn't offer her any further comfort. She didn't whisper soothing words or wipe Vhalla's tears away. But she stayed until the Deep Sleep took effect, and Vhalla's mind was finally forced to shut down. And Elecia never untwined her fingers from the grieving Easterner.

Vhalla stirred some time later when she was lifted into someone's arms. The momentary panic was quickly quelled the second she felt his warmth, heard his matching heartbeat slow and strong through his chest. Aldrik carried her off the chaise to the bed, settling her beneath the covers.

She whimpered pitifully. It hurt so much to be awake after sleep had been so blissfully void of everything. The bed sagged as he curled around her.

"Aldrik," Vhalla murmured, pressing herself into him.

"My Vhalla," he sighed heavily. "Sleep, it's not yet dawn."

Vhalla shook her head, earning another sigh. She needed to know what had happened. Cracking open her eyes, she was met with an exhausted shadow of the prince she knew. Dark circles perched upon his cheeks, taking up residence under his tired eyes. His hair was limp and tangled. She saw the makings of a bruise on his jaw that she wasn't sure she wanted to know how he got.

"Aldrik." One of the larger remaining pieces of her heart cracked and fractured at the sight of him. *It was her fault*, it was her fault he looked as he did; she had put him in this position.

"Sleep. You need your rest," he insisted again. No matter the state of his appearance, his voice was calm and level.

Vhalla pried herself away. "Don't you care?"

"*What?*"

"Larel, Larel is dead and I killed her!" Vhalla's words were wet with tears. "Don't you care?"

Aldrik pulled himself into a seated position, staring down at her. "*Don't I care?*" he breathed sharply.

She could hear the quivering tension he barely controlled. Vhalla instantly regretted her words but he spoke too quickly for her to revoke them.

"Do you still think I am the heartless Fire Lord?"

The look on his face alone made Vhalla hiccup with tears. "Aldrik, no . . ." She shook her head.

"Clearly you must if you somehow think I am blissfully unaffected by-by her death," he snapped.

"I'm sorry, I didn't mean it."

"Do you even know how we met?" Aldrik stood and began to pace the room. "How I met Larel?"

"She told me once," Vhalla whispered, feeling the anger radiating off of him.

"She told me I saved her, that I was the prince from all the stories who saves the helpless girl." Aldrik chuckled; sorrow waged a war against self-loathing in the darkness of his eyes. "I always told her she was foolish, and I never told her how much I needed those words. I never even *thanked* her for them. How silly she was thinking that I saved her when she was the one saving me."

"I know, you were close . . ." Vhalla pulled herself into a seated position.

"You have no idea." He rounded to face her. "You likely grew up surrounded by friends and people who enjoyed your company. Even in my best of years I was strange and distanced by nobility and magic. There was only one person among my peers who saw me as anything but their prince. *I had Larel.* And even-even after I pushed her away she came back. She was a far better friend than I ever deserved."

"That's not tr—"

"And when she came to me, paper in hand to march with you, I told her she wasn't ready."

It was her fault.

"I knew she wasn't trained enough, wasn't built for war. But I thought—" His hands gripped her shoulders suddenly. "I thought I could protect her. Just like I thought I could protect you."

Vhalla couldn't find words.

"But here you are, bruised and sliced open by an attempt on your life. There is no reason other than just . . . luck that you were not also in a pool of blood next to her. Don't you know I saw that?" He shook her and it made Vhalla wince from the pain in her back. Aldrik stopped and stared into her wide eyes, dropping his head. "Larel is dead and you may as well have died—I protected no one."

He sat gripping her shoulders, his hair covering his face. At the first breath she thought he was going to speak more, but he let it out slowly, then another shaky breath, filled with more silence. The quivers were small at first, and started in his shoulders before finding their way to his hands despite his fighting.

She heard it, *that breath*, the one his tears were let loose upon. Vhalla heard the strange, choked noise rise from his throat as he finally gave into his own overwhelming grief. He was tired, he was over-worked, and he had lost the person whom he had considered his best friend. Aldrik—the crown prince, the future Emperor, Fire Lord, ruler of the Black Legion, sorcerer—was only a man. And men could be broken.

His grip loosened and his hands slid down to her arms, but he still held onto her. It was the first tear that fell onto the bed sheet that finally drew Vhalla out of her own shock and pain. She reached out her arms and pulled him to her without hesitation, pressing his face against her chest to hide him. She knew in all his stubbornness he was likely shamed for simply showing his grief.

As his tears began to heave his chest, she found her own pain refueled by his. She held him tightly, stroking his hair, wanting to offer him all the comfort he would never demand himself. His arms moved and wrapped themselves around her waist as he finally gave in. The wound on her back protested as he grabbed onto her but Vhalla said nothing. He may not allow himself a second chance to cry, she realized, so she would do nothing to stop his grief.

She never fulfilled his original order of sleep as the sunlight began to fill the room. Even after the tears subsided, he remained curled in her arms. Vhalla knew the way he was twisted couldn't be comfortable, but she found as much comfort from him as she gave so Vhalla made no suggestion to move.

When Aldrik finally withdrew, he looked away before standing. He raised a hand to his face and Vhalla averted her gaze, allowing him his privacy. He turned back to her.

"We have a long day today." His voice sounded hollow and detached.

"What will happen?" She wasn't actually sure if she wanted to know.

"You heard it yourself; the attacks on you will be frequent and without mercy." He leaned over her, tilting her chin to look at him.

His face had already recovered itself and, other than red in his eyes, he didn't have the appearance of a man who had just cried for more than an hour. His jaw was set in determination, his brow furrowed with the weight of calculated planning. Vhalla wasn't sure what she felt when this desperate mix of emotion was directed at her.

"Today we are making three doppelgangers for you."

"Doppelgangers?" She blinked.

"Last night, the majors discussed who else among the host was the closest to your look, size, and build. Those women will come today, one by one, and we will turn them into you." He spoke with such precision that Vhalla knew this was not the majors' plan but his. "Each will ride with me, my brother, or my father, so from the beginning your exact location will be a mystery to everyone, including the soldiers."

"If there are three women, where will I be?" she braved.

"You will be hidden in plain sight." He caressed her cheek gently. "From today, your doubles own your name. It is no longer yours."

"What?" Vhalla was overwhelmed and confused.

"By tomorrow, one of them will be the real Vhalla Yarl. But none of them will be the real Vhalla Yarl. You will be a swordswoman of no merit or worth. You will have come with the Western footmen so no one will question not knowing you. Make up any name and story you would like but you will need it soon."

"I can't . . ." she whimpered softly, she didn't even know how to hold a sword.

"You can, and you will," he said firmly. Aldrik shook his head. "This is the best chance we have now, and I *will not* lose you."

"What about the other women? They will be targeted," she whispered.

"Exactly, and if one of them is slain the North may just believe they have killed the Windwalker," he said coldly.

"Aldrik, that's someone's daughter, maybe someone's mother, or someone—"

"I don't care!" Vhalla jumped at his sudden intensity. Aldrik stormed to the opposite side of the room. "I have to make a choice, Vhalla. That choice is your life or theirs, and it is no question for me. If they die, then they will die honorably for their Emperor." He turned back to her and she saw—to her horror—that his words were true, he really didn't care about their lives. They had been written off as expendable.

She fidgeted with her fingers.

"You will ride with Baldair—"

"What?" Vhalla exclaimed, jumping to her feet. Her calf stung in pain and Aldrik was quickly supporting her. "Aldrik, no, don't leave me. Don't leave me alone!"

"Quiet. *Hush.*" It was a command but his soothing words had their desired effect. "You must ride there for the illusion of a swordswoman. But it is only until we reach the North." Aldrik smoothed her hair away from her eyes. "When we reach the border, the host will split into smaller groups for movement through the jungle. You'll be with me then."

She sniffled loudly, tears returning anew.

"You'll be with me then, my Vhalla, my lady, my love." Aldrik pressed his lips firmly against hers, silencing any further objections.

"Do you . . ." she sniffled.

"I promise." Aldrik's jaw quivered briefly, and he was kissing her again. His mouth tasted like resignation, and Vhalla knew that was the flavor he would leave her with. "Now, promise me you will be strong."

"I promise." Her face twisted in agony.

Aldrik pressed her against him, and Vhalla clung to him so tightly her hands shook. His long fingers snaked through her hair. "I will sacrifice anything that must be sacrificed to keep you safe."

She believed him completely—evoking a new terror to swim through her veins.

He led her to a different room on the same floor and instructed her to wait. Vhalla had no idea what to expect when he reappeared later with the Emperor.

She clutched at the blanket Aldrik had placed over her tattered clothing. The Emperor regarded her with thinly veiled contempt. Aldrik was completely closed off.

"Well, let us begin." Emperor Solaris walked over to a table, opening a folio he was carrying, sitting before a handful of papers.

One at a time, Aldrik brought in majors who escorted women under their command. And one at a time Vhalla told them what it meant to be Vhalla Yarl. She told them of her childhood, her home in Cyven. She told them of the library, Mohned, her apprenticeship, Roan, and Sareem. She told them of the Night of Fire and Wind and of her trial. She laid herself bare to them with the Emperor and majors watching.

It felt like a Projection. She spoke and moved but her mind was more detached with everything that was said. Every word gave away pieces of herself and she became less and less Vhalla Yarl.

The last was a woman almost identical to her short stature. She appeared to be a mixture of Southern and Eastern with long dark blond hair. Vhalla felt she was the closest to her looks, despite her lighter hair and blue eyes. That woman thanked her before she was ushered out of the room. Vhalla was certain the woman had not listened to a thing Vhalla had said about her life if the woman was thanking Vhalla for the opportunity to be her.

Between Vhalla retelling her story to each doppelganger and the secrecy required to sneak each woman in and out of the room, it took all morning and into the afternoon to accomplish the task. By the time the last woman was led to her holding room Vhalla was exhausted.

Aldrik and the Emperor favored the same woman as Vhalla, which meant that woman would be the double who would ride in Aldrik's company. Vhalla was given the woman's bag as her new clothes. Aldrik also thrust a dagger and a bottle of black ink into her hands, telling her to do whatever she could to change her appearance.

Trembling and alone in the washroom, Vhalla carefully

sponged away the dirt and blood from the night before. She watched carefully as she applied the ink to her hair, changing the brown strands to black. After letting it sit for a moment she rinsed and repeated the process three times. She inspected her progress in the mirror; her hair had indeed changed color.

Vhalla bit her lip, remembering how straight and tame her hair had been when Larel had used her heat upon it. She choked down a sob and raked her fingers through her hair with pockets of wind trapped underneath. It was clumsy and took a few minutes to be met with any success. But it dried straighter, more Western looking, taking out her normal wavy texture. It was longer this way, and Vhalla made the conscious decision not to cut short it again. She had done so once and become no one. This time she would grow into her new skin.

But Vhalla still grabbed for the dagger. Pulling her bangs in the front Vhalla made a straight horizontal cut just below her brow. For the second time in a year, Vhalla was unable to recognize the person staring back at her in the mirror. She leaned over the washbasin, muffling her mouth with her hand as she struggled to suppress tears for the woman whose memory she had decided to honor.

Keep it together. Vhalla Yarl's friend died, Vhalla Yarl would mourn. *She was not Vhalla Yarl.* She looked back to the mirror, steeling her resolve. Looking at the hard eyes and foreign face she repeated to herself, *she was not Vhalla Yarl.* She cleaned up the bathroom quickly, changing into the other woman's clothes—she corrected herself—*her* clothes.

She left the washroom and returned to where the Emperor and Aldrik waited. Both men looked her up and down. The Emperor leaned back in his chair.

"It will do," he said, rubbing a finger against his lips.

"What is your name?" Aldrik asked her.

"Serien," she replied without hesitation.

"Serien, what is your family name?" he questioned.

"Serien Leral," she said and realized the moment he recognized her name.

Aldrik struggled to keep his composure. "Where are you from?" His jaw set firmly.

"A town called Qui. It's a mining town that I hope you never have to go to," she recited. Her story had been built for her.

"Where is Qui?" The Emperor leaned forward, folding his hands between his knees.

"It's about halfway to Norin, if you take the old roads."

"Your parents?" Aldrik asked.

"My father was a miner, and a drunk. My mother was a broken woman who left her home in the East because she thought it was love. They died when I was young, and I worked in the mines." Despite her small changes to account for her eyes she wondered if the Emperor would see the source of inspiration for her story. She smiled coldly; *of course he wouldn't*. Larel had meant nothing to him, she doubted he even remembered the girl his son saved from the silver mines of Qui.

"Why are you here?" The Emperor questioned her confident gaze.

"For a better life, to serve the Emperor," she said easily.

"Well done, Miss Yarl." The Emperor sat back in his chair.

She stared at him curiously. "Miss Leral," she corrected.

The man simply chuckled.

"Your armor is here." Aldrik stood to the side and allowed her to approach the table that was behind them. Basic plate and silver chainmail was displayed upon it. Vhalla was stunned a moment, one of the women would be wearing the armor Aldrik had made for her. *No*, she reminded herself, Aldrik had made that armor for Vhalla Yarl, and *she was not Vhalla Yarl*.

She scooped up the chainmail. This was Serien's armor, simple and unadorned. It was the kind of armor that would slip into a mass of soldiers and be undistinguishable from the next. Aldrik silently assisted in showing her how to strap on the plate. It was heavier than her scale, and the weight made her favor her uninjured leg as she pulled on the gauntlets.

He turned and presented her with a sword. Thankfully, it strapped over her left leg, her good leg, so she could draw it with her right hand. She shifted, adjusting to its weight on her hip.

"Any questions?"

There was a notable pause and their eyes met. She wondered what he saw in her then, *who* he saw then.

"Serien?"

The name was strange to hear coming from him, addressed to her. But if anyone could say it and make her believe that it was her new identity, it would be Aldrik. She shook her head no.

"Good, you'll be reporting under the Golden Guard. You are dismissed."

She nodded. Her eyes reflected the empty distance she saw in his. Grabbing her canvas bag off the floor, she turned and gave a brief salute. Her knuckles were white from attempting to walk down the stairs wearing armor with her injured leg. She was determined, but mindful not to rip her stitches.

It was almost sunset when Serien left the hotel though a backdoor.

CHAPTER 25

T HE RIGHTS OF the fallen were held at sunset so the Mother could usher the souls of the dead to the Father's eternal realms. Serien attended with the masses in the central square of the Crossroads, though none looked at her twice. She stared at the carefully crafted platform that held five bodies shrouded in red cloth.

One of them was Larel Neiress, the woman whom had spent countless hours putting Vhalla Yarl back together after the world had broken her. But this time, her hands had not been there, and Vhalla Yarl shattered into three pieces.

The crown prince stood before the bodies, stoic as a hooded crone sang the funeral dirge. Serien grit her teeth and walled her heart. She would not cry. She could not cry for a woman she had never met.

But her eyes were attentive and she saw as the crown prince was fixated on the fourth body. She felt the way his flames moved toward it at a base level that could not be explained away. She finally stepped out of the crowd as her stomach began to knot.

She was a drifter, a loner, the specter of the Crossroads with nowhere to be and no one to look for her. Serien perched herself under an archway of one of the many buildings, returning twice after being shoo'ed away. Eventually the owner finally stopped trying.

She watched the crowds move, blissful as life returned to normal. She saw a messy-haired Southerner go to the hotel with three large windows four times, returning to a familiar inn dejected and alone each time. The twinge of sadness crept up the back of her throat, which she quickly squashed—*emotions of another woman.*

When the army finally amassed in the square, prepared to march, Serien was an exhausted husk of a woman. She had barely slept out of fear, fear of what her treacherous mind may concoct and fear of sleeping in the open. She had no mount to speak of but instinctually fell into place in the center of the column. It was odd being surrounded by so much silver plate, but she quickly worked to accept it as her new normal.

Cheers erupted for the family Solaris as they left the hotel in full regalia. Six steeds had been lined up before the hotel, three were for the royals, the other three were for the dark-cloaked figures who walked at their side. Three women, almost identical in stature, with black hooded cloaks shrouding their faces walked next to each one of the royals. On the backs of their cloaks was a silver wing. It made for a beautiful target.

With vapid interest she watched one mount a black steed that had a white strip running down its face, like lightning. The woman was situated to the right of the crown prince, and Serien watched as the prince glanced at the woman before trotting toward his place in line.

"They could have at least tried to hide it," one of the soldiers around her remarked.

"Not very hard to tell which one is the Windwalker," another agreed.

"As if the Fire Lord would let his dark darling out of his sight."

Serien didn't join in their speculations as to the real

relationship between the crown prince and the Windwalker Vhalla Yarl, but her ears heard. Most seemed to be in agreement that there was something between the two, but their theories were wide-reaching. Two men and a woman joined the younger prince as he fell into line with the hooded Windwalker.

"That's enough, shape up!" an Easterner commanded.

Serien stared up at him as his horse found its way near her. The man with the golden bracer glanced down, meeting her stare. His eyes squinted slightly, and he opened his mouth to say something.

"Daniel, what is it?" a Southerner to his left asked.

Serien quickly returned her attention forward. She shouldn't have picked the center of the column. Serien tried to bring her hands together to fidget but it was difficult in the heavier gauntlets. She bit her lip instead.

"Nothing," the Easterner replied. "Sorry, it's nothing."

Keeping up with the horses was difficult as they marched double-time in full regalia, leaving the Crossroads. Serien's calf screamed in pain, and sweat poured off her from the exertion of smothering her cries. Even when the call to slow was made, it wasn't any easier. She was certain she had ripped her stitches.

Serien kept her eyes forward the whole day. The Great Imperial Way was going to stop soon. They would reach the last outpost before the North, and then it would be dangerous territory. Her somber mood didn't match any of the other soldiers', and she remained in her trance until the call to stop.

That was the first moment Serien felt lost. All the others knew what to do, where to go. They had their tents and their assignments. There wasn't any hesitation as they dissolved into normal life for swordsmen.

She moved slowly, trying to overhear a bit of conversation that would confirm if she could just go up to the tent cart and ask for one or not.

"Soldier," a man called from behind her.

Serien turned and her chest ached at the familiar eyes.

"You're a new recruit, aren't you?" Daniel stopped before her, a hand on his hip.

"I am," Serien mumbled.

"Your name?" The question was clearly forced.

"Serien Leral," she replied, hoping he'd take note.

"Let me see you use that thing." He pointed to her sword.

She looked back at the Easterner. What was he thinking? He was going to ruin her cover less than one day in. One or two others glanced at the Golden Guard addressing her, but it seemed normal enough that they didn't give it much heed.

Serien drew her sword, determined. It was too heavy, and she was instantly off-balance. She gripped it with two hands, trying to steady herself. Daniel drew his sword and in one fluid motion he sent her weapon flying from her hands and into the sand.

"That wasn't fair!" she protested.

"Do you think our enemy will be fair?" Daniel took a step closer. "How long have you practiced?"

Serien averted her eyes. She shouldn't have said anything. "Not long." It sounded a lot better than "never."

"The West is really letting their standards drop." He sheathed his blade, crossing his arms over his chest. Serien regarded him cautiously. "You *are* from the West, aren't you?"

"I am."

"Thought so." He sighed dramatically with a roll of his eyes. "Fine, I'll teach you."

"What?"

"I'm not letting a soldier under my command go into war helpless." A familiar tone echoed under his words. "Let's get out of the tents."

She followed him into the desert on the outside of the host.

They didn't go far, just far enough that there was room to move in a wide circle and not fear for swinging their blades.

"You don't hold it like that. Look at how I hold mine." He demonstrated on his own blade and ended up moving her hand placement anyways. "There, like that."

"It's heavy," she whispered.

"It's forged steel." Daniel chuckled. "Now, to swing."

If Serien had been exhausted, in pain, and sweat drenched from the march, it was nothing compared to working with Daniel until sunset. Every limb ached, her shoulders screamed in protest, and she could barely grip the blade to sheathe it.

"That's enough for today." Daniel made note of her condition.

Serien nodded in thanks. "Daniel," she said softly as they started back for camp.

"Yes?" His tone had changed to something she knew.

"Can I just get any tent?"

"You didn't already get one?" He seemed startled.

"No, I didn't. They didn't tell me anything." She bit her lip.

"There aren't going to be any left." Daniel ran a gauntleted hand through his hair. "Would you like to stay with me?" His question was so soft he clearly doubted it.

"I can't."

"Why?" Daniel asked sincerely. "Why can't you?"

"Because I . . ."

"I won't let you sleep in the sand, alone." It hardly sounded appealing to her either. "Are you travelling with someone, Serien?"

Daniel stole her eyes, and Serien struggled with finding an answer. "I'm sorry, I can't."

Serien pushed ahead of him and didn't look back.

It was just as he had said. She slept out in the open with her pack as her pillow. Even though the South would be in the throes of winter, it was hot in the Waste and that heat lingered through the evening. It wasn't until the moon was half in the sky that she began to shiver.

When Serien woke, a blanket covered her shoulders. There was no name stitched upon it, but it was finer than standard issue. Serien looked around, as if she could find the phantom who had placed it upon her in the night. But no one came forward.

She used it the next night, and the night after that. Once, Serien thought briefly about the other woman's powers, about reaching out her mind from her body in the cover of darkness to a certain prince. But the idea was quickly squelched. That prince did not belong to her, he and Serien were nothing. She drifted to sleep that night debating with herself. *If Serien and Prince Aldrik were nothing, then why was she sleeping alone in the cold?*

By the third night the other soldiers had begun to notice that she was aloof and different.

"You practice with Lord Taffl a lot," remarked one of the soldiers who marched next to her.

"It is an honor," Serien said dryly.

"You someone special to the lord?" they asked.

She didn't say anything.

"Hey, I asked you a question." The soldier waved his hand in front of her face.

She continued to look forward.

"What's wrong with you?" the man huffed.

"Leave the lady alone," Daniel ordered from atop his horse.

"Definitely someone special," the soldier mumbled to his friend.

The words stayed with Serien the whole day, and she confronted Daniel about them later. Serien threw her sword into the sand. Her leg was throbbing, likely from not taking off her greaves for nearly a week straight. Her calf was a mess she couldn't bring herself to look at.

"They think there's something between us."

"And?" Daniel sheathed his sword, picking up hers.

"We can't keep doing this or they'll think—"

"What?" He handed the sword back to her. "What will they think?"

"That there's something between us." Serien didn't take the weapon.

"So what?"

"They can't," she insisted.

"Why not?" Daniel shrugged but his eyes betrayed hurt.

"Because we're . . ." Her voice faded as he took a step closer to her.

"What? What are we?" he asked softly.

She finally took the sword sheathing it in frustration.

"I don't have words for it either, yet." Daniel laid himself emotionally bare before her. "But I want to help you, I want to look out for you. I know I'm not even supposed to know who you are, but I do and I'm thankful for it."

Serien shook her head, trying to unhear his words.

"Look at me," he said softly. She shook her head again. "*Vhalla*, look at me."

Her attention snapped to him at the mention of her real name. It crumbled her mask and tore down the walls she'd tried so hard to build. It made the pain worse and the truth harder to bear.

"Don't call me that," she begged. "Please, Daniel, don't call me that."

"It is your name." He quickly pulled off his gauntlet. She stilled when his skin made contact with hers, his hand along her jaw. "Why did they take it from you?"

"To keep me safe," she hiccupped softly, losing the fight with tears.

He sighed, unable to argue. "Then let me keep you safe as

well. Don't sleep outside on the ground again tonight. It has carved a hole into my chest that gets deeper each moment I think of you there."

"You know why I can't." She wasn't sure if it was Vhalla or Serien who looked at him then, but Daniel was unable to meet her stare.

"*He* would want you safe," Daniel mumbled. His hand fell from her face with the weight of resignation. "I won't touch you, I swear it."

The sun was setting over the dunes, turning his Eastern skin golden. Vhalla swallowed, trying to find Serien in her once more. Her heart hurt, her mind was heavy, but she didn't want to sleep in the cold another night and she was *so tired.*

Serien nodded.

Daniel stared at her in disbelief for a long moment. He was quick to lead her back to camp. Serien's heart raced as he led her toward a modestly-sized tent near the center. Two similar ones were placed near it, Baldair's not far away.

Her eyes lingered on the younger prince's tent. He would know. He would find out about her and Daniel, if he hadn't already. *What if he told Aldrik?*

She searched the soldiers in paranoia. But none paid her any mind. She was invisible, a no one. Daniel may be a lord and a major, but he was a freshly minted one and clearly not considered to be much above the common soldier. No one cared who went into his tent or why he took them there.

Inside it was larger than the average soldier's, comfortable for three people. Serien sat dumbly, her eyes adjusting to the fading light. Daniel wasn't a Firebearer, he couldn't summon flames for them to see by, so they were left to the remaining light of the sun and growing light of the moon.

"Do you know how to take this off?" He was already halfway out of his plate.

"Not really." She'd forgotten what Aldrik had shown her. It was more complex than the simple hooks he'd fashioned for her scale mail.

"Let me show you." Daniel moved slowly, as though the slightest motion could send her running. The moment he lifted the plate off her shoulders, she breathed a sigh of relief. She'd forgotten how heavy the blasted armor was. Serien was quick to shed her chainmail.

"What—" Daniel lifted her pant leg before she had time to object. Serien saw what had commanded his attention. Her calf was caked in blood, the bandages hanging limp and useless, her flesh was shredded from the stiches she'd ripped. "By the Mother, how are you even walking?"

"I've gotten used to it." There was a horrific fascination with seeing her own body mutilated. Serien wondered if she felt so calm because even her body didn't feel like hers. Nothing belonged to her anymore, not even her name.

"No, this is bad." Daniel rummaged through his pack. "I need to go to a cleric."

"No!" She gripped his wrist. "They'll ask questions."

"No, they won't." Daniel assured her. "Serien, you're no one. I'm mostly no one. Soldiers get hurt all the time. Stop worrying." He rested a palm on her head and quickly departed.

Serien struggled with the emotions silently warring in her that followed his absence: guilt, shame, pain, exhaustion, and *relief*. She was happy not to be alone.

Daniel re-bandaged her leg and refused to train with her for a week after that. She spent most of the time making up lost hours of sleep. As soon as his tent was erected, she disappeared and hid from the world. In the darkness she didn't have to be Serien or Vhalla. She could be no one, and that was the only thing that brought her peace enough to close her eyes.

Patrols and sentries were increased around the host, but

there weren't any further attacks. The march toward the North seemed so peaceful that it was unnerving. The soldiers were beginning to bore, and with their boredom came gossip.

"I hear he finally started taking her to his tent again." The chatty one next to Serien had been very excited for this particular piece of gossip.

"Who?"

"The crown prince and the Windwalker. Who else?"

Serien glanced in the direction of the talking soldiers.

"But I hear he's going through twice his usual spirits."

"Enough for him and her?"

"Well I can't blame her. I'd have to be out of my mind drunk to even think of sleeping with the Fire Lord!" They all laughed.

She wondered how Vhalla Yarl had been so deaf to their words. But those words stayed with her. They stayed until she practiced with Daniel that night, letting them go through her gradually less clumsy swings and footwork.

"You're getting better, you know," he encouraged as they rested side-by-side later.

"Am I?" She rolled to face him.

"You are." He smiled.

Serien did something she hadn't yet done. She smiled in reply.

The expression melted from Daniel's lips as he stared at her, as if realizing the same thing. "Vh-Serien," he corrected himself, remembering how she had pleaded for him not to the last time he'd used her name. It took away Serien's strength and reminded her of all the things that were broken in the world. Being Serien was becoming easier.

"Yes?"

"May I touch you?"

The question caught her off-guard, and she blinked at him, trying to see his face clearly through the darkness. She shifted closer in her attempt, but it was pointless. The moon was beginning to wane and with it their nights had become heavier.

"What sort of a question is that?" she whispered.

"I swore I wouldn't," he reminded her. "But I wish to."

"How?" Her heart was beginning to beat furiously in her chest.

"I don't know, just yet." Daniel shifted closer. "But, I want to find out. May I?"

Serien swallowed, her throat gummy. "You may."

The words escaped—she hadn't even known they had been hiding within her. The rough pads of his fingers, calloused from years of the sword, brushed up against her forehead, feeling where her face was in the darkness. They stilled, slowly tracing down her temple, over the curve of her cheek, along her jaw, to her chin. They brushed over her lips, and up her nose, as though he was an artist trying to recreate her likeness.

"Daniel . . . I . . ." her voice cracked. Tears threatened to spring forth from the ache in her chest that could split her in two. He was too kind.

"What? You what?" Sand ground beneath him as he shifted closer still. Serien could feel his warmth now. He was warmer than she expected him to be and it was such a soothing comfort. "What are we?"

Serien opened her mouth, trying to formulate an answer—but she didn't have one. She didn't know what she should call him, call *them*. He had gone beyond his call of duty as a friend and without her noticing he had begun to fill the holes her prior life had left in her. He comforted her in the night and he soothed away her fears for the day.

She pressed her eyes closed and pulled away. "I'm tired."

Daniel didn't ask the question again.

It took just over two weeks for Craig to finally confront Daniel about his new aloofness and odd habits. At which point

Craig was finally in on the plot. It shocked Serien that it took his being sat down before her and practically told to notice the woman whose body she was inhabiting.

The moment he realized who she was, he pledged to protect her as well, and she had two teachers after that. Serien hadn't realized her monopolization of Daniel's time had been taxing on him, but the moment he didn't have to be with her every second following the march, he was off doing other things, tending to Baldair's demands or helping run the camp. She was cross with him for not telling her she'd been a burden and made sure he knew it.

Daniel only laughed. He would have done it for her no matter what, he assured her.

Serien had been born of blood and death, but even she was beginning to see the sun rise in all its colors. Perhaps it was the tireless support of Daniel—and Craig. Or perhaps it was because every day carried her closer to the final outpost of the West, where the host would split, and she would be with Aldrik again.

Some soldiers had called the final outpost a "fort" but that term was a very loose one. It had a makeshift wall constructed of giant timbers and packed clay, but within it was little more than the glorified tent cities she had come to know. There was no pomp or circumstance here, no cheers or pennons or ceremony. This was the edge of war, and there wasn't time for such frivolous notions.

"We will rest here for the night," the Emperor shouted over the troops, his voice carrying across the desert. "When we march tomorrow we will move as three hosts."

The Emperor's sons flanked him to his left and right. Each of the royals had the black shadow that had never left their sides. Other than the dust on their capes, the Windwalkers appeared no different than they had when they left the Crossroads.

"Each legion will be divided among my sons and me. We three will each take a separate route to Soricium to increase our odds of all making it."

Serien recognized the name of the capital of the North, the last major blockade to the Empire's victory. She crossed her arms over her chest. Using the memories of the other woman, a smirk appeared on her face knowing that Vhalla Yarl once advised the Emperor about splitting royalty.

"Your commanding majors will announce your assignments tomorrow. Prepare for war."

Chapter 26

S ERIEN LAY AWAKE, listening to Daniel's breathing. She watched as his chest rose and fell in the moonlight, punctuated by the soft sighs of dreamlands. She wondered what he saw behind his closed eyes. His dreams could in no way be as tortured as hers.

Being next to him was becoming painfully normal. She missed Fritz and Larel with an ache that could never be filled. But Daniel was kind and attentive. He was thoughtful and preempted her needs to a surprising degree.

Serien rolled onto her side. If things had been different, *what would they be?* She bit her lip.

"Are you sure this is a good idea?" Even as a hushed whisper, Prince Baldair's voice carried.

"How many times must I tell you?" A voice, deep and dark as midnight, replied—its whispering tones echoing straight through Serien and into a woman who had been suppressed for weeks. "I will accept it no other way."

"You and her . . ." The voices grew near and Serien heard two sets of footsteps in the sand pass by Daniel's tent.

"Again, how many times must I tell you?" She could see him pinching the bridge of his nose in her mind's eye.

"I know," Baldair muttered in disbelief. "You've thought this through, right?"

The question went ignored. "How is she?" The voices began to grow faint.

"Well cared for. I have my own looking out for her. They're reporting into me and I've kept my promise, brother: she's had everything she's needed to be well."

Serien glanced at Daniel.

"You mean the Easterner."

"How did you know?" Baldair seemed as surprised as Serien.

"I must speak with . . ." Their hushed whispers were almost out of earshot.

He was there. *He was right there*, a voice in the back of her mind echoed. If she moved now she would see him. Serien knew she couldn't let herself. She'd been so careful to avoid the Black Legion at all costs. She knew what the sight of him would do to the other woman within her.

When his voice faded away entirely, her feet were under her, moving without thought. Serien made haste from the tent, praying she didn't wake Daniel. She saw them in the distance, the two princes side by side, walking toward Baldair's tent. A tiny mote of flame lit their path, and Serien staggered toward it, hypnotized.

His lean frame was swathed in black as if cut from the night itself. His elegant fingers curled around each other at the small of his back. His presence radiated the essence of poise to all who gazed upon him.

"Aldrik," she breathed.

It should have been impossible for him to hear, but he turned anyway. He stilled as though he saw a specter. Baldair turned as well, curious to see what had so enthralled his sibling. The second he saw her, he knew.

She took another step forward, and Aldrik said nothing,

his arms suddenly limp at his sides. Serien staggered across
the gap between them. Her eyes were lost in Aldrik's and the
crown prince seemed to see nothing else either. They were both
oblivious to Baldair's nervous glances for any onlookers.

"Vhalla," he whispered, holding out a hand to her.

Prince Baldair gripped his brother's wrist. "In my tent." He
gave her a pointed glance, and she quickly followed behind
them.

The moment they were both inside, Aldrik's hands were in
her hair. His long fingers wove themselves into the dark strands,
as if trying to entangle himself with her very essence. She felt
Serien melt away and, without the other woman's armor, Vhalla
was as naked as a babe, raw to the world and the emotions
fighting within her.

She tilted her head upward, grabbing Aldrik's face and
pulling it toward her. The prince obliged, dipping his tall frame
to crash his lips against hers. His chainmail dug into her chest
and her fingers scratched against it, searching for a grip to cling
to. She was desperate for him, for the life only he could instill
in her.

Baldair cleared his throat for their attention. Aldrik pulled
away only a fraction, his eyes searching her face. His hands ran
over her cheeks, down her neck and shoulders. He stared at her,
at the broken and scarred creature that she was, in amazement.

"I'll go stay with Raylynn tonight, I think," Baldair announced.

They both turned to see the tent flap falling back into place.
Vhalla felt a blush sneak across her cheeks for her forwardness
in front of Aldrik's brother. But the hand that hooked her chin
brought his lips to hers once more erased all thought of it.

Every slight turn of his head, shift of his wet lips over hers,
was an ecstasy she had not known until the first time she had
kissed him. It was the sweetest taste she had ever tried, one that
only improved in flavor with each passing moment. It was the

perfect thing to lose herself in and forget the pain. Aldrik pulled his body away, eliciting a whimper from her.

The arrogant royal grinned against her mouth. His hands fumbled with his chainmail, pulling it over his head between kisses. It fell heavily to the sand, and he pressed his body against hers once more.

It was a dance that only they knew the steps to, each movement purposeful. His hands, her hands, his mouth, her mouth, their bodies, all moved with perfect precision. The backs of her ankles hit Baldair's bed and Vhalla was forced upon it. Carrying such a thing on the march now seemed much more pragmatic than she had first given the younger prince credit for.

Her hands fell on Aldrik's hips, her thumbs finding their way under the hem of his shirt. Soft, *Mother, his skin was soft.* His palm ran lazily up and down her side, catching on her shirt now and then, pushing it up and exposing her own raw skin to the hot pads of his fingers.

Aldrik broke the kiss, breathless and flushed. Vhalla's chest heaved as she stared up at him, their faces close. He said nothing, but his eyes told her the promise of a world of barely containable desire. Vhalla hooked his neck and pulled his lips back to hers. *He couldn't look at her like that without kissing her.* Aldrik obliged her hungrily, and he discarded any previous timid notions of invading her mouth.

Her fingers walked around his neck, down his collarbone, and into the wide opening of his shirt. She indulged upon the exposed skin of his chest. He tilted his head, devouring her collarbone.

"I want to feel you," she moaned softy. It was a noise that she should be embarrassed at herself for making. But her head was too clouded for that. Her head wasn't in control.

Aldrik straightened, his knees on either side of her legs at the edge of the bed. He looked down at her uncertainly, insecurely, processing her words. Grabbing the back of his shirt he leaned forward, tugging it over his head and discarding it with the chainmail on the ground.

Vhalla stared at him. Her heart could drum or she could breathe, doing both was too much for her body right now. He was lithe, sinewy muscle cutting into and curving under the ghostly pale of his skin. The tiny flame cast deep shadows into his abdomen. There was an ugly scar on his right hip, another on his shoulder and a few minor ones here and there. He was almost too thin and the luster of his flesh could be borderline unhealthy. His nose was a little crooked and his face was angular and sharp.

"You're perfect," she whispered.

Aldrik seemed utterly taken aback. Other women clearly hadn't thought so.

Vhalla reached for him and he conceded, scooping her up and situating her farther on the bed. His mouth was on her once more, his palms exploring her form.

"I want you," he uttered huskily.

"Have me." Vhalla had never been so brazen. But this man was fire. He was life. He was the only thing that had felt good or right in weeks, and she loved him so deeply it made her ache to think of parting with him ever again.

"No," he said, as if the word was a curse.

"What?" Her eyes fluttered open to see him staring down at her.

He was heavy-lidded as well, he'd been indulging in the same cup of passion as she. "I won't take you like this." He caressed her cheek.

"Why?" she groaned.

"Because I care too deeply for you to have you in such a wanton way." He kissed down her jaw, his actions completely contradicting his words.

"What if I want you to?" Vhalla couldn't believe she was almost at the point of begging.

He couldn't either and Aldrik chuckled darkly. "Will you want me less come the dawn?"

"Mother, *no.*" She pressed her eyes closed—the thought of dawn, of being Serien again, of being distant from him threatened to crush her spirit.

"Will you want me less come the next dawn?" He nipped lightly at her collarbone, pulling back her shirt with his greedy fingers. "Or the one after?"

"No, no, no," Vhalla uttered, praying he never stopped his ministrations upon her.

"Then it shall be a fruit that will ripen with time and patience." Aldrik pressed his cheek against hers, his lips moving against her ear as he spoke. "And it shall be all the sweeter when it is finally plucked."

There were dark promises heaped between his words that were sealed with his actions. With nothing more than kissing and timid explorations he had a flush from her chest to her cheeks and her breathing heavy. Vhalla was driven crazy every time her fingers ran over the taut muscles in his shoulders. She was ready to scream his name when his fire glittered across her skin, crackling against her magic.

Eventually he rolled to his side, scooping her half onto him, his arms around her hips. Aldrik ran his hand along her back as she kissed him leisurely. Vhalla wasn't sure when or why the heat faded, but when it did she found herself curled against his bare chest, her head tucked up by his neck and chin and his arm around her. The passion had settled into a warm honey, simmering at the pit of her stomach.

"Aldrik . . ." Her whisper transformed into a yawn.

"Yes, my Vhalla?" he replied.

She felt his voice reverberate in both his neck and chest, and it made her shiver. "Nothing . . . I just wanted to hear you say my name."

"Vhalla, Vhalla, *Vhalla*," he obliged, punctuating each with a kiss on her forehead.

"If morning never came, I think that would be all right . . ." Her body was beginning to calm down, and the yawns becoming more frequent.

"I think it would be," he agreed, pulling her closer.

"We will be together, from tomorrow?" She hadn't dared ask, fearful of the answer. But if she had to brace herself for the worst, she wanted to know now. She would need the night to prepare herself.

"I wrote the list of soldiers myself." Aldrik nodded. "We will not be apart ever again from tomorrow."

"Isn't that a nice dream?" She yawned again.

"My Vhalla, my lady, my love." His words smoothed away the rough edges of her heart. "You make me do things far more dangerous than dream. You make me hope, you make me *want*." He sighed a sound that was part bliss and part pain. "Mother, I have yet to discover if you will be my salvation or my demise."

She twisted to look up at him, his dark eyes intense.

"I would never bring you harm." She pressed her lips against his.

"Salvation, then." He grinned against her mouth.

Morning threatened to burn through the canvas of the tent, and Vhalla felt as though the world began and ended with the man she was curled up against. His steady breathing and heartbeat were in perfect time with hers and created a melody that had a sweet timbre. Not quite awake, but no longer sleeping, Vhalla drifted through a blissful haze.

A haze that was abruptly interrupted by a broad-shouldered prince entering the tent. Vhalla sat quickly, as if doing so could hide the truth of spending the night in the crown prince's arms.

It was a contest to see whose face turned the reddest—hers or Baldair's.

"Good Gods, you're still here?" He cast a hand over his eyes as Aldrik sat as well, the covers pooling around his waist to reveal him only half clothed. "Brother, your debt to me is unfathomably great."

Vhalla looked back at Aldrik in alarm, only to see that he had a lazy grin spreading from cheek to cheek. He turned to her, looking five years younger with a good night of sleep. Aldrik grabbed her for a brief kiss—startling in its passion, given their audience.

"My brother is right," Aldrik whispered. "I must go or they'll wonder where I am."

She nodded.

"Wait for me until tonight?"

"Tonight?" She blinked at her prince.

"We will be together again with far fewer eyes upon us." Aldrik grinned.

"In enemy territory!" She punched his shoulder, surprisingly playful given the subject.

"I'll put the best men on watch." He gripped her hand, bringing it to his mouth, kissing her knuckles.

"Any time now," Baldair muttered, clearly uncomfortable by the lovers who had shared his bed.

"Unfortunately, no one will think twice about a woman leaving your tent," Aldrik muttered, standing and dressing. "So I'll go first." He turned to Baldair. "Thank you, brother."

There was a raw sincerity that Baldair was clearly not used to receiving from his brother. It brought a smile to Vhalla's lips to be privy to it. The two of them weren't so bad when they stopped fighting.

Aldrik gave her one last look, as if memorizing her form. Vhalla nodded. She only had to be strong for a short time more, *she could do it.* Then, that night, she'd find her way into his arms again. That knowledge alone kept her sane.

Baldair crossed over to the bed the second his brother left, assessing her. Vhalla regarded his gaze warily. "It's real then."

"What is?"

"You and Aldrik." Baldair could barely say it, as if the words would bring the Mother's wrath upon him.

"I love him." She nodded. "And he loves me."

"Vhalla . . ." Baldair sighed and sat beside her on the bed. "*Please*, be careful."

"More warnings?" She frowned.

"Not like before." Baldair shook his head. "I've never seen Aldrik like this, I know his feelings are not mirrors and manipulation."

"I tried to tell you that." She was unable to hide her frustration. "He would never hurt me."

"That's not what I now fear for." Baldair shook his head. "Vhalla, he is the crown prince."

"I know that." She gripped the blanket with white knuckles. "Why is it that you can be the playboy prince, chase whatever strikes your fancy, and he's chastised for spending time with me? We haven't even—" She stopped herself with a blush.

"Because I will not inherit the crown." The prince regarded her with a heavy sincerity. "I'm the spare, Vhalla. No one cares what I do, they care what *he* does."

"But they love you." It was no secret who the common people's favorite was.

"They love me because I never have to heap punishments upon them, or carry out executions, or levy taxes. I host parties and open casks of wine." Baldair shook his head. "They don't like him because Aldrik will be a fair ruler. He doesn't care about being loved, he cares about doing what's right."

"And what's wrong with—"

"Until you." Baldair placed his palm on the top of her head. "You're the first thing I've ever seen him want to take for himself."

"What's your point?" Vhalla knew already she wasn't going to like it.

"That it also means that you are the first thing the world knows it can take from him."

She froze in place and remembered Lord Ophain's words: *the chink in his armor.* As deeply as their Bond ran, she was still learning about her prince and Vhalla saw the man known as the Fire Lord in a new way. His reputation, his titles, they elevated him and protected him better than forged steel or boiled leather.

"But I'll try to make sure that doesn't happen." Baldair stood, helping her to her feet.

"Why?" She looked at him skeptically. "I have no interest in creating debts."

He chuckled aloud. "That isn't why I'm doing it. I have much to atone for when it comes to my brother. Maybe I didn't realize how much until I saw him happy again. Either way, consider me your sword, Vhalla Yarl."

She assessed him thoughtfully. He could be lying. But Baldair had never seemed to be intentionally malicious. Even the actions that had previously displeased her she couldn't resent him for. If he was to be believed, it all came from a good place.

Vhalla raised her hand. "Then consider me your wind."

Baldair smiled and clasped his palm against hers.

It was hard to be Serien when Vhalla was so happy, but she donned the guise of the other woman—mentally anyways. Serien was what she had to be, it was all she could be by daylight. To be anything else would make her worth noticing, and she was beginning to discover she enjoyed not being important.

"There you are!" Daniel waved her over for breakfast, and Serien sat between him and Craig. "I was worried."

"Sorry about that. I went for a walk," she lied easily and

neither man questioned her. Serien wondered if Vhalla's old friends would call her a bad liar now.

Daniel and Craig were easy going when other soldiers were beginning to fray at the seams. This was the two men's third tour, and they knew what to expect. Serien thought about asking what she would see, but doing so was pointless. What awaited her would be there no matter what words they shared. But she knew who she would face it with.

So when the host was being divided, Serien walked with confidence to Aldrik's group. None of the majors had instructed her to do so, but one catch of the prince's eyes and she knew she was in the right place. They would face the North together. Serien balled her hands into fists, opening a Channel she shouldn't possess.

The army began to settle, and the Emperor rode to the front. "Before we march, there have been a few changes to the groupings to better leverage the skills of our soldiers," he announced. "The following people will move to Prince Baldair's group . . ."

The Emperor listed off a few names and a handful of soldiers from his and Aldrik's groups found a new place.

He listed off a few more names, ". . . will move to Prince Aldrik's group." More shuffling followed. Serien shifted her weight from one foot to the next. She was ready to leave.

The Emperor continued with a few more names, suddenly drawing her attention, ". . . and Serien Leral. Will be under *my* command."

The most powerful man in all the realms had somehow found her among the hundreds of soldiers, though it couldn't have been hard as she had foolishly placed herself near Aldrik's side. Serien looked up at the prince, panic originating from the other woman and rising up like bile in her throat.

The prince alternated between glaring at his father and looking hopelessly at her.

She couldn't refuse, and her prince couldn't speak for her, not in front of all these people. Serien dragged her feet to life. *They were being separated.* The Emperor had done this just to spite them. Serien wanted to scream, she wanted to blow the Emperor off his high horse with the strongest gale he would ever feel.

Vhalla's emotions crept up on her: the fear of abandonment, fear of her friends dying while she was distant and helpless. Later Vhalla and all her emotions would escape. That shivering and shaking woman would break through Serien's strength and claw her way to the surface. She would cry at the injustice of it all, at the unheeded warnings and blind hope.

But at this moment, she would keep herself together. She would be Serien, and she would keep her dignity. Serien held her head as high as possible, high enough that it tightened her throat and held in the tears and screams. She would not give the Emperor the satisfaction of seeing the last shred of her hope being crushed under his boot.

CHAPTER 27

THE JUNGLES OF the North were unlike anything Serien had ever seen before. The Southern forests were tall timbers with a few low shrubs and trees but mostly a carpet of twigs and leaves covered the ground. The North was a dense and oppressive contrast. Bushes and trees closed in at every level, vines as thick as her arm spider webbed across the branches high above.

The ceiling the trees created was deep, and everything was cast in a hazy green shade. Despite the fact that it was the middle of winter, the humidity in the air instantly made it a little too warm for the amount of armor she wore.

The terrain slowed them, and everyone had been deathly silent from the moment they entered the forest. It was an abrupt line in the sand of the Western Waste. A clear marker created by burnt and cut down trees where the Empire ended. It was strange to think of herself as no longer being in the Solaris Empire.

With a step, the world she had always known ended.

But it hadn't just been one step. It'd been countless steps that had taken her here, and they'd all begun with a rainy night and an injured prince. Not all the steps had been made with confidence, and some had led her to pitfalls, but she was strangely glad she had made them.

Now, however, she didn't know where her feet would take her. Serien stood a stone's throw from the Emperor and fake Windwalker. She glanced at the man from the corners of her eyes. He rode confidently atop his War-strider, but his shoulders betrayed him. Despite his age he was attentive, alert, mindful of every place a threat could appear.

War was his arena, his art, and his legacy. He had laid siege to an entire continent and swept it under his banner in one lifetime. Serien turned forward again before he had a chance to see her attention. She wished an attack would come. She wanted to see this man at work with her own eyes.

But the day was uneventful, and by the time night fell there had been no attacks. They slept under fallen trees and huddled beneath brush. There were no fires or jovial discussions. There weren't even tents set up. Serien made herself small underneath a sapling, pulling moss around her. The nights outside had prepared her for this. She hardened herself and stayed the tears for one more hour, then the next hour, and the hour after.

By the third day she had yet to cry. Her emotions toward the Emperor and his switch were beginning to cool and mimic those of her feelings toward the Head of Senate, Egmun. She had seen it as Vhalla, and now as Serien, the actions of men who wanted to break her.

Unfortunately for them, one couldn't break what was already broken.

It was on the sixth day that Serien's ears picked up movement in the brush above. She looked upward to see the currents of air moving throughout the boughs of the trees. There was something unnatural that lingered on the edge of the wind, and Serien recognized a moment too late that it was the sound of breathing.

Northerners descended upon them in freefall. They rained

daggers that immediately found their way into the skulls of unfortunate soldiers. Serien reached for her hood of chainmail, forgetting with a curse that she was not in Vhalla Yarl's armor.

"Firebearers!" the Emperor shouted.

The Black Legion soldiers ran out to the perimeter creating a wall of flame. The Northerners were assaulted by arrows and magical tongues of fire to burn away the brush that reached out unnaturally to catch them. One fell straight before her, the body nearly exploding upon impact with the ground after such a long fall.

Serien took a breath, trying to assess their situation. The wind whispered to her once more.

"Incoming *left*!" she cried. Serien drew her sword as everyone, including the Emperor, stared on in confusion.

But her warning was validated the second Northerners were carried through the flames atop the backs of giant beasts unlike anything Serien had ever seen. It was a cat-like creature with double-jointed back legs and claws larger than a man's thigh. Its thick fur was slick and whatever was atop it was impervious to the flames it had leapt over.

Two more came, carrying even more riders, who quickly dismounted, entering the fray with their double-sworded stances. The first one was barreling toward the Emperor and Windwalker, their target clear. The Emperor drew his sword, positioning his mount fearlessly to face the Northerner head on.

It wasn't even a competition. The horse moved at the Emperor's command, and Emperor Solaris moved as if his enemy had told him all the attacks they would make. He sliced the man's head clean off, dodging all blades.

The Northerners didn't seem interested in engaging any of the soldiers, and the Imperial army was left to struggle to impede the enemies' leaps and jumps toward the Windwalker.

Yet somewhere amid the chaos, she managed to hear the sound of a bowstring. Serien turned, finding the archer immediately in their roost.

The arrow was headed straight for the Emperor, who was engaged in heated combat. She swallowed her pride and stuck out her hand. The arrow stopped just as the Emperor was about to turn his face into it. He wasn't able to conceal his amazement as the arrow dropped to the ground harmlessly.

Two cerulean eyes found hers. There was no love there, not an iota of appreciation. Serien set her jaw and missed the sound of another arrow being set loose.

By the time any of them heard it, it was too late.

The false Windwalker was knocked off her mount, she fell backwards and out of her saddle, an arrow protruding from her face. The Imperial company stared in shock, and the Northerners hollered in victory, making a calculated retreat. One by one the Imperial soldiers turned to the Emperor with apprehension.

"Leave her." The Emperor turned his horse forward.

Serien lingered, longer than she likely should have, to stare at the body of the dead woman. It could have been *her*. That woman had died for Vhalla Yarl, and Vhalla Yarl didn't even know her name.

The land became rockier as it elevated. Serien knew there weren't mountains in the North, not like the South, but some of the bluffs were beginning to grow to an impressive scale. That night they had the fortune of caves and caverns to hide within. It was the first time the soldiers could relax and most capitalized on the opportunity.

Serien huddled in a nook in the rock face, protected on all sides. She rested her elbows on her knees and stared listlessly into the sunset haze. They were already a week into the march. Another two weeks and they should make it to Soricium. She gripped her arms tightly. *She'd see Aldrik then.* Considering the alternative would be too much for even Serien to bear.

Given the fact that it was the first opportunity at privacy, she shouldn't have been surprised when a messenger tracked her down not long after sunset, leading her around the corners of boulders and into a small cave. He left quickly after.

"You wanted to see me, my lord?" she said, giving a formal salute—the salute of a soldier and not of the Black Legion.

"Yes." The Emperor stood, placing his hands behind his back. "I suppose you want thanks for your act of heroism."

She pursed her lips, waiting for him to get to the point. Waiting for him to arrive at the reason why he waited for days after that battle, why he waited for privacy.

"It's not every day a commoner has the opportunity to save the life of the Emperor." He walked to the opposite side of his small campfire. With the way the light illuminated his face she could almost see Aldrik's brow in his.

"It was my honor." He was going to make her play the game.

"Indeed," the Emperor agreed. "It was because you are *mine.* Your freedom, your life, your future rest in my hands, Vhalla Yarl."

The use of her name shredded through Serien, and it sapped the strength of her alter ego.

The Emperor didn't miss the wavering in her eyes. "I want you to be very clear on why you are here."

"I know why."

"Why?" he pressed.

"To win you your war." She didn't even bother with the nonsense of atoning for her crimes. Serien—Vhalla—wondered if he had decided her fate the moment he laid eyes on the whirlwind.

"Yes, very good." He began walking once more. "They said you were smart."

There was a predatory glint to his eyes that had Serien's hands balling into fists.

"Do you know who 'they' are?" the Emperor asked.

"Who?" She tried to stand to her fullest height so that he had less of a distance from which to look down at her.

"My eldest son." The gauntlet was thrown.

Serien's blood boiled. *That's what this was about.* "He is very smart, my lord."

"Usually," the Emperor murmured as he inspected her from head to toe. She already knew she wouldn't measure up. "Speaking of him, our two groups will merge again after the pass, during the final leg of the trip."

Serien struggled to keep her face neutral; she was sure she failed. The Emperor continued to stare her down. "Is that why you called me here, my lord? To tell me that?"

The Emperor chuckled in amusement at her bold front. "No, I simply wanted to thank you for your attentiveness. It is good to know that when you focus on your duty that you are, indeed, not useless."

"Thank you." She took a step away, feigning the dismissal that wasn't in his voice.

"Oh, and Miss Yarl." She paused. "I recommend you keep that focus where it should be, on making it to the front and giving me my victory. I will not tolerate your entertaining girlish fantasies or misplaced notions."

Serien clenched her hands into fists so tightly that the straps on her gauntlets threatened to break. She grit her teeth and set her jaw. She heard his threats loud and clear.

"Do you understand me?" The Emperor's voice was deathly quiet.

"Perfectly."

The conversation lingered with Serien as she stormed through camp back to her hideaway. It played on repeat through her mind as she struggled to find a position comfortable enough to sleep in. And, when she did fall asleep, the Emperor greeted her in her dreams. . .

The Emperor sat next to her. No, not her. Vhalla pulled herself away from Aldrik's dream form. His face was hard, and fire lit his eyes. She followed the line of his attention and saw herself, part ethereal and part concrete, in an all too familiar cage. She was huddled and shaking, blood dripping from the back of her head along her jaw and onto the floor. The strength that sparked in her brown eyes was a shadow play, it lacked true substance behind it. That much was apparent, not only to her, but to the man whose memory she was occupying.

His hand balled so tightly into a fist that the skin had gone ghostly from lack of blood. It was impossible for Vhalla to have seen from across the courtroom during the original trial but his jaw was clenched to the extent that his face shook and trembled. The Emperor was speaking, but to Aldrik's ears the words were blurred over the rush of hot anger in his head.

Aldrik's emotions radiated clearly, unfiltered through the Joining-induced memory, as he left the courtroom. He couldn't look at her. If he looked at her he would break. If he looked at her they would all know his worry on her behalf.

The moment the doors to Imperial quarters closed behind him and his family, Aldrik increased his strides, doubling the distance between him and his father. Vhalla could feel his magic trembling and pulsing with an undeniable need—a need to get to her.

"*Aldrik,*" the Emperor called.

He froze, turning. His face was expressionless, but she could feel the tornado of emotion ripping through his chest. The sight of his father filled him with panic.

"*I need you in the war council; the North is getting too bold, and we will need to counter this aggression with force.*"

"I will be there shortly," Aldrik replied stiffly.

"You will come now." The Emperor's tone was casual enough, but something dangerous shone through his eyes.

She could feel Aldrik gather his courage, a strange thing she never thought the man known as the Fire Lord would need to do. "Clearly the guard's definition of care is lacking," Aldrik's voice dripped venom. "I plan to educate them."

"That is not your concern." The Emperor waved the notion away, starting down a different hall.

"It is." Desperation flooded Aldrik's chest and overflowed into hers. "I told you, she can win you your war. I am merely protecting our interests."

"Which is why I didn't have the monster killed before she saw the light of day again." The Emperor paused, glancing at his son. "The Empire's interests, Aldrik?"

"Always for the greater good of our Empire." The words were rehearsed. They'd been said so many times they spewed from Aldrik's mouth without thought, completely void of emotion. They were so hollow that Vhalla could sense the dam that trembled in the prince, holding back a plea of, let me go to her. "You do not want her to die, Father. I told you, I can train her, mold her—"

"Right, right." The Emperor turned to Baldair, who Vhalla had almost completely forgotten was there. "Baldair, fetch a cleric to tend to Aldrik's pet."

"Father. . ." Baldair frowned.

"Thank you." The Emperor completely ignored the disapproving tones in his younger son's voice.

Aldrik continued to stand silently as the Emperor walked away. Vhalla felt his resignation. She knew his acceptance of a deeper truth that, despite all his wants, he couldn't go to the woman he wished to be nearest to.

"Baldair," Aldrik whispered once the Emperor was just far enough away.

"What do you want?" Vhalla felt a twinge of disappointment in Aldrik toward the disgust that laced Baldair's words.

"Go to her yourself," Aldrik demanded.

"What?"

"Go to her yourself, damn it," Aldrik hissed. "You owe me."

"I don't owe you anything." Baldair crossed his arms on his chest.

"What happened to being the noble knight who proclaims protection of the weak and innocent?" Aldrik sneered. Vhalla felt his satisfaction when he saw Baldair's expression change. The prince knew just what words to say to goad his brother in the direction he wanted. "You owe me for the last six Elixirs of the Moon I pilfered from the clerics without their noticing. Unless you'd like me to reconsider that arrangement."

"Fine, but not for you," Baldair huffed. "For the girl."

"Fine." Aldrik strode off, satisfied for the moment. His father was a few steps ahead and seemingly oblivious to the muffled exchange. Aldrik clenched and unclenched his fists.

He damned everything he ever loved. How could he have even thought being near her could end well? How could he have let himself blur the lines with the girl so far?

The questions radiated through Aldrik's mind and into Vhalla's consciousness as he stormed through the hall. A chair burst into flame by him, an outburst of emotion that couldn't be tamed. Aldrik scowled at it and extinguished the fire.

Vhalla woke shivering in the North with thoughts, pilfered from Aldrik's dream consciousness. *He had to get control. He couldn't let them see. He couldn't let them know what she was.*

CHAPTER 28

THE SOLDIERS SAID that "the pass" previously was the greatest river in the world. But it had long since dried up. It was hard for Serien to believe that the deep, rocky ravine could've ever held water.

But somewhere across the chasm was Aldrik. The Emperor may have wanted to threaten her into submission, but all he did was give her a point in time to wait for. Another day, maybe two, and they would be across the pass; she would be with him once more. She would be careful, but she would tell him of his father's threats, and somehow they would overcome them.

Serien looked at the Emperor from the corners of her eyes. He wouldn't get in their way, no matter how long and hard he tried. He couldn't fathom what his son felt for her and what she felt for him. But someday he would see.

It was halfway through the day when she first heard steel on steel and the sounds of combat echoing through the winds of the pass. Serien shivered, suddenly cold despite the jungle's heat.

Aldrik.

She wanted to run, to sprint, her heart beginning to race with a wild beat. He needed her. He did. She just knew it. Vhalla could feel it through the Bond.

Neither Vhalla nor Serien were prepared for the moment the troops rounded a curve in the pass. Fire burned the treetops as soldiers engaged on the opposite side of the pass. It was an all-out assault, and she was uselessly far. Vhalla searched frantically to try to find Aldrik among the chaos.

The North, however, was taking no chances with what side their query would approach from, and the Imperial soldier's shock was the ideal opportunity for a second surprise attack. Men and women, warriors in boiled leather, charged from the brush before them.

The Emperor frantically tried to call out orders but they were too disorganized and flat-footed. The Northerners cut through the front of the ranks with ease. The Imperial soldiers tried to compose themselves, the second and third rows of men and women drawing their swords. But shock made them clumsy and the points of their blades chipped off their enemies' magic stone skin.

What was an organized unit was quickly devolving into chaos. Trained soldiers tried to call for the new recruits to hold the line, but the battlefield was already stained with blood that was turning men mad. The Emperor shouted from atop his mount, trying to reclaim order. The might of the North pressed upon them, determined otherwise.

An odd calm had overtaken her. The bursts of flame across the ravine shone in her eyes, illuminating a deeper truth resonating within her. *You are a symbol*, Baldair's words echoed through her subconscious. Vhalla's fingers went to the belt strapping on her sword, dodging the first Northerner's blade in the process.

She would not meet these people in terror. If she was going to die, then she would die with dignity. Vhalla dashed backward and pulled off her gauntlets, feeling the wind beneath her fingers as they unlatched her plate. She would not die as Serien. If she was going to die, then she would die as the Windwalker.

The Northerner who had been attacking her charged forward and Vhalla's hand thrust forward to meet the woman. It was as if the wind had missed her commands and it responded in full force, knocking the woman off her feet and several other Northerners along with her. Vhalla swung another arm, sending the Northerners tumbling.

"The Wind Demon!" one shrieked, pointing at her.

Vhalla didn't shrink away, she charged forward. The wind was under her feet, and Aldrik's heartbeat in her ears. She drew from his strength. Together they would confront their foes. Together they would be invincible.

She moved effortlessly around the blades as they came. They couldn't touch the wind. Vhalla disarmed them with flicks of her wrists and waves of her fingers.

It was the first time she had truly fought without fear. Every time before, even sparring, she had been afraid. Her power had been strange, then the Joining, then the fear of killing once more . . . But she had learned how to shield her heart as Serien and she was a truly an agent of death now.

She'd show the Emperor, she'd show the world that they had finally gotten what they wanted in her.

Vhalla lunged for one of the warriors, and her palm covered his mouth. It was how Aldrik had killed the Northerner on the Night of Fire and Wind. But, from her, there would not be flame. The air trapped within the man's neck budged at her command. His eyes lolled in his head as it pressed outward, stretching the skin to its limit. The wind exploded free, taking strips of skin and hunks of meat with it, spraying blood over her face and arm.

The man fell before her and there was an almost audible hush as everyone seemed to pause and stand in horror. Vhalla looked at the soldiers, her allies. Her eyes met the Emperor's, who seemed equally stunned.

"Fight with me!" she cried. They needed a leader, they needed a symbol that was more than a man in golden plate. They needed a Fire Lord. Or, a Wind Demon. *"Fight with me!"* Vhalla punctuated her statement by lunging for another Northerner, who exploded at her hand.

Imperial soldiers sprang to life around her, heeding her wind, taking care to account for her movements. The Emperor wanted her to bring him victory. She would show him what it would cost.

All else faded to the drumming in her ears. She gave herself to her Channel with the wind and to her Channel with her prince. She dodged faster than a person should be able to, she jumped farther, and she lost count of how many died by her hand.

But she had never used her magic like this before—consciously—and Vhalla finally felt her power waver. What should have knocked back several soldiers only stumbled them. She paused, inspecting her hand, as if it had consciously betrayed her.

A large flame from the other side of the chasm demanded her attention and, for the first time since the fighting broke out, she looked across to Aldrik. Everyone, even across the ravine, stumbled at the wave of heat. Vhalla took a step in his direction. There were more Northerners, a lot more, on the other side of the chasm. She wondered what happened to all the other soldiers. Aldrik seemed to have five on him at once.

He was like poetry through fire. His body moved deftly, countering and parrying with flame. The fire swirled around him, and his dark armor seemed to be alive with it as Aldrik spun, commanding the blaze with his hands and thoughts.

She threw a hand, the sight of him inspiring her power again. A soldier was knocked into the flames, and they blazed about him as her air and his fire mingled. Aldrik turned instinctually and his eyes found hers.

His expression quickly turned to horror, and Vhalla felt the blade move through the air behind her. She dropped her shoulder and rose her hand, wondering if Aldrik saw the Northerner's face explode. Vhalla turned back to check, and her heart began to race for a different reason entirely.

He was being bested by two from either side. Aldrik dipped and swung, he dodged, but they were both clearly highly experienced combatants. Vhalla took a step forward. It was then she noticed four more had closed in, making a semi-circle around the prince and two Northerners. He was pinned against the edge of the ravine, occupied entirely by the two who dipped and dashed for any opening they saw.

Vhalla saw as Aldrik was forced back another step. The others on the edge of the semi-circle moved their lips fervently.

She took another step forward. Aldrik didn't notice them. *She had to tell him.*

Suddenly, the two soldiers jumped away, tumbling backwards. All six raised their fists in unison. Aldrik seemed too stunned to move. He barely was able to take a step as all the Northerners dropped their closed hands into the ground.

A groan, a rumble, and the ground rippled under his feet.

"No," she breathed.

Aldrik tried to run as the edge of the cliff cracked beneath him. He clamored, heavy in all his armor.

"No!" Vhalla cried, sprinting forward, past the blood and gore in an attempt to reach him. The swords faded away, the cries of the soldiers. She only saw her prince, losing his footing as the first large rock slid down into the pass below.

"*No!*" Vhalla screamed as she saw Aldrik tumble backwards.

The next thirty seconds stretched into eternity. Vhalla ran blindly to her prince, thinking of nothing but getting to him. His feet finally left the ground as the whole of the cliff shook away before the half-circle of Groundbreakers. Aldrik was falling, plummeting among the loose earth to the ground far below.

Her feet sped beneath her, carrying her away from the cries of the Imperial soldiers at her back. The wind was tangled around her ankles and caught beneath her heels. She had to get to him, she would save him. Vhalla leapt into the air, the wind at her back pushing her forward.

Aldrik was opposite the wide mouth of what was once a great river. And yet, with an expel of her power she crossed to him, propelled on the air, tilting forward. His hair whipped around his face and his dark eyes locked with hers in shock.

His lips formed a single word. "Vhalla," he whispered into the rush of wind around his plummeting body. Vhalla stretched her hand forward, desperate. *She would reach him.* The ground was coming up fast, and Aldrik finally began to reach for her as well.

His body tilted and twisted over the pockets of air she tried to create beneath him. There were too many unpredictable factors, she wasn't strong enough, and she wasn't skilled enough to stop a body like this. Panic propelled her to exhaust the last of her magic trying to slow him.

His hand groped at the air. Vhalla extended her arm, she had to reach him. The tips of her fingers touched his and Vhalla felt her body magically beginning to slow, the wind refusing to harm her. Aldrik stared at her, and she saw an emotion completely consume him that she had never seen from him before: *fear.* Vhalla's arm threatened to rip from her socket, *his hand was so close.* She almost had him, a moment more, a moment further, an ounce of energy that was not used to push the wind around her and him. The ground was relentless in its desire to violently meet their falling bodies, and she only had one last attempt before they were crushed upon it.

Vhalla took her chance.

She grasped the empty air, his fingers slipping past her bloody ones, and she screamed. The last thing Vhalla saw was the moment when Aldrik's body met the ground, blood pooling instantly about his broken and lifeless form, before everything went black.

EARTH'S END

BOOK THREE OF AIR AWAKENS

COMING IN FEBRUARY 2016

A woman awoken in air, a soldier forged by fire,
a weapon risen from blood.

Vhalla Yarl has made it to the warfront in the North.
Forged by blood and fire, she has steeled her heart
for the final battle of the Solaris Empire's conquest.
The choices before Vhalla are no longer servitude or
freedom, they are servitude or death. The stakes have
never been higher as the Emperor maintains his iron
grip on her fate, holding everything Vhalla still has left
to lose in the balance.

ACKNOWLEDGMENTS

MY COVER ARTIST, Merilliza Chan—I have to start with you, my dear, my "official fan art" creator. Your artwork for the *Air Awakens* covers continues to get better, time after time. The noises I made when seeing the final Fire Falling cover were inhuman. That armor? Aldrik's face? It's too beautiful. You inspire me to write better to make sure that the story I'm crafting lives up to the promises your artwork makes.

My editor, Monica Wanat—where would I be without you? With way too many "he said/she said", that's where! I can't tell you how many times I'd point excitedly at the screen and think, "Yes, yes! This is what I meant!" You're right there in my head and really elevate my work to a level of polished professionalism that I couldn't achieve without you. I know you've had a lot going on lately and I want you to know I have such a deep admiration for your perseverance.

Katie—I hope you truly understand how influential you are to everything *Air Awakens* has become. If I didn't have you to bounce ideas off and talk through things, I'm not sure what I'd do.

My betas, Nick, Dani, and Jamie—your contributions, viewpoints, opinions, and counterpoints really help me craft such a tight story. Thank you for taking the time to work with me, challenge me, and deal with all the times I'm freaking out thinking all the words are wrong.

My sister, Meredith—I don't think I can express exactly how important your excitement has been for me. It's pulled me out of the monotony of writing and editing and reminded me to be excited about this process. To be proud of what I've accomplished and really enjoy the steps of this journey. No matter how near or far we may be physically, you'll always be an essential piece to my life.

My mentor, Michelle Madow, author of the *Secret Diamond Sisters* and the *Transcend Time* Saga—you are so talented and wonderful. You've helped me go from unorganized ideas to a "real author." I'm so excited to read what you have coming out next! Thank you for including me in your world and giving me guidance.

Rob and the Gatekeeper Press team—you all have been absolutely amazing. The work you've put in, all your help, your insights, professionalism, how available you've been to me, it's an honor to work with you. You make things happen that I frankly could not on my own and I'm so glad I decided to work with you. I know I can be demanding at times, but I hope—I like to think—that we push each other to be better.

My Street Team—thank you for helping promote, love, and breathe life into *Air Awakens*. I love talking with you all, and I'm so glad you're with me on this journey. Each of you has done your part and more and I can only hope I continue to give you great stories to enjoy.

Jeffkun—thank you for not only tolerating this path I'm on but supporting it. When most brides are freaking out about centerpieces, I was freaking out about publication deadlines, and you just rolled with it. I can't do this thing called life without you.

The AAAPodcast Community—I know half of you must be tired of hearing about my books by now, so it's not lost on me how supportive you all continue to be.

My parents, Madeline and Vince—for being my biggest, unquestioning cheerleaders and the two people I know I can always count on. I love you both.

About The Author

ELISE KOVA has always had a passion for storytelling. She wrote her first novella, a high-fantasy, in sixth grade. Over the years she's honed her love of literature with everything from fantasy to romance, science fiction to mystery, and whatever else catches her eye.

Elise lives in Saint Petersburg, Florida, where she's currently working on the next installment in her debut YA fantasy series: *Air Awakens*. She enjoys video games, anime, table-top role playing games, and many other forms of "geekdom". She loves talking with fans on Twitter and Facebook. Visit her website, EliseKova.com, for news and extras about her books!

CONNECT WITH ELISE KOVA
http://www.EliseKova.com/
https://twitter.com/EliseKova
https://www.facebook.com/AuthorEliseKova

CPSIA information can be obtained
at www.ICGtesting.com
Printed in the USA
LVOW04s0040310116

473031LV00011B/92/P